Castles We Storm

Jessica Jude

Contents

Author's Note

WESBOURNE IS A FICTIONAL island country set in the middle of the Atlantic Ocean between North America and Europe. While the country is a fantasy concocted in the playground of my mind, all of my books are contemporary and take place in the modern world.

The following book contains mature content and potential triggers, including: fatal car accident, pet illness, sexual abuse of child (off-page), death of parent (off-page), terminal illness / cancer (off-page), parental affair, substance abuse and overdose (off-page), verbal / emotional abuse, language, and explicit sexual content (chapters 8, 30, 37). It is not intended for readers under 18.

Each chapter is named after a song that fits its vibe. Access the entire playlist on Spotify by going to https://jessicajude.com/castles-playlist

And finally, I am not responsible for any damages inflicted upon books or reading devices by the consumption of this book.

xoxo Jess

1

"Elastic Heart" - Sia

YOU KNOW WHAT THEY don't tell you about being queen? No matter your age, you require a round-the-clock babysitter as though you were still in nappies.

I thought it was bad before my coronation, but ever since the archbishop placed that crown on my head two months ago, I don't think I've been alone outside of my suite more than twice—and both of those instances were frowned upon.

Now, I'm stuck with a towering hulk of a nanny walking beside me. The only consolation is that I actually like this one. Davies was one of my first personal protection officers pre-coronation, so I like to think we have history. In reality, he's just the only one who will talk to me beyond "Your Majesty" and "Yes, ma'am."

"How is Tyson? Enjoying school?" I ask as we walk to my office.

Davies remains exactly thirty inches behind me and to my right. For the escorts who refuse to make conversation, I've invented a little game called "How Well Can You Trail the Queen at Thirty Inches?" It basically involves altering my speed or the length of my steps to make them get too close or lag too far behind. It's quite entertaining.

Davies has figured out that small talk is easier. "He's doing well, ma'am. Just entered secondary school."

Staff members scurry through the corridors like ants busy building a nest. They stop for a quick bow as we pass, their arms laden with pine boughs and red ribbons. The whole palace is starting to smell like a forest. I can't wait to sip hot cocoa in front of a roaring fire.

"He had a birthday recently, didn't he?" I say.

"He turned eleven two weeks ago, yes." Davies clears his throat. "Unfortunately, he's going to need braces."

"Ghastly things."

"With ghastly price tags."

I don't need to turn around to know he's blushing at his blunder. Etiquette around speaking of money to the monarch follows an unspoken—but no less rigid—rule: you don't do it.

"Forgive me. I didn't—"

I wave away his apology. "Please tell Tyson his queen is rooting for only a short stint with the braces, and that the colors lime and navy look smashing together."

We stop outside my office door, which is sporting a festive wreath studded with pinecones and bright red holly berries.

"Thank you, ma'am. I will," Davies says, and opens the door for me.

My office overlooks the southern terrace and the Parterre Garden via a bank of large windows, which let in both the sunlight and the cold drafts. The eighteenth-century trestle desk I inherited with the job sits in the center of the room. The sleek computer monitor on top of it feels sacrilegious amid the heirlooms and antiques furnishing the rest of the space, but it's hard to lead a country in the twenty-first century without electronics.

I take a seat behind the desk just as a brisk knock sounds on the door, immediately followed by the entrance of my private secretary. Her arms are laden with my green box of state papers, her trusty tablet, and a to-go cup that I desperately hope is my French vanilla latte. Through the open door, I can hear the grandfather clock sounding the nine o'clock hour.

Maisie bobs a quick curtsy and responds to my greeting with a meek "Your Majesty." With that, our ode to traditional deference is over. She pushes the door shut with a ballet-flat-clad foot, deposits the box and coffee on my desk, and sighs deeply as she sits down across from me.

"Traffic was awful this morning." She unlocks her electronic tablet. "I think they might be gearing up for another strike."

"Not again." Grabbing the cup, I take a sip of the frothy liquid and wince at the flavor of Irish creme. "This is disgusting."

She's already immersed in her screen. "Did they get it wrong again?"

"Unless you ordered an Irish latte, yes." I set the offensive beverage aside. "Apparently Her Majesty is just another customer."

Maisie grimaces. "Actually, they have no idea who I'm buying the coffee for. I figured it was safer that way."

"Safer maybe, but certainly not pleasant." I gulp down some water to wash the vile taste out of my mouth. "Give me the latest."

"First off, you received an . . . interesting request." This is Maisie-code for *strange*.

"Isn't it your job to filter those and politely decline?"

The number of requests I receive on a regular basis for asinine things like money, a tour of my bedroom, personal photos, lunch dates, and my "cast-off" clothing and jewelry was shocking at first, but I've slowly become accustomed to the weird stuff people have the audacity to ask for. With the exception of the request for my discarded nail clippings. I made Maisie burn that particular letter.

"Normally I would, but I thought you might actually be interested in this one," she says.

"I am not about to kiss some pregnant woman's belly."

"Not even close. The Duke of Sutherland requests a private audience."

My head jerks up from the planner on my desk. "The Duke of Sutherland?"

"You know, the former king?"

"I know who he is," I say. "What does he want?"

She glances back down at her screen. "His email says he has something to give you."

There is nothing he could give me that I want. "What's the policy on things like that?"

"Well, normally I send back a nice email politely declining, but given the circumstances . . ."

She's right. How does one refuse the former king? "Fine. Set it up."

Maisie gives a brisk nod. "Done. In other news, early reports show that overdose deaths in high schoolers have doubled in the last month. I just ran the numbers myself this morning. It's definitely gone up."

I jerk my head up. "Not insidion?"

"I didn't want to think so, but everything is pointing to that."

"How is that possible? Security at the ports is tight." Increasing it has been my most successful endeavor to date. Some might even argue it's my *only* successful endeavor.

"I'm not sure." She frowns at something on the tablet. "But these numbers are definitely accurate. I cross-checked them against the autopsies of over a hundred victims."

"One *hundred*?" It was alarming when there were seventy. One hundred is downright dreadful.

"That's what I'm seeing."

"And no one is talking about it?"

"I'm not sure anyone's put the pieces together yet," Maisie says. "It was just brought to my attention yesterday. It took me five hours to compile the data."

"It doesn't make sense. How is it coming into the country if the ports are secured?"

We've had nearly four months of freedom from the lethal drug spreading across Wesbourne like wildfire, taking the lives of hundreds of teens with it. Street-named *insidion*, the substance has a cultlike following among teenagers.

"Either they're finding another way to import it, or . . ."

"Or what?"

"Or they're making it here. In Wesbourne."

God help us.

"If I wasn't queen, I might be able to fight this," I say. As it stands, the monarch's job is to sit back, look pretty, and hope for the best.

"Actually, there might be a way you can fight back even from the throne." Maisie looks at me and pushes her glasses back up her nose. "They're holding a memorial downtown later this month to commemorate the victims. They've asked if you'd give a short speech."

Requests like these come in daily, usually by the dozens. I have to decline most of them, but this one is definitely going on the calendar. "Absolutely. I accept."

Her fingers fly over her small keyboard, probably already drafting the acceptance email. "Not to add fuel to the already roaring blaze that is your image in the press, but *The Sun* just released an article about"—she stops typing to read the quote directly—"your 'blatant overlooking of the working classes in favor of those below the poverty line, as well as her personal favorite, the wealthy peerage.'"

By the time Maisie looks up, my mouth has fallen open. "My 'personal favorite'? Is that some kind of joke?"

"I wish. You just took a factory tour last week, and you have an audience with the leaders of the Workers Union scheduled in December. It's libel."

"That's never stopped them before."

"Someone should have to pay."

"You know we can't—"

"'—deny anything or seek redress.' I know." She slumps back in her chair. "Doesn't keep me from wanting to, though."

I sigh and match her posture, taking another swig of coffee before remembering it tastes like leprechaun vomit. "It will blow over in a week or two. It always does."

"The weekend is only three days away. The Princess Royal will likely do something to make headlines by then, right?"

"I'm going to assume your brain malfunctioned while churning out that thought." As if my sister hitting the newsstand could ever reflect well on the royal family. Beatrice's popularity hasn't come from hosting tea parties and attending charity galas, and while being the sister of the queen has certainly helped her climb a few rungs on the social ladder, it has only increased her notoriety in the press.

"All I meant was that if Bea takes the heavy hitting from the press, it'll leave you to shine in all your glory. That's what the royal family is for—they're like a diversion from the monarch. A decoy!"

"You seriously need a filter."

"Okay, then. Let's get your mum to do something newsworthy. It will get the attention off you and polish the royal family's image at the same time," Maisie says.

While she is officially a working member of the royal family, I'm convinced my mother spends more time plotting my sister's love life than she does on anything furthering the interests of the nation. Her most recent scheme involves one of the princes of Denmark. She's not picky—either one will suit her purposes just fine.

"We will be leaving my family out of it," I say. "It wouldn't do any good anyway. Those vultures always circle back around. Besides, we have a press secretary to handle these kinds of things." I grab a ballpoint pen and click it open. "Why was this even on the agenda?"

Maisie bites her lip and quickly looks down at her tablet.

"Do I even want to know?" I mutter.

"No, and that's why I'm stalling," she blurts out.

I close my eyes and steel myself for whatever portent of gloom she's about to unleash. This job has given me more headaches than four years of statistics courses ever did. When I open them again, I see that Maisie's are closed and that she is subtly mouthing something, probably a petition for favor from the universe.

"Maisie."

Her eyes pop open, and she looks at me for two seconds before a string of words flies out of her mouth. It's completely incomprehensible.

"Could you repeat that? In English this time?" I say.

She takes a deep breath. "The Privy Purse is empty."

"Empty." I sip my coffee, trying to overlook the awful taste to get to the caffeine. "How is that possible?"

"I have no idea. All I know is that there is to be a payment plan installed on our wages. And you know I didn't take this job because of the money, and I have savings, so I'm fine, but I'm not sure how many other staff members can afford to receive only a portion of their salaries for the week, and—"

Her verbal faucet continues gushing, but I tune her out. How can the Purse be empty? I've only been on the throne for two months. It's not like I've gone on any major shopping sprees or commissioned palace renovations. I've barely had time to sleep, let alone spend millions on unnecessary things.

"Arrange a meeting with the keeper of the Privy Purse. I need to get to the bottom of this."

"Of course." Maisie's fingers begin a wild attack on the keyboard.

I click my pen rapidly, my thoughts spinning even faster. "Why has he not come to me about this himself? It doesn't make sense." The guy is in charge of the royal family's finances. How could an error of this magnitude have happened? Has he been siphoning from the accounts? Is he lazy, drunk, incompetent?

"I have no earthly clue," Maisie says. "I just caught word this morning about the wages. Payday is coming up, and everyone is freaking out."

Five hundred people are employed by this mammoth institution, and all of them are counting on me to put food on their tables and petrol in their cars. I think about Davies needing to pay for braces for his son.

"Arrange a meeting with my father's banker as well," I say.

"I— Yes. Absolutely. Um, your father? I'm afraid I don't . . ."

Maisie would rather confront a mouse than seem incompetent, but I should have specified more clearly. "Harold Bardman's. That's where my father's trust is located."

"Right. Got it." There is another flurry of typing, and then she says, "I don't mean to pry, but what exactly are you planning to do with the trust?"

"Use it to cover wages until we can get to the bottom of this debacle." I slide open my desk drawer for a notepad.

"You shouldn't be using your personal money."

"Why not?" I jot down a name and tear the paper off. "It's not like I need it to live off of. At least I didn't think I did," I mutter under my breath, and hand Maisie the slip. "This is the name of the banker who handles all of our trust funds."

My father left Beatrice and me each sizable trusts and the rest of his money to my mother. Prior to my coronation, we lived a comfortable lifestyle off the interest from those accounts, so the balance of mine should be enough to cover the staff's wages for a short period of time, but it's not a long-term solution. I'm embarrassed to say I don't know what the royal household spends on salaries in a month. I assumed that was something the keeper of the Purse was handling.

"I doubt your father intended for you to spend that money on other people. It was meant as a gift to you."

"He would turn over in his grave if I didn't do this. Besides, how can I parade around in the latest fashions while my staff can't even heat their homes? It's just common decency."

Maisie shakes her head. "Decency would be securing a loan to cover the wages. You have a bigger heart than you let on."

"Well, don't tell the press. It would ruin their day."

Despite the fact that I am doing the best I can with only a few months of preparation for being monarch, the press is determined to paint me as nothing but a money-loving, fame-hungry throne-snatcher. This is likely because of my recent divorce and everyone's opinion that I must be the stupidest woman on the planet.

If only they knew.

"I will warn the palace press office so they can stay on top of it," Maisie says. "That's the last item on this morning's agenda. I will let you know once I have those meetings scheduled." She rises to leave, eyes still glued to her screen, then promptly sinks back into her chair. Her face has turned ashen.

"What is it?" I ask.

She turns to me, her eyes large behind her glasses. "Please do not panic."

I'll never understand why people give such warnings. They always have the opposite effect, as evidenced by the tightening of my fingers around the pen in my hand.

"The press secretary just handed in his resignation."

2

"Stronger (What Doesn't Kill You)" - Kelly Clarkson

T HE AUDIENCE ROOM IS one of the more important ones in the palace. It's used for receiving special guests and dignitaries and for special meetings like the one I'm about to have with the keeper of the Privy Purse. The monarch enters through a secret door disguised as a built-in cabinet. Trickery like that makes us feel important.

It was previously named the King's Audience Room, but the "king" part was recently dropped, for obvious reasons. Someone decided just getting rid of it was easier than changing it, likely because the transition will be more efficient if we find another diary booting *me* from the throne.

The walls in here are covered in a mauve silk wallpaper that is worth thousands. While we could certainly take it down and auction it off along with the gilded mirrors, famous oil paintings, and antique furniture in the room, I would rather sell my organs on the black market than part with these historical artifacts.

Unfortunately, neither option is a long-term solution.

The door opens, and Lord Balmorran is announced. While a maid pours tea, we exchange the usual pleasantries that I swear will one day be the death of me, and after she leaves, we're finally able to approach the business at hand.

"Has the Civil List payment not come through yet?" I lift the china teacup to my lips.

"It did," Balmorran says. He's balding and wears glasses that remind me of Steve Jobs'.

"What happened to it all?" I ask. He has turned the color of the cranberries on the mantel behind him. He can't have thought I wouldn't find out. More than likely, he just hasn't come up with a plan for how to handle it yet.

"It was drained in the past few months, ma'am."

I set my cup down. "I don't understand. How is it that the royal family has survived all these years, and now suddenly we can't even make it three months? Did inflation skyrocket overnight?"

He takes a sip of tea. "It's not that, ma'am." His cup rattles on its saucer.

"Then what is it?"

I've seen people sitting in chairs with backpacks on look more comfortable than this man. "The royal family has never been able to support itself on the Civil List budget."

I wait a few beats. My brain is peanut-buttered to the sides of my skull. "Why not?"

"Well, the Civil List is nowhere near high enough to support the entire royal household."

"I see." I nod as if I understand, which I'm nowhere close to doing. "At least it's an easy fix. We'll ask Parliament to raise it."

Balmorran winces and sets his cup on the table. "I'm afraid it's not that easy. The Civil List is set in place for another four years."

A queen must not raise her voice. Must not raise her voice. Must not—

"Four *years*?"

He just looks at his lap.

"I'm sorry, but who set the Civil List so low that it couldn't support the royal household? That's the whole point of it!"

"Ideally, yes," he says. "But for centuries, the royal family has made enough of their own money that they haven't needed or wanted to ask Parliament for higher pay."

"You're saying the king was flipping burgers to pay for his butler?"

"They had *private* incomes, ma'am." Balmorran evidently can't read sarcasm any better than he can financial statements.

"And what if the monarch doesn't have a private income?" Using the interest from my trust to cover the costs would be the equivalent of trying to put out a fire with a snowflake.

"This situation is unprecedented."

"I understand that, but we need to come up with a solution—one that doesn't involve me taking on a second job. I'm working seventy hours a week as it is."

Yesterday, I had my weekly audience with the prime minister, the master of the household, and the lord chancellor in the morning. By 1:05 in the afternoon, I'd arrived in northern Wesbourne by train, received five local dignitaries at the station, traveled to the Wesbournian Soccer League, where I greeted another four dignitaries, and accepted a daisy from a little girl. From there, I toured the building, inspected trophies, met with more people, ate lunch, received a present, drank a local toast, signed the visitors' book, and unveiled a plaque. By 2:50, I was back in the car and on my way to the local civic center to do the whole thing again.

"Of course not, Your Majesty. I suggest we start by cutting salaries."

"Cutting salaries?" I stare at Balmorran over the rim of my cup. "You mean firing people."

"It's the biggest expense for the royal household."

"Yes, but those people are depending on us for their livelihood. We can't just wish them sayonara."

"I don't see what choice we have," he says. "There aren't enough funds to cover paychecks, let alone the rest of the household's expenses."

I can already see the headlines: *Queen Fires Staff to Buy More Gucci.* This will be the final straw in my battle with the press. "How many positions did you have in mind?"

"No less than four hundred."

I cough into my tea and set it down. "Excuse me. I thought you said four hundred."

"I did, ma'am."

"We employ five hundred."

Balmorran nods. "If the Civil List is our only means of payment, we need to cut at least that many jobs to stay within budget, in addition to closing the north and east wings of the palace and greatly reducing costs."

"I will not be the cause of four hundred people losing their jobs," I say. "I have a trust fund that should cover at least the staff salaries for a few months. Can we ask Parliament to bring the Civil List up to where it should be?"

"It's unlikely, but I suppose we can try. However, it could take six months or more before it goes into effect, and that's if it passes both houses."

"I will put my banker in touch with you. You are to prioritize staff salaries over any luxury or unnecessary budget line items." I stand to signal that the meeting is over. "In the meantime, we will both do everything in our power to come up with more reasonable ideas than a palace-wide layoff."

The Duke of Sutherland walks into the Audience Room with all of his former confidence and grandeur. I stop myself from curtsying just in time. Beside him walks the most beautiful dog I've ever seen. It has a glossy black coat, broken by a white cross covering its chest and rust-colored patches on its face and legs.

"Your Majesty," he says, and bows his head.

I swallow my revulsion for the man. "Good afternoon." Moving over to the animal, I offer it my hand. It sniffs eagerly before giving my fingers a big swipe with its wet tongue. "Your dog is beautiful."

"He's a Bernese Mountain Dog. And he's yours." William thrusts the leash at me.

I blink and take a step back. "I beg your pardon?"

"Consider it an act of gratitude."

"I'm afraid I don't understand."

"You stayed with me. The night Argos died."

"Yes, but"—I scramble for words—"a 'thank you' would have sufficed. You didn't need to get me a *dog*."

"I saw this guy when I went to replace Argos." He pats the animal on the head with more tenderness than I've ever seen him show toward a person. "I remembered you saying you've always wanted one." He attempts to hand me the leash again.

My chuckle sounds forced. "I appreciate the sentiment, but you can't give animals as gifts. That's a big commitment."

"You want me to take him back?"

I look at the dog. A giant pink tongue lolls from his mouth, and I swear he's smiling at me. His white muzzle stands in sharp contrast to his black coat and tapers into a white streak between his eyes. He has rich, chocolate-brown eyes, and they stay fixed on me as if he's awaiting the verdict of his future.

As a kid, I begged my parents for a dog for years, but my mum is allergic. After my father died, I forgot how it felt to want something so badly.

"No," I say, dropping to my knees. "I'll keep him." The dog easily weighs as much or more than I do, and kneeling in front of him puts us at nearly the same height. I loop both arms around his neck and am rewarded with a paw on my leg. I laugh and shake it. "What's his name?"

"Tundra."

"It suits him."

William shifts from one foot to the other, and I realize that I've kept him standing this whole time.

"Please, be seated," I say, and take the proffered leash. I lead Tundra over to the sofa opposite the duke. They both sit after I do. The only way this could be more awkward is if we were in our underwear.

I ring the small bell on the table next to me, and a maid immediately enters the room. "We'll take a tea tray, please." I glance down at Tundra. "What do dogs eat?" I ask William.

"Bah, just about anything." He waves a hand. "Except for chocolate. It'll poison them."

"Can they have ice cream?"

At his nod, I turn back to the maid, who's still awaiting my request. "And a small cup of vanilla ice cream."

She leaves to fetch our refreshments, and I address William again. "This was completely unnecessary, but it means a lot." I stroke Tundra's soft ears, and he pushes into my hand. "Thank you."

The duke gives another characteristic grunt. "I haven't always made the best choices, but having a dog is always a good idea."

I think about the things he did, how he violated his own child repeatedly and never paid for it. How can this be that same man?

He surprises me by continuing. "I wasn't a good father. I did some things I'm not proud of." He runs his hand over his shaved head. It sends a stab of familiarity through me I am not ready for.

"We can't change the past, only the future," I say.

His eyes meet mine, and I wonder what goes on in that evil mind of his. He molests children but adores dogs. It would be easier if he were just pure evil—then I could hate him with abandon.

The maid brings in our tea, and I watch as Tundra annihilates the small cup of ice cream in two seconds. He's huge. Huge dogs have huge appetites. And huge appetites cost money, lots of money . . .

"On second thought," I say after the maid leaves, "I'm not sure I'll be able to keep Tundra after all. We're cutting costs, and by the time we find a trainer, a handler, a groomer . . . I don't even know what dogs need. All of the supplies, the food, the vet bills." I press my fingers to my suddenly throbbing temples. "You should take him back."

At this, Tundra looks at me, tongue still searching his face for any leftover drops of ice cream. His eyes are pleading chocolate orbs. "I'm sorry, boy." I scratch the ruff around his neck. "I have other responsibilities that were here before you were."

"The palace is cutting costs?" The duke reaches for another tea sandwich. It's gone as quickly as Tundra's ice cream.

"Apparently, the Civil List is terribly inadequate to cover the budget." I wonder if the thread of accusation in my voice is as noticeable to him as it is to me. *You could have warned me.*

William grunts and leans back in his seat. "It's always been too low."

"Might I ask why you never had it raised?"

"I tried." He snorts and picks up another sandwich. "It was denied by Parliament on two separate occasions."

"But surely they could see that the amount was far below what is required to sustain the royal household."

"In the past, monarchs also had family estates that covered much of their living expenses. The Civil List was only increased at the rate of inflation. But maintaining an estate that actually makes money in the twenty-first century is hard."

"We had the same issue at Maison de Lierre," I say. "It costs much more than it makes."

Another sandwich disappears into William's mouth. Strong appetites must run in the family. "The Labor Party had control of Parliament at the time. You know how they disdain hereditary incomes."

"What did you do?" I nibble on my own sandwich.

"Did what I had to. Made a few investments that paid off over time."

"I don't know the first thing about that."

He shakes his head. "The Civil List should be enough to cover the royal household. You should petition Parliament. Maybe you'll have better luck than I did."

"We're talking millions, though. Where is Parliament going to get that kind of money?"

"Where they always do." William waves his sixth sandwich around. "The people."

"You mean higher taxes?"

He grunts in agreement.

"But taxes are high enough, don't you think?" I say. "I can't in good conscience raise them to pay for my own living expenses."

"Why not? The people want a queen. They should have to pay for her." His voice is lined with gruffness, but I can't tell if it's directed at me or just a product of his normal teddy bear persona.

What I wouldn't give to sit down with Adelaide right now and ask her advice on the issue. Unfortunately for me, she's currently holidaying in the Alps with her new lover and doesn't have cell reception. I'll have to make do with the duke.

"Maybe if we cut expenses as much as we can, it will only require a small tax increase," I say. It's not ideal, but I'm running out of options.

"Taxes are lower than they've ever been," William counters. "Wesbourne has one of the lowest tax rates in the world. They can stand to pay more."

He may be right. Wesbourne is known for its low taxes. And if a slight increase will allow hundreds of people to keep their jobs, that would be worth it. Right?

3

"Ghost" - Ella Henderson

"WHAT DOES ROSALIND THINK?" Maisie is sitting beside me in the back of a black limousine. There are security SUVs in front and behind us.

"My mother is the last person I would go to for advice on anything pertaining to the royal household," I say, "and I certainly would never ask her about money." She'd never recover from that major faux pas.

"Don't you think you're too hard on her?"

"I'm not any harder on her than she is on me."

I stare at the schedule for the Feed the World Foundation meeting where I'm about to make a twelve-minute appearance—just long enough to shake a few hands, take a quick tour, and present a plaque. My staff has even factored in a two-minute bathroom break.

"The duke was right," I say. "Raising taxes is the only solution."

"I have another idea, but you probably won't like it either," Maisie says. If she's prefacing it with that, I probably won't.

"What?"

"You have to promise not to shoot me, okay?"

I narrow my eyes.

She quickly immerses herself back into the digital world at her finger-tips before saying, with what I can only assume is fake nonchalance, "You could ask Henry."

I stare at her, waiting for the punchline, but she remains focused on the screen. "Henry?" I haven't said his name out loud in months. Doing so now feels like pushing on a squeaky, rusty hinge. Which is embedded in my heart.

"I know the two of you aren't speaking, but I thought—"

"If it involves Henry, you couldn't have been thinking."

"Celia, he could help with this. I know he could."

"I take back what I said about Rosalind being the last person I'd ask. At that point, I'd forgotten Henry existed." I flip to the next page, which contains a detailed map of the exact route I will take for today's walkabout, where I will have enough time to shake the hands of exactly twenty-seven people arbitrarily selected from the crowd.

"Come on. You two worked so well together when you were research-ing Helena and her lover. Surely you can put aside—"

"Put aside what? Our differences? Our mutual dislike?" *The fact that he broke my heart, drove over it with a military tank, and left the pieces to broil in the sun?*

"Didn't you say he improves businesses for a living?"

"The royal family isn't a business, Maisie."

"Doesn't mean it couldn't function as one."

I shake my head. "You're talking about taking a centuries-old institu-tion, steeped in history and culture and traditions, and commercializing it. You're out of your mind."

"Proposing a tax hike is going to sink your image."

"Believe it or not, there's more at stake here than the picture the press will paint of me. Including your job." I reach for my coffee in the cupholder. "Besides, I already submitted the request. Now we just sit back and wait for Parliament's decision."

"I know you don't think it's important," Maisie says, "but you can't lead the people if they hate you."

She's right, but I don't have time to think about my reputation right now. I have five hundred people waiting for the paychecks I owe them. Ever since the divorce, the press has painted me as the idiot who let the catch of the century get away. What's a little more fuel on the fire?

Meanwhile, Henry has retained his place as Wesbourne's golden boy, despite the fact that he hasn't set foot in the country for the past two months. A fact that proves the only thing he's good at is keeping his word.

"The decision is made," I say.

Maisie holds her palms up. "Okay. Fine. I just thought I'd suggest it." She chews on her bottom lip. "What happened between you two anyway?"

"Who?" By feigning ignorance, I'm hoping to convince my heart to slow the gallop it's currently taking around my chest.

"You and He-Who-Shall-Not-Be-Named."

I roll my eyes. "Nothing happened. It was a mutual split."

"That's the story you're selling?"

I jot down a question for my security team in the margin of my schedule. "I'm not selling anything."

"Celia, I'm not stupid or blind," she says impatiently. "I know something happened between you and Henry in London. You were caught kissing in a *pub*." To hear her, you'd think she wouldn't be caught dead in one herself.

"We were married. It meant nothing."

"So that's why you came home with streaked makeup and a cloud of gloom the next day?"

"Maisie, believe it or not, but I actually have the ability to fire you. And right now, it's very tempting. Where's the schedule for the president's state visit?"

"You can tell me if he broke your heart. We're friends, aren't we?"

"*Friendly* is not the term I'd used to describe us at the moment," I say.

From the back of my folder, she plucks a sheaf of papers that I swear wasn't there when I looked. "I don't understand how you can throw away good things like they're nothing."

I lower the folder and look over at her. "Just what 'good things' are we talking about?"

"Well, you threw away your engagement to Beckham as soon as a better opportunity presented itself." She holds up a hand to squelch my interruption. "And then you chased after Henry, only to walk away from that too. You don't even realize how lucky you are."

I'm rarely speechless, but there's a first time for everything.

"Don't look at me like that," she continues. "I know that was an over-simplification, but you have no idea what it's like to sit on the sidelines of your life while you work your way through some of the most eligible bachelors in the world. Meanwhile, I would love to go on a single date with a guy who can talk about something—literally anything—other than his bunions the entire evening."

"Bunions," I deadpan.

"I wish I was joking."

I snort out a laugh. "That's awful. Truly."

"Don't get me started on the one who brought his mother along, because apparently they were a package deal."

"You're right. I was lucky when it came to dating." Beck is the only man I've officially dated, aside from a few blind dates set up by friends. Even those weren't horrific. "But just because you don't see the pain, doesn't mean it's not there."

"I can understand the Beck situation. Your hands were tied. But I thought you loved Henry. Why walk away from that?"

I stare out the window as we ride through the streets of Wesbourne City. Pedestrians turn and wave when they see the flags flying from the bonnet of the car.

"Loving someone doesn't mean they'll love you back," I say quietly.

I am done trying with Henry, but that doesn't mean there aren't nights I lie awake thinking about the sound of his voice or his hands sliding down my body. I recognize the ache in my chest for what it is: a longing for him and what we never had. But I'm the queen, and I can't afford to waste my thoughts on a man who doesn't deserve them.

Maisie's right, though. He would be able to help me figure out a way to turn the royal finances around. He's brilliant at solving problems, even if he's equally brilliant at breaking hearts.

But brilliant or not, there's no way in hell I'm talking to him. Even if I could trust him, I don't know where he is. I haven't seen or heard from him since the day he left me in his hotel room in London, other than that brief flash at my coronation. He could have set up camp in Antarctica for all I know.

"I'm sorry," Maisie says. I can see in her eyes that she means it.

"Good thing I'm too busy being queen to have a love life, right? I'll have to live vicariously through you from now on."

"Oh boy."

"We'll have to find you some better candidates, though. I don't want bunions and IBS haunting my dreams."

"How about—"

But I don't find out what she's about to suggest, because the sound of screeching metal tears through the air. My body lifts from the seat, and I'm hurled forward. I slam into something hard, and then everything goes black.

I wake to the cloying scent of antiseptic burning my nose. My mouth is parched. There's something cool under my hands. When I blink my eyes open, it takes me a second to realize I'm in a hospital room and that the beeping is the myriad of monitors hooked up to me.

Panic grips me, and I begin to search for the nearest exit. I can't be here. I cannot be in this place where death waits in the halls, ready to snatch you as soon as you let your guard down. I can't die. I have people to lead. They may not like me very much right now, but I am still their queen.

I take several calming breaths. I can't be dying. There's no way death feels like this.

I do a quick assessment. I can feel all of my limbs, so that's good, but my head is pounding like it's recently been used as a battering ram. Whatever pain meds they have me on must be strong, because, while the pain is in check now, I can feel the monster rattling the cage.

A movement to my left makes me turn my head, which I instantly regret when the throbbing increases.

My mother hurries to the side of my bed. "Don't move. Are you able to talk?"

"Water," I croak.

She holds one of those nasty plastic cups to my lips. I obediently take a sip. Maybe this is death after all.

"How are you feeling?" she asks.

"Like I've been run over by a very large truck."

"Do you remember anything?"

"I remember being in the car. Everything's hazy after that."

"The limo struck a cement barrier. It's a miracle you're even here." She brushes her hand over the sheet covering my legs, smoothing away invisible wrinkles.

"Maisie?" I squeak out.

"She's very fortunate—minor injuries only. The car wasn't traveling very fast. You were thrown against the privacy divider."

I lift a hand and rub at my forehead. The IV tubing in my arm follows. "My head hurts like crazy."

"That's because you have a concussion and a fractured skull." My mother tugs my hand away and places it back on my lap. "You'll be in recovery for a while."

"How long?"

"As long as the doctor orders."

"I have responsibilities," I say.

"You have a *fractured skull.*"

"I'm going to be fine though, right? No brain damage or anything?" If there is, I'll probably need to abdicate, and then this whole thing will have been for nothing.

"They don't think so, but they want to keep an eye on you just in case."

I close my eyes and press my head further into the cracker masquerading as my pillow. "Is the driver okay?"

Her face pinches, and I already know from the way she continues to aggressively smooth the sheet. "He died on impact."

I don't even know his name, and now he's dead. "Please arrange for flowers to be sent to the family and cover the cost of the funeral."

My mum nods. "Of course. I'll make sure everything is taken care of. You don't need to worry about a thing."

"You said we hit a barrier of some kind? What happened?"

"The car lost a wheel, and the driver lost control. It all happened very quickly."

"What about the rest of the motorcade? Did they . . . ?"

She shakes her head. "They were able to avert it. They got you out immediately and brought you here."

I look around the room. It's spacious, and all of the curtains are pulled. Bouquets of flowers cover nearly every surface. I can already envision the approaching arguments between Rosalind and the nurses over the use of flat surfaces. Naturally, my mum will win, and the flowers will stay. Medication is second-rate to aesthetics, after all.

One bouquet in the corner has a yellow balloon floating above it. I move to sit up, and she pushes another pillow behind my back.

"Careful," she warns. "Moving too fast will make your head hurt."

"Yeah, I discovered that," I say around a wince. "Get rid of that balloon, please."

"Consider it done." She smooths my pillow once more.

"How does one increase the dosage of these meds?"

My mother shakes her head. "The doctor wanted you to wake up, so she's limited your painkillers for now. Try to go a little longer without another dose."

"Not all of us have the pain threshold of a stunt double."

"Try to rest. That will help." She pats my hand like I'm three years old again and in bed with a cold.

Someone knocks on the door, and she moves to open it. Instead of letting them in, however, she shuts it again after they exchange a few words.

"Who was it?" I ask when she returns to my side.

"Daphne. They've limited visits to immediate family only." She holds up the bag in her hand. "But she brought your salvation!"

"Indian take-out?"

"Don't be ridiculous. It's makeup." She opens the bag and starts rummaging through it.

"Mum, I'm in the hospital. Pretty sure looking terrible is a requisite for admission."

"Commoners are allowed to look terrible. You are the queen." She holds up a bottle of foundation and a beauty blender. "Now, I'm no Daphne, but I think I can manage to make my daughter look a little more like a human being."

"And here I was kind of digging the zombie look."

My mum shushes me and begins dabbing makeup on my face. "You need to call your sister when we're done. She's been worried sick."

"I hope you told her I'm fine."

"Of course I did. But she's threatening to come home and check on you yourself."

"That's nice of her." Bea would rush into a burning building to save someone's teddy bear. Her heart is huge. Her common sense isn't always up to speed.

"It's completely unnecessary," my mother says. "She needs to stay in England."

"I'm sure her professors would understand—"

"I'm not worried about her studies."

"Okay." I drag out the word. "Then what are you worried about?"

She swipes at my lashes with a mascara wand. "Men don't wait forever, and if she leaves now . . ."

"What, she'll become a spinster?"

"It's not outside the bounds of possibility."

"She's twenty years old, Mum. And one of the most sought-after women in the world." Beatrice is gorgeous enough to have been offered dozens of modeling gigs, famous enough to have landed the cover of every major publication in the world at least once, and has never had to attend an event alone.

"The right men get snatched up much faster than women."

I sigh. "Is this about the prince of Denmark?"

"I won't discuss the details of your sister's love life. You can ask her about it when you call." Mum carefully places all the makeup back into the bag and stands. "And tell her to stay where she is."

After she leaves, I tap Bea's contact on my phone. Her face fills the screen almost immediately.

"Oh my god, Celia! Are you okay?"

"I'm fine. A few bumps and bruises." I adjust myself ever so slightly and cover my grimace with a smile.

The video swerves as my sister walks across the room and climbs onto her bed. "Mum can't come to grips with the fact that we're both adults now and can make our own decisions. I can get on a flight tonight—"

"You don't need to leave England."

"But I should be there for you!" she says.

"Bea, seriously. There's no reason for you to come home."

She pauses, staring at me through the phone as though looking for reassurance that I'm not on the brink of death. "I just want to do something helpful."

"Then distract me by telling me about your latest fling."

Her head drops. It's hard to tell through the screen, but I could almost swear she's blushing. "There isn't much to tell. Yet."

"Do I know him?"

"You might know *of* him."

I'm reminded of a very similar conversation we had this past spring, the night I discovered we were both in love with the same man. "I hope it works out. You deserve to be happy."

"Don't tell Mum, because she reads way too much into these things, but I might move in with him next year."

My head rears back slightly. "Isn't that rushing things a little? How well do you know this guy?"

"I think he might be the one." Her face is glowing with happiness.

I take a deep breath. Probably better to change the subject than to remind her of the number of times she's thought a man might be "the one." "You're still coming home for the holidays, right?"

"Of course. I can't wait for a real Wesbourne Christmas."

This year, the holidays will be nothing like what we're used to, now that we are Wesbourne's royal family. Fireside board games will be replaced with walkabouts downtown, family Christmas parties will be traded for fancy charity galas, and the gingerbread baking will now be done by the staff at the palace. But I'm as excited as Bea is. It will be good to be together again, even if it's not at Maison de Lierre this year.

We hang up a few minutes later, and I close my eyes, hoping the drugs will pull me under quickly. This monster of a headache is starting to show its fangs. I'm just drifting off when a commotion in the hall outside drags me back to consciousness.

I can hear multiple voices arguing and the soles of the nurses' trainers squeaking against the tile floor. I'll have to see how quickly I can be released. How is anyone supposed to get rest with this constant noise?

My eyes flutter shut but immediately fly open again when one of the voices becomes distinct above the others.

"I don't give a damn about your bloody policies!"

My throbbing head now feels like a distant memory. There are more important physical matters to attend to, like the way my heart is about to pound right through my rib cage and bounce across the floor.

I know that voice as well as my own, and it's angry. Very angry.

Henry is back.

4

"Jar of Hearts" - Christina Perri

W HAT IN THE BLOODY hell is Henry doing here?

The sterile hospital air is clogging my throat. I think I'm going to be sick. He is the last person I want to see right now, but I am suddenly beyond grateful for Rosalind's quick makeover. I'm not stupid enough to miss the fact that he must be here because of me. I'm just too hyped on drugs to figure out *why*.

Speaking of meds, there has to be a buzzer nearby. If I can flag down a nurse before he finds a way to be allowed in, maybe I can convince her to give me enough painkillers to slip into a coma for the next few years.

The door to my room opens before I'm able to locate the button. I freeze, but it's only my mother. The ruckus in the hall has quieted down. Through the door, I catch a glimpse of several PPOs stationed outside. Davies is one of them, which gives me a breath of comfort.

"What's going on out there?" My nonchalance deserves an Oscar.

"I didn't know if you were still awake. Are you up for a visitor?" My mother has yet to remove her hand from the doorknob.

"I don't think so," I say. "I'm really tired."

"He came a long way."

"I should get some rest."

"I'll tell him to make it quick."

"I thought you said it was family on—"

She ignores me and opens the door.

And then he's here.

In my room.

At the foot of my bed.

Breathing the same air as me.

No. No, no, no, no, no.

He's wearing one of my favorite shirts. It's a pale blue linen, the top several buttons undone and the sleeves rolled up to the elbows. His hands are in the pockets of his white trousers, which are perfectly tailored to his body. He looks as though he's come straight from a modeling shoot where the vibe is "casually tousled" and "roguishly dangerous." All of the blood in my body rushes to my skin.

"I'll give you two some time," my mother says before closing the door on her way out. Neither of us looks at her. I couldn't break away from his gaze if I tried.

As the door clicks into place, Henry backs away, putting as much distance between us as possible. Maybe he thinks I'm contagious. He rakes a hand through his hair and slides his back down the wall until he reaches the floor, as if his legs are no longer able to keep him upright.

The last time I heard his voice, he said he regretted the two nights we spent together. His regret over our childhood friendship was unspoken, but implied.

Now he's here to rip the wound open again.

He doesn't give any indication that he's going to speak, just holds my gaze like it's the only thing keeping him afloat.

I can't handle it anymore. I tear my eyes away and focus on the thin blanket covering my legs. "Why are you here, Henry?" It's barely a whisper, but it feels too loud.

He doesn't answer.

Seconds tick by. When I finally look up at him again, his eyes are still on me, full of pain. My heart splits like a watermelon hitting the ground.

"When they told me about the accident . . ." He rubs his hand over his face. "No one had any details. Just that the driver was dead, and—" He takes a shaky breath. "And you'd been rushed to the hospital. When I left London, I still didn't have any updates." He folds his arms over his bent knees and rests his forehead against them, hiding his face. "That was the longest flight of my life. You can't imagine the horrific things I was imagining."

I need to staunch the bleeding, or I will succumb to him in a heartbeat. "Well, I'm fine."

He lifts his head. "Only by sheer luck."

"I'm not picky."

"Don't downplay this, C."

Shrugging, I study the geometric pattern on the blanket. "What's the sense in rehashing something that didn't happen?"

"You could've died!"

"Sorry to disappoint you."

Henry pushes off from the floor and stalks over to the bed, forcing the breath from my lungs as he does so. Then he leans down, hands propped on either side of me, until he's close enough that I can see the gold flecks in his eyes. "You must have hit your head pretty hard if you think for one second losing you would be preferable to death itself."

My lip trembles, and I can't think, not with his scent swirling around me, his intoxicating presence so close—close enough that I could kiss him if I wanted. Which, for the record, I don't.

"How did you get here so fast?" I manage to whisper.

"*Fast?* The accident was seven hours ago. It took them twenty fucking minutes to let me know."

Someone got fired, of that I am certain.

London is a six-hour flight away. He must have left immediately.

"Rosalind said they're only allowing family in." I swallow. He still hasn't moved away.

His lip curls derisively, and he shakes his head. "They weren't going to let me in." He finally pushes away from the bed, taking his addictive piney scent with him. "Stupid hospital policies."

"I'm surprised they didn't throw you out." God, how I wish they would've.

"They tried." A smirk lifts the corner of his mouth. "I can be very stubborn."

"I hadn't noticed," I deadpan.

"Glad to see your tongue wasn't affected."

"I told you I'm fine. You came back for nothing."

"As a matter of fact," he says, "I'm home for good."

"You're what?"

"I'm tired of London. And I have things to take care of here."

"But—" *You promised you'd stay away.*

"I'm not going to complicate things for you. But I need to be here."

I can't very well keep him from his home. But how the hell am I supposed to move on knowing he's so close? Watching him attend events with other women? Hearing his name on the lips of every person in the country?

"Where will you live?" This inane question is the one my brain decides is appropriate.

"I have a flat downtown."

Why does it feel like my heart is breaking all over again? I'm over him, damn it. "Why did you even come here?"

He looks at me like the answer is obvious. "I needed to know you were okay."

"I'm in better shape than I was the day you left me in London." Then, because I'm tired of restraining my tongue: "A car crash doesn't have anything on your ability to hurt me."

He sucks in a sharp inhale. "God, C."

I pluck at a loose thread on my blanket, avoiding his eyes. It was a low blow, but he deserved it. Unfortunately, it's not as satisfying as I thought it'd be.

"At least you're alive," he says.

"Staying alive just to feel like you're drowning isn't much of a life."

"I'd say I'm sorry again, but I doubt you'd believe me."

I cross my arms over my chest. "You're right. Might as well save your breath."

Henry's eyes close briefly. He runs his hand through his hair again and walks to the window, using a few fingers to push the curtain aside. "I know you think I don't care."

"You've said as much."

He spins around to face me. "I *never* said that."

"Then it was implied."

"There has never been a point in my life when I wouldn't have given up everything for you."

I scoff. "You have a strange way of showing it."

The sigh that drags itself from his chest is heavy. "I wish I could explain."

"I don't see anything stopping you."

"Not everything is visible to the naked eye."

I throw up my hands. "If you want to keep talking in riddles, please do so elsewhere. I'm going to get some rest."

"I'm sorry. I shouldn't have stayed so long."

"You shouldn't have come at all."

"I'm glad you're going to be okay," he says.

"That's debatable."

His eyes close. "Can I get you anything before I go?"

I shake my head.

He watches me for a few more moments, then walks over and kisses my forehead. His lips on my skin is all it takes. Suddenly he's the only thing I want, the only thing I can even comprehend. I scrape the bottom of my barrel of self-control to restrain myself from reaching up and pulling him down to my mouth.

"Take care, Celia," he says, straightening.

"Do you have any idea the hell I've been through since that day?" I ask as he walks toward the door.

He stops, his hand on the knob, and turns to look at me. "Yeah," he says softly. "I do."

5

"Look What You Made Me Do" - Taylor Swift

THE HOSPITAL DISCHARGES ME a week later, after confirming I suffered no brain damage from the impact. My list of prescriptions is as long as a grocery list, and I'm accompanied by a private nurse, because while I may be able to lead a country, I sure as heck can't be trusted to open a bottle of pills on my own.

"It's only for a few weeks, until you feel more like yourself," Maisie says. We're in the sitting room of my private suite, where all of my meetings are being held until a doctor deems it safe for me to walk through my own home.

"I feel perfectly normal," I say. "I don't need a babysitter."

She gulps down some of her coffee—likely her tenth cup this morning—before crossing and uncrossing her legs. "I have a favor to ask. Normally I wouldn't under the circumstances, but since you're not at full capacity for the time being anyway, I thought it might actually be a better time than ever, and I—"

"Maisie," I say. "Just say it."

"Okay." She huffs out a quick breath. "I was wondering if I could take off early tonight. If it's too inconvenient, I totally understand. I was just thinking that, since you won't be attending any events yet—"

"Of course." In the six months she's been working as my private secretary and assistant, she hasn't left early even once.

"Really?"

"Absolutely. Take off whenever you need to."

"Thank you!" Rather than providing an explanation for her request, she remains uncharacteristically quiet.

"Big date tonight?" I prod.

She turns violently red. "It's— I mean— I'm not sure what . . ."

"Come on, Maisie. Don't hold out on me. I'm practically bedridden."

"Well, I just— It's complicated."

"Let me guess: he has a foot fetish?"

"No! At least I don't think so." She pushes her glasses up. "This one definitely has potential."

"And? I need details."

She stares at me for a few beats. "I can't. Not yet."

"What do you mean? Why not?"

"I have this weird superstition that it won't work out if I tell anyone."

I open my mouth to argue, then close it. She's entitled to her superstitions. "Fine. But you'll tell me if things progress, right?"

"Of course," she says quickly, then turns her attention to her tablet. "By the way, this was sent out yesterday morning." She hands it to me, and I read the email on the screen.

To all employees of the Royal Family and the Palace,

Please be informed that heightened security measures have been put into place, effective immediately.

All visitors must be approved by the Head of Palace Security, no exceptions. No one is to enter the Palace or its grounds without a full-body sweep. This directive includes employees. All communication on Palace servers will be monitored more closely than ever.

Her Majesty is not to leave the Palace without six armed escorts at any point. She will also be accompanied by no less than five additional vehicles, for a total of eight in the motorcade.

"What is going on?" I hand the tablet back.

"I don't know. It was in my inbox when I got to work."

"Did something happen?"

A forced laugh slips through Maisie's nose. "You mean besides the fact that you were in an accident?"

"Besides that."

She shrugs. "The staff have seemed more tense than usual, but I just chalked it up to you still being in the hospital."

"Nothing else out of the ordinary? No break-ins or bomb threats?"

"Not that I know of," she says.

"How is the public responding to the whole thing?"

"Initially, everyone was freaking out. But once news got out that you were going to be okay, I think things calmed down."

"And now?"

"There are still some odd conspiracy theories out there, but they're all from crackpots."

"Conspiracies about what?" I ask.

"That the accident was deliberate sabotage."

I smooth the wrinkles from my skirt. "That's ridiculous."

"Some people will believe anything."

"So why the intense security then?"

"No clue." Maisie shakes her head. "Maybe you can talk to someone? Getting patted down before work is not my favorite part of the job."

I scoff. "And an eight-car motorcade? This is insane."

"Should I set up a meeting with the head of security?"

"Yes. And get rid of my nurse. One of my six bodyguards should be able to open a bloody bottle of pills."

Derrick Jameson, the head of palace security, is a large ex-military man with a buzz cut and a face permanently lined from what I imagine to be stress. He bows in greeting after being ushered into the small office in my suite.

"Good morning, Mr. Jameson," I say.

I motion to a chair opposite me, then sit down and fold my arms on my desk, hoping I present an intimidating picture. "It has recently come to my attention that security at the palace is being increased."

"Yes, Your Majesty, that is correct."

"I have taken a look at these measures, and they seem a bit . . . over the top."

Mr. Jameson doesn't so much as bat an eyelash. "I'm simply following orders, ma'am."

"Whose orders?"

"The risk analysis team works in connection with security."

"I see," I say.

"I take my job very seriously, ma'am."

"I'm sure you do. I didn't mean to imply otherwise. Can I ask what prompted these new measures? Has there been a breach recently that I'm unaware of?"

He hesitates a moment, and his face remains emotionless while he tries to decide what I should and shouldn't know. "Like I said, ma'am, I'm simply following orders."

I raise my brows. "So you're saying someone else ordered these new requirements?"

"I don't think I said that exactly, ma'am."

"You really don't need to keep referring to me as *ma'am*."

"I'd feel more comfortable doing so. Ma'am." He is proving harder to crack than I anticipated. What is he keeping from me?

"Mr. Jameson," I say, walking around to the front of the desk. I perch on the edge, allowing my Louboutin heels and my dress, which has ridden up several inches, to highlight my toned calves. "We both know you are excellent at your job and that the palace is already very secure. Which begs the question, why the sudden need for extra security?"

He rises to his feet and clears his throat, looking everywhere but at my legs. "Ma'am, I can assure you, it's only for your protection."

"I truly am grateful for your dedication. But I would still like to know who issued the command."

"I'm afraid I'm not at liberty to disclose that information."

"I am the queen, for god's sake. You work for me."

"Well—" He hesitates. "Not exactly."

"What do you mean? Palace security falls under the royal household, which is headed by the lord chancellor, who answers to me."

Mr. Jameson coughs into his fist. "Forgive me for the correction, ma'am, but palace security is conducted by an outside firm."

"An outside firm? What are you talking about?"

"I really don't know the details."

"And you're refusing to tell me the name of your employer?"

"My career will be in jeopardy if I do so, ma'am."

"Well, I don't want that." I straighten to my full height. "But you can tell your boss that I will get to the bottom of this."

I've been advised by my doctor to lie low for the time being, and Maisie has canceled or postponed all of my engagements for the next month.

This leaves me with more leisure time than I'm used to—more than enough for a little sleuthing.

My sitting room has become dull, so Maisie and I are settled in the conservatory, which has exploded with poinsettias in the past week. The late autumn sunshine is pouring in through the glass walls, and I discard the cashmere wrap Maisie insisted I bring along. She's almost as bad as the nurse she fired.

She stops clacking on her laptop and looks up. "I think I found something."

I sit upright on the bench. I'd almost given up on this pathetic search. We've been in here for nearly an hour, with only a few leads and more than enough dead ends.

Carrying her laptop, Maisie moves to sit beside me. "We already know that palace security is managed by Eastport Allied, because it's cheaper than keeping our own staff."

I nod. That information only took about ten minutes to track down.

"And whenever I try to figure out who owns Eastport Allied, I keep coming back to a shell company."

"CEEL Acquisition Corp."

"Right. It is a dead end, which is its entire purpose, but when I looked at the address on file, I got somewhere."

I stare at her screen, but it's a confusing mess.

"It turns out there are several other companies that use the same address," she says.

I beam at her. "You're brilliant."

"I know." She clicks a few more times until she finds what she's looking for. "Most of them are shells too, but there is one that isn't."

A flashy web page pops up, displaying a massive tower in downtown Wesbourne, all glass walls and steel. The slideshow changes to reveal the interior, which includes a dog-grooming facility, a therapeutic yoga garden, and the biggest pool I've ever seen.

"This is the Atlantis, Wesbourne's tallest, most expensive, and most drool-worthy high-rise," she announces. "That last bit is just my own opinion."

"It's impressive," I say. "But what does this have to do with palace security?"

She clears her throat. "All of the shell companies, including CEEL Acquisition Corp., use the Atlantis as their listed address."

"Is that legal?"

"It is if their business is conducted there or if the owner of the shell company lives there."

I sigh. "There must be a hundred flats in that place. How in the world will we know which one belongs to the owner?"

Maisie grins and holds up her index finger. "Tell me I'm brilliant again."

"Not until you solve this."

"Tell me now, because once you see this, you're going to be too pre-occupied to remember."

I frown and move to grab the laptop from her.

She snatches it back. "We can find the owner of CEEL because the Atlantis is also registered to the same address."

"Obviously. Where else would it be?"

"Let me finish. The Atlantis is also owned by a shell company."

"God, this person really wants to remain anonymous."

"You can't really blame them. They are protecting the royal family, after all."

I roll my eyes. "More like suffocating. But seriously, just tell me who it is."

"The shell company for the Atlantis? CeEl Capital Corp. You can't tell me that's a coincidence."

"Definitely not. But I don't see how this isn't just moving in circles."

"Oh, it is. It definitely is. That's why it took me so long to figure it out. What they didn't anticipate was my utter genius." She pulls up another page, this one listing the available amenities and businesses housed inside the Atlantis: restaurants, a health spa, and the like.

"What am I looking at?" I ask.

"That's the list of businesses owned by Atlantis Holdings Inc."

"Oh god, another shell?"

"Nope. This one is a *holding* company."

"Maisie, I swear to god, if you don't get to the point soon—"

"I found out who bought Atlantis Holdings Inc. last year."

"It is, I'm assuming, the same person who owns Eastport Allied?"

She nods. "Just promise you won't shoot the messenger."

I narrow my eyes. "I'll shoot you if you don't get this over with."

"Okay. But don't say I didn't warn you."

The computer screen switches to an overview of a basic database. I skim the contents until I get to the section naming the owner.

My blood runs cold in my veins.

That son of a bitch.

6

"Queen" - Loren Gray

"**W**E DON'T KNOW FOR sure that Henry was the one who changed the security protocol. It could have been some-one—"

"It was him," I say, blotting my crimson lipstick.

Maisie paces the length of my bedroom while I put the finishing touches on my makeup. "Even if it was, do you really think this is a good idea?"

"Why wouldn't it be?"

"If he's as stubborn as you say he is, I'm not sure how much good it will do."

I meet her gaze in the mirror. "You forget I can be stubborn, too."

"Oh no, I'm reminded of it frequently. Especially when you choose to ignore your better judgment." She waves a hand at my dress, which is definitely not modest enough for a state function. "Case in point."

I shrug. "Henry needs to understand who's in charge."

After several beats, she asks, "And who is that?"

I glare at her reflection. "It sure as hell isn't him."

"I don't like it. You're not as strong as you were before the accident."

"I'm perfectly fine." I feel frustration rise in my chest. "Your attempts to coddle me like a small child will only make it worse."

"Why can't you just email him?"

"Emailing Henry would be as effective as attempting to break into a vault with only your fists."

Her brows knit together. "Your doctor said you should wait a month before resuming your normal duties."

I stand up from the vanity and grab my handbag. "Then rest assured. This is anything but a normal duty."

My limo has been replaced with a revolving series of SUVs, all identical, and the one I ride in changes each time so that would-be assassins won't know if I'm in the third car or the fourth, although everyone knows it's never the first or last car.

The fumes from this eight-vehicle motorcade might be solely responsible for the thawing of the Arctic, not to mention the draining of the last bit of cash in the Privy Purse. What better way to let everyone in sight know that the queen is on the move than with an entire city block of cars bearing the Wesbourne flag? I'd be safer in a Toyota Camry I was driving myself.

The procession pulls into the underground garage at the Atlantis, which Maisie discovered houses the headquarters of all of Henry's businesses, as well as Henry himself. The garage looks more like an Italian ballroom than a place to park. The floor is brick, and the walls are a gleaming white tile. Giant chandeliers hang from the ceiling, giving off a soft glow.

My car pulls up beside a set of glass doors leading to a bank of lifts. Several of the PPOs exit to speak to the armed guards standing at the doors. After a few moments, they line up to create a barricaded tunnel for me to walk through, in spite of the fact that we waited fifteen minutes for them to do a full sweep of the space before we entered.

I can't wait to give Henry a piece of my mind.

The lift door opens immediately. I try to calm my nerves, but my pulse is a runaway horse with its tail on fire. This seemed like a good idea back at the palace, but now that I'm moments away from seeing Henry, I'm beginning to question the sanity of the whole thing.

The elevator slows to a stop, then opens into a lounge area, complete with sofas, a TV, and a kitchenette. Several security personnel are standing about. After a brief and hushed conversation between them and my guys, I'm ushered to a set of double doors on the other side of the room. A member of Henry's security team gives me a stiff bow and opens them for me. I step through to the flat on the other side, and my breath rushes from my mouth.

Opposite me, a wall of glass overlooks Wesbourne City, the lake in full view and the streetlights just starting to blink on. The ceiling soars above us, and even after living in the palace for months, the sight of this much luxury nearly makes my jaw swing on its hinges.

Music floats on the air, a peaceful, lilting melody that stands in contrast to the stark, cold feel of the modern furnishings. Groups of streamlined sofas and chairs are clustered in front of the giant windows, their sharp silhouettes softened by the glow from the lamps scattered around the room. The grand piano in the center looks ordinary rather than grand in this massive space.

"Her Majesty the Queen, sir," says the PPO who escorted me inside.

I turn in surprise. I didn't notice anyone during my gawking. The music stops, and Henry steps out from behind the piano, easily lost in the large surroundings.

My heart rate kicks into full gear, as if the band has just stepped onto the stage. Taking a deep breath, I order the weird hum surging through me to stop. It does not obey.

"Thank you, Roberts," Henry says, keeping his eyes on me.

The PPO nods and leaves the room.

Henry studies me through narrowed eyes. I wonder if he suspects why I'm here. "Celia." He motions to the sofa behind him. "Have a seat. I'll get us some drinks."

Instead of obliging, I opt to stroll through the room. Everywhere my eyes land, there's chrome, glass, and squint-inducing white. Sharp lines and harsh edges define every single object, and there isn't any decoration that even hints at the approaching holiday.

I manage to find the one item in the whole room that looks out of place. It's a small wooden frame on a round table tucked into a corner. I move closer to see it better. As recognition dawns on me, so does regret.

The picture is of Henry and me twelve or thirteen years ago. We're sun-tanned and grinning at the camera. My arms are thrown around his neck as he gives me a piggyback ride, and his hand is resting on my arm. A woven friendship bracelet dangles from his wrist.

"One of my favorites."

I jump at the sound of Henry's voice and turn to find him standing a few feet away, holding two glasses of wine. He hands me one, and an electric current rushes up my arm as his fingers brush mine. I move back to the sofa and take a seat. It's softer than it appears, and I allow myself to sink into it just a little. He settles in across from me.

I sip the wine and try to get my bearings. Being here has completely thrown me off my game. This is Henry's *home*, the place he spends his time, where he lives his life. This is what he chose instead of me.

Something hard and achy forms in my chest.

He's wearing a long-sleeved Henley and soft blue jeans. The buttons of his shirt are undone, and his hair is a disheveled mess. My body wants nothing more than to curl up in his arms, inhale that scent that I am missing so much it hurts, and listen to the steady beat of his heart. My head, on the other hand, reminds me that he will never be mine.

I should have settled for an email.

I manage to find my voice in spite of the tightness in my throat. "Do you always play piano before receiving visitors?"

"Only when it's you."

I sip my wine to hide my discomfort. "This place is impressive. You've got your own castle in the sky."

"It has the best security in Wesbourne," he says.

"Not surprising, considering it's also home to the most elite security company in the country."

His left eye twitches. "What are you talking about?"

"Come on, Henry. You're not the only one with crafty people in your employ." I slowly cross my legs and enjoy the look of momentary stupefaction that crosses his face. "Imagine my surprise when I found out who owns Eastport Allied."

His features have pulled into an expressionless mask, but I know I've shaken him. He thought he was safe behind his wall of shell companies. Maisie needs a raise.

I take another sip of wine and rest my arm on the back of the sofa, aware that it highlights my body in the best possible way. The movement attracts his eyes. When he looks back at me, he seems to be holding back a smile.

"And you're here because . . . ?" he says.

"You promised you wouldn't complicate things for me."

"I did."

"Well, you failed to keep that promise the day you increased my security detail."

He narrows his eyes. "I guess Mr. Jameson will be looking for a new position."

Leaning forward, I set my glass on the table. "Don't you dare fire him. He didn't say a word, even when I threatened him."

"You threatened him? With what, your Louboutins?" Henry smirks into his wine.

I shoot him the filthiest glare I can muster. "Has there been a breach of security recently?"

"I'm not sure."

"You're not sure?"

"The risk analysis team doesn't have any conclusive results yet," he says.

"So you'll let Mr. Jameson know the new protocol isn't necessary after all?"

"Uh, no." Henry drags the word out.

"What do you mean, no?"

"I mean the security protocol stays."

"But there isn't even a threat!"

He crosses his arms. "I feel the need for increased protection."

"Then increase your own damn security!"

"I meant protection for you."

"Bloody hell, Henry! I am perfectly capable of making those kinds of decisions for myself."

He leans forward and rests his elbows on his knees, his wine glass dangling from his fingers. "I disagree. The fact that you're here to argue with me over this proves my point. You should be grateful for the extra security, not resenting it."

I gnaw on the inside of my lip, hoping the right words will present themselves. "We can't afford the extra security. We can't even afford the normal routine."

"What are you talking about?"

"I'm talking about the fact that when your father was king, the royal household was almost entirely funded by his private income, of which I have next to none. The Privy Purse is empty. I'm scrambling to find a way to pay the salaries of all of my staff. Increasing the security detail is out of the question, I'm afraid."

Henry's brows pull into a dark *V*. "What about the Civil List?"

"Not up for reconsideration for another four years. And nowhere close to being enough."

"What about—"

"Henry, please." I swallow the desperation creeping into my voice. "I'm not here to discuss financial matters. Just agree to drop the extra security, and I'll be out of your hair."

He shakes his head and sets his glass on the table. "Absolutely not."

"I just told you I can't afford—"

"We'll do it at no extra charge."

"I—" I am aware my mouth has fallen open, but it refuses to listen to orders to close. "You can't do that."

"I can do whatever I like. It's my company."

"I appreciate the offer," I say, "but I would feel better if we just dropped the whole thing. My staff is getting uncomfortable."

"Celia, this isn't about comfort. We're talking about your life." His voice has grown lethal.

"Since when has my life been in jeopardy?"

Standing abruptly, Henry walks to the window. The city lights glimmer like stars in the growing darkness. "You were just in an accident," he says quietly.

"Exactly. It was an *accident*. Enhanced security wouldn't have prevented it."

"We haven't confirmed that it wasn't something else."

"That's nothing but a conspiracy theory."

He turns to face me. "Until we can completely rule it out, I'm not about to gamble with your life."

"It's not your decision to make."

"Actually, as the final word on palace security, it is."

My hands ball into fists at my sides as I stand. "You lost the privilege to influence my decisions the day you walked out on me. And you certainly lost the right to interfere with my life."

He lowers his head and rakes a hand through his hair. "I know. But it's not going to stop me."

Is he serious? That isn't the way this works. "You promised you'd stay away. Making decisions like this behind my back, *against my wishes*, is the opposite of staying away."

He stalks over, stopping right in front of me. "Then get used to it. Because this is how it's going to be until I can confirm there isn't a threat."

His scent permeates my senses, begging me to give up, to melt into him. But that way madness lies. I blink to clear the fog that's creeping in.

"What qualifies you to know what's best for me?" I ask.

He gives me an amused smile. "Well, there isn't a thing I don't know about you."

Except how easy it would be for me to spiral again. My mouth is full of sand, and all I can do is whisper, "Prove it."

His eyes search mine. "I know that every nerve ending in your body is on fire right now. If I so much as touch you, you'll combust on the spot. I know that kissing that spot behind your ear lobe makes you whimper. And I know that you'd rather die than admit it when you're scared."

I will also die before I let him see the effect he has on me. "You cocky bastard."

"It's all true, isn't it?"

"Fuck you, Henry."

He grabs my chin in his hand. "Fuck me all you want, baby. The security stays."

It's like he's touched me with a branding iron, my skin seared by his claim. I jerk away from him and stumble backward. "I guess we'll see about that, won't we?"

He shakes his head, and another small smile plays on his lips—lips I can still taste when I close my eyes. "You won't get anywhere with Mr. Jameson, no matter how short your skirt is."

My mouth drops open again. I snap it shut. "You are positively abhorrent." Is there anything the man doesn't know?

"So you've told me, on more than one occasion. It doesn't change the fact that your safety is more important than your comfort."

"You don't even know that I'm in danger!"

Henry props his hands on his hips, and I can almost feel the tension leaking from his body. "Your car lost a wheel, C. The only way that could have happened is if the lug nuts were loose. The cars are inspected before they leave the palace, so either there's an employee who will be lucky to be alive after I get my hands on him, or someone intentionally sabotaged the car while you were gone."

"Lug nuts can loosen over time, can't they?"

"No," he snaps. "Not like that."

"Think about all of the extra work this will require of the security team because of something you don't even know was intentional."

He scoffs as if I'm a ridiculous child. "Like I would risk your life to keep up company morale."

"Too bad you didn't show the same consideration for my heart," I say bitterly.

"C." His voice breaks.

I look away from the hurt in his eyes. "Just leave me alone, Henry. Please."

7

"Fight Song" - Rachel Platten

THE THING MOST PEOPLE don't realize about royals is that we're actually quite normal. We bleed red, we don't like Brussels sprouts, and we get bored during three-hour-long dinners. This particular one happens to be my first since the accident, and you'd think that would make it more interesting.

It doesn't.

The best thing that happens is the serving of the bûche de Noël, which I haven't had since last Christmas. The worst is discovering Henry at the table, something Maisie conveniently forgot to warn me about. He's wearing a navy-blue suit expertly tailored to his body, and I can't deny that the sight makes my blood charge through my veins like a herd of stampeding cattle. I take it easy on my heart and keep my eyes directed elsewhere.

The meal proceeds as usual: three hours of footmen bringing dishes to the table while everyone watches me as though I'm the queen or something.

With each dish, the rule is that as soon as I set down my fork, the course is over, which causes more anxiety than you might think. I pay close attention to everyone else's plate and wait until it appears they have all finished. I've never been a slow eater, so this is absolute torture. At my first state dinner, I got so lost in trying to do all the right things that I forgot to pace myself and finished my soup in less than five minutes. Some people hadn't taken more than two bites.

So far tonight, things are going swimmingly, and by that I mean that no one has asked me anything I don't know how to answer, there's only one course left to be served, and I've almost forgotten my ex-husband is at the table.

But this, of course, can't possibly last.

Lady Crawford leans forward from her spot a few seats down from me, breaking protocol by speaking over the person on her left. "Your Majesty, is it true you'll be giving a speech at that memorial downtown next week?"

I nod. "It's an important cause."

"It's such a shame that all the hard work you did to eradicate that nasty business was all undone," she says, taking a sip of her wine.

We now have the attention of the whole table. I'm no fool—I know they're all waiting to hear how I will respond to this subtle affront. I can feel my mother's eyes boring into me, entreating me to remember everything she's taught me about poise and self-restraint.

I force a smile onto my lips. "I like to think things would be even worse if it wasn't for the steps taken earlier this year."

"Yes," Lady Crawford croons. "One must find comfort where one can."

Three hours after it started, the dinner is over, the guests have all left, and I'm free to meet Maisie to wrap up the speech she's helping me write for the memorial. Normally I'd leave it to the communications team, but this one needs to be perfect.

I'm heading down the corridor that leads to the staircase when I hear footsteps behind me. I turn when they pick up speed. Henry is following me, and I suddenly feel like I'm trapped in a dark alley. I'd rather talk to Lady Crawford again. Outwalking him is impossible, thanks to the long evening gown and heels I'm wearing, but like an idiot, I try anyway.

He catches up to me in five stupidly long strides, but I ignore him and keep moving toward my office. "C, I need to talk to you," he says, keeping up without any effort at all.

"I thought I told you to stay away from me," I say without breaking stride.

"You're not going to that memorial."

I halt abruptly. "I'm sorry. It sounded like you just tried to tell me what to do."

"You heard me. It's far too dangerous," he says.

"In case you've forgotten, you're talking to the *queen*. You can't lock me in a tower for the next fifty years in case I stub my toe."

"I would if I thought you'd let me," he mutters, then moves closer, his hands on his hips. I take a step backward. "We're talking about much more than a stubbed toe. If I let you go, you may never come back."

"If you *let* me go?" I let out a high-pitched laugh.

"I'm in charge of your security, Celia."

I wave him off. "You're being paranoid, and it's stifling."

"Someone wants you dead, and you're calling me stifling?"

"You don't know anyone is after me. What would they possibly stand to gain?"

"There are a million possibilities. I'd prefer to learn which one it is *before* they try something, not after," he spits out.

"How about you work on figuring that out, while I do my job as queen?" I spin away from him and resume my trek as fast as my heels will allow.

When I get to my office, Maisie is already waiting for me, and she jumps when I burst through the door, Henry right behind me.

"Sorry I'm so late," I say.

She shakes her head, a confused look on her face. "No worries. Um, aren't we working on your speech tonight?"

"Yes, why?"

"Is he helping us?"

"Who?"

Sighing dramatically, she tucks a strand of hair back into her braid. "And here's me thinking we could go back to using his name."

"I have no idea what you're talking about." I sink into my chair and kick my heels off under the desk.

"What are you two doing? It's nearly midnight." Henry directs this question at Maisie.

She shrugs and scoots her glasses back up her nose. "This is pretty normal."

I didn't think he could get any madder, but that comment seems to have done the trick. "Normal? She just got out of the hospital."

"Try telling her that," Maisie mutters under her breath.

"As you can see, she's ignoring me," Henry says. "Any recommendations?"

"Switching her latte flavor usually penetrates that armor."

"You're both children," I growl. "Maisie, you can kiss your job goodbye if you ever use the word 'penetrate' again. And Henry, for the love of god, will you please go away?"

"I'm not leaving until I have your agreement." He crosses his arms over his chest, and I do my best not to notice the way his jacket strains against his biceps. I'm not entirely successful.

"In that case, enjoy sleeping on the floor. Maisie, let's get started on the speech." I keep my focus on my computer screen. Meanwhile, Henry's eyes are burning a hole through my dress.

"Don't bother. You won't be needing the damn thing." He leans over my desk and fills my field of vision until I have no choice but to look at him.

I lean back in my chair to put as much distance between us as possible. "What do I have to say to make you leave?"

"Simple. Five words." He ticks them off on his fingers as he says them. "I. Won't. Attend. The. Memorial."

"Ha. Try again."

"Celia, I'm dead serious. You're not going."

"The fact that you think you can march in here and tell me what to do is actually kind of sad," I say. "Maybe you should see someone."

"I am bound by law to make decisions concerning your security."

"It's your own security you should be concerned about, because I'm about to kill you with my bare hands."

He smirks. "As much as I relish the thought of your hands on me, it's going to have to wait for another time."

I slug his shoulder with as much force as I can, but it probably hurts me worse than it does him, because that sucker is hard.

Maisie pipes up. "God, are you two always like this?" I'd forgotten she was even in the room.

We both ignore her, preferring to nail each other with murderous glares instead.

"Okay, why don't we talk about this? We can sit down, I can get some coffee, and we'll discuss it like adults," she says.

"This isn't a mediation, Maisie," I snap. "I'm going to that memorial, and I *am* giving a speech."

"You would do that to your country?" Henry says.

"I'm doing it *for* my country."

He scoffs. "You're useless to them if you're dead."

"You really think it's that serious?" Maisie asks.

He tears his gaze from me long enough to say, "Yeah, I think it is. The square downtown would be nearly impossible to secure. It's surrounded by not only crowds, but buildings, windows, and doors in all directions."

"It's the perfect location for drawing a lot of attention," I say.

"It's also the perfect location for a shooting—or god knows what else."

Maisie belatedly covers her mouth to hide the gasp that just slipped out. "A shooting? In that case, maybe—"

"I cannot believe this." I swivel toward her. "Are you seriously taking his side?"

"It's not about taking sides!" she says. "But if you're in danger . . ."

"I won't be. It's ludicrous, based on nothing but a bunch of theories and zero proof."

"C, I told you." Henry leans closer, until his face is only inches from mine. I can almost taste the spearmint on his breath. "I'm 99 percent positive that was no accident." His eyes beg me to believe him.

"Ah, yes, but what about that pesky 1 percent?"

He pushes away from the desk and mutters *fuck* under his breath.

"Celia, do you really think it's a good idea? What if he's right? What if something happens to you?" Maisie says.

I shift my glare from Henry's anger-strained back to her wide-eyed face. "And if I don't go, how many children will die this month? How can I value my own life over theirs?"

"That's hardly a fair compari—"

"Of course it's not," Henry interrupts. "But she's determined to be a fucking martyr."

"Maisie, would you please call security to have him removed?" I say, before remembering that the entire team answers to his rotten ass.

"I wouldn't bother," he says to Maisie with a wink. "But if you wouldn't mind giving us a few minutes of privacy, I would be very grateful."

Dread crawls up my spine. Maisie is only too happy to acquiesce, and she's gone before I can get out the words to stop her.

Henry circles the desk and crouches in front of my chair. He places a hand on each armrest, and the delicious heat of him seeps through my clothes. My brain is screaming, *Danger! Wolf!*

"We can find a different way. Please trust me on this, C."

I drop his gaze. "I'll never trust you again."

"I know I hurt you," he says, "and I don't expect you to forgive me for that. But this is your life we're talking about."

"I appreciate your concern, but I'll be fine." My hands long to trace the muscles outlined by his shirt. I clench them into fists. *Wolves bite,* I remind myself.

"Celia, I'm not asking." The steel in his voice scrapes against my skin like the flat side of a razor.

My defenses are crumbling. I can feel them toppling brick by brick. Everything would be so much easier if I just surrendered—until the moment he decided to break my heart again. And I don't know if I'd be able to get back up next time.

I swallow the gigantic lump in my throat and say quietly, "May I remind you that we don't have the kind of relationship where you're entitled to give input on what I do?"

Henry drops his arms and stands up. "Is there anything I can say to make you change your mind?" His voice is raw and pained.

The sultry tension in the air is replaced by an electric hum. I lift my chin. "Absolutely not. I'm not backing down on this. It's too important."

"As if your life isn't."

"Henry, you don't even know if there's a threat."

"By the time we confirm there is one, it may be too late," he hisses. He stalks back to the center of the room, frustration rolling off him with every step as he paces. After a few minutes, he turns back to me. "Since you're determined to be completely unreasonable about this, I'll make you a deal."

The nerves along my spine stand up straighter. "The last time I made a deal with you, I wished I'd made one with the devil instead." The memory of that kiss still has the power to make me flush, which it is happily demonstrating right now.

"Well, don't worry. I won't require your soul for this." His gaze lands on my lips. Apparently, he hasn't forgotten either.

"What do you want, then?"

"Change the venue to the palace."

I consider this for a moment. "Why?"

"There's plenty of room in the back gardens for a stage and a crowd, and it will actually be possible to secure the area."

My mind whirls as I think about everything it would take make it happen. The memorial is less than a week away. But if it gets Henry off my back, I'll work around the clock if I need to. "Fine. Deal."

"That's not all," he says. "If you do this, I'm going to be in your security detail, all up in your business and happy to use my hands to accomplish whatever needs to be done."

My jaw clenches at the insinuation, and my temperature rises for the same reason. "I'm used to that kind of treatment already. It doesn't matter who it's coming from."

Henry blinks and takes a tiny step backward. "Sounds like we have a deal."

"Sounds like I'm still getting my way and you're just coming along for the ride."

8

"Fire Meet Gasoline" - Sia

They couldn't have chosen a better morning for the memorial. The sky is overcast, but there's no chance of rain, and the air is that perfect combination of brisk and clear, encouraging you to suck in lungfuls at a time.

I do and end up in a coughing fit, so maybe not the best idea.

The palace's back gardens have been transformed into what can only be described as madness. There are people everywhere. I don't even want to think about the screening process they had to go through. The dozens of TV crews set up around the perimeter give me hope that at least those who couldn't attend will be able to watch the footage.

I push aside the curtain to get a better view through the window. The massive terrace stretching across the back of the south wing will pose as the stage for the event. It's already crawling with personal protection officers.

"Hang tight," Henry says from my left, where he stationed himself first thing this morning and hasn't so much as budged from since. "You won't be leaving this room until it's your turn to speak."

"Says you."

He gives a sharp laugh. "Yeah, says me." His attention is focused on the crowd outside, probably scanning for anyone with *SHARPSHOOTER* scrawled on their T-shirt. "The area has been turned inside out and is as secure as we can possibly make it. But there are going to be some rules. First, you will act like a drunk penguin when you're on-stage."

"Excuse me?"

"Do not hold still. Ever. A target moving in unpredictable patterns is harder to hit than a stationary one."

"You want me to bob and weave?"

"Yes. I want you to drop your pen, move around, and act like you've drunk two bottles of that Pauillac you like so much."

My laugh is abrasive. "You're out of your mind."

Henry turns from the window to look at me, nostrils flaring. "I'm serious, C. The other thing I want is for you to trust me explicitly. If I tell you to move, duck, or run, you're going to do so immediately—without asking a single damn question. Got it?"

"I'd rather be shot."

The hard look melts from his face, and he turns and cups my cheeks in his palms. My heart leaps for my throat. "I know I hurt you. But I will do everything in my power to prevent anyone else from doing the same."

"Don't like sharing your voodoo doll?"

"Damn it, Celia." He drops his hands and closes his eyes, then lifts his hand to his earpiece. After a few seconds, he barks, "Confirmed. Exiting in thirty."

"What's going on?" I say.

He ignores me, and I bump his thigh with my fist. Eyes focused on his watch, he grabs my hand and twines our fingers together. Tendrils of electricity shoot up my arm. I try to pull away, but he holds on tightly. A moment later, he gives me a tug. "It's time."

He pulls me onto the terrace, never letting go of my hand. We are surrounded by PPOs, and it's like walking inside a moving box. The podium is in the center, and as I approach it with my own personal football team, the crowd begins waving and cheering.

"Remember what I said," Henry hisses in my ear before releasing me and positioning himself no farther than twelve inches from my left elbow.

Another PPO stands on my right. There is a wall of them behind me and in front of me, although the ones in front are stationed a few steps down to allow the audience to, at the very least, see my face. The whole thing must look absolutely ridiculous, like I'm some kind of terrorist who could be taken out at any second.

I clear my throat and step closer to the microphone. "Hello. Thank you all for coming. It's unfortunate that we're meeting under these circumstances, but what's the purpose of life if we don't pull together during the hard times?"

The crowd cheers.

I wait for the noise to settle before continuing. "Wesbourne has gone through a lot. We've fought for and won our freedom, we've built a great nation, and we are not about to let an evil force steal our children from us!"

The people go wild. Henry nudges me and mouths, *Move around.*

I frown but make a few swaying motions while continuing my speech, expressing sympathy as well as encouragement, stressing that we need to pull together as a nation. I can't help but notice the faces around me, grief chiseled onto them, leaving them hard and bitter. "To the families who've lost their loved ones to this fatal drug, I offer my deepest condolences. You are not alone, and your children are not forgotten. We as a nation stand—"

Henry knocks me and the rest of my speech to the ground. I register a sharp whiz and panicked screams. It's like I've entered a dream, the kind where everything you hear is at a distance and has a hollow echo. The breath has been evicted from my lungs by Henry's full weight bearing down on top of me. All I can feel is the cool stone floor of the terrace pressing against my cheek.

After what feels like an eternity but could just as easily be a few seconds, I'm hauled to my feet and sandwiched between Henry and another PPO. They all but carry me into the palace, and from there, we wind through the corridors until we reach the garage. I'm hoisted inside one of the large black SUVs. Henry crawls in behind me, and the car screeches out of the gates.

My head is throbbing. I wonder briefly if the impact gave me another concussion. Henry is panting beside me, and a glance at his lap shows his fisted hands are trembling.

"What happened?" I ask.

"There was a shooter." The thin veneer of calm in his voice is threatening to crack from strain.

"How did you . . . ?" I can't even process what just happened, let alone how he knew it was going to.

"I saw a flash and acted on instinct."

"From where? I thought the palace was secured."

"It was. It came from one of the buildings next door. He must have been using a long-range scope."

"How did you know it was a gun?"

"I didn't, but I wasn't about to take the chance."

"They were aiming at me?"

Shoving his fingers into his hair, Henry exhales. "Yes."

The breath rushes from my lungs. I feel dizzy.

Someone actually tried to kill me. Henry was right. That means the car crash wasn't an accident either. If it hadn't been for his suspicions and protection, I would be dead right now.

I fold my arms across my stomach and lean forward. Nausea washes over me. I consider asking the driver to slow down, or at the very least not take the curves so fast, but no words come out. My body sways of its own accord.

Strong hands slide across my shoulders and under my legs, and Henry pulls me into his lap. I curl into the security of his chest, the scent of his pine-and-amber cologne bringing more comfort than I could have imagined. He rubs his palm over my back in circles.

The trembling starts in my bones. Once it rises to the surface of my skin, it's impossible to stop. He tugs me closer, tucking my head under his chin, and says quietly, "Breathe, baby. Breathe."

I try to obey, but my chest is constricted. All that comes out is tiny gasps. Henry continues moving his hands over me and encouraging me to inhale slowly. When it becomes clear that it's not enough, he pulls back and takes my face in his hands, forcing me to meet his eyes.

"C, I need you to breathe. Deep, calming breaths."

I shake my head, still gasping. "I can't."

"Do it with me." His chest expands, and I try to follow suit, but short, pulsing breaths are all I can manage.

"I almost died." It's nearly a wail.

"But you didn't. And you're safe now, okay? Everything's going to be okay."

"If you hadn't been there, if you hadn't—"

"Shhh." He cuts me off and buries my face in his chest again, his heartbeat thrumming through my body. I try desperately to match my breaths with it.

"What if they come after me again?"

"They'll have to get through me, that's what." The words rumble through him. His hands are still on me, their rhythmic strokes calming my pulse.

The car slows and pulls into an underground garage. "Where are we?" I ask.

"The Atlantis," Henry says. "We don't know yet if the palace has been compromised."

Fresh chills break out over my skin, and I shiver. Five months ago, I lost my family's estate and the only home I've ever known. The palace isn't what anyone would describe as homey—nothing with fifty-five private apartments, more priceless art than the Louvre, and five hundred staff members could be. But at least I feel—*felt*—safe there.

I must be shaking again, because Henry's arms tighten around me as we wait for the all-clear to exit the vehicle. I'm still sitting in his lap, and I realize with surprise that this doesn't bother me. His hands haven't stopped moving since he pulled me onto him. That's probably the only thing keeping me from a full-blown panic attack.

Several minutes later, there's a crackling in his earpiece. I listen to the vibration of his response without comprehending the words. He pulls the earpiece out and shifts me so I'm upright. "The penthouse is clean. We're good to go."

We get out of the car and walk to the lift amid a sea of PPOs. They should have asked me to wear a suit and tie so I'd blend in. My fuchsia dress is like a billboard advertising my every move.

The elevator hums with tension as we ride to the top floor. The PPOs riding with us murmur among themselves. Henry is still holding me tightly against his chest, and the only thing I'm focused on is his heartbeat and slowing my breathing.

When we reach the penthouse lobby, Henry stops to talk to the man I assume is in charge of his security team, keeping me curled against him like a small child. After this brief exchange of short, clipped sentences, Henry leads me inside.

His flat is just as I remember it, but none of it has any impact on me. My head is still throbbing, and I'm still trying to wrap it around the fact that someone tried to kill me. Twice.

We stop in the center of the large living space, which consists of great room and kitchen. Henry grabs both my shoulders and holds me at arm's length. I'm still shaking, so I clasp my elbows with my hands and will myself to calm down.

"Do you want some tea?" he asks, leaning down to try to meet my eyes.

I shake my head, my vision blurry—whether with tears or dizziness, I'm not sure. Maybe both.

"A warm bath? A glass of wine?"

I just close my eyes against the throbbing in my temples.

"Celia, tell me what you need. I can't help you if I don't know what you need." A warm palm cups my face. "Look at me, baby. How can I help you relax?"

I wish he'd stop calling me *baby*. My body keeps interpreting it as a term of affection, and it spikes my blood pressure every time. I open my eyes to find him staring at me intently, a thick furrow between his brows. His eyes dart back and forth across my face, then resolve hardens his expression.

Before I can process anything, his other hand joins the first in cradling my chin, and he holds me firmly in place as he steps closer. He waits two beats before kissing me.

It isn't a gentle caress or a slow dance. It's a burning fire. At the first taste of him, my body goes electric, screaming after finally getting another dose of the drug it's been craving for months. He still tastes exactly as I remember, yet somehow even better, if that's possible. Everything flees my mind except for the way his lips are eating at mine, the way he completely invades me.

Our movements become frantic, a frenzied mess of limbs. Henry's hands slide into my hair, and I groan with pleasure. My fingers have become tangled in his shirt, and I'm clinging on for dear life as he makes me forget my own name.

I push at the jacket impeding me from exploring his shoulders. He lets go of me for one brief moment to shrug it off, then his hands are back, their warmth searing through my skin and right into my blood.

We stumble further into the flat. Correction: I stumble, but he is all grace, leading me without missing a beat.

Memories often become exaggerated with time, leading to disappointment when we try to relive those remarkable moments. That book we loved isn't nearly as good when we reread it. The dream vacation becomes a blur of frustration when we try to recreate it. The one that got away isn't quite the catch we make them out to be in our head.

And then there are times—truly magical ones—when our expectations are exceeded, completely blasted away. Even in our wildest dreams, we never imagined things being so good.

This moment with Henry falls into the latter category.

I'd be lying if I said I haven't fantasized about what it would be like to be with him again, feel his hands sliding over my hips, taste his spearmint-flavored mouth, touch the lines of the body I barely got to know before it was snatched away. I've spent countless nights in bed, pretending he was with me, touching myself the way I imagined he would, and falling asleep ashamed of not having been strong enough to resist the thought of him.

But now he's here, and we're doing this, and it's so much better than even the most scandalous of my fantasies. It's better because he's real and solid beneath my hands, his scent vivid in my nostrils, the heat between us so much bigger than anything I could generate on my own. It's better because he still has the power to surprise me and take my breath away. No amount of sex dreams could prepare me for the way he makes me gasp when he bites my neck or shiver when he rubs his stubble against my cheek or melt when he whispers my name over and over in my ear.

"God, Celia. You wreck me," he says in a choked voice. His hand finds the zipper of my dress and lingers there, a question in his eyes.

I don't hesitate, just seal my mouth against his once more. He understands completely and slowly tugs the zipper down. My dress splays open at the back, and he chases away the chill with his ever-moving hands. I disengage my own from his hair just long enough to let the dress slide off my shoulders and onto the floor.

Henry helps me step over the discarded fabric, and we move toward what I assume is the bedroom. I'm too distracted by the sensation of his hands on my bare skin to pay attention to trivial things like location.

He's only stopped kissing me for the absolute essentials, and my lips are already swollen, but that doesn't stop me from wanting him for the rest of eternity.

Before I can register what is happening, he swoops me up in his arms and carries me the rest of the way. "You deserve to be taken to a bedroom," he says.

I can't stop the thrill that races up my spine. He claims my mouth again.

It's cooler in here and smells more sharply of Henry than the rest of the house. I can't decide if I prefer a hit directly from his skin or the secondhand scent that permeates the space where he spends most of his time.

Lowering me to the bed without breaking stride, he climbs over me like he owns me, and quickly divests me of the remainder of my clothing. Then, as if he's been in withdrawal for an eternity, he begins his slow attack on my body. His hands rake over me, cupping my curves, drawing out shivers, coaxing out tiny moans. He takes my breast in his mouth, moving his tongue back and forth over the nipple until I cry out.

When I arch up toward him, he slides his hand down to where I need him most, the other still wrapped around my breast. His finger slides inside effortlessly, and I nearly combust. It's a startling reminder of just how much of a knock-off the generic thing is. No one else has ever made me feel this good.

We shouldn't know each other's bodies this way. We've spent the night together only twice, but from the way he is touching me, you'd think we'd been together for years. There is no awkwardness, no hesitation. His hands are possessive and confident. He knows better than I ever could exactly where I want him.

My orgasm hits like a tsunami, much faster than I anticipated. I guess that's what happens when you don't have sex for months. Henry holds me as I bury my nails in his back and ride it out.

I've barely come down from the peak when he flips me onto my stomach. "Get on your knees," he growls in my ear.

I do so obediently, silently aching to know what he has planned.

He reaches between my legs and spreads them farther apart. Then I feel the heat of his mouth, and it takes everything in me not to fall apart all over again.

After several minutes of blissful anguish, he pulls back, and I hear the familiar sound of his zipper. I drop my head to peer at him between my legs, just in time to see him slide a condom over his very considerable length. A spike of heat flares through my belly.

He winks when he catches me watching, then grabs a pillow. "Rest your head and arms on this." He helps me position it under the upper half of my body. That done, he strokes my face and murmurs, "Press into the bed if you need to. I plan to fuck you senseless."

My breath catches in my throat. He wraps his fingers tightly in my hair and presses a kiss to the spot behind my ear. A few seconds later, he lets go, and I feel his hands on my thighs.

He moves them up and down, each stroke bringing him a centimeter closer to my apex. His hands finally reach me, and I muffle my cry with the pillow.

He gives a satisfied chuckle. "That's only the beginning, baby." His fingers circle me, taunting me, and then I feel him press up against my entrance. "I'm going to take you on the count of three, okay?" He grabs my hips for leverage, and there's a small amount of pressure as he positions himself just inside.

I forbid myself to press backward against him, and it's the hardest thing I've ever done.

"One." The pressure increases infinitesimally. I tremble and rest my head on the pillow like he directed. "Two." He pulls my hips back ever so slightly, arranging himself perfectly.

I am burning with anticipation. I force myself not to move, to sink into the pillow, which smells like pine and amber, to feel every sensation in my body right now. I don't know when his final count will come, and it's driving me mad with desire.

"Three." He grunts and thrusts inside of me in a single, fluid motion, pulling back on my hips while pushing his own forward. He rams home like he belongs there, like there isn't anywhere else in the world he'd rather be, and a loud cry rips from my throat.

He continues thrusting, his fingers now branded into my hips as he moves them exactly where he wants them. My body jolts forward with each motion, completely at his beck and call.

His hand moves from my hip to between my thighs. I press into the heat of his palm, seeking the friction I know I'll find there. He cups me roughly and presses me backward against him with his forearm.

His thumb swirls over my clit, taunting and begging me to give him everything. Bright spots of light flash behind my eyelids, and I shudder as my climax builds to its breaking point.

When it hits, it sends me screaming into the pillow. He follows right behind, and collapses on top of me when it's over.

I couldn't care any less about what is raging in the world outside right now. Henry has a way of consuming me that leaves no room for a single thing in my mind but him.

9

"Bad Blood" - Taylor Swift

I N MOVIES WHEN SOMEONE sleeps with someone they shouldn't, you can see the realization of what they've done dawn on them like the sun slowly rising. In reality, it's nothing like that. I'm smacked in the face with it before I even open my eyes, more like a lightning bolt than a sunrise.

The first thing to hit me is Henry's scent. No one should smell that good. A quick peep through my eyelashes reveals the bed beside me is empty. The manly woodsy scent is coming from the pillow beneath my face, not the actual person, thank God.

The second thing I notice is the fact that I feel incredible. I haven't felt this good since London, and that was long enough ago that I'd almost forgotten it was possible to feel like a giant bowl of Jell-O and be okay with it.

This is quickly followed by the realization that I *shouldn't* be okay with this feeling. These loose muscles and the urge to let out a satisfactory purr need to be murdered immediately. What happened here was a mistake—a huge, life-altering mistake that will never be repeated as long as I live.

The last thing to slam into my conscious is the fact that I am naked. I'm fortunately covered by a duvet, but I remember with vivid clarity my dress lying puddled on the floor of the great room.

A gentleman would carefully have laid the dress at the end of the bed for me. One glance shows that Henry is not a gentleman. He is probably waiting for me to walk out wrapped in a sheet like some tramp he brought home from a club.

I've made some questionable choices in my life, but this one—*this one* ranks so high on the list it obliterates every other entry. At the moment, I don't have the mental capacity to figure out what the hell I was thinking, let alone formulate a plan for going forward. The only thing I know is that I will not be leaving this room anything but fully dressed.

I paw through Henry's walk-in closet looking for something comfortable to wear. It's harder than it sounds, because my hormones have yet to accept that Henry is, in fact, the enemy. And just because one temporarily loses one's sanity due to an attempted assassination and sleeps with said enemy does not make it appropriate to bury one's face into each item of his clothing and inhale deeply.

I finally locate a pair of gray sweatpants and a worn Harvard sweatshirt and slip them on. They both smell like him, and I allow myself one final sniff of Henry-scented fabric. I whisper a million and one prayers that he won't be in the great room to witness the world's most humiliating walk of shame when I step out.

God grants my request but decides to have a little fun at my expense. Henry's not in the great room. He's in the kitchen, which has a direct view of the great room and the path I must travel to get to the door. Of course, I don't realize this until I've already tiptoed out of the hall and into sight, the tile floor cool beneath my bare feet.

Henry's leaning against the counter, typing on a laptop. He's changed out of his suit and tie and looks absolutely devastating in a soft cashmere sweater and black-rimmed glasses. I allow myself one brief fantasy of dashing across the room and into his arms, then shove it back into the recesses of my mind and stride fully into view.

Glancing up from the screen, he looks me over from head to toe. "How are you feeling?"

How am I *feeling*? A few hours ago someone tried to kill me. Since then, I've had a panic attack and sex with my ex-husband. "Great," I say.

His brow furrows. "I'll make you some tea."

"Actually, I'm going to head home."

He doesn't even bother turning around, just sets the kettle to boil. "Sit down, C. We need to talk."

"What could we possibly have to talk about?" I scoop up my discarded dress from the floor while his back is still turned.

"We can't just ignore what happened."

"You mean someone trying to kill me? Or us losing our bloody minds?"

His eyes rise to meet mine as he sets an empty cup on the counter in front of me. "Both."

"Fine. I'll have Maisie set up a time for us to meet."

He chuckles and remove the wrapper from a tea bag before dropping it into the mug. "You don't have anywhere you need to be. We can talk now."

"I've already blown off so many engagements this afternoon, they'll probably fire me."

"Trust me, no one expects you to be anywhere except somewhere safe."

I try to think of something terrible to call him, but my attention is riveted by his hands preparing my tea. They're strong and graceful, his fingers long and lean. My face heats with the memory of where they just were and exactly what he can do with them.

"How long did I sleep?" I finally say.

Henry flips his wrist around to see his watch. "Around two and a half hours."

"Why'd you let me sleep that long? Now I'll have insomnia tonight."

"You were exhausted. You just had the shock of a lifetime." The kettle starts to whistle, and he removes it from the stove.

"Yet you clearly thought it an appropriate time to take advantage of me."

"Take *advantage* of you?" He waits until he's finished pouring the hot water to glare at me. "What the hell, C," he mutters.

It isn't a fair accusation, I know that, but I can't help throwing it at him all the same. "You knew I was shaken up."

"You were on the verge of hysteria. Kissing you was the only thing I could think of to get your mind off of what had just happened. You're the one who started humping me."

The picture that flits through my mind is anything but pretty. "I was probably trying not to pass out."

"I can show you the scratch marks on my back if you'd like."

"Defense."

"The hickey, then."

I snort out a laugh to cover my mortification. "Hard as it may be to believe, not every girl is desperate to get into your bed, Henry." This sentence is absolutely ridiculous when considered next to the fact that I would very much like to be back in that bed this very minute.

He leans across the counter, his jaw clenched so tightly I can picture it snapping. He sets the cup down. "Sit. Drink. And find your damn sense while you're at it."

I plop onto the sleek, modern barstool with a huff. How did we go from not being able to get enough of each other to wanting to gut each other in a few short hours?

Henry sticks his head into the fridge. "What are you hungry for?"

"I'm not," I snap, and take a sip of tea. It's jasmine, my favorite. What guy stocks jasmine tea?

He pulls out a loaf of bread and several kinds of cheese. The frying pan clatters as he sets it on the stove. "Now why don't you tell me how you're really feeling?"

"We just had sex. How do you think I'm feeling?"

"Based on the sounds you made, I'd say pretty good."

My cheeks burst into flame. I'm well aware of the noises he's able to coax from me. "I hate to break it to you, but smoke doesn't always mean flames. Sometimes it's just the remnants of a fire that was put out a long time ago."

I swear I see his shoulder muscles tighten, and I congratulate myself for getting under his skin. The sooner he gets tired of me, the sooner he'll let me go.

"Are we really going to do this right now?" he says. The scent of browning butter fills the kitchen.

"I thought you wanted to talk about our panic-induced lovemaking."

"Unbelievable. Someone just tried to kill you, and all you can focus on is the fact that we had sex."

My heart rate doubles. "Because it's the only thing I know how to feel about!"

Tossing the spatula onto the counter, he walks around the bar to me. He takes my face in his palms in a way that is becoming dangerously familiar. "I'm here to help you process it. I'm not going anywhere, okay?"

A mirthless laugh slips past my lips, and I pull away from him, causing his hands to drop. "Right. Just like all the other times." I turn back to my mug. "Please stop touching me." The same words he used in that stupid hotel room.

From the corner of my eye, I see him deflate. I refuse to feel even a smidgen of sympathy. He brought this on both of us. Nothing I say or do will ever equal the pain he has put me through.

"Something's burning," I mutter before taking a long swig of tea.

Henry walks back to the stove and flips the toastie in the pan. The silence that fills the room is louder than our raised voices were. After a few minutes, he slides the sandwich onto a plate, cuts it in half diagonally, and sets it in front of me.

"I said I wasn't hungry."

"You haven't eaten anything since this morning," he says.

I push the plate toward him. "And I still don't have an appetite."

He shoves it back. "You can't function on an empty stomach."

"A sniper nearly shot me a few hours ago, so forgive me if I can't eat anything right now!" I send the toastie whirling across the bar. He catches it right before it sails off the edge.

Closing his eyes, he braces himself against the counter, his veins bulging against the tight skin on his arms. "I'm sorry," he says softly. The look on his face is so apologetic I nearly cave. "Are you finally ready to talk about this?"

I drop my gaze. How do you go about discussing the fact that someone hates you enough to kill you? "What is there to talk about?"

"If you don't want to talk to me, fine. But you need to talk to someone. You can't bottle this up."

"What is there to say? 'Please tell me what's so horrible about me that someone wants me dead?'"

"That's a start."

I look up. He's watching me, arms crossed over his chest, looking like a sexy nerd in those glasses. "I don't know what else you want me to say." I shake my head.

"I just want you to be honest. Honest about how you're feeling, about the fears you have." He pauses. "Honest about the danger you're in."

Ah. So that's where this was headed. "Surely they've caught the guy by now."

"Trust me, if they have, I will tear him to pieces with my own hands. But I don't think there was much to go on."

I tear off a small piece of crust from the now cool sandwich. "What about fingerprints, shoe prints, DNA? Isn't that how they catch the bad guys in the movies?"

"I don't think I need to remind you that this isn't a movie. And this guy is good. Really good."

A needle of fear enters my bloodstream. "What aren't you telling me?"

"Just that until whoever is behind this is caught, you're in more danger than I think you realize."

I refuse to give in to the fear that wants to envelop me. "Good thing I have the best security team in Wesbourne, huh?"

Henry sighs. "They can't protect you if you don't follow orders."

"If I hadn't attended the memorial, that guy would have found another way to get to me." I brush crumbs from my fingers.

"That doesn't mean you need to make it easy for him."

This is getting exhausting, and I'm regretting ever leaving the bedroom. "How many times do you think we'll have this conversation?"

"As many as it takes for you to quit being so stubborn and admit that you need help." He grabs one half of the sandwich and takes a huge bite.

"And by help I assume you mean *you*?"

"I'm the one best equipped to protect you, yes."

I smirk and shake my head. "Wouldn't you say the one being protected needs to be able to trust the one doing the protecting?"

"C—"

"Save it, Henry. You annihilated my trust. Completely blew it to shreds. I'll never trust you again." I slide off the barstool, grateful when the room doesn't start spinning.

"Where are you going?"

"Home."

"You're not leaving the penthouse," he says.

"That's what you think."

He doesn't respond, and when I look back, he's still standing in the kitchen watching me, his arms folded across his chest.

"You can't be serious," I say.

"Dead serious."

"You can't lock me in your castle."

"Watch me."

"Go to hell, Henry."

My handbag is on the table in the foyer, and I swipe it up as I walk past, dress draped over my arm. I have enough sense to wonder what the PPOs will think when I walk out in Henry's clothes, but not enough to care.

The doors open well enough on their own, but my leaving is impeded by the two large men blocking the doorway.

"Hello," I say. "I'm ready to go home now."

"I'm sorry, Your Majesty," one of them says, bowing his head. "You'll need to stay here until the palace can be secured."

"I'm sure Henry is overreacting. Palace security is unbreachable." Even as I say this, I wonder if it's true. Someone did nearly kill me on the back terrace.

"All the same, ma'am, we have orders to keep you here until further notice."

I briefly consider darting past him, but one look at his huge arms tells me he'd snatch me up before I made it two steps. "I'm your queen. Surely that must count for something."

His face colors, and he glances down at his shoes. "Beg your pardon, ma'am, but we don't answer directly to you."

I scrunch my eyes shut, then turn and head back to the kitchen. Henry is exactly where I left him, polishing off the last of the toastie.

"You're a psychopath," I say.

He shakes his head. "That's harsh, considering I'm trying to protect you."

"I'm not staying here." I *can't* stay here.

Wiping his hands on a towel, he walks around the bar. "My job is to protect you. The best place to do that is right here. The Atlantis has the best security in the country. You'll be safer here than anywhere else."

It makes sense, in a way. No one can slip in through the back door unless they also know how to scale a hundred-story skyscraper. The palace has a thousand doors and windows on the ground floor alone. Henry's flat is comfortable enough, even if it lacks personality and warmth. The only problem is that he lives here too.

"I can't stay, Henry," I whisper. This place could be over ten thousand square feet, and it still wouldn't be big enough to keep me from falling for him all over again.

"I'm afraid you don't have a choice." His voice has softened with apology.

I imagine eating breakfast with him at this bar or him walking out in nothing but a towel. There is no way in the world I can do this. "There has to be another option."

"The royal safe houses haven't been needed in so long, they've fallen into disrepair," he says.

I don't have to ask why. I'm sure there wasn't funding for renovations.

My stomach lurches as another thought crosses my mind. "I guess this means I'll have to witness your nightly parade of women?"

He lets out an amused sigh, a faint smile playing at the corners of his mouth. "You don't have to worry about that."

I'm not sure what that means—maybe he has a private lift in his bedroom?—but I can't handle this conversation anymore, or the way I can still smell him on the sweatshirt I'm wearing. I excuse myself to go change.

The penthouse may protect me from my wannabe assassin, but what will protect me from Henry?

10

"The Great War" - Taylor Swift

HENRY'S BATHROOM IS MASSIVE, with a sunken tub next to the floor-to-ceiling glass wall, twin shower stalls—because why have one when you can have two?—and a marble vanity that stretches the entire length of the space. The mirror wall above it shows that my dress is just as wrinkled as I was afraid it would be, but that can't be helped. Smoothing it out as best I can, I toss Henry's balled-up clothes in the hamper.

I place my hands on the marble counter and breathe—slow, lung-filling breaths just like my private yoga instructor teaches. It helps calm my pounding heart, but it can't slow the thoughts racing around in my head.

I know Henry's right. The threat is real. If it wasn't for his paranoia, I'd be in a coffin right now. But that doesn't negate the fact that he is just as much of a threat to me as a sniper is. If I allow him even a grain of trust, he will use it to exploit me and leave me for dead. I will not recover from another broken heart.

I walk to the window of the great room. The city looks the same as always. You'd never know the monarch had just narrowly escaped assassination. I pull my phone out of my bag, ignore the dozens of missed calls, and dial Maisie.

She answers on the first ring. "Oh my god! Are you okay? I've been so worried—"

"I'm fine," I break in. "It looks like I'll be staying at Henry's penthouse for a few days until this whole thing blows over."

"You're staying with *Henry*?"

"Yeah." I blow out a breath. "The security here is amazing, so . . ." No need for her to know I'm being kept against my will. "Could you bring my things, including all of the financial records? I may as well get to the bottom of this while I'm stuck here."

"Of course. I'll have Daphne pack your bags, and I'll get everything from the office. What about Tundra?"

"Bring him too, please." I completely forgot about him in the mayhem. What kind of dog mom am I? I don't know what the Atlantis's pet policy is, but since I'm currently being held hostage by its owner, he can either put up with my dog or let me go home.

Two hours later, Maisie appears at the door with coffee and three PPOs laden with bags. Tundra strains at his leash when he spots me.

Maisie releases him, and he vaults across the room toward me, making me nearly topple into the table in the foyer. We'll need to work on his approach. I bury my face into his soft black fur. A month ago, I wouldn't have believed it if someone told me a dog could be this therapeutic.

"Where do you want this stuff?" She hands me my latte. Henry's security team doesn't look excited about their new status as bellhops.

I realize I have no idea where Henry is intending for me to stay, nor do I know where he is. "Just drop everything there," I say, motioning to the middle of the foyer. If he's going to treat me like a prisoner, he can carry my bags himself.

The security officers seem uncertain but do as they're told before quickly skirting out of the room. Tundra has lost interest in me and is sniffing the various objects in the great room.

I take a tentative sip of coffee, then raise my brows. "I'd forgotten what French vanilla tastes like."

Maisie grins. "New coffee shop."

"Thank you for that. And for bringing all of this. Although I don't intend to stay more than a few days." I arch a brow at the pile of suitcases. "You've packed enough for an entire year."

"Not for the queen of Wesbourne," she says. "We didn't know what you'd need, so Daphne thought we should include different options."

"And here I thought you brought my whole closet."

Shrugging, she looks around. "I'm sure there's room for it here. My god, this place is huge."

"It's ridiculous," I say. "Wait until you see the master bath."

If Maisie is surprised that I seem to know my way around Henry's flat, she doesn't say anything. I give her a brief tour of the rooms I've seen so far, and together we gape in awe. I may live in a palace, but it's old, drafty, and its furnishings carry their value in age, not sleek beauty.

She runs her hand over the smooth curved edge of the bathtub. "I could sleep in here. No joke. Give me a duvet and a pillow, and I would 100 percent curl up in this a happy girl."

We walk back through the master bedroom, where I draw her attention to the glass wall and away from the rumpled bedding. Before we reach the door, she lays a hand on my arm. "I actually wanted to talk to you about something. I've been waiting for the right time, and after everything that happened today, I'm not sure I'm doing the right thing, but they say time is fleeting, and it could have gone so wrong today, and I—"

"Maisie," I say. "Just tell me."

She takes a deep breath and bites her lip. "Okay. Remember I told you I met someone? Someone amazing?"

"Of course. I want to hear all about it."

"Well, I—

"Celia!" The yell comes from the great room.

I roll my eyes. "Keep going."

But before she can continue, we hear the sound of breaking glass. "Good god," I mutter and stalk out there.

Henry is standing in the middle of the room, hands on his hips, a pile of broken ceramic at his feet, and tongue-lolling Tundra at his side. His irritated gaze collides with mine.

"Care to explain why there's a dog in my house?"

I study him for a moment. "He's mine." Turning to Maisie, I say, "I'll walk you to the door," ignoring her curious glances as we walk to the foyer. I refuse to feed her fantasies that there will ever be anything between Henry and me besides hostility. Feeding hers only leads to feeding mine.

"Now tell me about this guy," I say once we're in the foyer.

"It can wait for another time. It looks like you have your hands full. I'll be by tomorrow with your latte."

"No, seriously." I grab her arm. "I've got time." Talking to Maisie means not talking to Henry.

She looks over my shoulder. "I've got a ton of stuff waiting for me at the office. But we'll catch up soon, okay?"

After she leaves, I force myself to walk back to the great room, but Henry has disappeared, along with Tundra and the broken glass. I briefly wonder what it was he broke before landing on the more important question of what Henry has done with my dog.

I scan the large room before finally spotting them in the furthest corner, near a small sofa. Henry is sitting with Tundra between his legs. If the look on the dog's face is any indication, he is receiving the world's best pets.

"Glad to see you're not holding a grudge," I say as I move toward them.

Henry looks up but keeps his hands on the massive animal at his feet. "I'm not a monster. Who could stay mad at this guy?"

I pat my leg encouragingly, but Tundra only looks at me with calm indifference as Henry keeps stroking him. I scowl at both of them. "You're not stealing my dog."

Henry chuckles but doesn't look the least bit remorseful. "I might. He clearly likes me more than you do."

I like who you used to be.

"Tundra," I say softly, and pat my leg again. "Come here, boy." My cajoling has no effect until Henry finally releases him. Then he bounds over for his second serving of pets. And they say dogs are loyal.

Several hours later, the sky has turned black and is glowing with the lights of the city. I've settled into the corner of one of Henry's sofas, Tundra at my feet, papers strewn upon every surface within arm's length.

I still can't make sense of the financial state of the royal household. How have royal families in the past managed to pay for multiple state dinners a year, not to mention designer wardrobes and luxury cars?

The Civil List covers about 20 percent of our annual budget, meaning I need to scrape together millions from somewhere to cover the rest, and that's assuming we greatly reduce expenditures. I toss a stapled copy of last month's expenses aside. This is a nightmare.

Henry walks into the room, carrying a bag of pretzels and a bowl of peanut M&Ms. He sets them on the coffee table and sits down next to me, a box of papers between us. "You got bored enough to rob a"—he picks up a sheet and scans it—"filing cabinet?"

"Very funny." I yank it from his hand and place it back into the box. Trying to get this reorganized may be the death of me.

"What is all this?" he asks, reaching for a handful of pretzels.

"Just monarch-related things."

"Since when is the monarch required to wade through boxes of financial papers?"

"Since today." I study the page in my hand. It shows that the previous royal family—Henry's—received a very large income from outside the monarchy, but there are no details as to where it came from. Likely an estate or two, but how they were able to generate that kind of money from a dying industry escapes me.

"Careful. I've heard that those furrows in your brow can become permanent if you hold them too long."

I relax my forehead on instinct. My mother would suffer a collapsed artery if she could see me right now. "I'll relax when you leave."

"Why don't you tell me what you're looking for, and I'll help."

"No, thanks." I move the paper to the bottom of the stack in my lap.

"Come on, C. It's late and you should be in bed."

I shake my head and study the figures on another page. "I told you earlier. I won't be able to sleep."

"Then at least let me help."

I toss the pile back into the box. I have no idea how I'm going to get to the bottom of this, and despite what I said, I'm exhausted. I study Henry. He's still wearing that soft sweater and his slutty glasses, both of which do funny things to my insides. I look away. "Fine. Tell me how your family makes its money."

He coughs into his fist. "Excuse me?"

"If you want to help, that's what I need to know."

"Why do you need to know that?"

I shuffle through the documents on the table and pull one out. "The royal household can't keep the lights on with what we're getting from the Civil List, let alone pay someone to change the light bulbs." I hand the paper to him. "I need to know how you did it."

He glances over the budget before handing it back. "We've always lived primarily off private income."

"I know that, doofus. What I don't know is what you did to earn it."

His eyes meet mine for a few seconds, then he reaches for the candy bowl. "I'm not sure. I think my father has quite a few investments and businesses."

"You *think*? How do you not already know this?"

Shrugging, he pops several M&Ms into his mouth. "I never cared. Probably one of the reasons he hates me so much."

He offers me the bowl, but I shake my head. My stomach feels queasy enough without carb-loading before bed. "I have no idea what I'm going to do," I say.

"I'm assuming you've already trimmed everything you can?"

"We've reduced by 17 percent, but that's nowhere close to where we need to be."

Henry frowns and pulls a stapled sheaf from the table. "What about investments?"

"The Royal Estate has very little, and what my father left isn't even worth mentioning." Not when we're talking about a multimillion-dollar annual budget.

He studies the pages for a few minutes. I take that time to run my fingers through Tundra's fur. Maisie must have had him groomed before bringing him over, because his coat is glossy and fluffy.

"I have an idea."

I look over at Henry, whose brow is now the one furrowed. "Waiting with bated breath," I say.

He lowers the papers and meets my eyes. "Why not turn the royal collection into assets?"

"What are you talking about?"

"All of the art, antiques, gardens—display them to the public and charge admission."

"We can't commercialize the royal collection."

"Why not? The British Crown did it years ago. Plenty of other monarchies have done the same thing."

I press my lips together tightly. How he doesn't understand this is beyond me. "Wesbourne is different from other countries. We have a poise the Brits lack."

He huffs out a laugh and tosses the documents back onto the table. "I'm not sure anyone who's been following Wesbourne in the news this past year would use the word 'poise' to describe us."

"Okay, fine. We've had a rough year. But to turn the palace into a museum? That's insanity."

"You wouldn't have to allow tours of everything, just the state rooms, galleries, and a few drawing rooms. No one's going to go through your underwear drawer. Except maybe me." He grins wolfishly and pops another M&M into his mouth.

"You're disgusting." I return my attention to the pages in front of me so I don't dwell on what that grin does to my insides. "Besides, I already submitted the request for a higher Civil List payment."

"And what, raise taxes?"

I let out a long sigh and grab a pretzel from the bag. "I'm out of options. Your father seemed to think it was a good idea."

His head snaps up. "You talked to my father about this?"

"It's not like I requested a meeting. He was there anyway, and it just came up."

"You need to stay away from him," Henry says.

I spread my hands in front of me. "Um, hello. Kind of locked up here away from *everybody* at the moment."

"I'm serious, C. He's bad news."

"Believe it or not, I'm actually not as helpless as you seem to think. Now, if you will leave me alone, I can keep working on this."

He gives me a tired look. "You should go to bed. It's nearly one o'clock."

I'm well aware of the time. I'm also aware of what I'll see if I close my eyes. It's imperative that I keep them open. "I'm wide awake," I say.

"Your left eye has been twitching for the past five minutes."

"That's due to the sterile environment in this place. Seriously, would it kill you to hang some tinsel?"

"You want to argue over holiday decorations right now?"

"Christmas is less than a month away, and you don't even have a tree."

"You're getting delirious," he says. "I'm putting you to bed."

"Fine, jailer. Lead me to my cell." One can stay awake in a bedroom as well as on a sofa.

I hold my wrists out to him, and he gives me an unamused look. "You're staying in my room."

"I'm sorry," I say around a laugh, "but just because I accidentally had sex with you under duress does not mean we are sharing a room."

"I meant *alone*. And for the record, you can't accidentally have sex with someone."

"Yes, you can, and I'm not taking your room." I stand up. "This place must have a million guest rooms."

His brows rise. "So close," he says. "It has four."

"Great. I'll take one of those, then." One that isn't tainted with memories of rolling in the sheets with him.

"Mine has the best view."

"Hardly necessary while sleeping."

"All the same, I've had it readied for you." He beckons with his hand.

I notice my luggage is gone from the foyer, presumably already ensconced in Henry's massive closet. "That was hardly necessary. I would have been just fine in a guest room."

"And what kind of guy would I be if I did that?"

"Um, normal?" I take a step in his direction.

"You're the queen, C."

Good thing he cleared that up. Fantasy-loving Celia was going to run with it, right into he-cares-about-me territory. "You're right. I momentarily forgot, since all of my other rights have been stripped from me." I smile sweetly.

"You know I'm doing it for your own good."

I brush past him toward the bedroom. "Spoken like a true dictator."

The shots wake me.

I sit up in bed and scream. I know I shouldn't, because it will only lead them to me, but what else am I supposed to do? The room is dark as sin, but all I can think about is that they've found me.

I don't hear any more gunfire, but my screams don't stop. I don't think my throat is capable of closing.

The bedroom door bursts open, and somehow my screams increase in intensity. The man rushes toward me. I know that this is it. This is how I die.

It isn't until he's beside me that I realize it's Henry, not a gunman. He grabs me and slides into bed next to me, pulling me into his lap. My screams stop as I melt into him, his arms wrapped around me and my face pressed against his chest.

"Where is he?" I whisper.

"Who?"

"I heard shots. They found me."

His hand strokes my hair away from my face. "It was just a dream, baby. There's no gunman."

"But I heard them."

He whispers "shhhhh" in my ear. "Trust me, no one can get in here, okay? There are a dozen guys outside the door. They've all sworn to protect you with their lives."

My fingers curl into Henry's T-shirt as he gently rocks us back and forth. Twice in one day, this man has had to comfort me. This needs to stop. I need to be stronger, more resilient, and far less emotional. But every time I decide to pull away, the fear yanks me back into his embrace.

I don't know how long we sit like that, but it's long enough for my heart rate to slow and for my brain to convince me of just how pathetic I am. "Sorry," I mutter, and shift upright.

"Nothing to be sorry for," he says, one hand still stroking my back. "You just had a major shock."

"I'll be fine now, but thank you for coming."

"You sure? I don't mind staying."

"I'm sure." The nightmares might keep me from going back to sleep, but I know I definitely won't be able to if Henry is beside me.

He crawls off the bed and turns back to face me. "You'll let me know if you need something?"

I nod. "Of course." *We'll see.*

He props his hands on either side of me. "I promise I won't let anyone hurt you."

I wish I could believe him.

11

"We Found Love" - Rihanna + Calvin Harris

"WHAT'S THE CATCH?" BEA asks.

"Why would there be a catch?" I've just asked my sister to spend the holiday with me, an invitation I thought would be met with more eagerness, considering the fact that I was nearly killed yesterday. As I grab a bottled water from the fridge, I spy a tub of chocolate chip cookie dough that definitely wasn't there yesterday. I pull it out and find a spoon.

"The only reason you'd ask me to stay with you is if there's a catch. And you're acting weird."

"I'm not acting weird." I pop a piece of cookie dough into my mouth. "And what's so bad about wanting to spend time with my little sister?"

"First off, you're acting *very* weird. And secondly, you never call me your little sister unless you want something, so spill." Damn, she's become more intuitive than I realized.

"I wouldn't call it a catch, exactly . . ."

"Now I'm terrified," she says.

"You have to promise not to breathe a word of where I am to anyone. Security reasons and all that."

"Yeah, duh."

"Swear it?"

"Yes, I swear. Quit stalling and tell me what you're up to."

I scoop one more ball of dough from the container before putting it away again. "I'm staying with Henry." I'm not interested in hearing her thoughts on the subject, so I plunge ahead. "There are plenty of extra bedrooms, and it would be so nice to have someone else here."

Bea doesn't say anything.

"Well, what do you think?" I say when the silence stretches too long.

"You're living with Henry," she says in a monotone.

"I'm not *living* with him. I'm staying here. Temporarily. Obviously."

"Are you two together?"

"What? No, we're not together."

"But London—"

"You know very well we weren't together after London." I never shared the details with her, but it's not hard to put two and two together when your sister returns with puffy eyes instead of the guy she went after.

"Okay. So you're staying with him platonically, and you want me there to make it less awkward?"

"No, of course not." I'm getting better at these lies. "But I can't leave the penthouse, and it—"

"You're staying in a penthouse?"

"Yeah, at the Atlantis."

"Isn't that the place that does diamond microdermabrasion?"

"I have no idea. But probably." This place has literally everything, including a grocery store on the third floor.

"I'm in. I am so in. Mum's flat barely has running water."

Rosalind is staying at the Carlton during palace renovations, so she probably has sparkling water on tap, but I'm not about to contradict Bea now that she's agreed. "I'm glad it was the sisterly bonding that won you over."

"Absolutely! We can bond over deep-sea mud masks."

"God help me."

"About Henry." She takes on a more serious tone. "Will he be there much?"

I can guess why she's asking, which is exactly why this plan should work. "Well, it's his home, so I would think so. Although I do need to warn you that he's a bit of a scrooge. Not a single Christmas decoration in the whole place."

She gasps and launches into an account of her holiday plans, which include way more activities than she'll ever have time for, but I just let her talk, because my plan has worked. I need a wall between Henry and me, and Bea is the perfect fit.

The golden whirlwind that is my younger sister arrives on Monday as promised in a cloud of silk, Chanel No. 5, and more luggage than I think I've seen in my entire life, and I've been to a lot of airports.

I watch as bag after bag is deposited into the penthouse foyer. "I'm positive you left with less than half of this," I say after Bea releases me.

"Darling, what do you think I *do* on the weekends?"

"I'm going to go out on a limb here and say it's probably not study-ing."

She laughs like I couldn't be any more ridiculous. "With London an hour away and Paris only a few, you can't possibly expect me to spend my time studying."

"Of course not. Studying at uni would be preposterous." I guess asking for a loan from her trust fund is also out of the question. "I'll let Henry know you'll need a separate room just for your bags."

She starts to follow me toward the guest bedrooms but stops and squeals when she sees Tundra. "Who is this?" She drops her handbag and just manages to hold on to her fancy water bottle as he barrels toward her. She sits back on her heels, but he nudges her backward until she's on her bottom.

"Henry has a dog?" Her voice is muffled by Tundra's thick coat, which she is burying her face in.

"Actually, he's mine. Come on, Tundra. Let her up."

I've given Bea a quick tour of the flat, turned down her request to swap bedrooms with me, and am just heading back to the foyer to supervise the moving of her luggage when Maisie arrives, vanilla latte in hand. She holds the cup out to me while her gaze flits over the pile of Louis Vuitton suitcases. There isn't time to explain before Bea floats into the room.

"Maisie! How did you know I was dying for caffeine?" she asks, and snatches the cup from my assistant's hand before either of us can object. She takes a long sip, then makes a face. "God, how boring. This must be yours." Handing the to-go cup to me, she claps her hands. "Now, which of you fine gentlemen is planning to move all of my bags?"

The eyes of the PPOs clustered near the doors were already glued to her, and now they move so quickly I'm sure someone is going to get trampled. Bea's luggage is swallowed up within seconds. The entourage follows her down the hall, Tundra included.

Maisie's eyebrows settle back into their normal position. "This ought to be fun."

"At least she'll keep us entertained," I say.

Bea bounds back into the room, plate in hand. "I almost forgot. Addison's mum made these right before I left and forced me to take some."

"Please tell me those are not pot brownies."

"God, I wish." She shoves the plate toward me. "We have so much to catch up on. But for now, I'm going to take a nap. I need my sleep, because you know what tonight is!"

"I don't, actually."

"Party time!"

It takes Henry approximately twenty minutes to convince Bea that neither she nor I will be leaving the penthouse tonight, and me another fifteen to convince her that even if I could, I would never attend a club with her. Ever.

The three of us eventually settle on a compromise.

"You're like a boring old couple. Movie nights are a complete snooze fest. Can't we at least have some people over?" Bea says.

Henry's hands are still on his hips, where they've been stationed for the past half hour. I'm settled on the sofa, watching him duke it out with someone other than me and thoroughly enjoying myself. He received the news of Bea's arrival with a cocked brow and a mildly amused look that said *Dear god, what have I signed up for?* I can only hope it makes him regret his decision to keep me locked up here.

"Absolutely not. Celia's location—and yours for that matter—is a matter of national security."

Somehow, Bea makes her pout look enticing rather than childish, and a prickle of unease crawls down my spine. I invited her here as a buffer, but it's not like I hope they actually start something.

"Well, how about baking some *special* cookies?"

I recognize the discomfort in Henry's laugh. "Afraid not."

"When did you become so boring?" Bea steps close enough to him to grab his tie. She tugs on it, and had his feet not been firmly planted, he probably would've stumbled. His Adam's apple bobs as he swallows.

"Bea, come on. Let's just have a quiet movie night here. It'll be fun." He pries her fingers off his tie, so she grabs his hand instead.

"Fine. But I'm picking the movie." She spins away, stretching out her arm until their fingers finally release.

An hour later, we're watching *I'll Be Home for Christmas* and listening to Bea wax poetic about the hotness of Jonathan Taylor Thomas "for a nineties kid." I glance at Henry to see if he has regrets, but he's busy giving Tundra a vigorous belly rub.

Instead of reclining chairs, Henry's home theater has several suede-covered sofas the size of king beds, piled high with pillows. We all share one of them, and in an ideal world, we would each have a section to ourselves, with no less than twelve inches separating us. In reality, I have half the sofa to myself. Bea, Henry, and Tundra are sharing the other half. To be fair, Henry doesn't exactly look thrilled about the situation, but he isn't trying to change it either. Bea may not be in his lap, but my bet is she will be by the end of the night.

Henry needs a beautiful, vivacious woman at his side. Someone who sparkles and draws the eye of the entire room. Someone he won't get bored with and cheat on. Someone who isn't hampered by her duty to her country but has enough rank to make her the catch of the century, just like him. And Bea needs someone who will lavish her with gifts, who will push back when she's out of line, who will treat her like the princess she is.

But even if they're meant for each other, they're not meant to have my dog.

"Tundra," I call. "Come here, boy."

He lifts his head and looks at me but doesn't move from his position atop Bea.

She giggles and continues stroking his head. "He's so comfy. Don't make him move. Besides, he's warming my legs."

Maybe you should've worn something that covered more than your butt. Giving myself a mental slap for the thought, I scoot off the sofa. "I'm going to grab some snacks."

I pad into the kitchen in my thick woolen socks and flannel pajamas, much more suitable December attire than Bea's satin boxer shorts. I rummage around in the kitchen until I've gathered an array of food: the brownies Bea brought, some popcorn I found in the pantry, the tub of cookie dough, and those honey mustard pretzels Henry likes.

Yes, I'm stalling.

I'm sliding the popcorn into the microwave when I feel him enter the kitchen. I don't even need to turn around—my body reads his presence like a scanner. I shut the microwave door and program it, a churning lump of nausea now residing in my stomach.

Henry leans back against the counter, arms crossed. "You okay?"

"Why wouldn't I be?" I dump the pretzels into a bowl.

"You seem a little withdrawn."

"Just tired." I pop one in my mouth. "I think I'll head to bed, actually."

"The movie just started."

I turn to face him. "Don't pretend you aren't eager to spend time alone with Bea."

"Why would I want time alone with Bea?"

Laughing, I open the tub of cookie dough. "I'm not a fool, Henry."

"Then I guess that makes me one, because I have no idea what you're getting at."

I slam the container onto the counter. "Really? That's the way you want to play this?"

"You still think I have a thing for your sister?"

"I think you have a thing for women." The microwave dings, and I pull the bag out. Stream rises from the seam, and I let it dissipate before pulling it open.

"I would never sleep with Bea."

I empty the popcorn into another bowl. "What's wrong with Bea?"

"For one thing, she's your *sister*."

"I didn't realize you had standards."

"Yeah, I'm aware." He stares at the floor and rubs the back of his neck.

"Exactly how long did it take you after London? The next day? That night? Did you even bother changing the sheets?"

Henry crosses his arms again and narrows his eyes at me. "Three months."

"Three months what?"

"Three months before I had sex with anyone."

I bark out a laugh. "Right. Okay. I wouldn't believe you if you said anything longer than a week." I crumple the popcorn bag and toss it into the bin.

"It's the truth."

"London *was* three months ago, genius. So unless you're about to confess to sleeping with my sister after all, I don't believe you." Grabbing a spoon, I use it to scoop out a ball of cookie dough.

"I had sex with you five days ago."

I stop scooping, my hand frozen. The lump from my stomach has moved to my throat. I try to swallow it. It doesn't budge.

He takes a tiny step closer. "I knew one time with you would ruin all other women for me." Another step. "I was right."

I hold up the spoon. "Don't. Move." It's only a whisper.

"I haven't been with anyone since you."

"And I'm a two-headed horse. I'm not *stupid*, Henry!" I throw the utensil into the sink and spin around.

He's right there, right in the space where I want to be, and then his hands are cradling my face, and they feel so good, so right. I know I should push him away, but his touch is exactly what I've been craving, and I want his words to be the truth even though I know I'd have a higher chance of winning the lottery.

My nausea grows stronger. I place both palms on his chest and shove. He goes easily, as if he was expecting it. "Don't you dare say things like that to me," I tell him.

"Just because you don't want to hear them doesn't mean they're not true."

"Fuck you, Henry." I whirl out of the kitchen before he can see the tears that have already formed in my eyes.

12

"Demons" - Imagine Dragons

T HERE ARE A NUMBER of ways one can organize one's ties: by color (the obvious choice), by texture, by fabric. Or, if someone happens to be particularly evil-hearted, they can avoid organization entirely and simply hang them up with no semblance of order whatsoever.

I may not be able to rectify much else right now, but I can certainly do something about this situation.

I dump all of Henry's ties into the middle of the closet floor. He must have over fifty of them. I briefly consider taking a Sharpie to each one as revenge for the lies he told last night but decide it's beneath me.

I settle down next to the pile and press play on the latest episode of my favorite history podcast. They're doing a deep dive into the first settlements in Wesbourne back in 1274. I rummage through the ties for all the reds. I've decided to go the color route.

I knew one time with you would ruin all other women for me.

Bloody hell. Is that line going to haunt me for all eternity?

I roll up a maroon tie and shove it into the organizer with extra vehemence. If I had a dollar for every time I've wanted to stab Henry, I'd have enough money to keep the royal household afloat.

What possessed him to say that? It must give him some kind of sick pleasure to know he can still mess with my heart. And mess with it he did.

Even after retreating to my bedroom last night, my screwed-up heart could only wish what he said was true. But I established a long time ago that Henry isn't capable of telling the truth, so I simply kept circling the issue again and again. I didn't fall asleep for hours.

I tuck a crimson tie into a small cubby and scream when someone touches my shoulder. I whip around to find the man of the hour standing over me. Yanking my headphones down to dangle around my neck, I stand up. "What are you doing, scaring me like that?"

Henry has the audacity to look bemused. "What are you doing playing with my ties?"

"I'm not playing, I'm organizing," I say before thinking better of engaging him. "Why would you just barge in?"

"I knocked." He gestures to the door, then my headphones.

"What do you want?"

"Um, something to wear?" He glances at his clothes hanging along the wall.

My cheeks must be as red as the ties. I step back so he can get inside. What I thought was a spacious closet yesterday has now become the size of a locker. I cross my arms over the flimsy nightgown covering my still braless chest. Even though it's nearly nine in the morning, I'd prefer to stay locked in here than venture into the rest of the flat in the hopes of avoiding the man currently browsing through his shirts. He finally settles on a pale blue one that will look amazing against his skin tone. As a matter of principle, I ignore the way his back muscles ripple through his T-shirt.

He looks down at the tangle of ties on the floor again and clears his throat. "Any chance you could choose one for me?"

I quickly bend over and grab a navy tweed one. I hold it out, and his eyes flit down toward my perky chest.

I knew after just one time with you . . .

If he meant that, he went without sex for three months.

If he meant that, I'm a circus monkey. I should strangle him with the tie instead.

He takes it from my hand, his eyes lingering on mine, probably trying to get a read on how deep his words cut last night. I cover a yawn with my hand.

"Tired?"

"Insomnia."

Henry frowns. "Nightmares?"

"Awful bed."

His eyes crinkle at the corners. "The worst."

He's likely remembering the same thing I am: me gushing about his incredible mattress post coitus. I shut my eyes and take a deep breath. Surely this must be the apex of my life's humiliation.

He rests his hand on the doorknob. "I'll move my clothes to the guest room so this doesn't happen again."

Before I can say anything, he's gone, leaving me with a feeling akin to homesickness.

Late morning brings several inches of snow, a weird feeling in my stomach, and my mother.

"You didn't think you could keep her all to yourself, did you?" she asks as she sweeps inside the penthouse. She floats over to where Bea is still finishing her egg white omelet and plants a quick kiss on her cheek. "Hello, dear. How was London?"

"You know she's at Cambridge, right?" I swallow the rest of my coffee. Maisie brought it nearly two hours ago, and I regret the decision as soon as the lukewarm liquid hits the back of my throat.

Rosalind waves her hand and unwinds the cashmere scarf from her neck. "Technicalities, Celia."

"Morning," Bea mutters, still half-asleep.

"Good lord, child. It's nearly eleven. The least you can do is greet me properly."

Bea murmurs an apology before taking a long sip of her own hot coffee. "I'm so tired."

"I can see that. How many times have I told you it's better for your face if you get at least eight hours of sleep?"

"About a thousand more than necessary," she says into her mug.

"Evidently not." Mum settles herself onto the stool next to her. It's a little like watching a cat trying to drive a car. "I assume a boy played a hand in this sleep deprivation." She is a pro at questions without question marks.

All too quickly, my mind flashes back to last night, when I left Henry and Bea alone to finish the movie. He must have come to the kitchen to sabotage the fragile state of my heart before returning to ravish my sister. I cover my mouth and will the vomit to stay down.

"We were just talking," she says, as if in answer to my thoughts. "I didn't realize how late it was."

"A woman must put her own self-care above men. That's why the three of us are going to the spa today."

I cough into my hand. "Excuse me?"

"You heard me. I already arranged everything. They'll only have a minimal staff, everyone has signed an NDA, and we'll have the whole place to ourselves."

"I get to leave?" I don't care if my mother planned a trip to Snake Island if it means I can see the outside of this flat.

"I've already spoken to Roberts about it. He helped me arrange everything."

Bea stands and throws her arms around Mum's neck, late-night exhaustion forgotten. "You're the best, Mummy. I was starting to decay in here."

"You've been here twenty-six hours," I deadpan.

"And that was twenty-four too many." She tosses a wink over her shoulder and heads to her room. "I'll be out in a few minutes!"

My mother sneezes into a tissue she managed to grab just in time. "Bless you," I say, just as Tundra rounds the corner from the hallway. "Oh, boy." I stick him in my bedroom and shut the door before he can send her into hives.

We head to the spa at the Atlantis, which is every bit as glamorous as Bea wanted—and as private as I hoped. If I can prove to Henry that there's no threat in my leaving the penthouse, he might let me out more often, even if it's only to come here.

Bea signs us up to be "pampered to within an inch of our lives," and we follow the tiny receptionist down a hall to the sauna.

"I still don't understand why I'm paying to do something I normally actively avoid," I say, taking a seat on one of the wooden benches along the wall. I tuck the fold of my towel in more tightly and shudder. "Sweating."

"You're not paying for it," Mum says. "I am."

"For which we are both eternally grateful." Bea sprawls her towel-clad body out on the bench opposite me. Her sigh is no less dramatic than my shudder.

A tinny rendition of "Jingle Bells" wafts through unseen speakers. Steam begins to cloud the room, and I remind myself it's a detox, not the road to death. "Whoever thought getting wet without water was a good idea should be hung."

"You take hot showers all the time," Bea says.

"Yeah, there's *water*."

"Girls, quit bickering." Mum sighs and settles into her seat. "This is supposed to be relaxing."

"This is going to be the best holiday ever," Bea says. "I still cannot believe I'm staying at the Atlantis! It's a million times better than the palace. No offense, sis."

I cock a brow while the rest of my face remains frozen. "None taken."

"The only thing that would make it better is if Rhett could come visit. I'm going to see if he can fly over for a few days."

I may have just imagined the tensing of my mother's jaw, because her voice is perfectly calm when she says, "Who is this Rhett boy you've become so obsessed with?"

Last time I checked, neither of the Danish princes were named Rhett. In fact, the only time I've encountered that name was within the pages of *Gone With the Wind*. Rosalind's blood pressure has likely spiked ten points.

"Rhett Cole. He's a musician. I thought I told you."

"Define *musician*," I say.

"He writes his own songs." She says this like he has cured cancer in dogs. "He's not famous yet, but he thinks he'll get a record deal soon. He's had a few songs go viral."

"He's British?" Rosalind is trying her damnedest to look interested, but I catch the twitch in her eye.

"He's from here. And he told me last night he's coming home next week." Bea squeals and clasps her hands together.

"That's who you were talking to last night?" I ask.

"Yeah, *obviously*. He calls me every night."

I sink further into the bench. Not Henry then. Wiping away the sweat already beading on my upper lip, I tell myself my relief is because I don't want to see Bea get hurt.

"Does Mr. Cole have any family I might know?" Mum asks.

"Actually," Bea says, "his dad was in a band when he was younger."

I hardly think those are the kind of connections Rosalind is fishing for, but she smiles. "Well, which band was it?"

Bea waves her hand. "You probably didn't know them. They were a rock band."

"Not the Cole Brothers?"

Bea and I both stare at the woman we thought was our mother but who may have been replaced by a doppelganger. "You listened to rock music?" we both say at the same time.

"Girls, please." She laughs. "I have a life outside of motherhood."

"One that consists of electric guitars and drumbeats?" I use the corner of my towel to wipe my face. Are saunas always this hot?

"You listened to the Cole Brothers?" Bea says. "Randy Cole is Rhett's dad."

Mum's smile is foreign, one I've never seen on her face before. It looks young, lighter. "Even better, I saw them in concert once."

"You saw the Cole Brothers in concert?" Bea sounds skeptical.

Rosalind nods, her smile still lighting up her face. "They were incredible."

"I can't believe Dad took you to a rock concert," I say.

I'm watching her closely, and I don't miss the tiny slip of her smile before she drags it back into place. "I didn't go with your father. He would've never endured it. Said it gave him a headache." She waves her hand casually before tucking a strand of damp hair back into her chignon.

"So who'd you go with?" Bea says.

"Oh, just a friend."

There's something fishy about the way she says it. Bea must pick up on it too, because she says, "A *friend*? Which of your friends listens to rock?"

Mum laughs, her head tipped back against the wall, eyes closed. "Okay, he was more than a friend."

Bea's eyes meet mine across the small room. Never once has Rosalind shared any of her romantic history with us, no matter how many times we've tried to pry it out of her. Turns out, the secret was good old-fashioned sweat all along.

Several beats pass, then Bea says quietly, almost timidly, "Mum? The Cole Brothers didn't start touring until 2002."

Rosalind's eyes fly open and settle on Bea. For a long moment, none of us say anything. I think of all the secrets we each carry, the lengths we go to to keep them hidden, to make sure they are buried with us in the grave. But sometimes, despite our best efforts, one manages to find its way to the light.

"Mum, did you have an affair?" Bea finally asks.

She doesn't answer. She doesn't need to. The truth is written in her eyes, which drop Bea's and land in her lap, where her fingers are twisting together in a knot.

"So it's true?" I say. "You cheated on Dad?" Bea's voice had a soft inquisitiveness to it. Mine is all sharp edges.

Rosalind gives a tiny nod. A singular tear runs through the sweat on her face. "I didn't mean for it to happen." She wipes her face. "I know everyone says that, but it's true. It only lasted a few weeks, and I felt awful for betraying your father, especially when he forgave me."

"Wait, Dad knew?" I don't even try to hide my surprise.

Rosalind nods again. "He knew and chose to forgive me. Later that year, we got pregnant with Beatrice."

We sit in stunned silence for a few minutes. Some things you're just better off not knowing. And thinking about my mum with anyone but my dad—

"How could you do that?" I say. I don't mean it to sound harsh, but it comes out as a hiss anyway.

She looks at me for the first time since slipping up. "I didn't plan it. Sometimes things just . . . happen."

How dare she make me reconsider my stance on accidental sex. My situation is completely different from hers.

"No offense, Mum, but how could Dad trust you again after that?" Bea asks.

"I know I wouldn't," I say under my breath.

My mother lifts her chin the way I've seen her do many times when faced with an obstacle. "Knowing he trusted me was more motivating than any sense of right or wrong. I think he knew that. I haven't so much as flirted with a man since, not even after he died."

This much, at least, I'm pretty sure is true, because the thought of Rosalind flirting with anyone is akin to picturing a robot attempting to dance. But that doesn't change the fact that she cheated on my father, and she cheated on us. Being good afterward doesn't excuse the sin.

Bea scoots over beside her and lays her head on Mum's shoulder. "Well, if Dad forgave you, that's enough for me."

Rosalind smiles and kisses the top of my sister's blonde head, which somehow doesn't manage to look any worse for wear after sitting in this bloody steam room. They both look over at me as though expecting me to echo the sentiment.

I stand and readjust my towel. "I need to get out. It's too hot in here."

I don't wait for them. I don't even bother changing back into my clothes before taking the private lift to the top floor. The spa should add an additional warning to their already lengthy list of the dangers of saunas: *Mothers may rearrange your life while under the influence of detoxifying steam.*

God, will the bombs ever stop falling? I'm tempted to hire a private detective to uncover my parents' entire past just so I can have all of the facts. Apparently, nothing is sacred anymore.

13

"Castles Crumbling" - Taylor Swift ft. Hayley Williams

S NOW HANGS FROM THE corners of the windows, but I have to imagine the biting chill, because I haven't left this tower in seven whole days. The most shocking part is how much I miss my people.

Before my coronation, I wouldn't have considered myself an extrovert, but something changes when you realize an entire country is looking to you for leadership.

While I didn't have the endorsement of every citizen before becoming queen, I was well-liked. Divorcing Henry changed that, however. Even some of my most loyal supporters questioned whether I was the right woman for the job. The people were scandalized, especially the ones who think Henry hung the moon. Which accounts for 98 percent of the population.

I try to make out the streets below from where I'm standing in the living room, but we're up too high to see the ant-sized pedestrians scurrying to work. I wonder if their lives have all gone back to normal since the shooting, or if everyone else is on hold the way I am.

I feel foolish for spending so much time worrying about Henry and the effect he has on my heart. There are so many bigger problems in the world, but as long as I'm stuck here, there's little to nothing I can do about them.

Now the foyer doors open, and Roberts announces Maisie. I eagerly accept the latte from her hands as she passes on her way to deposit my green box of state papers onto the dining table. Once we sit down and I get a good look at her face, dread creeps into my stomach.

"What is it now?" I ask.

She takes a deep breath and lets it out. "The press found out about your appeal to Parliament for the tax raise."

"Terrific." What's a little more gasoline on the fire?

"I would recommend staying away from the news for the time being."

"You may as well tell me. It can't be worse than I'm imagining."

Her eyes grow large. "How good is your imagination?"

She hands her tablet to me. The home page of the *Wesbourne Sun* fills the screen, the headline taking up nearly the whole thing. *Queen Stages Assassination to Garner Sympathy for Tax Hike?*

My eyes fly back to Maisie. "They actually think I hired the shooter myself?"

She shrugs and takes back the tablet. "They're certainly speculating that you did. Everyone is covering the tax proposal. The *Sun* is the first to suggest a correlation, but you know the rest will follow."

I sink back into the pillows. She was right. This is worse than I was expecting. "Surely someone has mentioned the fact that it's impossible to run the royal household on the current Civil List?"

"Unfortunately, they are conveniently leaving that part out. At the risk of saying I told you so . . ." She winces. "I did warn you about this."

I brush at my lint-free pants. "Yeah. You did. I just assumed people would understand."

"We just need a really good plan to bring this around," she says.

"Please do not tell me you have a scheme in mind."

"Absolutely not. I was just thinking that maybe we should find you a husband."

I take another swig of coffee. "If that's not a scheme, I'm curious what you *do* consider one."

"The British royal family's support sky-rocketed when William and Kate became engaged."

I scoff. "They were in love. It wasn't a forced match to gain publicity."

"Okay, you're right. What we need is a really good press secretary," Maisie says.

"How is the hunt coming?"

"Nothing promising yet. Apparently, no one wants the job of repairing your image. Personally, I don't see what the problem is. It's not like you're Hitler." She glances back down at her screen and murmurs, "At least not before the tax thing."

"Is this supposed to be helpful?"

She glances up and clears her throat. "My apologies, Your Majesty. My lips are sealed on the subject forever."

"I'll believe it when I see it," I say. "What if we released a statement of some kind? Or I could make an appearance?"

"I don't know how much good a statement would do, but an appearance would be great. Maybe you could fake a few tears or act like you're scared for your life?"

I raise a brow. "I *am* scared for my life."

"Of course you are. I just meant— Well, you're not exactly acting like it."

"Because I'm locked inside Fort Knox!"

"Right, I-I know," she stammers. "Do you think *he* will let you out to make an appearance?" Her stage whisper is atrocious.

"God, Maisie. You can say his name."

"I'll believe it when I see it. So, will he?"

I blow out a breath. "There's only one way to find out, isn't there?"

Henry's office is in a wing of the penthouse I haven't spent much time in, aside from that awful movie night. Besides his large workspace, there is also a gym (evidently the three communal ones the building offers aren't enough), the home theater, and a billiard room.

I'm about to knock on his door when Bea spots me.

"There you are!" She approaches, and I lower my hand. Her eyes are red and watery. "I've been looking everywhere for you."

That's impossible, since I was in the great room for the past hour and only left a minute ago.

"You found me," I say with a smile. My head is throbbing with pain, but I push it to the back of my mind.

"I need to talk to you."

I motion to Henry's door. "I'm kind of in the middle of something. Can we chat later?"

"This is really important," Bea says. "I feel like my life just ended."

I force my eyes to stay on her when what they really want is to roll across the floor. Maybe I've coddled her too much, because Bea thinking I will drop everything every time she has a blowout gone wrong is concerning.

I am the queen, which means I have responsibilities beyond my little sister. And right now, those responsibilities include doing something to regain the people's favor and support.

"I'm sorry, Bea, but I need to handle this right now. I'll find you in an hour, okay?" Without waiting for her answer, I knock on Henry's door.

He calls for me to come in, and I do. The far wall is all glass, and the L-shaped desk is sleek and modern. A large table is situated on the other side of the room, surrounded by chairs. This space is a cold cousin to his cozy office in the palace.

He looks up when I enter. It's impossible to ignore the little dip in my stomach when his eyes crinkle up at the corners. He immediately stands and motions me over.

"Sorry to interrupt," I say, taking a seat in the chair across from him.

He moves aside several large blueprints. "I needed the break anyway."

"Are you buying another business?"

"No, just a pet project I'm working on." Interlacing his hands behind his head, he leans back in his chair. "What's up?"

I bite my lip. This seemed like a good idea while Maisie was still here, but now that I'm facing him, my hands have grown clammy, and I can feel the fabric of my sweater growing damp under my armpits. "I don't know if you've seen the news," I say.

"I have."

"Then you're aware that the press is dragging my name through the mud."

Henry nods. "A pastime of theirs, I believe."

"I can handle their usual blows, but now they're saying I staged the assassination to gain sympathy."

His nostrils flare ever so slightly. "Vultures."

"We thought, if I could show the people that the threat is real and that I really am under heavy protection, they would ease up a bit." My abdomen has decided to join my head in a competition to see which can cause me the most discomfort. I declare a tie in hopes they will both give up. They don't.

"Who's we?"

"Maisie and me." I press my teeth into my lip again.

"And how exactly do the two of you think you can prove the very real threat on your life?"

"We haven't covered that part yet."

"Allow me to save you the trouble," Henry says. "It's not happening." He pushes several paper clips into his desk drawer.

"There has to be a way to do it safely."

He laughs and cracks his knuckles. "You're hilarious."

"I'm sorry," I snipe, "which part of this conversation is humorous to you?"

Smile vanished, he sits upright in his chair. "The part where you thought for a second I would allow you to put your life in any more danger than it already is."

"Henry, sometimes you have to take risks for the things that matter."

He raises his eyebrows. "Only if the benefit outweighs the risk."

"And in this case, it does."

He stands and leans over the desk. His spicy scent, combined with the warmth from his body, reminds me of hot cider on a cold day. "So if you died, at least everyone would love you?"

"I—" That's not what I meant, but somehow I've lost the ability to make sense with my words.

"You will not make a public appearance until this guy is caught." Henry sits back down with a sigh. "And maybe not even then. There's always the risk of copycats."

"You cannot be serious."

His eyes flash to mine. "Do I look like I'm joking?"

No, he doesn't. He looks like his anger is simmering just below the surface, and for some reason it's hot. Very hot. I wave a hand in front of my face to cool it. "What about a live stream on social media?"

"Absolutely not."

"It's not like anyone would know where I am."

He studies a paper on the desk, ignoring me. "Not a risk I'm willing to take."

"But *I'm* willing." I'm practically pleading now. "Doesn't that count for anything?"

He looks up from the page, but only to glare at me. "It's not your decision to make."

"My life, my decision."

Folding his hands in front of him, Henry says, "Let me make something very clear. You gave up the right to make decisions for yourself the moment you accepted that crown. Because like it or not, you no longer belong to yourself, but to the people of Wesbourne. They expect a leader who is strong, confident, and smart. Not someone who makes impulsive decisions based on how she's feeling that day. Got it?"

I narrow my eyes, my jaw clenched tight. "The only thing I 'get' is that you're an arrogant asshole who likes to boss people around."

He shrugs. "Good luck finding someone else who can give you three orgasms in an hour."

I inhale sharply, and my entire body breaks into goose bumps. He has already turned his attention back to his work and doesn't even acknowledge my anger. When it becomes clear he isn't planning to discuss this further, I excuse myself and walk out.

It isn't until I'm back in the hallway that I realize his talk of orgasms chased away my headache and abdominal pain entirely.

14

"Fight For You" - Jason Derulo

I CHECK THE TIMESTAMP on the text. It came in nine minutes ago. It took me eight to locate my phone after I heard the ping. I glance in the mirror and run a hand over my hair before deciding it will have to be good enough.

The great room is dimly lit when I walk through, still void of any kind of holiday decorations. I scan my memory for anything pointing to Henry hating Christmas but come up blank. Then again, we haven't exactly spent much time together in the past decade, so what do I know?

His office door is closed when I reach it, so I knock softly a few times. It opens immediately, and he stands back to let me in. My face heats from the memory of his last words to me, but if he remembers them, he gives no indication.

Placing a hand on the small of my back, he leads me to the large conference table. I ignore the thrill that shoots up my spine at his touch. I recognize Jameson and Roberts, who are already seated there. They both stand and give a stiff bow when I approach. There are two other men at the table as well, whom Henry introduces as O'Falloran and Ramos. I shake all of their hands and offer a feeble smile.

I'm suddenly nervous as hell.

Henry indicates that I should take the chair next to him. "What's the latest?" he says, directing his gaze at Jameson.

"Progress is a little slower than I'd like because we've run into a few snags. Around 25 percent of the windows in the west wing have been replaced, and teams are working on the installation of the biometric system, sir."

"Very good. And the next step?" Henry asks.

"After the windows are completed, the plan is to move to securing the entrances. There have been some issues with structural damage, which is adding time," Jameson tells him.

"Okay," Henry says. "Do what needs to be done. No cutting corners."

He's already shifting his attention to one of the others, but before he can ask another question, I interject, "What's the time frame on completing the west wing?"

"It's hard to say at this point, Your Majesty, but I'm hoping we can have it done by the end of the year."

"The end of the year?" We're still in the first week of December.

Jameson nods. "That's what we're aiming for. It might end up taking longer, depending on what we run into. It's an old building, and so far, it's resisting security upgrades."

I take a deep breath. It's not his fault it's taking so long. "And after the west wing is complete, I can move back in, correct?"

Henry straightens in his chair. The pen in his hand makes a sharp click. Jameson shoots him a quick glance before returning his attention to me. "That's not advisable until we have the palace fully secured."

"But surely if the residential wing is secure—"

"It's impossible to fully secure the west wing if the rest of the palace is unsecured," Henry says.

"But that will take months!"

Jameson nods gravely. "I'm afraid so. But rest assured, the teams we have in place are working around the clock to get this done as quickly as possible without sacrificing the quality of the work."

I take a deep breath. "But surely—"

Henry places a hand on my leg beneath the table. "Relax, C," he says, quietly enough that I'm the only one who can hear him. "There's a good chance we'll catch the guy first."

He takes charge of the meeting again, this time turning to Roberts, head of Henry's own security team. "Do you have anything to report?" He doesn't remove his hand from my thigh. That small point of contact between us is stealing all coherent thoughts from my head.

Roberts clears his throat. "I've already shared everything of significance with you, sir. But just to recap for the others in the room: The security at the Atlantis is the tightest in the country. The only issues to date have been miscommunications among the security personnel and a possible press leak through the building staff."

"Do you have a list of suspects for me?" Henry asks.

The stocky man called Ramos pulls a sheaf of paper from the folder in front of him and slides it across the table to Henry.

Henry rifles through it, growing more and more irritated. I can't focus on anything but the sheer length of it. There are five pages of names of people who potentially want me dead. Single-spaced.

One name jumps out at me. "Why is my *cousin* on this list?" I snap.

"He would inherit the throne if you and the Princess Royal were both eliminated," Ramos supplies.

Eliminated. Like we're nothing more than pawns on a chess board. "So Beatrice is in danger as well?"

"We can't be sure, but we've increased her security detail just to be safe."

I briefly close my eyes against the nausea. "And you actually think Benjamin might be behind this?"

"We're considering everything a possibility," Ramos says.

"How did you come up with all these names?" I ask.

"By making a list of anyone with even the slightest motive to want you dead. People who have sent angry letters or made threats, people who would gain politically if you weren't on the throne, as well as those with personal vendettas."

"Personal vendettas. What, like Salome Jenkins? She hated me for winning the spelling bee in third grade."

Ramos blinks a few times before picking up a pen. "I'll add her to the list." He starts scribbling something on a notepad.

"She's kidding," Henry growls, increasing the pressure of his fingers on my thigh ever so slightly. He tosses the pages back to Ramos. "This list is impossible to work from. Why the hell is it so long?"

Ramos darts a quick glance in my direction before replying. "The press ran a story accusing Her Majesty of some unsavory things—"

"I know that. How is that relevant?"

"As a result, there have been more threats than usual made against Her Majesty, sir."

I might actually be sick pretty soon.

The lean man with close-cropped hair Henry introduced as O'Falloran scratches his head before saying, "Her disappearance from the public eye has caused some outrage, sir."

"I told you I should show everyone I'm fine." I try to stand, but Henry's fingers are still grasping my leg. He pushes me back into my chair. My stomach flops over, and the queasiness rises. I dig my nails into the back of his hand as hard as I can. He inhales sharply and clamps down harder.

"How close are we to getting this bastard off the streets?" he asks.

"Unfortunately, the room where the shots were fired from was clean, sir. We swept it three times and didn't produce a single hair, fiber, or fingerprint." Ramos looks disgusted with himself.

"Fuck," Henry mutters. "He was prepared."

"It looks that way, yes," Ramos says. "I have someone who's been deep for years, waiting for something like this, and he's getting me a list of names of the best assassins for hire. Until we have something more to go on, it's our best shot."

"What about the limo? Were you able to get anything more from it?"

Ramos shakes his head. "Every mechanic on staff has been fired, with the assurance they'll get their jobs back if we can verify they had nothing to do with the crash."

I'm about to object again, but Henry's hand is so close to my hip now that it doesn't seem advisable.

O'Falloran clears his throat. "Is it possible this guy has given up? He hasn't tried anything in a week."

I fear for his neck, because Henry looks like he's on the verge of snapping it. "I'd like to think that's due to us having the best security in the country. This guy doesn't strike me as one to 'give up.'"

After a few closing remarks, Henry ends the meeting and they all exit, leaving the two of us alone. I'm about to excuse myself, not in the mood for more of his brooding anger, but he surprises me with a soft hand on my arm. "Are you up for a little adventure? I want to show you something."

I open my mouth a few times before finally nodding.

He grins. "Dress warmly. I'll meet you in the foyer in fifteen minutes."

I expected to be taken to the rooftop terrace, which Henry presumably has had cleared. I did not expect to be led to the helipad at the other end of the roof. When we arrive, a chopper is there, blades already spinning.

I halt. "Please tell me you're not about to fly that thing."

"Relax," he says, and tugs on my hand. "I've played a ton of video games."

His grin is way too big as he settles me in the back seat, fastening my buckles before sitting down beside me. "Come on. You didn't actually think I was a pilot, did you?"

I glare at him before turning my gaze out the window. "Where are we going?"

"Surprise."

I want to tell him that his surprises suck, but the reality is that they're always kind of amazing. We soon lift into the air, and my gut clenches in anticipation. It suddenly hits me: I'm actually leaving the penthouse.

We soar over the city, which is dotted with thousands of twinkling lights. Eventually, they give way to the occasional village marked only by traffic lights and the faint neon glow from pubs.

I lose track of time as we fly farther and farther from the city and the castle Henry has me trapped in. When we finally land, the time on my phone says we've been in the air for an hour.

It takes me a minute to orient myself when Henry helps me out of the helicopter. We're on a deserted beach, inhabited only by some pieces of driftwood and large boulders. The air whips around us, but I'm too ecstatic to feel the cold. I'm finally out of prison.

I race down the sandy stretch, my arms splayed wide, not caring who sees me. Henry is waiting with a grin when I return.

"Happy to be outside?" he asks, hands in his pockets.

"Happier than you know."

"Come on." He reaches for my hand and leads me to a cluster of rocks that create a tiny sheltered alcove. Inside, a blanket has been laid out on the sand. A thermos sits to the side of it, along with two cups.

"What's all this?" I ask.

Henry sits down and pats the spot next to him. "I knew how badly you wanted to get out. This was the best I could come up with."

I glance around. The ocean is in front of us, dark and rolling. The sand stretches in both directions, brightened by the light of the moon. Behind us and scattered along the beach are dark figures I didn't notice before. Of course there's a security team, but for the first time, I don't care. If it means I can get some fresh air, they are welcome to watch me all night.

I plop down beside Henry, and he hands me a cup of hot cocoa. "Thank you," I say. "For all of this."

He smiles. "What kind of prison warden would I be if I didn't allow you a little yard time?"

We both stare at the vast expanse in front of us and sip our hot chocolate. The ocean has the power to make me feel very tiny.

"Where did it all come from?" I say into the darkness.

"What, the ocean?"

I jerk a thumb over my shoulder at the chopper sitting somewhere behind us. "The money to do all of this."

"I told you. I own multiple businesses that do very well."

"But how did you get started?"

He drops his gaze to his lap and shrugs. "I had some money I wanted to invest."

"That must have been some allowance."

A hard laugh slips past his lips. "My father doesn't believe in money that isn't earned."

"That certainly hasn't slowed you down," I say.

He murmurs something in agreement.

"Don't you have any weaknesses?"

He glances over at my legs, which are stretched out in front of me. "Never ask a man what his weakness is."

"Why? Afraid I'll expose you?"

"Not all of us are strong enough to reveal them."

You wouldn't have to flip over too many stones to discover my weakness, but I don't think that's necessarily a sign of strength. It's just that my soft spot for Henry is so all-encompassing, it only takes a faint brush against the bruise to make it smart.

He pulls a backpack out of the shadows and unzips it to reveal a collection of snacks. "I need sustenance if I'm going to do this."

"What, play guard dog?"

"Keep my hands to myself."

"Please." I blow on my steaming mug. "We both know I present no temptation to you."

He just laughs and opens a bag of crisps, then offers it to me. I take one, and we munch in silence until I can't stand it anymore.

"I used to think that maybe I was your weakness," I mumble. Damn this stupid romantic gesture that isn't supposed to be the least bit romantic. Three minutes in, I'm already spilling secrets. I can feel Henry's eyes on me, but there's no way I'm looking at him now.

"You don't think so anymore?" He rests his arms on his bent knees.

Now it's my turn to laugh. "You killed that fantasy a long time ago."

"Maybe you just misread the situation."

"Or maybe I'm just a fool."

His gaze feels soft, like a caressing hand on my cheek. I still don't look up.

"You're not a fool, C," he says quietly.

I swallow, but the lump in my throat only grows bigger. "I thought you were going to be my first kiss that day in the Sunken Garden."

"Not kissing you was the second-hardest thing I've ever done."

What are we doing out here? This feels like a tightrope over Niagara Falls.

"What was the hardest?" I'm not sure I really want to know.

He drains his cocoa and lets the mug dangle from his fingers. "Leaving you in London."

This time I can't help but look at him. He seems completely serious, but I can't be sure anymore. I'm so tired of this. I'm physically exhausted from the rollercoaster that is loving Henry.

"I don't know why you say things like that." Pulling my legs in, I wrap my arms around them, rubbing them to chase away the chill.

"To be honest," he says, "neither do I."

"You told me we can't be together. That you don't want it."

"Yeah. I did."

"But then you say those things. What am I supposed to do with that?"

"I don't know." He rubs his hand over his face. "I'm sorry."

Something suddenly occurs to me. "Are you gay?"

For a minute, I'm scared his eyes are going to pop out of his head. Then he throws his head back and laughs.

My fear changes to irritation. "Haha. So funny," I mutter.

Henry wipes tears from his eyes before looking at me. "I'm sorry. That was just very . . . unexpected."

I drain my cocoa. "Glad you found humor in it."

"Celia, come on. You of all people should know that I am as straight as they come."

"At this point, I don't know anything."

"You know who I am, behind all the facades."

"I thought I did," I say. "But you've made me question everything."

"Who I am with you, that's real."

"Yeah, the heartbreaker. He's a real catch."

Closing his eyes, he rubs the bridge of his nose. "That guy is the one trying to do the right thing."

"Oh, by hurting me?"

"By protecting you."

"And just what are you trying to protect me from?"

He scratches at the stubble on his chin. "Myself?"

"Then why," I say, "when I try to move on, are you always there?"

"Maybe you weren't wrong about being my weakness."

Running a finger through the fleece of the blanket, I smooth it in one direction, then another. "If I'm your weakness, you're stronger than Hercules himself."

He exhales an amused sigh. "I've fallen prey to you many times."

"So now I'm a predator?"

"More like a siren."

The heat from his body seeps into mine even though we're not touching. It's going to take me a long time to work through everything he's just said, weed out the lies from the truth—if there's any truth in it at all.

Standing, he offers me his hand. "We should head back, or we'll be dead on our feet tomorrow."

I nod and let him help me up, but he stops me before I can leave the alcove. "It was always supposed to be us, you know." He brushes the backs of his fingers across my cold cheek. "But sometimes life fucks it up."

15

"Back to December" - Taylor Swift

I FEEL LIKE I'M stuck in a really bad country song. And what's worse, I don't even listen to country music, so I can't enjoy it. Tundra offers to be my sounding board while I do my makeup, and I gladly take him up on it.

"He said it's hard to stay away from me. Explanation: he's a red-blooded heterosexual male, and I'm a heterosexual woman who isn't bad looking. Fair enough. He's at least somewhat attracted to me, even if it's only on a primal level."

I glance down at Tundra. He is staring up at me as if he desperately wishes he could give his two cents. "Thanks, buddy. That's kind of you to say." I scratch behind his ears, and he nearly passes out from happiness.

"He also said that leaving me in London was the hardest thing he's ever done. Explanation: he's trying to protect me. Side note: the guy has an unhealthy preoccupation with safety, and I should probably suggest he get help."

Tundra barks his approval of this plan.

"Then he implies he's the one I need protection from. Explanation: I don't have a bloody clue." I rifle through my lipsticks, looking for the perfect shade. Not that there is such a thing when you're locked in a penthouse and the only person you have a hope of seeing is the security guard bringing your dinner. "Men are insane, you know that?"

Tundra cocks his head at me and whines.

"No, of course I wasn't including you in that statement. Strictly referring to human males."

I turn back to the mirror and begin applying the crimson lipstick I settled on. As I replay Henry's words in my mind, I realize he never really made any statements. Questions, vague references, but no straight-up declarations of any feelings. Explanation: he's a player, through and through.

"I'm giving up on men. You and I can rule this country together."

Tundra huffs out a snort and lays his head on his paws.

"Sorry, boy. Obviously you're meant for bigger things." I swipe a final coat of mascara onto my lashes and appraise my work. It's not Daphne-perfect, but it's good enough for someone who won't be leaving the flat all day. Not that I'm not thankful for Henry's surprise trip last night, but it only made me want to escape all the more.

It's time to put him out of my mind and work on coming up with a solution to the royal family's financial dilemma. I need to have a backup plan in case Parliament denies my request to raise the Civil List. I'm already beginning to question the wisdom of that move, considering the people's response to it.

I can't get on board with Henry's idea to commercialize the royal collection. Exposing those valuable items to the general public puts them at risk for damage and theft. The insurance costs alone would probably wipe out any profits.

There has to be another option. What I need is someone who understands the delicate situation I'm in without being directly affected by it.

Someone who knows how important this is but also understands why it's important to keep the royal family's privacy.

I can't believe I didn't think about him before.

I pull up his contact info in my phone. I didn't have the heart to delete it earlier, and now I'm glad for my reluctance to let go of our three-year relationship.

There's a two-second pause before he speaks. I visualize the wheels in his head spinning as he decides what to say to me. He settles for a classic "Hello?"

"Hi, Beck." My voice sounds way too chipper. "It's me. Celia."

"Yeah, I know."

I close my eyes against the onslaught of memories. "Look, I know this is weird, but I was wondering if I could talk to you about something confidential. I need some professional advice."

There's a long beat of silence, long enough to make me question my decision. This was a stupid idea.

"Um, I guess?" My heart breaks at the unease in his voice. I did this to him.

"I promise I won't make it weird. It's not personal. It pertains to the Crown."

"I was actually trying to work up the courage to call you myself."

"Oh." I blink at myself in the mirror. "You were?"

"Yeah. Listen, I, uh—well, I was wondering if I could have the engagement ring back."

The words fly out of my head. Of all the things I expected him to say, that was at the bottom of the list. "Sure. Yeah, absolutely."

"I hate to ask. I mean—"

"No, it's totally fine," I say. "I shouldn't have kept it as long as I did."

"Normally I'd never ask. It's just—"

"I get it, okay? We're not getting married anymore. I shouldn't keep the ring. It's fine."

He sighs. "Okay. I'm really sorry."

"Please don't feel bad. I can get it back to you today if you're able to meet?"

"I can do lunch," he offers.

"Perfect." I bite my lip. "I'll have to send a car to pick you up."

Getting Beck clearance into the penthouse proves easier than I'd anticipated. Apparently Henry didn't issue a strict no-visitors policy before he left for wherever he disappears to every day, and when I assure Roberts that Beck works on the Crown's legal team, he agrees to the visit.

Maisie brings over the ring from the palace, and I open the box for one final look. A year ago, I was imagining myself wrapping Christmas presents for my new sisters-in-law on this day, not locked in my ex-husband's penthouse, about to return my ring to my ex-fiancé.

"Thank you," I tell Maisie.

"Of course. Are we done here, or . . . ?" She locks the screen on her tablet.

"Actually, I was wondering if you'd look through these records with me, just until Beck gets here."

She chews on the side of her lip. "I kind of have a lot of things to do back at the palace."

"This won't take long. He should be here in the next thirty minutes, but if we work together, we'll get an hour of work done on it."

She doesn't argue, and we start tackling a small section of the huge collection of financial documents. We've managed to get through an inch-tall stack by the time Beck is escorted inside, bringing the smell of curry with him. My heart does a little dance when I spy the familiar brown bag in his hand.

He holds it up enticingly. "Hope you're hungry," he says. "I took the liberty of assuming you hadn't eaten yet."

He stops abruptly when he spots Maisie. Before the diary and my subsequent coronation, the three of us had dinner together a handful of times. Now they're looking at each other as if they're strangers. Apparently our broken engagement made things awkward for more people than just the two of us.

I clear my throat. "That's all for today, Maisie. Thank you for everything."

She nods and scrambles to collect her things. Less than a minute later, the foyer door closes behind her.

"How did you know I was craving chicken biryani?" I say, taking the bag from Beck and setting plates on the bar.

We settle into our old routine the way you help yourself to your mum's pantry after moving out. Beck opens the foil containers, and I divide the naan bread between us.

"I haven't had this in ages," I say after inhaling several bites.

"Best Indian food in the city." His smile is a little too tight, and now my heart is as well.

"How are Alexa and Jasmine?"

"They're good, really good," he says. "Alexa is switching her major again. Jasmine is doing her first-year residency at Billings Memorial."

"That's right. She graduated this summer, didn't she?" While I was getting married to another man.

Beck nods and takes another bite. I want to ask more questions, to find out how his sisters are *really* doing, not just the pat answers he'd give the receptionist at his office. But I know why he's holding back, and I can't blame him.

I know the financial strain he's under. He works tirelessly on a salaried solicitor's income to put both of his sisters through university and pay off his own loans. But he'd never deny them anything that was within his power to provide. And this is the kind of goodness I walked away from.

"I really am sorry about . . . everything," I say. The curry congeals in my stomach, and a wave of nausea crashes over me. "I know I said I wouldn't make this personal, but I want you to know how sorry I am about the way I handled everything."

"Celia, please. It's fine. I've moved on."

"I—" I blink at him. "You have?"

He nods and takes another bite of chicken. "What was it you wanted to talk to me about?"

My mind still reeling from this revelation, I do my best to sum up our financial problems as succinctly as possible. Beck has moved on? Already? We just broke up a few months ago.

He frowns and wipes the corners of his mouth. "Parliament isn't going to approve the tax hike."

"What?" I drop my bread. "Why not?"

"They pride themselves on Wesbourne's low tax rate. They're not about to jeopardize that."

"You're sure about this?"

"Yeah, pretty sure." He works on the Crown's legal team, so if anyone would know, it's Beck.

"What do they expect me to do?"

He wipes a few crumbs from the counter with his napkin. "Probably find a way to generate another income."

I groan. "Why does everyone keep saying that?"

"I'm sorry, Celia. I wish I had better news for you."

"Do you have any idea how I could quickly generate a residual annual income of ten million?" I offer him a full-wattage grin. "Preferably overnight and with no investment."

He gives me a grim smile in return. "You know I'm not cut out for business matters. I assumed . . ." He shakes his head. "Never mind."

I almost ask what he was going to say, but I stop myself at the last second. Something tells me it has to do with Henry, and I don't need any more arrows pointing in that direction.

"Do you ever think about where we'd be if that diary hadn't been donated?" The words slip out before I can stop them.

He nods. "I used to. But like I said, I've moved on." Folding his napkin into a neat square, he lays it on the countertop. "That's why I brought this stuff back." He lifts his work satchel onto his lap and pulls out a shopping bag.

I take it from him and look inside. I recognize the scarf I gave him last Christmas, the toothbrush I kept at his flat, a picture of the two of us in Rome. I slide a Valentine's card out and hold it up. "You're giving this back?"

He shrugs, as if the life we built together was of no consequence, and clears his throat. "It's not exactly a clean break if I still keep mementos lying around, is it?"

I stick the card and my pride back into the bag. "No, I guess not." I say, scooting off the barstool. "I'll just go get the ring."

Beck has stacked our take-away containers on the counter when I get back. "I wasn't sure where the bins were," he says, sticking his hands in his pockets.

"I'll take care of it." I hold out the velvet ring box, and he takes it from me. I can almost feel the rush of air from the story of us slamming shut.

"Thanks. I'm sorry to make things awkward."

"It's fine." I wave my hand like this isn't tearing out a chunk of my heart. "So. You're seeing someone?"

He lifts his eyes to meet mine. "I am. But that's not what this is for."

"You don't owe me any explanations," I say.

"I don't want you to think I would ever give another woman the ring I bought for you."

"Really, Beck. It's fine." It took him two and a half years to propose to me.

"Alexa is changing her major again." He holds up the box. "I need the tuition money."

I laugh as though I'd assumed nothing less. "Of course she did. Give her my best wishes."

"I will." He moves toward the doors in the foyer, but before he can open them, Henry walks through and nearly into us.

He looks up from the phone in his hand and takes in Beck and me standing there. His expression changes from one of distraction to one of very strong irritation, the way it would if you realized someone had completely rearranged the drawers in your desk.

"What's going on?" Henry looks directly at me and ignores Beck entirely.

I glance at Beck. Disgust hides in the lines of his face, and I realize the conclusions he must be coming to. "We were just— I'm staying with him, but just until the palace—"

"Celia," Henry barks. "Not another word." He turns to Beck. "You need to go."

"I was just on my way out. Sir." There is no mistaking the icy way he splits it into two sentences.

After he leaves, Henry and I stand facing each other.

"You didn't have to be rude." I turn back to the kitchen.

"Entertaining guests in my flat while I'm gone?" he says, following me. "I'll admit, I was expecting shaving cream in my shoes or holes in my pants, but this?" He leans on the counter, palms flat against the marble.

"I wasn't entertaining. I was soliciting advice," I say, refusing to look at what his posture does to his shoulders.

"Advice about what?"

"None of your business." I begin to stack the dirty plates into the sink. "But since I know you won't leave it alone, I needed advice on the budget."

Henry looks incredulous. "You wanted that bugger's advice but not mine?"

"He's a solicitor. Besides, I already asked for your advice."

"And I gave you a damn good idea."

I shrug and start rinsing the dishes. "Depends on who you ask."

He shakes his head, muscles popping in his arms, which are still propped on the countertop. "No one is to know where you are."

"Don't be ridiculous. It was only Beck."

"How do you know we can trust him?"

"I trust him more than I trust you." I keep my eyes on the sink, but I can feel Henry's glare.

"You don't mean that," he says.

"Cross my heart and hope to die."

"When have I ever hurt you?"

My eyebrows fly so high they're in danger of getting lost in my hairline. "Are you serious right now?"

"Besides that."

"Excuse me? *Besides* that?"

He sighs. "You know what I mean. Have I ever hurt you physically or put you in danger?"

"No. And neither has Beck." I load the plates into the dishwasher and dry my hands on a towel, steeling myself against the bile clawing its way up my throat.

"Well, at this point, the only people I'm confident won't hurt you are me and my security team. So until we can prove otherwise—"

"Oh, please. My mum? Beatrice?" I don't bother to hide my disgust.

Henry opens the refrigerator and pulls out a bottle of nasty-looking green sludge. "Obviously I don't regard your family as suspicious."

"Just your own."

"Can we be done with this conversation?"

I tear off a big hunk of naan and wave it at him. "Feel free to leave whenever. I was just trying to enjoy my lunch when you came barging in like a jealous caveman."

He points to the sloppy take-out containers littering his pristine kitchen. "Since when do you like Indian food?"

"There's a lot you don't know about me."

"Not as much as you think." He takes several long swallows of what looks like pond scum. His Adam's apple bobs, and my mouth grows dry.

"Let me guess. You have a three-inch dossier on me in your office," I say.

"Try three and a half."

"And here I thought the boarding school scandal got hushed up."

"Do go on. This sounds juicy."

"It really wasn't a big deal," I tell him sweetly. "He was only ten years older—"

Henry chokes on his green smoothie.

"But I'm boring you." I hop down from the stool and gather the garbage into the bin.

He picks up the shopping bag Beck brought. "What's this?"

"Just reminders he no longer wanted." I snatch the bag from his hands.

Henry tugs it back. "Let me see," he says, sifting through it. "Seriously? He returned this stuff to you?" He holds up the political thriller I gave Beck on his last birthday.

"Yeah, well, I guess the memories were too painful."

"Then he could've thrown them away. Giving them back is a dick move." Opening the bin, he drops the whole bag inside. "You're better off without him."

"Some people would say the same about you."

"And I'd agree with them. But at least I'd never give your stuff back."

"What stuff?" I say.

"If there was stuff."

Another wave of nausea hits, and this time I have to grab on to the back of the barstool to stay upright.

Henry is beside me in an instant. "What's wrong?" he asks. "Is it your head?"

I shake my head. "Stomach," I manage to get out, before clamping my hand over my mouth and rushing for the trash. I lose my lunch on top of Beck's things, and Henry holds my hair and rubs my back until I'm done.

He grabs a bottle of water from the fridge, takes the lid off, and hands it to me. I rinse my mouth out and spit into the sink.

"Thank you," I say, just as I feel it hit again. I lean over the bin again and heave until I'm sure every last intestine has been deposited in there along with my lunch.

"That bloody tosser," Henry mutters. "He gave you food poisoning."

16

"Faded" - Alan Walker

ADD "BECOMING AN ENTIRE bed for my dog while he naps sitting up" to the list of things I didn't expect from life.

"Tundra," I say, and push back against him. He's leaning on me so hard that I'm about to fall over. Jerking upright, he looks at me, tongue lolling out of his mouth like he also doesn't know who the idiot was who almost knocked me over.

"Sorry, buddy. I'm not upset at you. It's this stupid financial crisis." I scan the budget in my hand once more.

He whines and cocks his head.

"I know, but I don't have a clue how to handle it. No one seems to have any ideas for me."

This time he barks.

"Okay, fine. *One* person had ideas." I frown at him. "But they weren't any good."

Were they? Even Beck seemed to think I'd go to Henry for help solving this. Maybe if I heard him out, we could meet in the middle with a plan.

"All right," I say, standing up. "You convinced me. But I'm only going to listen to him. I'm not agreeing to anything yet." I hold up a finger as Tundra looks at me expectantly.

I leave the bedroom to find the whole flat quiet. All I hear is the sound of the vacuum running in one of the guest rooms. I try the gym first, but the lights are off. Next I check the home theater and the billiard room, but they're both empty. That leaves Henry's office, where I'm unlikely to find him given that it's evening, and his bedroom, which I'm not about to enter.

I open the door to his office, fully expecting it to be as empty as the rest of the place, but the lights are still on. I'm about to step inside when my blood runs cold.

They're on the other side of the room, near the window, and they don't seem to have heard or seen me. I only wish I could say the same for myself.

Henry is standing with Bea cradled against his chest, his head bent near hers. I can't make out what they're saying, but I can see his hand running up and down her back. I know exactly what that embrace feels like, because I've been on the receiving end of it more than once.

I quietly pull the door shut behind me and run to the bathroom. I haven't eaten much today—some eggs for breakfast, some take-away Bea had delivered for lunch—but it all comes back up as I heave over the toilet. I use bathroom tissue to wipe my mouth and rest my head on my knees. My hands are shaking when I press the flush lever.

What was I thinking? He told me nothing was going on with Bea, and I actually bought it. I wanted to believe that Henry could change, that I was special enough to warrant that kind of character arc in someone.

But I'm a fool. A pathetic fool.

Henry isn't ever going to change, and certainly not for me. I refuse to let tears fall. This is my punishment, the consequence of allowing myself to go there. Isn't this what I was waiting for anyway? The whole reason I invited Bea to stay at the penthouse in the first place? I knew it would happen. It was only a matter of time.

Leopards don't change their spots, and tigers don't change their stripes. Only a fool would expect a player to change his ways.

I decide to explore the flat, to distract myself but also to put as much distance between those two and myself as I can. Tucked between two of the guest bedrooms is a small library I've never seen before. I slip inside and close the door behind me. Even Tundra doesn't know where I am. He'll have to play Leaning Tower of Pisa with someone else.

The space is small and cozy. It holds only a fraction as many books as my father's library at Maison de Lierre or the massive one at the palace, but there's something about its intimacy. This is the only room in Henry's entire flat that feels remotely homey.

I pull out my phone and make the call.

The Duke of Sutherland answers on the second ring. "Your Majesty."

"Hello, William. I trust this isn't a bad time?"

He grunts his assent, and I dearly hope this wasn't a bad move. "I'm calling about the royal budget."

"I heard about Parliament's denial."

"I'm not sure what to do next." I pause for a few seconds. "I was hoping you could help me."

He doesn't say anything right away, then finally tells me, "Aside from cutting expenses and petitioning to raise the Civil List until they finally give it to you, I only see one other option."

"And that is?"

"Marrying someone with a private income."

I cross the room to the single window overlooking the city. "Excuse me?"

"You're free now, and you'll need an heir eventually. The way I see it, you can hit two birds with one stone this way."

Good lord, he's actually serious. "And you think there's a line of gentlemen just waiting to be married for their money."

"You'd be surprised."

I cough out a laugh. "Thank you for your advice, Lord Sutherland. I will certainly consider it."

After ending the call, I sink into one of the two armchairs. I really am out of options. Loathe as I am to ever see his face again, listening to Henry's plans is my only choice.

My phone pings in my hand. It's the scheming prick himself.

Henry: We're setting up Monopoly in the billiards room. You in?

I toss my device onto the other chair. Like I'm going to be party to their canoodling for another night. But on second thought, if I don't text back, he'll come looking for me.

I grab the phone again.

Me: No thanks.

I'm still glued to my chair when the door opens ten minutes later. "There you are," Bea says. "I've been looking everywhere."

Rolling my eyes, I turn to face her. "You found me." I hold up the book I was trying and entirely failing to read. Turns out reading while angry doesn't really work.

She looks fresh and glowing in a baby-pink cashmere lounge set. It sets off the flush in her cheeks. I, on the other hand, am still in my day dress and heels.

"Henry said you weren't going to play a game with us. I'm here to beg you to reconsider."

His name coming out of her mouth grips my heart like a vise. I want to scrape it from her tongue. "I'm not feeling well," I say. "I'm going to pass tonight."

"Come on, Celia." She sticks out her lower lip. "I'm only going to be here for a few weeks. The least you can do is spend time with me before I leave."

Bea's manipulations are so thin even a child can see through them, but it doesn't matter because she's so irresistible. She is Odysseus's siren, and not even the strongest of men can deny her.

Especially those whose names start with an H and end in "enry."

Sisters also tend to become her prey, which is why I find myself laying my book aside and saying, "Fine."

I follow her down the hall to the game room, using the back of her ponytail-swinging head as target practice for my mind darts. Which isn't fair, if I'm honest, because I invited her into this trap knowing this would happen. I set up my own sister, and now I'm angry that she fell for it.

Well, fuck if I care. I aim one last mental dart. It hits her smack in the parietal lobe. Perfect score for me.

We find Henry already sitting at the baize-covered table in the corner. I hate his perfectly tousled hair. I hate the stupid Harvard sweatshirt he's wearing, the same one I wore last week. I hate the stupid grin on his face when we walk in. I hate that I have to sit beside him and smell that bloody awful scent of his.

I hate that he picked the Scottie piece for me like he knows what I want.

"I don't want the dog," I say, tossing it back into the box. Tundra lifts his head from where he's lying at Henry's feet and looks at me mournfully. "Not you," I say to him, and add "stealing my dog" to the list of things I hate about the man.

Henry looks at me for a beat, then hands me the box. "Okay. What do you want to be?"

I grab the race car and place it next to the top hat and sack of money on Go. I imagine myself driving over both of them in my shiny vehicle.

"I'll be the banker," Bea announces.

We move around the board in relative silence until Henry serves drinks, and about three sips into her margarita, Bea starts giggling. "You're all going down tonight," she says. "I'm feeling very lucky."

"You're gonna need it," I mutter into my wine glass.

Henry shoots me a look before rolling the dice. He buys Illinois Avenue, which leads to Bea exclaiming, "I was collecting the reds!"

He chuckles. "Sorry, princess. It's mine now."

He passes the dice to me, and I wait for him to release them before reaching out my hand. I land on Free Parking, but there isn't even any money under it, making this one of the worst games in the history of mankind.

Crossing my arms over my chest, I take a long swig of wine. I'll give them an hour of my time, then I'm done.

Bea throws doubles. "See? I told you I'm feeling lucky." She rerolls, and it happens again.

"One more and you're in the jailhouse," Henry teases.

Licking her gloss-covered lips, she tosses the dice again. It's her third set of doubles.

Henry makes a mock moan as Bea moves the money bag into jail. She looks seriously pissed. Losing isn't something she's had much experience with.

"Hey, cheer up." Henry bumps her arm. "I'll come visit you."

"Promise?" she asks.

"Absolutely." He refills her glass. "Your luck is just getting started."

"I need to use the restroom," I say. "Excuse me."

They barely look up as I walk out.

When I reach the hallway, I stop and lean against the wall, sucking several deep breaths into my lungs. I don't know how I'll be able to tolerate another hour of this. The vision of them together in Henry's office is still seared into my mind. And Bea's only been here five days. How will I ever get through another three weeks?

I square my shoulders. I'll do it the same way you get through any-thing—by gritting your teeth and deciding that this will not be the thing that brings you down. If Henry and Bea want to hook up, what's it to me? Bea is old enough to make her own mistakes, and Henry—well, Henry can go rot in hell for all I care. He's only proven that I was right in not trusting or believing him. I should be grateful. Lifting my chin, I walk back into the room.

"Finally," Bea says. "Hurry up and take your turn. I'm wasting away in jail, remember?"

"I'm surprised you didn't take it for me."

"I wanted to, but Henry wouldn't let me." She shoots him a faux-an-noyed look. The one I give her is real-annoyed.

Bea doesn't roll the necessary doubles to get out. "I'll be stuck in here forever," she says, chin in her hand. "Does anybody have a Get Out of Jail Free card they'll sell me?"

I toss mine across the table. "Just take it if it means you'll stop whin-ing."

The pout melts off her face. "What's your problem?"

"You okay?" Henry reaches across the table for my arm.

I yank it back and hiss, "Don't touch me."

He blinks and moves back. "Sorry."

Play continues around the board, but the mood has shifted. They are both regarding me as though I'm a loose tiger, which is ridiculous con-sidering they're acting like a pair of mating rabbits. My nausea intensifies.

When I have to mortgage Baltimore Avenue to pay the school tax, I finally realize how little I've been paying attention to the game. I have a measly four properties and no upgrades. Henry, meanwhile, is putting his second house on Boardwalk.

"I think this is the first time I've ever owned Boardwalk," he says. "You're off your game tonight, C."

"Yeah, that seems to be the trend of late."

I can feel him looking at me, but I refuse to meet his eyes. He can take his fake concern and go shove it. He's not fooling anyone.

Tundra pads over to me and rests his head on my leg. My fingers wind their way through his fur. Apparently even he is picking up on the hostility in the room.

As Bea and Henry take their turns, I plot a way to bankrupt myself and leave the game. I'm in the process of mortgaging my second property when the nausea hits again. Clapping my hand over my mouth, I run for the powder room in the hall.

Once I've finished vomiting what little I had in my stomach, including the wine, which makes my throat burn, I rinse my mouth with cold water from the faucet.

Henry is standing outside when I open the door. The concern in his eyes is real. "You're sick again?" he says.

"I'm feeling better now."

"What did you eat today?"

I try to remember, but my brain feels foggy. "Eggs. Some take-away for lunch."

"What take-away?"

"It was Thai," Bea says from beside him. I didn't even notice her there.

"That's the second time you've eaten take-away and gotten sick," Henry says. "I don't like those odds."

"I think I'll go to bed now," I say, and start to move past them.

He slips an arm around my waist. "I'll walk with you."

Loathe as I am to admit it, that's probably a good thing, because my head keeps spinning until I'm finally lying down. Henry tugs my heels off, pulls the comforter up to my chin, and smooths the hair from my brow.

"No more take-away, okay?"

"You want me to starve?"

"I'll hire a private chef. But no outside food."

I murmur my assent before falling asleep, already sinking into dreams that consist of Henry taking care of me and, for once, not breaking my heart.

17

"loml" - Taylor Swift

I'M ON MY THIRD video tutorial on how to use the bloody steam wand on Henry's espresso machine when he walks into the kitchen. Yawning, he leans against the counter to watch me, arms crossed. I surreptitiously avert my eyes from the way his flannel pajama bottoms dangle from his hips.

"Feeling better?" he asks, reaching for the questionable cookies Bea baked yesterday.

"I'm fine, but I wouldn't eat those if I were you." I bob the pitcher of milk up and down as demonstrated in the video but obviously don't do it right, because milk splatters all over the front of my dressing gown. "Bloody hell." I toss the pitcher into the sink.

"Easy," Henry chides. He tosses the remainder of the cookie in the bin, then spits out the piece in his mouth. "God, what did she put in those things?"

I bite my cheek to hide my smile. Serves the bastard right. "I warned you. Now be a gentleman and show me how to use the steamer."

"I don't have a clue."

"It's your machine!"

"I just use it for espresso."

I groan and use a dishcloth to dab at the stains on my gown.

"Doesn't Maisie usually bring you a latte?"

"It's Saturday."

"Okay, we'll just order something. There's a coffee shop on one of the lower levels. One of the guys outside can grab it."

"That will take too long. I need caffeine now." I'll also need a morphine drip if I am to endure Henry.

"Then we'll just have to figure out the steamer."

He fiddles with the machine, refills the pitcher with milk, and two minutes later presents me with a beautiful vanilla latte.

"How did you do that?" I ask.

He shrugs and pulls a double shot of espresso for himself. "I was highly motivated by the look of pure rage in your eyes."

I take a small sip, but my caution is unnecessary, because it tastes better than the ones Maisie's been bringing me. "This is actually really good."

"Don't sound so surprised," Henry says. "I am a man of many talents."

"I'm well aware." It comes out before I can stop myself. I slap my hand over my mouth.

He has the courtesy not to meet my eyes, but a small smile tugs at his lips.

I clear my throat. "Thank you for the coffee. I should get ready." I dash out of the room before I forget exactly how much I despise him.

It takes a person three days without fresh air to start to go insane. Apparently, it's the same for dogs. I glance up from my laptop as Tundra starts mounting the suede ottoman.

"Tundra!"

He glances back at me, and I swear he's grinning from ear to ear.

"Tundra, stop it!" I set my laptop on the sofa next to me and move to pull him off. He dismounts and tries to mount my leg instead. "Good god, you're restless."

One of the PPOs has been taking him to the rooftop dog park, but clearly it isn't doing the trick. Besides, if I have to breathe this recycled air much longer, I'm going to turn into a corpse. However, we're currently eighty-seven floors above ground with James Bond and his team right outside. Leaving won't be as simple as walking out the door.

"Come on, boy," I say. "Let's sneak out."

Whether he understands my words or not, his entire demeanor changes, and he follows me to the bedroom. I decide to leave on my leggings and oversized sweatshirt (stolen from Henry's still-half-full side of the closet, because his are way comfier than mine and *not* because I like to randomly sniff the cuffs). I pull on a pair of trainers and rifle through Henry's things to find a ball cap that fits.

A look in the mirror confirms that I look nothing like the queen. The sun has already set, and there's no way I'll be recognizable in the dark.

Tundra barks when I pull out his leash. My own tongue nearly starts lolling at the thought of fresh air. I haven't left this flat since Henry took me up in the chopper. I still don't know how I'm going to slip past the army stationed outside, but I plan on crossing that bridge when I get to it.

Unfortunately, it blows up before I even reach it. Just as I'm leaving the master bedroom, Henry walks down the hallway from the guest bedrooms.

"Going somewhere?" he asks.

"Tundra and I are just going to ride the lift up and down."

"Nice try."

"Come on. No one will recognize me like this, nor expect me to be out walking my dog."

He gives my derrière an exaggerated stare. "Definitely recognizable." He continues his perusal, then frowns. "Is that my sweatshirt?"

"See? People will think I'm you."

"Funny. You're not going out." Walking to the kitchen, he pulls a bottle of water from the fridge.

I stalk over to him, Tundra right beside me, and yank it from his hands. "I'm going to explode if I have to stay inside another minute. And Tundra needs a walk."

Henry considers us both for a minute, then sighs. "Fine. Let's go."

I hold up my hand, not intending to touch him, but he takes a step forward and collides with it all the same. That warm, broad chest under my fingers is tantalizing. I drop my hand. "You're not invited."

"All the same, I'm coming."

"I don't think so."

"Then inform Tundra that he will need to take his walk inside this flat, because you are not going out alone."

"No one will even know it's me," I snap.

"That's not something I'm willing to take a chance on," Henry growls, bringing his face close to mine. "It's either me or the entire security team. Your choice."

There's no way in hell I'm walking down a city street flanked on all sides by PPOs, and he knows it. But I don't want his company tonight either. Still, if it's the only way to get outside, it's the lesser of two evils.

"Fine. But you're picking up after Tundra." I hand Henry the poop bag dispenser and rejoice when tiny frown lines appear on his face.

The ride down to the lobby is as awkward as one might expect when riding with your ex-husband-turned-prison-warden. By the time we're about halfway down, Tundra assumes we are stuck in here for life and jumps up on me, giving me a good whiff of his lack of hygiene.

"Down, boy. God, your breath stinks." I push him back down. I think we're all a little relieved when the chime that announces our arrival in the Atlantis's lobby sounds.

The crisp evening air is so welcome that I gulp in several lungfuls. We could be in the middle of a blizzard and I'd still rejoice at being outside, but fortunately, the temperatures are hovering in the midfifties. Tundra strains at his leash, eager to get moving, while Henry sticks to the street side of the pavement, keeping a close eye on our surroundings. I have to admit, I feel safer with him next to me.

"Are you ever going to relax?" I ask him as Tundra heads for a patch of grass to relieve himself.

"Not until this guy is caught."

"Where did you learn all of your"—I motion to his torso—"spy moves?"

His brows quirks upward. "Impressive vocabulary."

"You know what I mean. Protection and everything." We continue our walk down the street.

"Military, remember? Not that I need to be taught how to protect you."

"Just that good, are you?"

"I have good instincts," he says, scanning the area. "And nothing to lose."

"Except your life."

"Like I said, nothing to lose."

Tundra chooses that moment to dart after something in a bush and yanks the leash from my hand. Proving his point, Henry's reflexes are much faster than my own, and he recovers the dog within two seconds.

"That was slightly impressive." As I take back the leash, his fingers brush against mine, and I feel like I'm in secondary school with the way my heart races at the touch. My mind flashes back to that one blissful day walking the streets of London, my hand tucked in his, and the way I didn't think I could possibly be any happier than I was at that moment.

Turns out, the higher the mountaintop, the harder you fall.

"Any updates on the palace renovations?" I ask as we turn a corner.

"Just that it's taking twice as long as it should. The security is horribly outdated."

"It's done a fine job all these years, hasn't it?"

Henry cuts me a sharp glance. "There hasn't been an attempted assassination before."

"I'm not sure whether I should be offended or flattered that I'm the first monarch deemed worth killing."

"Don't be glib, C. We're talking about your life."

Tundra squats in the grass next to the pavement, and I grin at Henry. "Looks like you're up."

He scowls but dutifully cleans up after the dog. I have to admit I feel an extraordinary amount of satisfaction watching him.

While he's tying a knot in the bag, I glance around. We're a few blocks east of the Atlantis, in a strip known as Restaurant City because of its five blocks of nothing but tiny eateries, with cuisines ranging from Malaysian to Ecuadorian. Strings of white lights illuminate the street, creating an otherworldly effect. There are red bows tied to all the lamp posts. A woman with long black hair is standing across the street playing a sad song on her violin.

"Beautiful, isn't it?" Henry says. As we're watching her, he slips his hand in mine, lacing our fingers together. I startle and instinctively pull back.

"Shit. I'm sorry, C," he says. "I wasn't thinking."

I frown and rub my upper arms. "It's fine. We should keep walking before Tundra destroys those flowers."

He nods and calls the dog away from the potted poinsettia he's investigating. I walk beside them numbly, not even cognizant of where we're going. What the hell was that? He wasn't *thinking*? In what universe would holding my hand be natural for him?

I'm lost in my deadly spiral of thoughts and almost don't see the couple until it's too late. They're just walking out of a cute little Italian place I've been to hundreds of times. The owners are old friends of Beck's family, and we visited at least once a week when we were still together. I know what every item on the menu tastes like. I know the kitchen smells, like garlic and tomato and a secret ingredient the family will never reveal. I know how rickety the tables and chairs are. I've walked out that door with my hand wrapped around Beck's arm exactly the way—

"Celia?"

I finally look away from Beck long enough to take in the blonde woman at his side. Her hair is long and flows down her back. She's wrapped in a black peacoat with a red scarf around her neck. She looks so familiar.

Tundra agrees, because he bounds up to her and starts humping her leg. She laughs and pushes him down, and then it clicks.

It's Maisie.

On a date.

With my ex-fiancé.

It's stupid, I know. I should have recognized her immediately, but I've never seen her without her hair up, glasses on, and wrapped in a cardigan like the ones my grandma used to wear. And also, forgive me for it never crossing my mind that my assistant might date my *ex-fiancé*. To say things are awkward would be like saying the sun is bright—true, but a gross understatement.

Beck coughs. "What a surprise."

"Surprise. Yeah," I say in a monotone. Kill me now.

"Actually, can I talk to you for a minute?" It takes me a second to realize he's talking to me.

"Um . . ." I glance at Henry. His opinion is evident on his face, but before he can object, I quickly add, "I'll be right back." I hand him the leash and custody of Tundra, who is still trying to mount Maisie's leg, and follow Beck down the pavement.

He stops a few yards away. "I am so sorry you had to find out like this," he says.

"When you said you'd moved on, I never expected . . ."

"I know. I'm sorry. I wanted to tell you the other day, but I lost my nerve."

I tuck my hands into the sleeves of my sweatshirt and bring one up to rest against my chin. Henry's scent fills my senses, and I inhale deeply, allowing it to give me strength. "So, what? You two are seeing each other? Is it serious?"

Beck looks like he'd rather bungee jump off the Eiffel Tower than have this conversation. I share the sentiment. "It's new, but yes, I care about her."

Something in my chest tears, as if someone is ripping my heart apart with their bare hands the way TV chefs shred barbecue. "Well, I'm happy for you both," I manage to get out.

"Thank you," he says. "If you really mean that."

A smile is all I can give him in return. "We should get back."

Henry and Maisie look even more uncomfortable than Beck and me, if that's possible. There is a painful exchange of goodbyes and the usual strained politeness as we try to navigate around each other without actually touching or making eye contact.

"What just happened?" I ask Henry once we're out of earshot.

"One of the most awkward moments of my existence."

"You were awkward? How do you think *I* felt?"

We continue our walk through the shadows, Tundra leading the way to sniff out rabbits, squirrels, and leftover burger wrappers.

"Do you want to talk about it?" Henry asks after a few minutes.

"Not really," I mutter. But five seconds later, I add, "I just don't get it. What does he see in her? We are nothing alike."

"I thought she was your friend."

"She is." One of my closest friends, actually. "Which makes this a double betrayal, right?"

"In what way?"

"You don't date your friends' exes! And you don't date your ex's friends!"

He offers me a sad half smile. "Maybe they didn't read the rule book?"

I punch his arm. "It's not funny."

"I know," he says, and pulls me against his side. His scent wraps around me like a hug. "It's okay to feel upset."

"Is it, though? After all, I'm the one who left him."

"Do you have regrets?"

Regret giving my heart to Henry? Yes. Regret breaking up with Beck for the good of my country? "No. I just didn't expect it to hurt like this." Beck gets to move on, while I'll forever be stuck on the wheel of pain, circling the same heartache over and over.

"You wouldn't take him back if given the chance?" Henry asks.

I shake my head. "I don't want him back, but I guess I hoped he would pine over me a little longer. Does that make me a horrible person?"

"Of course not. It makes you human. For the record, how anyone could choose her over you is beyond me."

"You're forgetting *I* dumped *him*."

"Technicalities."

"Then maybe you also forgot that you had the option to be with me and passed? More than once."

He turns and looks at me, the streetlamps reflected in his dark eyes. "As if I could forget something like that."

18

"Ghost" - Halsey

Maisie and I have worked together for nearly three years, and she's been my private secretary for six months. She is nothing if not reliable, which is why I find myself watching the clock with dread as it creeps closer to nine.

When she arrives for our morning meeting, she looks different. Her glasses are gone, and while her hair is pinned into its usual chignon, she's wearing more makeup than she normally does. I get a whiff of floral perfume as she approaches. I could sum up this whole transformation in one word: confidence.

"Maisie." The ice coating my greeting is thin, but it's there.

"Your Majesty." She drops into a lower curtsy than usual. "I have your box of papers. And your coffee." She hands me the cup, and I briefly wonder if she's poisoned it.

"You look . . . different," I say.

Her fingers fly up to smooth her hair as she keeps hold of the green box in her arms. "Oh, I got contacts. Life-changing," she says with a tight smile.

Life-changing enough to steal my fiancé?

"Won't you sit?" I take a seat at the round dining table on the far side of the room.

She sets the box down on the table but stays standing. "Celia, can we talk first? About . . . personal things?"

I turn around to face her. "What things could we possibly have to talk about?"

"I didn't want you to find out like that."

"And yet you didn't tell me yourself. How long were you planning to keep me in the dark while you snuck around with Beck behind my back?"

"I wanted to tell you. I *tried* to tell you. There was just never a good time." She twists her fingers together. "And I wasn't sure what you'd say."

My laugh is short and abrupt. "I can't imagine it was very hard to deduce."

Maisie's features tighten. "I've never had a connection like this with anyone."

"I thought we were friends."

"Of course we are."

"So you'll break it off with him?" I say.

She lifts her chin ever so slightly. "I won't."

"Friends don't date each other's exes. Especially not ex-fiancés."

"We're not children, Celia."

I turn back to the table and lift the lid of the box. "I'm sure you can appreciate how awkward it would be if you were to keep seeing him."

"You'd rather see me lonely?"

"There are thousands of single men in the city." I pull out a stack of letters. "Take your pick."

"I did."

I shoot her a glare. "Pick again."

"What if he's my soulmate?"

"There's no such thing." And if there is, Beck was *my* soulmate until fate intervened.

"Says the woman who can't have a normal relationship with anyone because she's still hung up on Henry."

I slam the lid shut, causing Maisie to jump. "Everything about this conversation is inappropriate."

"Agreed. I'll be sure to keep it entirely professional from here on out." With that, she turns and marches to the door.

My preferred way of coping with finding out my assistant is sleeping with/dating/possibly in love with/probably going to marry my ex-fiancé one day? Cookie dough. But since I can't afford to gain five pounds, I'm resorting to my second favorite way: organizing.

I'm rifling through Henry's nightstand wholly without shame (but more than a little embarrassment—there are way more condoms in there than anyone wants to see, especially me) when I spot a box under the bed.

A million possibilities flit through my mind—none of them good—but I pull it out anyway. It's a keepsake box, meant for storing photos and cards. I don't even hesitate. If he didn't want me going through his things, he shouldn't have locked me in his house.

Lifting the fitted lid, I can see that the box is full but unorganized. I remove the first item, which looks vaguely familiar, but it's not until I open the card that I realize it's the one I gave Henry on his seventeenth birthday.

Happy birthday to the best friend a girl could ask for!!!

I lay the card aside and lift out a stack of photos. Henry used to have an old film camera that had been his mum's, and he carried that thing with him everywhere when we were young.

The first picture is of us at his seventeenth birthday party. It was a small, with just a few friends—friendships are a luxury most royals can't afford. We spent the night playing games on his PlayStation and eating pizza. It was the last birthday we'd spend together.

The next shot is also of us, earlier that same year. Our faces are pressed close together in ridiculous poses. I quickly flip to the next one. I remember the day clearly, although I didn't realize he'd taken a picture. It's of me sitting cross-legged in the Sunken Garden, wearing lipstick for the first time—my mother has rigid beliefs about the appropriateness of makeup before age fifteen—my hair falling forward and partially covering my face. There's a book in my lap. It was the day we finished *The Catcher in the Rye*. I hated it. Henry loved it.

"It's the perfect dramatization of life," he said.

"It was perfectly pointless," I countered.

"Do you regret reading it?"

"No," I told him, pulling our list from my pocket. "Because it gets us one step closer to one hundred classics." I drew a neat line through the entry.

"What do you want to read next?"

I scanned the list. We always took turns choosing. "Let's do *Wuthering Heights*."

It would be the last one we read together. Our copy of it is probably still decaying at the bottom of the garden fountain.

The rest of the photos are more of the same. Henry and I, sometimes with others, most times alone. Some are of just me. Little Bea makes an appearance in a few, although she usually didn't spend time with us at the palace.

It isn't until I reach the end of the stack that I realize what I'm holding in my lap. It's a box of mementos of our friendship, not of Henry's childhood the way I initially assumed. All of the cards are from me, each one cheesier than the last.

There was a period of time when we exchanged letters. The ones I sent him all neatly stacked and held together by a rubber band. I move them aside. I have no desire to read the thoughts of twelve-year-old me.

A plastic zip-top bag holds a dandelion I once gave him, now dried, after he said he'd never been given flowers before. There are movie ticket stubs from the time the Crown bought out an entire theater so the two of us could see a movie without the media madness. A handful of puzzle pieces lie scattered across the bottom, each seemingly from a different puzzle. They click together with sudden clarity when I recall that every time we put a puzzle together, there would be a piece missing. The little bastard.

The box holds other odds and ends, little trinkets that I have no recollection of. I do remember the woven friendship bracelet stuck in one of the corners. It's the same one he's wearing in that photo in the great room. I received the kit for my birthday, and we each made one, then exchanged them. I have no idea what happened to the one Henry gave me.

I slip the bracelet onto my wrist, curious if he'll notice or recognize it. Then I stuff everything back into the box and shove it under the bed. If I look at these things much longer, I'll start reading into why he's kept them.

Which is not something I can afford to do.

It isn't until I leave the bedroom that I realize how much time has passed. The lights are on in the great room, the sky already dark. Through the glass wall, the city lights twinkle like the stars they've replaced. The smell of something delicious reminds me I forgot to eat lunch.

Henry is in the kitchen, stirring something in a pan on the stove.

"You can cook?" I ask, peering over his shoulder.

"Out of necessity. Sorry we don't have a chef yet. I conducted interviews, and he starts in two days."

"No worries." I open the fridge to see what's available.

"You want some of this? I've got plenty." He arranges lettuce, tomatoes, and cucumbers over what looks like lamb meat.

"I'll just eat some crackers and peanut butter."

"Absolutely not." He grabs another plate from the cupboard. "You're going to eat real food."

We settle in at the bar and scarf down our gyros. It feels both weird and perfectly normal to sit here with him, eating and not feeling the need to say anything. Every time he brushes against my arm, my skin prickles with goosebumps.

"There's ice cream in the freezer if—" He stops, his eyes focused on my wrist. "You went through my things?"

I spin the bracelet around several times. "You said there wasn't stuff."

"I don't think I said that exactly."

"Well, a lie by omission is still a lie."

"You didn't ask."

"Because it never crossed my mind." I adjust my feet on the metal bar of my stool. My soles have been hurting all day.

Henry takes both our plates to the sink and opens the freezer. "It's not exactly the kind of thing you broadcast. Not if you're a guy, anyway."

I watch his back as he scoops ice cream from the container, definitely not enjoying the way his shoulders bunch up with the movement. "Why do you have it?"

"Sometimes you need a reminder of happier times."

I thread the beads through my fingers. "I was your happier time?"

"You sound surprised."

He sets a bowl of ice cream in front of me. It's cookie dough, drizzled with the perfect amount of Hershey's chocolate syrup. I stare at it.

"Shit," he says. "I wasn't thinking. You probably have a new favorite by now?"

I shake my head. "It's been so long since I've had it." Beck only ever had vanilla in the freezer, and Rosalind wouldn't dream of stocking something with so many calories."

The first bite is bliss. A little moan escapes my lips, and Henry chuckles. "That sound never gets old."

My face heats immediately, in spite of the cold ice cream. I mentally scrub away the memory of him coaxing that same noise and many others from me. I clear my throat. "Favorite childhood memory?"

He sucks air between his teeth like he's wincing. "That's too hard. I need it narrowed down to an era."

"An era? What, you're T Swift now?"

"We had eras. You know we did."

I stare at him. "I have no clue what you're talking about."

"Okay." He leans his elbows on the countertop. "First was the Make-Believe Era. We had enough imaginary worlds to fill our own Disney Channel."

"That wasn't first. We were both in diapers the first time we had a playdate."

Henry shovels a massive bite of ice cream into his mouth. "Are you going to dissect every single thing I say? Or can you just hear me out?"

"Get it right the first time and I won't have to."

Faster than lightning, he smears chocolate syrup on my cheek. I gasp and lunge across the counter, but he's too quick. He's still wearing a giant grin when he hands me a wet washcloth.

"Just wait," I say. "You know what they say about payback."

"Mmhmm," he says around his spoon. "But first you'll have to catch me."

I narrow my eyes and fight to keep my smile hidden. God, I've missed him so much. "What era was next?"

"Next was the Artsy Era."

"Artsy."

"You know, that weird spiral thing you had. The black paper you could scratch off. Those things." He gestures to my wrist.

"Okay. Fair enough. It was kind of artsy."

"Then came the Adventure Era, which was the best, in my opinion."

"Why?"

"Because when you're a kid, what's better than getting dirty, playing hard, and falling into bed exhausted every night?"

I lick off my spoon. "Might I suggest about a million things?"

"No way. You loved it."

"I loved aspects of it."

"Our fort down by the stream? The treehouse that only ever had a floor? Spying on the stable hands?"

I grin. "Okay, spying was a lot of fun."

He laughs. "See? Told you. Although our Classic Era was also top-notch."

"Classic? I'm sorry, but I'm going to have to question that one too."

"I'll admit it's a stretch, but hear me out. Remember the summer we worked on the '67 Mustang? A *classic* car."

"*You* worked on it. *I* read to you."

"Yeah, but from what? *Classic* literature."

I snort out a laugh. "That's hardly enough to label an entire era after."

"You were also obsessed with classical music."

"Still am."

"And we spent hours around the piano."

"I nominate that as the best era."

"We'll call it a tie," he says.

"What era are we in now?"

Henry holds my gaze for several seconds before replying. "I like to think of it as the Fight to the Death Era."

"Is that what we're doing? Fighting each other to the death?"

"Not each other. The rest of the world."

My eyes snag on his again. They're big and dark and full of a lot of things I don't dare think about for risk of falling into places I'm not willing or ready to go again, because lord knows they haven't worked out for me in the past.

"I know I've hurt you," he says softly. "A lot. And I know I don't deserve your trust. But it doesn't keep me from wishing I had it."

I swirl the chocolate soup around in my bowl, not because I have any intention of eating it, but because I can't look at him any longer. My stomach feels a little like this melted ice cream. "Well, Rome wasn't built in a day."

"I'm in it for as long as it takes."

"Here." I slip the bracelet from my wrist and hand it to him. "A reminder that you were once my favorite human being on the planet."

He takes it and runs it through his fingers. "I'm still the same person I was."

"I hope so," I say. "I really hope so."

19

"Firestone" - Kygo + Conrad Sewell

THERE ARE A FEW places on earth I'd prefer not to go if given the choice. The spa is one of them. But when I wake to the soles of my feet hurting even more than they did yesterday, I don't have a lot of options.

Roberts & Co. arranges for me to have the spa to myself for an hour-long massage, and while I don't relish the thought of a stranger putting their hands all over my naked body, I do relish being able to walk. If I don't do something about these weird pains soon, that might not be an option anymore.

The receptionist has a small Christmas tree on her desk. It's white with pink ornaments and doesn't look the least bit like a Christmas tree should, but even that small symbol of holiday cheer feels good after the Scrooge wasteland I've been living in.

Once I've stripped down and wrapped a towel around myself, she leads me down a corridor, stopping outside the sauna.

"I think there's been a mistake," I say. "I booked a massage, not the steam room."

Her ever-present smile doesn't falter. "The sauna is included in all of our packages. It helps you relax those muscles before the massage."

I debate whether to stand here and explain to her that sweating does *not* relax my muscles but decide it will probably be faster to just do what she says. Opening the door, I step into the inferno. I startle when I realize my sister is already inside.

Her eyes fly open as I enter. "I thought you hated the spa," she says.

"I do," I grumble, and take a seat against the wall.

Since catching her with Henry, followed by that atrocious game night, I've managed to avoid her. She spent the weekend with Mum at the Carlton, so it wasn't too difficult. If I weren't already naked under this towel, I'd turn around and leave, sore feet be damned.

I was looking forward to spending the holidays with Bea, and now I can barely stand to be in the same room as her. Maybe it's time to act like an adult.

"How's Rhett doing?" I ask. "You never said if he's able to come for a visit or not."

She drops her gaze. "He's not."

"Everything good between you two?" Maybe he also found out about her fling with Henry.

My sister's smile is as fake as plastic, and I can see tears forming in the corners of her eyes. "No, actually. He broke up with me."

"Bea, I'm so sorry. I know he meant a lot of you."

"Yeah, he did." She sniffs and wipes at her nose. "Turns out he just wanted my fame to help him reach his own."

The bastard. "Why didn't you tell me?"

A garbled laugh floats across the steam-filled room. "I tried to when he started acting strange, but you said you were too busy for me."

The vision of her tear-streaked and standing outside Henry's office flashes through my memory. "I'm sorry, Bea. I had no idea."

She shrugs. "I'm not upset anymore. I just wish I hadn't gone to Henry instead."

Oh god. This is it. Can I still make a run for it? I really don't want to hear about her rendezvous with Henry.

"He was great, of course. Told me I was beautiful and that Rhett was a jerk. Held me while I cried." She swipes at the tears hanging in her eyelashes. "But then I had to make a fool of myself."

The ever-present nausea churns in my gut.

"I tried to kiss him—because I'm an idiot—and he pushed me away. Said he cares about me but could never see me that way. And that's about the time I almost died from mortification. Hence the real reason I decided to stay with Mum. I get stupid around him."

I try to swallow down the bile. *You and me both.* "He knows he's not good enough for you."

She sighs. "He can't love me like that."

"Or anyone, for that matter."

"Come on, Celia. Please tell me you are not still blind where he's concerned."

"If by blind you mean realistic," I say, "then yes I am."

"I was here all of three minutes before it was painfully obvious how he feels about you."

I adjust my towel, which is nearly soaked by now. "I'm afraid you're mistaken. We tried that before, and I discovered it was nothing but a game to him."

"Trust me. It's not a game to him."

"I hate to play the older sister card, but you really have no idea what you're talking about."

Bea rolls her eyes. "One of these days you'll realize I'm smarter than you think."

"Don't hold your breath," I say with a smirk.

"And maybe someday I'll find a guy who's not a jerk."

"Of course you will." I move over to sit beside her and wrap my arm around her. "You've got plenty of time."

"I'm not like you, though."

"What do you mean?"

"You're strong and independent. You don't need a man to make you feel beautiful."

I give an awkward chuckle and remove my arm from her shoulders. "It's too hot in here to touch," I say, moving back to my original spot. "You know, independent or not, I'm just as susceptible to being wrecked by a guy as the next girl."

"Then you do a better job of hiding it than me."

"Um, were you there when I got back from London?"

She straightens and smooths the towel on her lap. "Okay, good point. But either way, you've inspired me to become Beatrice 2.0."

"Ah. And what is she like?"

"For starters, she doesn't need a man's approval to feel good about herself."

I give her a small smile. "That's great, Bea. Truly."

"And she doesn't get upset when people don't do or say what she expects."

"Maybe you are smarter than I gave you credit for."

She grins. "Told you. Oh, by the way, I'm going to stay with Mum for the rest of my holiday."

I glance up from where I've been tracing lines on the tile with my toes. "What?"

"She begged me, and I thought it might be nice after all." Bea's dainty shoulders lift in a shrug. "I think she's lonely."

"But—" All I can think is that the last time we were in this room, my mother blasted away every positive image I had of her. "But what about what she told us?"

Bea looks completely unconcerned. "Ever since then, I feel like she's a real person, rather than this statue of perfection."

"She cheated on *Dad*, Bea."

"I know. But we all make mistakes. It was a long time ago, and we don't know the circumstances. She said she was sorry, and I chose to forgive her." Bea crosses her legs, the picture of poise in spite of the heat.

"You chose to forgive her? Just like that?"

"What's the point of holding on to it?"

"She needs to know that what she did was wrong."

Her forehead wrinkles. "But she does know that. It's eaten at her for years."

"I don't understand how you can just forget about what she did," I say.

"I could choose to hang on to this, sure. But all that will do is keep me from enjoying a relationship with my mum. And personally, I hate grudges. They're total buzzkills." Bea rewraps her towel around herself and walks to the door. "I know she hopes you will come to the same conclusion."

She leaves, and all I can think is, *No way in hell.*

20

"My Boy Only Breaks His Favorite Toys" - Taylor Swift

T HE PENTHOUSE IS EMPTY now that Bea has moved to the Carlton. The next morning, I make myself a cup of jasmine tea and let the hot ceramic warm my fingers. The days are getting colder, and I vaguely recall the meteorologist mentioning a chance of snow this weekend. It would be amazing if we got a white Christmas.

I should keep puzzling my way through the financial documents, but I'm afraid if I look at another column of figures, my brain will revolt indefinitely. I decide to browse the small library instead in the hopes I'll find something interesting to read.

I've come to think of the room as my own, since I've yet to see anyone else using it. It's the perfect size for one person and much cozier than the great room. I even asked Roberts to get a small Balsam pine to put in the corner. I don't have any ornaments for it yet, mostly because I'd normally ask Maisie to bring some from the palace, and the two of us aren't saying more than necessary to each other these days.

Despite the fact that I notice the strip of light under the door, I'm not expecting to find anyone inside, least of all Henry. When I enter, he looks up and smiles—just a genuinely happy smile like he's pleased to see me, and not one of the myriad others that can mean so many different things.

"I'm sorry," I say, my hand still on the doorknob. "I didn't realize anyone was in here."

He straightens, and I can see that he was bent over what appear to be documents, which cover every available surface, including the chairs. "Don't apologize. Come in."

I glance around the room, which now feels the size of a coat closet thanks to Henry's giant presence. "It's okay. I was just going to read." I start to back into the hallway.

"Celia, wait." He moves to the door before I can close it and grasps the knob.

I look up at him, his face only inches away. My heart feels like it's participating in a race at Royal Ascot. My swallow is loud, and I hope he doesn't hear it.

Henry's eyes flicker over my face. "Please stay," he says. "I want to show you something."

I couldn't leave if I wanted to. His magnetic field has complete control over mine.

Following him into the room, I point to the papers strewn around as if a tornado just blew through. "Let me guess. You have something against Marie Kondo?"

He gives me an amused smirk and pushes a few of them aside until he gets to the bottom of the pile. "I know you said you don't think it's a good idea, but just hear me out."

I study the page in front of me, and it takes a minute before I realize I'm staring at a blueprint for the main wing of the palace. "I don't understand. What is all of this?"

He digs another paper from the stack and hands it to me. It's a mock-up of an art gallery. Before I can ask, he hands me another page, this one full of figures. My brain immediately starts to spin.

I hand it back. "I'm sorry. I've been looking at numbers all afternoon. You're going to have to interpret this for me."

"Okay, take a seat." He clears one of the armchairs.

I sit down and watch him bring some semblance of order to the chaos. He has a weird energy buzzing through him, and after he straightens the same stack twice, I realize he's nervous. "Henry, what is it?"

He looks over at me and blows out a breath. "I wasn't planning to show these to you yet, but Davies needed to use my office. Promise you'll keep an open mind?"

My heart is still zipping around the racetrack, especially looking at Henry in that white shirt. It's straining over his arms, and several of the top buttons are undone, as if he got restless and a little warm while working. There's something about a man so casually—

"Are you done undressing me with your eyes yet?"

My gaze snaps up from that triangle of bare chest to meet his smirk.

"Don't worry," he says conspiratorially, "I've done it to you plenty of times."

My face is officially on fire. "What did you want to show me?" The faster I can get out of here, the better.

He leans back against the table and kicks his feet out in front of him, crossing them at the ankles. It does not help my war with my wandering eyes, only makes them aware of my direct line of sight being his—

"I know the financial issues with the royal household are eating at you, so I've taken some liberties."

I open my mouth to object, but he holds up his hand. "You don't have to agree to any of this, but please, at the very least, listen."

I was on the verge of giving him a second chance to explain his ideas before catching him with Bea. Now that I know nothing happened between them, the least I can do is hear him out. I nod and smooth my dress over my legs. "Okay, I'm listening."

"You said that opening the palace to the public would be commercializing the royal family. But I propose that maybe that's exactly what Wesbourne needs."

I frown but don't say anything. I still have veto power.

"The royal family, specifically the monarch, is the personification of her country to the rest of the world. Her job—your job—is to satisfy the emotional needs of the people of Wesbourne. What better way to earn their respect and win their adoration than by sharing something with them that only the luckiest have gotten to enjoy so far?"

I ponder this for a minute or two. I've always thought of the monarch as the ruler of a country, but since ascending to the throne myself, I've realized just how little power a queen really has. I'm meant to inspire greatness in my people, encourage them through difficult times, and provide a moral compass for them—something to aspire to. So far, I've done none of this.

"Go on," I say.

Henry grins, and I see the little boy he used to be in that face. He pulls the palace blueprint back out of the stack. "With a few small changes, we could open the main wing of the palace to the public for guided tours. Making twenty staterooms and the gardens accessible would allow for a comprehensive tour that wouldn't invade your privacy. I estimate this alone would cover 30 percent of the household budget."

My eyes widen. "There's no way."

"Unless my numbers are completely off"—he cuts me a glance—"which they're not, it's very possible. People want to see how royals live. It's a fact of life. They're intrigued by what they don't have. It would also help exponentially with tourism for the country as a whole."

"It sounds . . . intriguing. What else do you have?"

He pulls out the mockup. "We turn part of the east wing into an art gallery. The palace has enough art to keep it stocked as well as host a rotating collection in a separate room. We could also invite local artists to display their work, giving them exposure and boosting the economy at the same time."

"Those pieces are valuable, Henry. What about damages? Or theft?"

"We'd have top-notch security. It's a lot harder to steal art than it looks in the movies."

I bite my lower lip. "I don't know. Those pieces were entrusted to the royal family for safekeeping."

"Come on, C. Don't you want to share all of that beauty with the world?"

Henry's right, of course. Keeping priceless art locked up to be enjoyed by only a handful of people is selfish.

"I'll consider it. Was that all?"

A huge grin splits his face. "I'm just getting started. Did you know there are roughly thirty-six thousand acres of farmland in the Royal Estate, most of which isn't being cultivated or put to use?"

"You're kidding." I haven't gotten to those records yet.

He shakes his head and continues. "I propose we turn some of it into organic farms for produce. Some can be converted into grazing pastures for grass-fed cattle, sheep, goats, poultry, and pork. The land least suitable for farming can be converted to nature preserves that provide habitats for wildlife. In five to ten years, we should be able to create a wildlife park that celebrates the beauty of Wesbourne's rarest creatures."

"I love it," I say, a little breathless imagining it all.

I can see the surprise in his eyes as he glances up from the pages in his hands. "You do?"

"Absolutely."

"In that case, I've got more." He pulls another paper out. "Nearly 80 percent of Wesbourne's seabed belongs to the Royal Estate. For years, we've been asked to sell the mineral rights to it, and it's always been denied. Selling those rights on an annual renewal would cover 10 percent of the budget."

"You're serious?" At his nod, I say, "I want to hear more before deciding, but it sounds great. I'm worried, though, that most of these things would only add to our expenses rather than our income. That's a lot of staff we'd be adding, not to mention renovations."

"I'm guessing there isn't the greatest efficiency at the palace at the moment. By bringing in a few experts, we should be able to free up 20 to 25 percent of the staff, allowing them to move to other positions such as tour guides and museum security. As far as the renovations go, the palace is already undergoing massive reconstruction for security reasons. Adding in a few more things shouldn't impact the budget or the time frame much."

I stare at him in amazement. "You've thought of everything."

He offers me a small smile. "I tried."

I take a sip of tea before setting the cup aside and getting to my feet. I need to study these plans a little closer, so I move toward the table and the massive amount of papers strewn across it. "This is what you've been working on?"

I knew Henry was preoccupied with a project, but I just assumed it was renovations at the palace or something with one of his own businesses.

He doesn't shift away when I reach around him for the gallery mock-up, making me graze his body with my chest. My nipples harden at the contact.

"It's still pretty rough," he says.

"I didn't realize you cared so much about this country." I don't mean to sound rude, but exiling himself to London hasn't exactly scored him patriotism points.

"Of course I care about Wesbourne." He turns and ensnares my gaze with his own. My stomach does a little dip.

"Okay, so Wesbourne makes sense." I finally free my gaze and look back down at the print in my hand. "But why do this for me?" He could just as easily have left me to figure this out on my own. It's not like we're married anymore.

Henry doesn't speak for a long minute, not until I finally look back up at him. Then he says quietly, "I assumed that was blatantly obvious by now."

I shake my head. "It's not."

He sighs deeply and runs his fingers through his hair. His movements are short and jerky, finally ending with him putting his hands in his pockets. His eyes grip mine again, overflowing with emotion. "Because I love you, C."

My breath hitches on the inhale, expanding my chest like a balloon. I want to let everything out, to hear the whistle of air wheeze past, but it remains inflated, waiting for the pin that will pop the whole pretty picture.

He's never said it before. All this time, he's been holding the trump card close to his chest, waiting until the perfect moment to play it. He's implied that he has feelings for me, he's whispered sweet nothings that turned out to be bitter nothings, but I've never once heard him use the L-word.

The stakes in whatever game he's playing must have risen. He would never have made this play otherwise.

"I've always loved you." He edges a few inches closer to me, bringing the delicious heat of his body nearer. "For as long as I can remember. God, I am so in love with you, I can't think straight." He tucks a strand of hair behind my ear with gentle fingers.

He's saying things that have the ability to rock my world, and all I can do is stand here clutching my elbows. I'm completely frozen, transfixed by the power he wields over my heart.

"Please say something, C."

I lick my dry lips without looking at him. "What would you like me to say?"

His body exhales backward, as if my words have physically knocked into him. "Nothing, I guess." He returns to the table and rubs the back of his neck. After a few more tense seconds, he gathers the pages into a crumpled heap and moves toward the door, pausing with his hand on the knob. "Nice tree, by the way."

I glance at the small evergreen in the corner, still devoid of ornaments. "You can't say things like that!" The words tear out of me before I even realize I'm thinking them.

Henry slowly turns, a puzzled look on his face. "About the tree?"

"Of course not."

He tosses the pages into the closest chair and stalks over to me. Cupping my trembling jaw, he pulls me against his chest. "I said it because it's true."

It takes every grain of discipline I have to keep myself from sinking into his embrace. This is exactly what I've always wanted, isn't it? To hear him profess his undying love, to tell me the whole thing was just a big misunderstanding, that he's been mine all along.

I can hear the sickening lurch as I grasp the knife he buried long ago and pull it from my belly, where the suction wants to hold it in place, because at least the pain reminds me that I'm still alive, that I'm capable of loving someone with every cell of my body. That I can feel, even if it's pain I'm feeling.

"It doesn't matter." I drop the hypothetical knife, and it hits the floor with a clatter.

"Of course it does. This changes everything, baby."

I close my eyes as he moves even closer, close enough that I can feel his breath on my lips. I know what his next move will be.

As badly as I want to kiss him, I force myself to pull away. I tug my face from his grasp and step backward until I feel the table pressing against my tailbone. "You think you can whisper a few words in my ear and I'll come running?"

"I—" He closes his mouth. Several seconds pass before he finally starts again. "Frankly, yes. I thought this was what you wanted. For us to be together."

The laugh that floats past my lips is anything but amused. "What I want is for you to leave me alone."

"You don't mean that." He steps closer. My heart goes into overdrive.

I hold up my hand to stop him. "Of the two of us, I'm the only one who actually means what they say."

His eyelids drop lower, hooding his eyes. "How long are you going to hold that over my head?"

I cross my arms over my chest. I need to put a barrier between us before I do something stupid. "As long as it takes for you to get the message that I want nothing to do with you."

Henry takes another tiny step closer, squishing the distance that separates us. The table is still digging into my back, and I have nowhere else to go. "You can push me away all you want, but you know we always find our way back to each other."

My throat births a choking sob. I wish I knew how to make it untrue. "There's a first time for everything," I whisper.

"You'd rather never see me again than move past this?"

"How am I supposed to move past it, exactly?" I pause, trying to swallow the lump in my throat. "Do you know how many nights I cried myself to sleep over you? Or how many times I picked up the phone to tell you something, only to remember that you didn't want me anymore?" My voice cracks. "My dad *died*, Henry, and you weren't there."

His face crumples, and he runs his hand over it. "You were better off without me."

"How dare you make that decision for me!"

"There are so many things you don't know."

"Then tell me."

"I can't."

"Why not?"

His sigh is deep, like it's been pulled from the pit of his belly. "I'm trying to protect you."

"I told you, I don't want your protection."

"You say that, but I've held you through two separate panic attacks. Clearly, you're more scared than you're letting on." He props his hands on his hips. I can feel the frustration emanating from his muscles.

Of course I'm scared. I'm bloody terrified. Someone out there wants me dead for reasons unknown. It's enough to make anyone quake. But what Henry doesn't seem to grasp is that I'm even more petrified of what *he* might do to me if I allow him to get too close.

"Fear doesn't give you the right to make decisions for me," I say.

"I'm trying to do the right thing. I couldn't live with myself if I let something happen to you."

I push away from the table. "Something did happen to me! You, with your wrecking ball excuses."

"Damn it, Celia. What do you want me to say? 'I'm sorry for protecting you from myself'?"

He's so close, too close. I can smell the spearmint from his gum and feel the heat from his chest. I shift my weight backward again, which puts a sliver of distance between us.

"That's just it. You didn't protect me. You left me gaping and vulnerable."

He closes his eyes and flexes his jaw. "I didn't know you would take it so hard."

I don't want to think about that summer and the fall that followed. Losing the boy you love, your best friend, or your father would be devastating for any teenage girl. Losing all three at once was absolute destruction.

"Maybe you didn't know back then." I fiddle with a thread on my sweater. "But you had to know in London . . ." I can't even bring myself to finish the sentence. London was a different kind of heartbreak altogether.

"You're right," he says. "I did know. I suppose it's too much for you to believe it was for your own good?"

I look up to find him watching me earnestly. "That would be correct."

He deflates like a balloon. "Is there anything I can do to get you to trust me again?"

"No, Henry. There isn't."

Henry left the library a while ago, after our conversation shuddered to a halt and there was nothing left to say. I've been staring out the window at the city ever since, trying to decide how best to dismantle everything he dumped on me.

With some things in life, it's better late than never, but you know what's not? Finding out the man you've loved your entire life loves you back, but that he'd rather watch you suffer the heartbreak of his rejection than trust you with the truth.

My mind is still trying to process this information. It's as if a giant recycling truck pulled up to the back entrance of my brain, unloaded all the scraps, and now I'm left to sort it all into piles. With every single thing that Henry told me, I have to hold it up, inspect it, and determine if it's true or not. But how can I do that when everything about our relationship has been a lie?

Snow has started gathering on the roofs of the buildings closest to the Atlantis. In the park below, the branches of the trees are quickly becoming white. It's incredible how things can change in a matter of minutes.

My heart has turned into a hunk of concrete in my chest, unsure what to believe or hope for. My first instinct is to doubt Henry on every count. He's betrayed me so many times that I'd have to rewire my neural pathways to accept his confession as truth now.

But as resistant as I am to believing him, I have to admit that there's a tiny echo of truth to what he said. There were signs when we were kids, signs that he felt the same way I did, that we had a future together. It's why I felt the courage to confess my own feelings in the first place. I still have the memories of him reaching for my hand, brushing my hair from my face, telling me I was beautiful and that he couldn't imagine being with anyone else.

But I have to assume it was all just a game to him. *Let's see how hard I can make Celia fall when I yank the rug out from under her.*

I don't know what his endgame is this time. He has certainly done his part to protect me, so he must not want me dead. Maybe he just gets sadistic pleasure from watching me suffer a heartbreak he's caused.

The sky has grown dark enough that I can see my reflection in the glass. I look pale and tired, which I suppose is understandable given my present circumstances.

Henry and I were supposed to do this together. In being jointly crowned, we were meant to help each other with the myriad of issues monarchs deal with. Instead I'm left on my own and somehow supposed to come up with a solution to this whole mess.

My mind wanders to Henry's plans. They're actually pretty solid. If his projections are correct, his suggested changes would enable us to keep all five hundred people employed by the royal household without raising taxes. There's no guarantee his ideas will work, but they're better than anything I've come up with.

The only problem is that enacting them will require trusting him. I'm not sure I can do that. I'm all too aware of the devastation he's capable of wreaking on my heart. What if he does the same to this country?

Even as I have the thought, I dismiss it. Because no matter how much of a player Henry is, he does care about Wesbourne. That has always been evident, in spite of his recent relocation to England. He knows business, and he's familiar with the royal household. I definitely can't trust him with my heart, but I think I can trust him with my country.

He's at the dining table in the great room wearing those ridiculously sexy glasses. I shut off the part of me that wants to turn into a pile of goo. The documents he had in the library are spread out on the table, and there's a sandwich sitting next to him, but it appears untouched.

He hasn't spotted me yet, hidden as I am in the dark hallway, so I stay here for a bit, watching him study the pages in front of him with a frown. He scribbles a note, then sticks the pen between his teeth as he shuffles them around.

I'm about to join him when Davies comes around the corner from the foyer followed by his son, Tyson. Henry drops the pen and smiles as they approach. Their conversation is too quiet for me to hear, but Henry says something to the boy, who grins.

Curiosity drags me out of the shadows in time to hear Henry tell him, "Sick gear, man."

Tyson lights up like a glow stick.

"Don't forget to wear that retainer. You don't want to end up with a smile like mine," Henry adds, which is ridiculous considering the effect his oral wattage has on people.

"Yes, sir," Tyson says.

There's a dripping in my chest, and I realize it's my heart melting like an icicle in the sun. Who knew Henry had a soft spot for kids?

I'm close enough now that they notice me. All three bow in deference as I approach.

"Davies," I say. "How are you?"

"Very good, Your Majesty."

"Tyson was doing homework in my office," Henry says.

"And how are the braces?" I ask Tyson.

He gives me an open-mouthed grin.

I return his smile. "Navy and lime. Told you they're a winning combination."

He and his father take their leave, and the air prickles as Henry and I are left alone. "You're good with kids," I tell him.

He looks at me like he's trying to find the hidden barb in my words. "Can't wait to have my own someday," he finally says after giving up on discovering any malice.

I mask my surprise. I can't imagine Henry having children. That would require settling down, another thing I can't reconcile with the image of him in my head. I rest my hands on the back of one of the chairs, facing him and trying not to be done in by those glasses. "I wanted to apologize for earlier. I shouldn't have lashed out. Apparently I'm still a little sensitive on the topic."

He cocks his head and clicks his pen several times. "If anyone should apologize, it's me. I shouldn't have expected to earn your trust back so quickly."

"Baby steps, right?"

The corner of his mouth pulls up. "Yeah. Baby steps."

I wave at the papers on the table. "Can we start here?"

"With the estate plans?"

I nod. "I think they're great. I want to put them into action."

21

"What About Us?" - P!nk

MAISIE'S AT THE PENTHOUSE for our morning meeting, and I watch her slide on her mask of neutrality as she approaches. I just saw her chatting with one of the PPOs at the foyer doors, her head thrown back in laughter, but by the time she reaches me in the great room, she looks like nothing more than a cool professional.

She slides the green box onto the low table in front of me and quickly curtsies. I'm pretty sure the icy chill I feel is coming from her frosty demeanor and not a draft from outside. She hands me my coffee, and our eyes meet. Hers betray nothing, and I wonder again how we got to this place.

"Thank you," I murmur, and sip the hot latte, hoping it will fight the nip in the room.

She doesn't stay long. Our business has been taking less and less time these days. I don't know if it's because there are actually fewer things to handle or because neither of us wants to prolong things any more than necessary. Where we would have laughed and joked before, there's only a gaping awkwardness now.

I lift out a stack of correspondence from the box. Every week Maisie sorts through the letters the palace receives and selects the ones she thinks

I will be most interested in, then I read each one in the stack and choose a few to personally respond to.

After reading several of them, I come across one clearly written by a child. There's usually a couple in every pile, but the return address on this one is a nearby hospital. I slice it open.

Hello Your Majesty,

My name is John Matthews Manchester. I am seven years old. I am staying at the hospital. Would you please join me for some tea? I'm in room 308. I hope you come.

Yours truly, John Matthews Manchester

There's another note inside the envelope, written in a different hand.

Your Majesty, I am John's nurse at the Wesbourne Cancer Institute. He has been diagnosed with stage IV leukemia. They do not expect him to see Christmas. His one request for weeks has been to have tea with the queen. I realize this is an impossible ask, but I wanted to do my part in helping John. If there is any way at all you would be able to pop in for a visit, or even send a card, you would be brightening the life of a small boy who won't be here much longer.

I swipe a tissue from the table and dab at my eyes, being careful with my mascara. I will have Maisie send him the biggest gift basket the hospital has ever seen. Obviously a visit in person would be better, but it's out of the question. Not only would Henry explode at the idea, but there's no way I could bring myself to willingly walk through the doors of another hospital with that sickening smell of death hovering. My father may have died over a decade ago, but that stench has never left me.

I continue reading through my correspondence, but the words are blurring together. Many of the messages contain ridiculous requests, and I know Maisie has stuck them in for humor's sake. I warm to her ever so slightly for not giving up that part of our routine.

By the time I've read through the sixth letter without processing what it said, I toss the entire stack back into the box. Grabbing my coffee, I walk over to the large windows. Outside, Wesbourne is covered in a layer of snow, the sunlight glinting off it like it has something to prove. It's a world full of possibilities. I only wish I could be out there doing my part to make them happen rather than stuck in this tower, unable to do a single thing that will make a difference.

I glance over my shoulder at the box. The blue envelope containing John Matthews's letter winks at me from the sea of white. I know it's impossible, but what if I *was* able to get in to see him? I can't handle the thought of him dying with his one wish unfulfilled.

Henry will never go for the idea, but I haven't seen him all morning anyway. What's keeping me from sneaking out if I want to?

The mob of security at the doors, that's what. I can't exactly slip out the back door, since I don't know how to rappel down the side of a skyscraper.

I walk to one side of the great room before turning and walking to the other. There has to be a way. John Matthews Manchester may only be one subject in my kingdom, but getting to him has suddenly become the top priority on my agenda.

All I need to do is convince the security team to let me out of the penthouse. The rest shouldn't be too difficult.

And just like that, I have my solution.

The lift stops at the floor for the spa. Convincing Roberts of my new-found love of pampering was way too easy. Davies moves out of the elevator first to do a quick scan, then motions for me to follow him.

"Actually, can you come back in here?" I say.

He frowns but steps back into the lift. I bite my lip and hand him the card. He scans both John's note and the one from his nurse, his face unreadable the whole time. When he's finished, he hands them back. "A very sad situation, ma'am."

"It is," I say. The next few seconds will determine the outcome of my plan. "I found myself asking what kind of queen I am if I don't help those who desperately need it. If I only do the things that are expected of me, or that keep me safe, how am I supposed to hold my head up?"

He stares at me impassively, but there's a softness around his eyes. "I don't like where this is headed, ma'am."

"Come on, Davies. Imagine if it was Tyson lying in that hospital room. Wouldn't you want me to do everything in my power to honor his final wish?"

"No offense, ma'am, but his final wish would probably involve the latest *Minecraft* edition." The side of his mouth quirks ever so slightly.

"Undoubtedly. And you know I would bend over backwards to get it for him."

He takes a deep breath and releases it through his nose. "I could lose my job over this."

I touch his arm. His suit jacket feels stiff under my fingers. "I'll make sure that doesn't happen. A queen's power must be good for something, right?"

After studying me for a few more moments, he sets his mouth in a grim line. "Let's do it."

Davies may be breaking all kinds of rules and protocols to get me to the Cancer Institute, but he's still doing everything in his power to keep me safe. We took one of the less conspicuous SUVs from the garage at the Atlantis (no flags flying from the bonnet), and he made sure I was strapped securely into the center seat before pulling out of the lot.

Now we're parked at a back entrance to the hospital while he talks to someone inside on his phone. Before embarking on this mission, he assured me he will not be leaving my side for anything, including the restroom, in case I wanted to change my mind. I didn't.

He hangs up and turns back to me. "They are sending an escort to walk us inside, but the idea is to keep your presence here a secret."

I couldn't be more in favor of that plan.

A group of six hospital security personnel exit through the back doors. They surround Davies and me as we walk the short distance to the main building. It's not until we're inside that I realize I haven't panicked once about setting foot in here. The smell hits me like a strong gale, and I cling to Davies's arm to steady myself.

"You okay?" His face is tightly drawn.

I nod. "I'm great. Let's go. Room 308."

We're given access to a private lift used by the cleaning crews. A dull throbbing starts at my temples as we ascend to the third floor. One of the security officers assured me they would have a pot of tea brought up straight away.

The doors open onto a hallway decked out with red and green streamers. An evergreen wreath hangs outside each patient room. Davies walks close to me until we reach the right one, the placard outside reading *J. Manchester*.

"This is it," I whisper.

Davies knocks on the door with his giant fist. It opens to reveal a young woman with auburn hair dressed in Disney-princess scrubs. At first, she looks at Davies in confusion, but when her eyes land on me, she covers her mouth and starts chanting, "Ohmygod, ohmygod, ohmygod."

Davies pushes past her, leading me inside with a hand on my upper arm. He quickly shuts the door behind us. The room is dark, the TV on the wall turned to some kids' channel, several animated characters dancing around what appears to be a massive sleeping dog. The bed takes up most of the space. The little boy in it hardly takes up any space at all.

His head is bald, his eyes sunken in their sockets. His skin looks pasty, and his lips are dry and cracked. My heart splinters open at the same moment my stomach does a nauseating lurch.

John Matthews looks up at Davies and me as we enter. Recognition lights a spark in his eyes, and he does his best to sit up. His nurse rushes to his side to raise the bed for him.

"Your Majesty." His chapped lips pull into a smile. "I knew you'd come." He turns to his nurse, whose name tag says *Amanda H, RN*. "Didn't I tell you she'd come?"

For the next half hour I have the sweetest and most unconventional tea of my life. John Matthews is surprisingly upbeat for a kid who may not live another two weeks. He tells me about his two rabbits, Beatrix and Potter, and about his favorite teacher, Miss Emily.

"Where are your parents?" I ask.

"Mum's at work. She'll be by after." He runs his fingers along the stripes on his blanket. "I haven't seen my dad for a long time."

Bloody hell. This kid is on his deathbed, and neither of his parents are here.

I've hardly noticed the nausea plaguing me like a telemarketer, or the dull ache behind my eyes. John and I invited Nurse Amanda and Davies to join us, but they said they preferred to stick to their duties—Amanda bustling around the room arranging medications, and Davies alternately peering through the glass in the door and the window.

Presumably the rest of the security team thinks I'm still at the spa, although how long we can keep that ruse up, I'm not sure. We've already been gone for nearly an hour.

Davies catches my eye, then glances at his watch. "We really should be going, ma'am."

I say my goodbyes to John Matthews and thank Amanda for helping him get in touch with me. Davies and I head back to the lift, my spirits strangely buoyed in spite of the tepid stench filling the place and the knowledge that John Matthews will never walk out of here.

In the lift, I turn to Davies. "Please see to it that his mother is able to take off work to be with her son. He shouldn't be alone here."

"I will do my best, ma'am, but it's likely they need the money."

"I will take care of the financial aspects," I say. John Matthews's mum should spend his last days with him, even if it means I have to use my personal spending budget.

Davies pushes open the back door of the hospital, and we are immediately greeted by both fresh air and a throng of reporters. A dozen mics are shoved in my face as the newscasters yell over each other. Davies yanks me against him and rushes for the SUV parked a few feet away. Opening the door, he pushes me inside, then jumps into the driver's seat.

The press is closing in when he puts the car in gear and drives away with a squeal. I'm half-scared he's going to run one of them down. My heart is thumping so hard I can almost see it moving my bodice as I fasten my seatbelt.

Inside, the car is quiet. I can see Davies scowling in the rearview mirror.

"How did they find us?" I finally say.

"I don't know." His voice has a low, ominous tone. I wonder if he's plotting revenge or hoping he doesn't lose his job over this. "We have another problem, ma'am."

I lean forward between the seats. "What is it?"

"They're tailing us." He flicks his eyes between the road and the rearview mirror.

"Who?" I ask, turning around. "The press?"

"Those bloody vultures won't stop at anything to get a scoop. Hang on. This next part could get a little choppy."

The car lurches to the side as he whips it around a corner. We sail down another street. When that still doesn't shake them, he tries again. We fly through the city like Jason Statham on the run. The only thing missing is a gun fight, and that thought hits a little too close to home to be humorous.

After what feels like an eternity of tight corners and even tighter alleyways, we pull into the parking garage at the Atlantis. My stomach has never felt more relieved.

When we arrive on the top floor, no one seems the wiser about our shenanigans. "Thank you," I whisper to Davies as he escorts me to the penthouse. "You were great."

He nods as I step through the doors. "It was my pleasure, ma'am."

An hour later, I've washed the hospital smell off and sent an email to Maisie, asking her to send a deluxe hardcover copy of the Beatrix Potter stories to John Matthews. I'm just pulling the ingredients for a chicken Caesar salad out of the fridge when Henry walks—or rather, stalks—into the room.

"What's this?" Anger bleeds through the thin veil over his voice.

"What's what?" I turn around to see him holding up his phone, a video playing on the screen. It's footage of a car chase downtown, shot from a chopper above.

"Looks like a high-speed chase," I say, before returning to my lettuce. I reach for a plate from the cupboard, but he slams it shut before I can grab one. "What is your problem?" I glare at Henry's hand holding the door closed.

"Look closer." He shoves the phone under my nose.

I yank it from his hand. This time I take a look at the headline scrolling across the top of the screen. *Queen Visits Terminal Cancer Patient.*

"Bloody hell," I whisper, and hand the device back. I offer him a weak smile. *Fuck.*

"What. Were. You. Thinking." He chops each word apart like an onion.

I hold my hands up, both in supplication and to keep him from coming any closer. "I can explain. Just promise me that you'll listen and not jump to conclusions."

His nostrils flare, and he looks at me with crazy eyes. I take this as permission.

"There is a little boy, John Matthews, who wrote to me asking me to come visit him. He's only seven and doesn't have much longer. It was the sweetest card, really. His nurse helped him mail it off, and—"

"I don't care if it was hand-delivered by carrier pigeons!"

I stare at Henry, a slight flutter starting in my own nostrils. "You said you'd listen."

"No, I didn't. And now I'd like some explanation as to why you put yourself directly in danger, against my orders and against your better judgment."

"He's going to die soon, Henry!"

"Are you planning to put yourself in harm's way for the thousands of others who also won't see the end of the year?"

"Don't be ridiculous." Shoving him aside, I grab a plate from the cupboard. I toss a handful of chopped greens onto it, even though my appetite has vanished.

"You think I'm being ridiculous?" He leans against the counter, propping one elbow on the marble, hedging me in between himself and the fridge.

I scatter pieces of grilled chicken breast over the bed of greens. "It does seem to be your default state of late."

"I am trying to protect you. Why do you insist on making it so damn impossible?" He's leaning even closer now, the heat of his breath tickling my neck.

"I had Davies. It's not like I was without protection," I say, ripping open the package of Parmigiano Reggiano.

"Davies." Henry spits the name out between his teeth. "I hope you made it worth his while. He's going to have a hard time finding another job in this city without a recommendation."

I drop the cheese onto the counter and spin to face him. "You didn't."

"Fuck right I did."

"He has a family, Henry!"

"He should have thought about that before he drove you around the city like he's Tom fucking Cruise." He crosses his arms over his chest, muscles nearly shredding the sleeves of his T-shirt. The veins in his arms are popping out like a drug addict's.

"He didn't want to," I say. "I begged him. Please, don't fire him."

"He directly disobeyed an order, Celia. Besides, it's already done."

"Can't you undo it? For me?"

Henry closes his eyes and doesn't say anything.

I let out a shaky sigh, then place my hands on his arms. His skin is hot, searing my palms, and his eyes snap to mine at the contact. "I thought—" I stop, trying to force the words out. "I thought you loved me." I move my fingers slowly back and forth over his forearms. The hair on them is soft. I can feel his pulse jumping beneath my fingers.

His eyes flash with anger as he takes a step backward. My hands fall and hang at my sides. The line of his mouth is flat and grim. "I do." His voice is a low growl. "But don't you dare use that as a weapon against me."

22

"Never Forget You" - Zara Larsson + MNEK

I F DODGING THE GUY who makes you so mad you can't see straight was an Olympic sport, I would have a gold medal in it—bronze at the very least. I should also get a trophy for all of the times I've wanted to drive over him with my car and refrained.

After our confrontation in the kitchen, I managed to avoid Henry for the rest of the day and all day yesterday. But this morning, I wake with nausea severe enough to send me scurrying to the kitchen without scouting for the enemy first.

The newly hired cook is already there. Musa appears to be in his late twenties, and I learned yesterday that he's originally from Jaipur, India.

"Of course," he says after I request a cup of tea. He sets the kettle on to boil.

I'm just about to sink my face into my hands when Henry walks around the corner. My heart leaps the way it does when someone sneaks up behind you, only now it also sends a sickly sweet chemical through my veins. His eyes flit over me where I'm seated on the barstool, but he doesn't say anything, just pulls out a frying pan.

"Can I get you something to eat, Your Majesty?" Musa asks. He apparently doesn't mind sharing the kitchen with his employer.

"No, thank you," I say.

He cocks his head, a faint smile on his lips. "Are you sure? Some eggs? Or maybe some of the yogurt you had yesterday?"

"I appreciate the offer, but I'm not feeling well this morning." I don't relish the thought of hurling into the garbage bin again, and tea seems like the only safe option at the moment.

"I can make you my yumma's famous stew. It is said to cure even the most stubborn of ailments." He waggles his eyebrows.

I offer him a weak smile. "Just the tea for now, thank you."

He nods and pours the hot water over a bag of jasmine leaves. I'm about to take it and head back to my room when Henry props an elbow on the bar beside me.

"You're feeling sick again?" His tone is low and concerned.

I take a sip of tea. "Your presence intensifies it."

"Any more throwing up?"

I turn my head just enough for him to see my scowl. "What are you, my doctor?"

"Just answer the question, Celia." The ever-present edginess in his voice tickles its way through my belly.

"Not since a few nights ago." I blow across the surface of the hot beverage. "It's not that bad. Just mild nausea." Okay, *mild* might be a stretch, but Henry doesn't need to know everything.

"I'll have your doctor make a house call." He pushes away from the counter.

I grab his arm before he can walk away. "Absolutely not. I told you, I'm fine."

He tosses a glance at Musa, who has taken over cooking Henry's eggs, before lowering his voice. "You're not eating, and you're throwing up what you do eat. It's concerning."

"You may be in charge of my security, but I'm still in charge of my health." I dig my nails into his arm. "No doctor."

He yanks free of my grip. "Fine. Then tell me what you've been eating."

"Well, since you cut off my take-away, not much."

"You haven't brought in any food from outside?" He puts a hand on the back of my barstool and hovers over me like a dark storm cloud.

"Not unless you count me sneaking out for the sushi buffet on North Thirty-Third and buying a questionable burrito from a street vendor on the way home."

"This isn't funny, C."

"Glad we agree on something." I take a long gulp of tea and promptly burn my mouth.

"I have another question, but you have to promise not to get mad," he says quietly. Musa is still floating around the kitchen, humming show tunes to himself and apparently oblivious to our less-than-friendly conversation.

"Too late."

Henry closes his eyes and inhales through his nose. Then he leans in close and whispers, "You're not pregnant, are you?"

My jaw hits the floor, and I jump off the stool. I can't do this anymore.

Henry grabs my arm this time. "I said not to get mad. It's a legitimate question."

"It's a *stupid* question."

He throws his hands up. "Fine. Stupid question. But do you mind answering it anyway?"

I narrow my eyes into the deadliest glare I can. "You're insane. No, I'm not pregnant. *God*."

Until he said it, the thought hadn't even occurred to me. I quickly scan the calendar in my head. With everything that's been going on, I've completely lost track, but I'm positive this is not pregnancy-induced nausea. "Even if I was, it clearly wouldn't be yours."

Lines of confusion cross his brow. "But we just . . ." he whispers.

"That was too recent," I hiss back. My face must be the shade of a strawberry right now.

"What about London?"

I do some mental gymnastics, but while the timing would work, I've had my period since then. I shake my head. "Definitely not."

His eyes flick back and forth between mine as though he's wishing he could crawl into my head and know exactly what I'm thinking. "So then . . . you're definitely not?" Something like disappointment threads through his voice.

I will not dwell on that.

My tea has finally cooled, and I take a long drink before answering. "I guess it could have been one of the others."

The hand Henry has clamped on the marble countertop turns white. His face is frozen, looking much like the marble itself. "Others?" He doesn't move his mouth as he says it.

Shrugging, I run a fingertip around the rim of my cup. "Probably not, though. We were careful."

His face loses its remaining color, and I focus on the delicate china in my hands so he won't notice how much I'm enjoying watching him squirm. From the corner of my eye, I can see him rake his fingers through his hair. He blows out a long breath and finally walks back into the kitchen.

Does he actually think I've been sleeping around? I'm the queen of Wesbourne, for god's sake. And more importantly, did he actually think I was carrying his baby?

Sunday passes much like the day before, which means avoiding the common areas for fear I'll run into Henry and eating at odd hours—if I can get any food down at all. I miss Bea. As annoying as she can be, at least she was a good distraction.

I'm planning to slip into the library with a book because, beautiful as it may be, I'm getting tired of spending all my time here in the master bedroom. When I open the door, Tundra barrels past me before I can stop him, straight into the great room.

Unfortunately, Henry's also in the great room, along with a spruce so massive it nearly hits the chandelier. When I join them, Tundra is standing beside him, looking up at the tree with a mixture of awe and joy. He probably thinks Henry brought him his own territory to mark.

I finally find my voice. "What are you doing?"

Henry looks over at me, a boyish smile tugging at the sides of his mouth, and my stomach dips. He stretches out a hand to steady the tree as Tundra leans closer for a sniff. "Happy Christmas."

"You got a Christmas tree? How did you get that thing on the lift?"

He chuckles and shakes his head. "You don't want to know." Evidently deciding Tundra can be trusted, he releases his hold on the trunk and walks toward me. "Consider it my peace offering."

Cocking a brow, I glance over his shoulder at the incredibly large spruce. It must be over ten feet tall and probably just as wide. "Chocolate would have worked, too."

His face splits into a grin. "Yeah, but that wouldn't have done anything for my reputation as Scrooge." Stopping a few paces away, he jerks a thumb over his shoulder. "My mum sent over some old ornaments. Wanna help me put them up?"

Of course I want to. The tree is the epitome of holiday decorating. But my stomach clenches at the thought of spending time with Henry, of making myself even more vulnerable than I already am.

His brows flick upward slightly. "I thought we could talk about the plans for the Royal Estate while we do it. Kind of a two birds, one stone deal." He sticks his hands in the front pockets of his jeans. I try unsuccessfully to look away from the way his T-shirt is fitting so perfectly over that wall of muscle.

We do need to discuss his ideas, and I did decide to trust him with this. "Sure," I say. "I'll help."

The grin that takes over his face is infectious, and I find myself smiling in return. I inspect the tree, which Tundra has already claimed as his own, while Henry grabs the boxes Olivia sent over. He sets them down and leaves the room, probably to get food.

The staff had to move several of the sofas just to fit the tree. It's the biggest I've ever decorated. A thrill races up my spine at the thought of a real Christmas, even if it is spent in Henry's sky-high castle.

I open the first box of ornaments, expecting to find those plastic-y balls that were popular in the early 2000s. At this point, I don't care if Olivia sent over one hundred inflatable Santas. I'm too excited by the prospect of actually having a little holiday cheer around this place.

I'm not prepared, however, for the tediously packaged antique ornaments that greet me. They are hand-painted and made of a thin, fragile glass I know from experience breaks with hardly any effort at all.

Henry walks back into the room carrying a plate of tiny sliders and sweet and savory tarts. "I should have hired a chef a long time ago," he says, popping one of the pastries in his mouth. He sets the food on the coffee table and peers over my shoulder. The skin on my neck is suddenly three times as sensitive as usual. "Are the ornaments any good?"

I move a bit to the left and away from his warmth, even though sinking backward into him sounds like heaven. "They're incredible." I gently pry a blue-and-gold dreidel from the packing foam and hold it up. It spins between my fingers. "They look like they're from the thirties."

"She said they were my great-grandmum's, so that would make sense."

"Are you sure this is a good idea? These are family heirlooms, and"—I glance at Tundra, who's currently fascinated by a piece of tissue paper that has floated out of the box—"well, one of your houseguests isn't known for gentleness."

Henry grabs a pink-and-white sphere and tosses it into the air, catching it again with ease. "I trust you," he says, and winks.

"Henry!"

He assumes a look of innocence before setting the ball back into the box. "What? She'll never know if a few go missing. There must be hundreds here."

His good mood is rubbing off on me despite my best efforts. "In that case, we'd better get started. Do we have lights?"

We've got lights on the tree, the first box of ornaments emptied, and some preliminary ideas in place for refilling the royal household's coffers. Our only disagreement has been over the seabed mineral rights.

"Okay, we'll scrap that idea for now," Henry says.

I glance over at him. Even perched on a stool he has to strain to reach the top branches of the tree. His right arm inches upward, and I see the small tattoo on his upper arm, a calligraphic black *C* with hydrangeas twining around it. I inhale sharply, and he turns his gaze to me.

"You okay?" he says.

I nod, momentarily scrambling for words. "Um, actually, what if we did a trial run on the mineral rights? Maybe find a sustainable and responsible company to do some testing, see what's there."

"Great idea." He points to the box of ornaments. "Mind handing me a few more of those?"

I gather a small armload and carry them to the ladder. The lower branches are mostly covered by now, meaning the rest will need to go up high. I hand him a sea-green finial. His fingers brush over mine as he takes it, sending an electric shock up my arm.

"I'm sorry about earlier." His eyes hold mine. "I was an ass."

I flush as I recall his pregnancy question. "It's fine. You were just worried."

He turns back to the tree to hang the finial. "Was there . . . someone else?"

I'm pretty sure my face outshines the glass balls around us right now. "You know there wasn't." I hand him another ornament.

He lets out a deep breath, as if he's been holding it for a while. "I'm not going to pretend that isn't a huge relief." There's a note of discomfort in his tone when he laughs.

We're quiet for a few minutes as he hangs the rest of the decorations. I do my best to hand them to him with minimal touching. The brush of his fingers does things to my pelvic region better left unexplored. It wouldn't take much for my common sense to flee the premises.

Henry climbs down from the ladder, but instead of moving toward the outlet to plug the lights in, he edges toward me until our toes are touching. My blood is rushing through my body like a bullet train. I can't stop the trembling in my hands.

He tilts my chin up with a finger, and I meet his gaze, his eyes dark and gentle, his face beckoning me to relax. This is Henry, my one-time best friend, my short-time lover, my all-time nemesis. He holds more of my secrets than anyone else on the planet.

"We are literally living my nightmare," he says.

I swallow loudly, my mouth suddenly dry. "What, a Christmas tree in the living room?"

He tucks a loose strand of hair behind my ear. Goosebumps flood my face and neck. "For years I've tried to protect you. And now it's like the whole fucking world is conspiring to tear you away from me."

I think about everything he's done in the past few weeks. The gestures, the protection, the worry, the thoughtfulness. He said he loves me.

Maybe he actually does. Maybe there's a part of him that can actually override the twisted side, at least for a while. After all, no one is that good of an actor, right? Eventually, we all slip up.

Maybe there are more things than the mineral rights that can be considered on a trial basis.

I move closer, until my nipples brush against him. The sensation is incredible, but I can't focus on that right now. "What if I was willing to try?" I say, biting my lip. I'm pretty sure I know how he's going to respond, but that doesn't stop my pulse from racing.

His eyes narrow as he focuses on me and what I'm offering. "What changed?"

I open my mouth, but nothing comes out. This is one question I haven't prepared for. "Maybe I had a change of heart," I say with a shrug.

Henry crosses his arms over his chest, which draws my eyes. Curse those damn biceps. "So you no longer think I'm trying to hurt you? Or sleep with your sister?"

"Bea told me what you said."

He looks off to the side in disgust. "So you believe her, not me."

"What do you expect? You've lied to me so many times, I don't even know what the truth sounds like coming from your mouth."

A vein in his temple throbs. "I have proven myself to you over and over. I shouldn't have to keep doing it."

"I said I believe you. Or . . . I'm choosing to be optimistic."

"'Choosing to be optimistic'? God, are you listening to yourself right now?" He starts pacing the room, hands on his hips. "You can't build a relationship without trust, Celia."

"I'm ready to try."

"It doesn't work like that. One wrong move and you'll be out."

"You're the one with commitment issues, not me."

"I do *not* have commitment issues," Henry growls. "I've been in love with you for the past fifteen years. If that's not commitment, I don't know what is."

I roll my eyes. "Not exactly what a woman dreams of."

His fingers plow rows through his hair. "What do you want from me, C?"

"I want you to give us a shot."

He looks down at the floor and shakes his head. "Not if you don't trust me."

"I do." *Or at least I can fake it.*

"Prove it." He stalks over to me, thrusts his hands across my jawline and into my hair, and buries them there like a stake in the ground. His lips meet mine, hard and vicious. I clamber for breath, but he won't give it to me.

He pulls me closer, his lips not leaving mine for even a second. Our teeth clash together, and it's all I can do to stay out of his way. His tongue forces its way into my mouth, exploring every inch like a conqueror surveying his lands.

His hands are still cradling my head, but that doesn't keep him from pressing my body against his as tightly as possible. Then, so suddenly I barely have time to gasp, he wraps an arm around my waist and turns me until I'm up against the dining table. The wooden edge cuts into my back as he pushes against me further.

Grabbing my thighs, he lifts me onto the table, then fills the space between my legs with himself. He leans me back with one hand behind me, and I can feel tissue paper being crushed by our bodies. In all this time, he hasn't once let me come up for air, claiming my mouth like it's a prize won through blood and tears. I can already feel my lips grow swollen and the chafing from his stubble.

He's leaning over me, his weight nearly pressing out what little air I have left in my lungs, when he suddenly pulls back. Then he leaves me lying across the table like some kind of tramp while he walks away and wipes his mouth.

I catch my breath and slowly sit up. The paper rustles around me. "Care to explain what the hell that was?"

Henry turns back to me, hands on hips. "That was a test. Which you failed."

"Excuse me?"

"I told you to prove you trust me. You resisted the entire time."

"Because you practically mauled me! What was I supposed to do?"

He walks closer but remains a foot away. "Remember the last time we had sex? You completely surrendered to me. I had just saved your life, and you trusted me with everything." As he steps closer, I can smell the spearmint on his breath, can still taste it on my tongue. "I know the difference between surrender and resistance. And the last thing you are is surrendered."

My jaw tightens. "Maybe I was performing a test of my own."

"Yeah, I gathered that. But it doesn't work that way. I'm not some bloody business proposition. You can't take me for a test drive, see how well you like the steering. You're either all in, or you're out."

"Dating is, by definition, a test drive."

He props his hands on either side of me on the table and leans down until we're at eye level with each other. "I am not interested in dating you. I already know you're the only person I want to spend the rest of my life with. I would take a bullet for you. I nearly did—and I'd do it again. I haven't looked at another woman in months. I have proven myself to you in as many ways as I know how, and if that's not good enough for you, you need to walk away right now, not string me along for six months before deciding I'm not what you want." He stands up straight. The air is charged with electricity and devoid of oxygen.

I'm still panting, trying to grab hold of my racing heart.

Henry stares at me for a few more seconds, then walks toward the hallway. Near the kitchen, he stops and turns. "Your heart isn't the only one capable of being broken, you know."

23

"Believer" - Imagine Dragons

WHEN YOU'VE MADE A complete fool of yourself, it takes a full bottle of chardonnay to forget—maybe less if you have something cheaper than the organic limited ten-bottle run I found in Henry's wine cooler.

My lips are still chapped from his assault on them last night. Every time I expect him to respond a certain way, he does the opposite, which usually ends with me looking like an idiot.

My hangover this morning isn't terrible, but I take Musa up on his offer of his yumma's cure-all stew. Fortunately, he has some already prepared in the fridge. The savory mixture of vegetables, beef, and chicken tastes as if it took hours to prepare. I devour every spoonful while telling myself this is the absolute last time a man ever drives me to drink. I am the queen, for god's sake. Time to start acting like it.

Maisie arrives promptly at nine o'clock, latte in her hand, face implacable. I'm beginning to think we might never get our friendship back. The only thing to hope for at this point is that she breaks up with Beck soon. Lord knows *he'll* never do it.

Tundra greets her with an enthusiastic hug, by which I mean he football-tackles her, and she nearly ends up on the floor. I admit I take a certain a certain pleasure in the spectacle. After I pull him off her, he circles back to hump her leg. It seems everyone wants a piece of Maisie these days.

"Tundra," I snap. "Down."

He gives a few more thrusts before finally placing all four feet back on the floor and walking to his bed in the corner of the great room.

Maisie laughs. "He's just excited to see me."

"He does it to everyone," I retort.

She blinks at my sharp tone. "Still, it's nice to know he likes me."

"He likes everyone."

"Are we still talking about Tundra?" She's more astute than I give her credit for.

"Of course," I say, and head for the great room. As I pass the kitchen, Henry glances up from the breakfast he's wolfing down. I wonder how much he's heard.

Maisie sets the box on the dining table, and I have a sudden flashback to Henry pinning me on that very table last night.

"Let's move over here." I lead Maisie to a spot near the windows.

"There's been a lot of buzz around your visit to the hospital," she says after we settle ourselves on opposite ends of the sofa. "The people seem to be responding favorably. Even the media appears impressed, although there's talk about it being a publicity stunt."

I roll my eyes. I'm never going to be able to do anything that can't be construed as that. "I'm glad something good came of it all." I'm still furious it cost Davies his job.

"The press office is spinning it as best they can."

"And the search for a new press secretary? Any luck?"

"We've been interviewing, but no one seems to be the right fit."

The royal family's image is in shambles, and I don't know the first thing about how to fix it myself. And with this sudden surge of warmth toward me, now is the perfect time to act. I need someone who isn't daunted by a challenge and understands how to best present themselves.

I need someone like Rosalind.

My mother may not have been successful in her bid for her daughter to marry the future king, but that wasn't due to any failure on her part. I was the perfect candidate for princess by the time she was done with me.

If only she hadn't stuck a knife in the back of our relationship when she told us of her scandalous affair. She's nearly at the bottom of my list of people I'd like to talk to, right above Maisie and Beck.

But what other options do I have? If I can put aside my irritation with Maisie to continue doing my job, I can surely put aside my disdain for my mother's choices if it means the betterment of our family.

I call her an hour later. It rings six times before she finally answers. It seems my propensity for misplacing phones is an inherited trait.

"Mum?" I force more warmth than I feel into my voice. "Can you meet me at the Atlantis? I need your help with something."

"Of course. I'll be right there."

I shouldn't be surprised by her quick acquiescence. She's probably as close to rotting away in her hotel as I am. "Don't forget your allergy meds," I remind her before hanging up.

She arrives half an hour later, looking like she's about to play a hotshot lawyer in one of those TV shows that value ruthlessness and grit. She glances around the great room, presumably for Tundra.

"He's locked in my bedroom," I say. "He likes to hump things." I don't think she would appreciate that as much as Maisie seemed to.

"Isn't he fixed?" she asks, setting her handbag on the coffee table.

"He is. I don't know why he does it."

We each take a seat on the sofa Maisie and I vacated not long ago. "I have to say, I was surprised you called," my mother says, her sharp eyes analyzing me.

I glance down at my lap, smoothing the fabric of my fuchsia dress. "Me too." I meet her eyes again. "I'm not ready to forgive you for what you did. But I need help, and I think you're the best candidate."

She doesn't even flinch. If there is anything one should know about Rosalind, it's that she has nerves of steel. She gives one short, brisk nod as if she expected nothing less. "What's the problem?"

"Have you been watching the news?"

Two hours later, my mother leaves, and I'm left holding a detailed plan for exactly how to get back into the good graces of the people of Wesbourne. According to her, the monarchy has been way too aloof for centuries. England overhauled how their royal family relates to the people decades ago, and she suggested we do the same. "In today's society, people want to see their queen up close and personal."

I grimaced at this. "I'm not sure I'm comfortable with that."

"Then get comfortable with being disliked. This is what our culture demands, and if you're not prepared to give it to them, it won't reflect well on you."

"What do you mean by personal?" I asked.

"Many more public outings. Giving people a chance to meet you, shake your hand, that kind of thing. They should feel like you're *theirs*."

"My schedule is pretty full as it is."

Mum nodded, her chin lifted. "It will have to become fuller."

I'm pretty sure my mouth fell open at that point. "With what exactly?"

It was then that she brought out a paper and pen from that deep-bottomed bag of hers. "You're already doing the stately things. Galas, ribbon cuttings for hospitals and galleries, launching ships," she said. "But we need to add more things for the commoners." As though she could feel me bristle at the term, she added, "For lack of a better word."

Her list grew with each new suggestion.

Visit the Soccer League Association.

View soft play areas for children with disabilities.

Observe displays in sports halls.

Have tea with citizens in retirement homes.

Watch young children in rough-and-tumble gymnastics.

Inspect civic centers.

Plant trees.

Lay wreaths on graves.

Visit schools and factories.

Walk around exhibitions.

Tour shipyards.

Admire paintings from local artists.

Unveil plaques.

Accept invitations to dedicate churches.

I have to admit, by the time she tore the three pages of ideas from her notebook, I was excited. Adding these things to my schedule will make me busier, but they actually sound like fun. She assured me that the more events I do like this, the more invitations will roll in.

I can only hope she's right.

24

"Lights" - Ellie Goulding

AFTER SAVING THE CHRISTMAS tree from what surely would have been fatal destruction, I finally decide to do something about Tundra's mounting. William answers on the second ring, his voice as gruff as ever.

"William," I say. "I'm calling about Tundra."

He grunts, and I wonder if rough monosyllables have always been his response of choice, or if that's what being monarch does to a person. "What about him? Is he okay?"

I chuckle as I pull Tundra away from the shelf of antique globes. "Oh yes, he's quite well." A little too well, maybe. I'm in the penthouse library because it's reminds me the most of home. Unfortunately, this leaves little room for Tundra to roam and all too many breakable objects within his reach.

I finally get him to sit beside me. "You did say he was neutered, didn't you?"

"Yes," the duke harrumphs. "A few years ago."

Tundra looks up at me, mouth open, like he's expecting a prize for being such a good boy. "That's strange. Any chance they didn't do it right?"

William snorts. "I don't think so."

"It's just that he's mounting everything, and it's really starting to become a problem."

His laughter rolls through the phone so loudly I have to pull it away from my ear. "That's normal."

"Normal? How is it normal? I thought they took away his ability to . . ."

He laughs again, and it's really starting to annoy me. "He doesn't have the ability to perform, but that doesn't mean he won't try."

"You're saying there's nothing I can do about it?"

I feel his shrug through the phone. "Train him not to."

I move to the small Christmas tree in the corner when Tundra appears on the verge of testing his performing abilities on it. "And how exactly do I do that?"

"Same way you taught him other things."

I'm quiet for a few beats. The truth is I haven't taught Tundra much of anything. He was already trained when I got him, and I'm planning to hire a handler once I get the royal household back in running order. "Okay," I say finally. "Thank you, William."

Ending the call, I sink back into the sofa. "Great," I mutter. "One more thing to do."

I jump up again when the library door bursts open. It doesn't exactly slam against the wall, but only because Henry's hand is still clamped around the knob. A look of irritation is etched onto his face, but I expect no less these days.

"Please tell me that was a friend or family member named William and not who I think it was." He closes the door behind him.

"Family member," I say.

He narrows his eyes. "You don't have a relative named William."

"Ah," I say, and hold up a finger, "but I do. My ex-father-in-law."

A vein in Henry's jaw pops, and his nostrils flare as he inhales. "I thought I told you to stay away from him."

"Relax. We were only talking about Tundra, not taking over Russia."

I realize my mistake the moment his eyes narrow. "Why were you calling my father about your dog?"

I have no idea how much of our conversation Henry overheard, but I decide to take the chance that he only caught the tail end of it. "He's an experienced dog owner. I thought he might know how to get him to stop humping everything."

Henry crosses his arms and leans back against the fireplace. "I don't buy it."

I return his glare with one of my own. "You're right. We're actually secret lovers."

"I'd laugh if I wasn't too busy vomiting," he growls. "I'll find out eventually, so just tell me."

I hate that he's right. Somehow, he always manages to sniff out everything. "Tundra was a gift. From your father." May as well throw the truth in his face.

The only indication Henry registers my words is the twitch in his right eye. Apart from that, he could be watching the weather report. He turns and grabs the fireplace poker, jabbing at the logs smoldering in the grate. Sparks fly up, and the blaze slowly grows larger. He spins around so quickly that Tundra lets out a startled yip. "Why the hell did my father give you a dog?"

I cross my legs and settle further into the sofa. I could watch those back muscles ripple all day long. "How should I know?"

"Because you've never accepted a single thing in your life without tearing it apart looking for the reason behind it."

"Maybe I'm full of surprises."

"Maybe you're full of shit."

If I could turn my look into a sound, it would be a snarl. "It was a gift of gratitude. I was with him when Argos died."

"My father wouldn't know gratitude if it bit him in the ass." Henry pulls his phone from his pocket. "Roberts, I'm going to need a tech team in the library ASAP."

Seconds later, the door opens and several security personnel file into the room. Roberts is at the front of the group. "Sir?" he says, looking at Henry.

Henry motions to Tundra, who thinks I'm unaware of the ornaments he's trying to swipe from the tree. "I want a full sweep, X-ray, and medical examination."

I stand up. "What is going on?"

"Yes, sir." Roberts takes ahold of the dog's collar and begins leading him from the room.

"Leave him here," I yell, attempting to follow, but Henry's arms wrap around me from behind. "Tundra," I scream. "Tundra!"

"Let them go, C. He'll be back."

I try to pry his arms from my chest, but it's useless. He doesn't let go until Tundra has disappeared through the door. I swivel on him and smack him across the cheek.

"You told them to take my dog!"

Henry rubs at his face. "It's temporary. Provided they don't find anything life-threatening."

"What are you talking about?"

"If my father gave you that dog, you know there was a damn good reason for it."

"And you think that reason was what—to blow me sky-high with TNT?"

"I'm not willing to rule it out."

"How do I know you're not the one behind everything?" I say. "Maybe you're locking me in here so you can find the perfect opportunity to do me in."

Henry rolls his eyes and turns his attention to his phone. "If I wanted you dead, I could've killed you a million times already."

"You're suspecting your own father."

"I have to suspect everyone. It's part of my job."

"I thought your job was sitting in a cushy office and buying business-es," I counter.

"It was until your car lost a tire."

I stare at him. "Tell me that's not why you came back."

He puts the phone in his pocket. "Okay. That's not why I came back."

"Why don't I believe you?"

Shrugging, he walks to the bar cart in the corner. "Suit yourself." He pours a glass of wine and one of whiskey.

"I have a security team," I say. "I don't need *you*."

"Tough luck. You got me anyway." He holds out the wine.

I shake my head. "One of these days, I will find a way to get rid of you."

"Well, until then, darling, you're stuck with me. And let's get one thing straight. You are not to see or talk to my father again. Not under any circumstance. Got it?" His whiskey disappears in one long gulp.

"No, I don't 'got it.'" I cross my arms over my chest but am under no illusion that I appear intimidating. It's simply a defense mechanism at this point.

"Celia, for god's sake." Henry sets both glasses down on the bar.

"Have you ever noticed how our entire relationship consists of you telling me what to do?"

"No, it consists of me saving your ass because you refuse to listen."

"Because everything you want me to do is ridiculous," I say. "And also, you could try asking occasionally, instead of barking orders like a drill sergeant."

"Fine. Will you please stay away from my father?"

"No. Not without a good reason."

The growl that leaves Henry's throat is low and threatening, and also undeniably sexy. "I told you, he might be dangerous. Why can't you just trust me?"

I level him with a lethal glare. "*I* told *you*. I'll never trust you again."

I cannot believe they took my dog. William may not be a peach, and he did some pretty awful things to Henry, but to suspect him of trying to harm Tundra? This has gone too far.

I pace the library, both to release some of the anger I feel and to come up with a plan. If I could get Henry and William to talk through their issues, I think they could be reconciled. The problem is how to get them in the same room.

The plan comes out of the blue.

An hour later, I have my laptop set up in the library, and I accept William's video call. "Thanks for agreeing to this," I say as his face comes into focus on my screen. He's sitting in a desk chair, looking as grumpy as ever.

"Show me what he's doing," he says.

"Tundra isn't in here right now," I say. "Let me just ask someone to bring him."

I pull out my phone and text Henry.

Can you come to the library? I need help with something.

Hopefully they don't both murder me for this.

"While we're waiting, I was wondering if you know why Henry is so angry at you."

The duke's look is so cold, I'm sure he's going to hang up on me, but finally he says, "I wasn't a good father."

The admission is so stark, it takes me by surprise. "Have you ever apologized to him?"

He shakes his head. "It wouldn't make a difference."

"It might make one for you. Hanging on to guilt and bitterness will only make you miserable."

"My father was a terrible man," he says. "I know that doesn't excuse anything, but I didn't know how to be a good person. He did things to me—" His voice breaks, and I sincerely hope he's not about to confess everything from his sordid past. "He did horrible things, and I did horrible things to my son."

Flashbacks of what Henry told me play across my mind. This man is a monster. But even the worst monster can change, can't he?

"You might be surprised at how much better you'd both feel if you talk to him," I say.

William laughs, but there's no humor in it. "Henry would rather kill himself than talk to me."

The library door opens, and Henry walks in, much more calmly this time. I jump up from the sofa and cock my head to motion him over. "Please keep an open mind," I say quietly.

He's lowering himself onto the sofa beside me when he sees his father's face on the screen. He slams the laptop shut and stands up. "What the *fuck*, Celia?"

"Henry, just talk to him."

He whirls around on me. "I cannot believe you called him, minutes after I warned you to stay away from him."

"Maybe if you would explain why, I could understand!"

He steps closer, now inches from my face. "I told you he's dangerous. That's all you need to know."

"You want me to trust you. Why can't you trust me?"

"This has absolutely nothing to do with trusting you." He backs away and begins pacing the small room.

I perch my hands on my hips. "You're withholding information."

He shakes his head. "Not because I don't trust you."

"Then why?"

"I don't trust him. It's safer if you don't know why."

"You need to work through your anger toward him."

He levels a glare on me. "My anger toward him is the least of your concerns."

"I'm only trying to help."

"You want to help? Make up with Maisie. It's practically frigid in here every time she shows up." Henry walks out of the room, slamming the door behind him.

25

"Wake Me Up" - Avicii

I HIT SNOOZE. AGAIN. Normally I'm up the second my alarm goes off, but lately, by the time it rings, I've just fallen asleep for the first time all night. Instead of looking forward to mornings, I've started dreading them, which is almost worse than the insomnia.

I squeeze my eyes shut. I'm supposed to be going back to sleep, not lying here thinking about sleeping. But as always, it's eluding me. Maybe Henry's right, and it's time to consult my doctor.

It takes another forty-five minutes of scrolling my phone for natural sleep remedies before I finally break down and make the call.

"Your Majesty," Dr. Lahoussaye barks. "Everything okay?"

My palace-appointed doctor has treated the royal family for the entirety of his career. While he looks like a grandfather with his white hair and wrinkled skin, if my grandfather had acted anything like the good doctor when I was a child, I would have cried.

"Actually, I've been struggling with insomnia." I do my best to ignore the nausea plaguing me.

"Insomnia?"

"Yes. I've hardly been able to sleep for days."

"I know what insomnia is," he mutters. There's a clatter, as if something has been knocked over. "When did it start?"

I think back over the past few weeks. "It's hard to pinpoint the exact day—"

"Try."

I fill my lungs with air. "I think it was soon after the shooting. Maybe a few days?"

"That'll do it. I assume you're wanting some pills?"

"Um"—I bite my lip—"yes?"

"I'm supposed to ask about your sleeping habits first," he says. He doesn't sound excited by the prospect.

"Okay," I say. "What about them?"

"What time do you get up, go to sleep?"

"Well, like I said, I haven't been sleeping much—"

"Are you doing the right things before bed?"

I blink at my reflection in the mirror. "I'm sorry, what are the *right* things?"

Dr. Lahoussaye sighs as though I'm rain during his picnic. "No screens before bed, nighttime routine, proper bed."

"Yes, I do all of that. And I try to be in bed by eleven." Or midnight. But only because I know I won't be able to sleep anyway.

"Diet?"

"I'm sorry?" Is he suggesting I go on one?

"Has your diet changed recently?" he snaps.

"Maybe a bit healthier?" Thanks to the lack of eight-course state dinners.

There's another crash, followed by a low curse. "What about your bed?"

My eyes immediately land on Henry's king-size one in the center of the room. I'm assailed by memories of his body pressed against mine, the heat of his skin searing through me, his mouth traversing me like a map. I close my eyes against the vision and swallow. "What about it?"

"Is it comfortable?" The doctor sounds like he's talking to a small child.

"Yes." The word squeaks past the agonizing knot in my throat.

"What about stress?"

A maniacal laugh slips out before I can stop it. "Stress? Are you asking if I have it?"

"Obviously," he retorts.

"I was just in a car accident. Then someone tried to shoot me. On top of that, I discovered several months ago that I am meant to be the sole monarch of this country, a role I've been trying to fill ever since. So *what do you think?*"

He's quiet for a few moments, long enough for me to wonder if he regrets his harsh manner. That question is quickly answered when he says in the same tone as before, "A yes would have sufficed."

I clench my teeth and ball my hands into fists. How anyone can tolerate this miserable human is beyond me.

"Relationships?" he says.

"I don't understand the question. Are you asking if I have them?" I grab a tube of lipstick and apply it.

"Just answer the question, ma'am."

"I don't understand the question!" I consider my lips in the mirror. I look like a clown. I miss Daphne.

"Are your relationships causing stress?" He stops after each word, enunciating it like it's a prized possession in his mouth.

I think about everyone I'm close to at the moment. I think about everyone I *should* be close to at the moment. The scales seem unrealistically unbalanced. "No," I say. "They're not."

"I'm prescribing zolpidem," he says.

Apparently the only thing he needed were the correct answers to his pop quiz. "Thank you."

"This is a month's supply. We'll have to do this whole thing again if you want a refill." His tone informs me that he would much prefer that didn't happen.

You and me both.

I verbalize my consent and end the call. A text from Henry waits on my screen.

> **Henry**: Tundra will be back within the hour.

My fingers fumble as I type out a response.

> **Me**: Did they find anything?

> **Henry**: Nothing but a sock that looked suspiciously like mine.

Relief turns my muscles to jelly.

> **Me**: Maybe you shouldn't leave them lying around.

I swipe my mascara wand through my lashes, then spritz perfume on my wrists and head to the kitchen. Tundra is going to be okay. I almost want to skip.

Musa hasn't even finished preparing my yogurt parfait when Maisie arrives. The sight of her makes my stomach clench, even though she's carrying my vanilla latte. Interacting with her every day is probably giving me an ulcer.

She curtsies as she hands over the coffee. I used to look forward to her filling me in on the latest scandal among the staff or whatever her nephew had shoved up his nose that landed him in the ER. Now I dread it, dread it enough to want to stay in bed with the covers pulled over my head.

We walk toward the dining table in silence. This is ridiculous. I'm literally making myself sick by letting a man get between us. A man I don't even want, for god's sake. I stop and spin around.

Maisie's eyes are glued to her tablet, and she nearly runs into me. "I'm so sorry," she stammers. The look on her face is the one I imagine you'd have if you were facing a serial killer in a locked room.

"No, I'm sorry," I say, before realizing that's a stupid intro. "What I mean is, I want to apologize for the way I've been freezing you out. I made some stupid demands before, and I'm sorry."

She gapes at me. Evidently, my new reputation as Miranda Priestly has superseded any prior notion she had of me. "You're—you're sorry?"

I pull out one of the chairs and take a seat. "I'm ready to put it behind us if you are."

Slowly sitting down, she reaches to push up the glasses she no longer wears. Her eyes narrow. "You don't care if I see Beck?"

"Not at all." Okay, that part might not be completely true, but I'm confident I can get there. "I wish you all the best."

"Omygosh," Maisie says, her expression illuminating like a kid's at a carnival. She momentarily rests her face on the table, then lifts it again. "You have no idea what this means to me. It has put such a strain on our relationship, knowing that you didn't approve, but the whole thing just feels so right, and I didn't know what else to do." She studies me more closely. "You're sure you're okay with it?"

My eyebrows flick upward, and I cough into my hand. "Positive."

She claps her palms together. "I'm so glad. Now I can ask you what I should get him for Christmas. He already has everything, and I—"

"Maisie." I hold up my hand. "Not happening."

"Yep, right. Got it."

They bring Tundra home an hour later. He's still groggy, but that doesn't stop me from smothering him with kisses. "My sweet boy," I murmur in his ear. "I was so scared." I settle him on his dog bed so he can sleep off the rest of his sedation. Hopefully I will be doing the same tonight.

I find Henry in the home gym, which has more equipment than most public ones. He's wearing the most useless piece of clothing I've ever seen. Between the low-cut sides, the thin straps, and the low neckline, he may as well be shirtless, something I certainly wouldn't complain about. It gives a very nice view of his collection of tattoos. His athletic shorts stop a good four inches above his knees, revealing more black ink. It takes little to no imagination to remember exactly what he looks like under those clothes.

He drops from the chin-up bar in front of me, hands on his hips and panting. "Like what you see?"

My eyes snap up from his impeccable set of pectorals to meet his smirk. "Actually," I say haughtily, "I came to share some good news."

He grabs a towel from a nearby bench and rubs it over his glistening muscles. Muscles I have the strange inclination to lick. "I'm all ears."

"You wanted me to make up with Maisie. Just thought you'd want to know that I did." There's a twinge in my stomach I now recognize as nausea building.

Henry grins and tosses the towel onto the bench. "That's amazing, C." He breaks the seal on a water bottle and gulps down the whole thing, Adam's apple bobbing, my mouth salivating. He swipes his lips with the back of his hand and tosses the bottle into the bin. "Was it as hard as you thought it would be?"

"Harder," I say, even though we both know it's a lie.

"Feel better?"

I shrug my shoulders. "Maybe a little." My heart feels a bit lighter, but my stomach is churning.

He smiles. "I'm proud of you."

I don't know what else to say and feel a little foolish for coming in here like this. I just needed to tell someone. The space between us grows thick and uncomfortable. All of a sudden, I wonder if he's waiting for me to say I forgive him.

Chancing a glance at him, I see he's looking at me, and I swear there's a question lingering in those eyes. I want to, but I can't say it. I can't form the words. If I tell him that the past is forgotten, that I'm ready to move on from everything he did to me, it will be nothing short of a bald-faced lie. I trust him to help me, but I do not trust him to handle my heart without crushing it.

I clear my throat and look down at my shoes, toeing one of the rubber mats in front of me. "You know, I think William was sincere about—"

"No." His body has gone rigid, a hard mass of muscle in front of me.

"Henry, just think—"

He shakes his head. "I appreciate what you're trying to do, but there are so many things you don't understand."

"Then tell me." I take another step closer. If I can just crack through his facade, I might be able to help.

"Celia, you need to stay out of it." His brow furrows as he looks down at me. "I mean it. My father is more dangerous than you realize."

"What if he's changed? What if you've misjudged him?"

Henry leans down until our noses are nearly touching. "Not something I'm willing to take a chance on. Stay away from him, C."

I'm in the shower when the door bursts open. I instinctively scream before my body registers that it's Henry. I try to cover myself as best I can, but the walls of the stall are glass and visible from the door.

He stalks over and grabs a towel from the shelf. "Get out."

"Excuse me?" I say. "Is this about earlier?"

He looks momentarily confused. "What? No." He thrusts the towel at me again. "We need to go."

"I'm not going anywhere with you until you tell me what's going on." Turning off the water, I accept the towel from him but don't budge from the shower.

"There's been a security breach." I see now that what I mistook for anger is actually fear. He's literally trembling with it.

"What, here? I thought the Atlantis had the best security in the country."

"We don't have time to discuss this. We need to move. Now."

I allow Henry to help me out of the shower but stop in front of the mirror. "Wait. I still have conditioner in my hair."

He glares at me in the glass. "I'll give you thirty seconds. You can either use that time to rinse your hair or put clothes on."

He waits outside the walk-in closet while I slip into a velour tracksuit. It's not the cutest thing in my wardrobe, but at least it will keep me warm. I can't seem to shake these chills.

Henry gives me a once-over when I open the door. "You're going to need warm boots, a coat, and a hat."

I lower my brows. "Where are we going?"

"Right now, to the roof. I'll update you after that. Please hurry." Stepping into the closet, he rifles through one of the drawers, then tosses me a pair of gigantic wool mittens. "Put these on too."

Once I'm bundled up enough for his liking, we take the private lift to the roof. The helicopter is already running. "Please tell me we're not going to the beach again," I say as the wind whips around us and finds every tiny gap in my clothing to slip through.

Henry wraps his arm around me and steers me toward the chopper, then helps me inside. The door closes behind us, and we strap into our seats. The air is warmer than outside, but I can already tell I'm going to need every layer I'm wearing for this trip.

"Now will you tell me where we're going?" I say.

He looks over at me, and I can see the anxiety still etched on his face. "Roberts's mother-in-law has a hunting cabin up north. We're going to hide out there."

"We're what?" I force a laugh. "For a second there, it sounded like you said *hunting cabin*."

Henry's eyes narrow a tiny bit before resuming their anxious patrolling. The chopper lifts into the air, and my stomach drops. "You heard me," he says.

"You cannot be serious."

He whirls toward me, the light from the instrument panel in the cockpit reflecting in his eyes. "What part of this do you think I'm joking about?"

"Why can't we stay at the Carlton?" I hold up my hand. "And before you say anything, I'm aware I sound like a pretentious princess right now. But a hunting cabin?"

He rubs his palm against the side of his neck. "Trust me, if we had any other options, I wouldn't be taking you there. It was the most remote place we could find on short notice."

"Isn't remote bad, though?" I say. "With people around, there's less chance he'll try anything, right?"

"It didn't stop him at the memorial."

Bloody hell. He's right. "So what's the plan then?"

"Lay low until we catch this guy."

"I'm going to need more than that."

Henry shrugs and glances at me. "We're making this up as we go. I realize you don't want to trust me, but you don't have a choice at the moment."

26

"Why Why Why" -
Shawn Mendes

I'M NOT SURE WHAT I expected when Henry said hunting cabin, but I'm pleasantly surprised by the small lodge. Plaid was at the forefront of my mind, and there's plenty of that, but it has a certain charm about it too. And I don't know how they managed, but someone got here before us and lit a fire in the fireplace, so the chill in the air is already starting to vanish.

The whole place is a blend of warm browns. The walls and floor are made of wooden planks, the furniture constructed from either supple leather or pine logs, and the wooden canoe hanging from the ceiling is polished a golden honey. The tapestry on the far wall is a vibrant red and perfectly complements the plaid throw pillows on the sofa.

"Thank god there's indoor plumbing," I say after opening a door to reveal a commode and the world's tiniest shower.

Henry cuts me a glance from the small round table, where he's unboxing what appears to be a set of security cameras. "Like I would have let you pee outside."

The door I imagine opens into the bedroom turns out to lead to a small closet. I turn in confusion, and that's when I see it: a single bed, tucked against the wall near the fireplace. I thought it was a futon.

"Don't worry. I'll take the sofa," Henry says without looking up.

"I was just worried about bed bugs." I shrug as if he didn't just read my mind. "I'm going to take a shower. Hopefully I can finish this one."

Henry isn't in the cabin when I get out. My heart takes a nosedive to my toes before I spot him through the window. He's outside, perched on a chair and fastening something over his head. His shirt has ridden up, revealing a sliver of those rock-hard abs that still torment me in my dreams.

I watch him, his muscles expanding and contracting as he mounts a security camera. I imagine him pressing me against the wall, hips rolling against mine, pinning me into place. I can almost feel his fingers tunneling through my hair as he tilts my head and takes my mouth with his. He needs so little of his strength to capture and contain me. The thought makes me feel both small and protected.

It's that last one that gets to me.

Henry has always made me feel protected. The fact that he's currently outside in this brutal weather, installing cameras for my safety, is only one of the reasons why. The thought hits me with a bang.

I should be terrified out of my mind right now. Someone is out there hunting me, and they won't stop until they either accomplish their mission or are stopped. If Henry hadn't come back from London and made it his responsibility to protect me, and by some miracle I was still alive, I would be an anxious mess.

Wind blasts through the door as he opens it. He rushes inside, carrying the wooden chair in one hand and slamming the door shut with the other, then stops abruptly when he sees me. I'm still standing in the middle of the room like an idiot, water dripping from my hair all around me.

"God, Celia. You're going to freeze to death." Henry drops the chair and grabs a towel from the bathroom. It should be called a bath cupboard. The shower was hardly big enough to turn around in.

Standing behind me, he begins to dry my hair, squeezing the rest of the water out of it. Without all of my products, it's going to be a frightful mess tomorrow.

The room tilts, and he drops the towel to grab me instead. "C?"

"I'm fine," I murmur. "Just very tired." I try to hold myself upright, but my legs aren't following instructions.

Henry half carries, half drags me to the bed. After helping me lie down, he tugs my boots off. "You sure you're okay?" he asks, tucking the plaid coverlet around me.

I hum in agreement. "I forgot I took sleeping pills before we left." I realize as I'm drifting off that I forgot to tell him just how safe he makes me feel.

I wake to the scent of frying eggs. From my dwarf-sized bed, I can see Henry in the kitchen. He's turned away from me, and I use the remaining moments until he realizes I'm awake to admire the strong lines of his back.

His soft T-shirt hugs his shoulders, then loosely falls to puddle around his waist. The sleeves are tight around his biceps. Before I can stop myself, I imagine shredding the whole thing off.

Enough of that. As I swing my legs over the side of the bed and stretch, I realize I slept the whole night through despite the lumpy mattress, which smells faintly of cat urine.

Henry pivots from the stove and gives me a devastating smile. "Good morning, sunshine. I hope you're ready to be locked in here for the day." He gestures to the window before turning back to plate the eggs.

A thick blanket of snow has smothered the world outside, leaving nothing but blinding white everywhere I look. I thought the penthouse was bad. How can I be expected to survive in a tiny five-hundred-foot cabin with Henry as a roommate?

But the day goes better than expected. We find a few battered board games stowed in a closet, and for tradition's sake, I smoke Henry's ass in Monopoly. There's an old VHS player hooked up to the antiquated TV, and we laugh our way through a small stash of terrible American Westerns.

Whoever made the fire last night also stocked the cupboards, so we haven't starved yet. Now it's close to dinnertime, and Henry pulls out several questionable-looking boxes. "So, deluxe cheeseburger macaroni or"—he eyes the second box with a raised brow—"tuna tetrazzini?"

I pull a face. "Isn't there more roast chicken in the fridge?"

"You polished that off at lunch." He opens the refrigerator. "Are you sure you're not pregnant?"

I launch the TV remote at his head, and he ducks behind the door.

"There is a little bit of cheese, enough milk for a family of eight, and approximately six grapes."

We end up eating bowls of cereal on the sofa. "You know, this would be great for your rebranding campaign," he says.

"What would?" I slurp another spoonful of milk, not caring that I'm acting like a slob right now. "Me dressed like a hobo, eating dinner in what is essentially your bed?"

He laughs. "The fact that you eat breakfast cereal for dinner in your pajamas."

"Somehow I don't think that's what Rosalind has in mind."

"It makes you relatable."

I set my bowl on the coffee table and tuck my feet under my large sweatshirt, stolen from Henry. "I thought the whole point of the monarch was to be this mysterious entity that no one truly knows."

He shrugs and devours another mouthful of cereal. "Not necessarily. You'll always be a bit of a mystery, but it's good for the people to see that you're human, too."

"And here I thought 'ice princess' was a good image."

Setting his bowl down, he angles his body toward mine. "You couldn't be an ice princess if you tried."

"That depends on who you ask. Maisie, for instance."

"I thought the two of you made up." He takes one of my hands between his and begins rubbing warmth into it.

"We did, but I was pretty cold before."

Henry presses his thumbs into the pad of my palm, and I fight the urge to moan. "It's not like you didn't have a reason," he says quietly.

The same uncomfortable silence swirls around us, and I let my gaze wander. I can't meet his eyes, not when we both know I can't give him what he wants.

"Do you remember when you were thrown from that horse?" His words surprise me out of my determination.

My head jerks up. "I still have the scar." I tug my hand from his grasp and push up my left sleeve. Heat races through me as he touches the puckered skin.

It was a bright day with a faint breeze, perfect for riding. One minute I was astride a beautiful mare from the palace stables, and the next I was flying through the air. The impact broke my arm in two places. I told Henry it looked like a swan. He held me as we waited for help.

The memory isn't painful. In fact, it's almost sweet to remember a time when Henry and I did nearly everything together, and that most of my childhood memories are entangled with him in some way or another. Breaking my arm was painful. Doing so while my best friend and the boy I was falling for held me made the moment tender.

But when I look at Henry's face now, he doesn't appear to be reliving a sweet shared memory. His brow is furrowed, and the hard set of his jaw tells me he is barely containing his anger. He yanks the sleeve of my shirt back down and stands abruptly. I watch him attempt to pace the room, but he can only take two steps before he's met by a wall.

"Would you care to explain what's going on? Because I'm officially confused," I say.

The silence stretches around us, growing thick and elastic. His fingers bury themselves in his hair, and in that moment, I know he's scrambling to find a story to sell me—something believable and as far from the truth as possible.

He turns toward me slowly, the indecision on his face as clear as if I had written it there with a Sharpie. He still doesn't trust me, even though he wants *me* to trust *him*.

"You know what? Never mind. I don't want to know." I push off the sofa and move to the bathroom, shutting myself in before he can do anything to stop me.

"Celia, please," he says through the door.

"I'm not interested in your fabrications."

There's a pause. "What if I tell you the truth?"

I look in the mirror. I'm not tall by any means, but I can only see myself from the chin down unless I duck. Roberts's in-laws must be tiny, or else someone doesn't know how to hang a mirror. I lean my head back against the door and remind myself to take slow, calming breaths. *One, two, three, four, five. Exhale. One, two, three, four, five.*

"I'm not sure you'd recognize the truth if it bit you on the nose," I finally say.

"Will you listen if I try to explain?"

"Give me one good reason why I should."

"Because," Henry says, "despite all of the lies, you've always believed that what we had was real."

No. It's just another trap, and I'm so far gone, so deep into my obsession with him, my need for him, that I'm at a greater risk than ever of falling into it. And even this knowledge isn't enough to protect me, because no matter what I tell myself, no matter how much my heart knows the truth, I will always pursue that path if it carries even a tiny flicker of hope. Hope that this time it's real, this time he'll tell me what I want to hear.

That this time I won't break.

"I can't, Henry. I just can't." I force my feet to move away, away from him and the door. His words are nothing but a bomb fuse masquerading as a beacon of hope he's holding out to me like a candle in a dungeon.

His words are muffled by the heavy door, but they cut through me all the same. "I love you, C. I've always loved you."

There's a rough brushing sound. I imagine him sliding against the wood until he's sitting on the floor. I don't move a muscle.

"My bastard of a father knew, probably before I did," he continues. "You falling from the horse was his doing. I learned that later. He said the next time you'd leave in a body bag, not on a stretcher."

My heart ices over.

"It was his way of controlling me," Henry says. "He's always hated my guts, and it gave him the power he craved. At the end of summer, when you told me how you felt, I knew the only way to ensure he couldn't hurt you was to put distance between us. If you were out of my life, he couldn't use you as a weapon anymore."

I let out a trembling breath and hold on to the sink while I ease myself to the floor. The agony of that day sears through me like a poker hot from the fire. It was a painful break, but at least it was a clean one. The ones since have been as messy as black-market amputations.

"The women, the tabloids, the parties—I needed you to hate me. I had to keep you away, and I couldn't think of anything that would repulse you more than that. I lost myself in it for a long time, hating myself more the longer I stayed. But it was effective, wasn't it?" His laugh is full of scorn. "You hated my guts."

I never could, try as I might.

"Are you even listening?" Henry asks after a long pause.

I don't say anything. I'm afraid if I do, he might think I believe him. Or worse, stop talking.

He sighs heavily, and for a minute I'm afraid he's going to leave, but then he says, "Remember the night you came to my room and we played Monopoly?"

Like I could forget. It was magical, up until the minute he ripped my heart from my chest.

"He sent that fucking bottle of champagne to mess with me. Somehow he found out about us—I swear the man has eyes everywhere—and he wanted me to know that he knew.

"I knew it wasn't fair to you to keep playing with your heart the way I was. But god, how was I supposed to stay away? You're the only good thing in my life. When you showed up in London, I didn't know what the hell I was going to do. I thought I was hallucinating at first. I thought maybe I'd conjured you out of my own need to see you.

"You said no one knew, and like a fucking idiot, I thought maybe he wouldn't find out. But he always finds out. As soon as the paparazzi caught us, I knew it was only a matter of time. I had to make him think it was only a fling for me. The only way to do that convincingly was to send you home with a broken heart."

I wish now I hadn't listened, that I'd jumped in the shower and drowned his words in the hot water. At least then the wound wouldn't be gaping open like it is now, the pain fresh and all-consuming, exactly the way it was that day.

But it's too late. I'm paralyzed, a victim to any other pain he decides to dole out. My heart desperately wants everything he's saying to be true. But how many times has he played me for a fool in the past?

I can hear movement on the other side if the door, probably Henry getting to his feet. Without giving another thought to what I'm doing, I approach and slowly turn the knob. I can't decide if I want him to be gone or not, but when I open the door, he's still there, and my heart skids through my chest. He looks so tired, as if sharing this has literally sucked something from his body.

"Is William the one behind the assassination attempts?" I ask quietly.

"We've been keeping a close eye on him, but I don't think so."

"So why are you telling me this now?"

Henry leans a shoulder against the doorjamb, hands tucked into his pockets. "I want you to know that you can trust me."

"So this is the truth? All of it?" I cross my arms over my chest before he can eviscerate what's left of my heart.

"C, I—"

"Just answer the question, Henry."

He waits a long time before he answers. His silence tells me everything I need to know.

Finally, he sighs and says, "No, it's not all of it."

"Because you still don't trust me."

"Because it's not safe for you to know." The vein in his forehead throbs.

"I'm not a small child who needs coddling," I tell him.

He rubs his hand over his face. "I know that. But I'm terrified something will happen to you."

"How do you expect me to trust you when you won't even tell me the truth?" I shut the door, ignoring his pained expression. Then I sink to the floor and sob.

27

"Young Men Dead" - The Black Angels

H ENRY IS GONE AGAIN the next morning. This time I don't see him outside any of the windows. My suspicions are confirmed when I spot Roberts in a chair near the fireplace reading a biography of Chiang Kai-shek.

He looks up from his book when I approach. "Your Majesty." He nods respectfully and stands. "I can make some breakfast. What would you like?"

You've never experienced humiliation until you wake with terrible bedhead and no bra to find your personal bodyguard in a perfectly pressed suit offering to cook you breakfast.

"Um, I'll just have some cereal," I say, clutching the warm flannel blanket to my chest. I wait until he has his back turned before running to the bathroom.

Forty-five minutes later, I'm ready to face the world. Roberts is absorbed in his biography again, but there is a bowl of cornflakes awaiting me on the counter, accompanied by a small jug of milk and a spoon. After I sit, he joins me at the table.

"Where is he?" I finally allow myself to ask.

"He had some pressing matters to attend to in the city," Roberts says.

I guess my protection isn't the most important thing on Henry's list after all.

"I'm sorry that you're stuck with me out here," I say.

Roberts cuts me a wry smile. "I've always liked the place. Besides, we're heading back today too."

I lower my spoon without taking a bite. "We're going back?" I was already envisioning spending Christmas trapped in the middle of Timbuktu playing Monopoly with Roberts for the five-hundredth time.

He nods. "Just as soon as the chopper returns."

Which means Henry only left this morning, likely just a few hours ago. Why couldn't he have waited if he knew I would be going home today as well?

"Is the Atlantis safe?" I ask.

"We secured the breach. It won't happen again," Roberts assures me.

When we arrive back at Henry's penthouse, the security lobby outside is fuller than usual. As Roberts and I step off the lift, the entire room stands straighter and breaks into salutes. "You'll find a few heightened security measures, ma'am, but only until we catch this guy," Roberts says quietly as we approach the double doors.

Bloody terrific.

Several PPOs are standing in the foyer, and Roberts hands them my luggage. Musa is bustling around in the kitchen when I round the corner.

"Something smells delicious," I say.

He turns with that breathtaking grin, all stark white teeth against his brown skin. "I just pulled some orange-cranberry scones from the oven," he says. "Would you like one?"

"I think you know the answer to that," I say. "I'm going to freshen up, and I'll be right back."

When I return, Musa has plated a scone along with a small bowl of fruit and a cup of tea. "I wasn't sure when you last ate a good meal," he says.

"Does cereal count?" I settle onto one of the barstools and laugh at his look of disdain.

My good mood evaporates the second Henry walks in. He was fixated on his phone when I came out of the bathroom last night in the cabin and gone when I woke up. He's one of the last people I want to see right now.

He gives me a long, piercing look before settling on the stool next to mine. My scone suddenly doesn't seem so appealing.

"The usual?" Musa asks him, and Henry nods. "How are you feeling today, ma'am? Any more sickness?"

I force a smile and shake my head. "Not since the day before yesterday. I think I'm on the mend." It must have been the lack of sleep.

Henry is staring at me. "You've been sick that long?" His voice is hard. "Why didn't you tell me?"

"I'm sorry that my illness is so offensive to you." I pop a blueberry into my mouth and refuse to look at him.

"Musa, what have you cooked for her since you've been here?" he asks.

To his credit, Musa pretends to be unaware of the tension between Henry and me. "I've made salmon meuniere, lamb and veal Bolognese, garlic filet steak," he says. He rattles off a few more dishes that would be at home at some of the finest restaurants in Wesbourne.

"If you're done questioning me," I say to Henry, "I think I'll go to my room now." I've lost my appetite.

He clamps a hand on my leg. "Stay." Turning back to Musa, he asks, "The salmon—was it fresh or frozen? Where did it come from?"

"I only source from the best fisherman in the country. He brings his fresh catch into the city daily."

Henry frowns. "What about the other meat? Was it fresh?"

"Henry, this is ridiculous," I say. "I just have a virus of some sort. I'll be fine in no time."

"Then let's get a doctor to confirm it."

Like I'm going to talk to that weasel again. "Absolutely not. I'm feeling better already." I turn to Musa. "Your food is delicious."

He gives me a slight bow and grins. Claws click against the tile floor, and I look over to see Tundra padding toward the kitchen. "Look who finally decided to get up," I say, sliding down to greet him. Wrapping my arms around him, I bury my face in his fur. I missed him while I was gone, but Henry insisted there was no way we could take him with us.

"Roberts," Henry barks. I look up to find him on his phone. "Pull up the tests the lab did on the dog." There's a brief pause, and then he says, "Did they test his fur for toxins?"

I walk to the fridge, pull out a prepackaged raw meal, and scrape it into Tundra's bowl. I crack an egg over the top and set it down in front of him. He starts chomping as though he hasn't eaten in a week. I grab another meal, this one frozen, and stick it in the fridge to thaw for tonight.

Henry is off the phone when I return to my cooled tea. "The lab said he's clean."

"Of course he is. You thought someone was poisoning me through my dog's fur?"

"I needed to rule it out."

"Why can't you just accept that I caught a bug?"

"Because if I accept that, you might end up dead."

I sigh. "You're being ridiculous."

"Someone tried to kill you. Twice. Now you're getting sick. It's not unreasonable for me to suspect poisoning."

"I already told you, I'm only eating the food Musa cooks. You've confirmed Tundra is clean. Hey, maybe your housekeeper is poisoning me through the towels."

Henry gives me the side-eye. "Joke about it all you want, but I'm determined to get to the bottom of this." Musa slides a plate of six over-easy eggs onto the bar in front of him. Nothing else, just six eggs. And the man questions my diet.

"You do that." I climb down from my stool, then startle when Maisie walks in from the foyer. I'm glad to see her, but the jerk in the kitchen is killing my mojo.

"I wasn't expecting you today," I tell her.

She hands me my coffee—a relief, because tea isn't cutting it. "Roberts updated me on your schedule. Besides, I knew you'd want that." She nods at the latte, her hands still full of my box of papers and her bag.

"You're an angel."

I lead the way into the great room as I inhale the aroma of freshly ground beans. But before I can take a sip, Henry snatches the cup out of my hands and gives Maisie a hard look. "What's going on?" I say.

"How often does she bring you a latte?" he asks without taking his eyes off my assistant.

"Every day but the weekend. Why?"

"You told me you weren't eating outside food."

"Well, technically coffee isn't—" Henry shoots me a look, and I swallow my argument. "It didn't cross my mind."

"Where do you get these?" He holds up the offending cup in front of Maisie, who appears frozen in place. I've never seen her eyes so wide before.

"The shop on the corner of Bradley and Eighth. Cafe Lumière," she says. There's a tremble in her voice.

"Do you watch them prepare it?" he asks.

"Not every time, no."

"Henry, what's going on?" I say. "You're freaking her out. Me too, for that matter."

He ignores me. "And the coffee remains in your possession until you hand it over to Her Majesty?"

"That's right, sir."

He pulls out his phone. "Roberts, I'm going to need a team for escort and someone to make a delivery to the lab. Yes, we're inside." He slides the phone back into his pocket. "You can both have a seat."

Maisie follows me to the sofa and sits at the opposite end. Her hands are clenched so tightly in her lap they're turning white. "What's going on?" she asks quietly.

"I have no idea," I say. "But we'll get to the bottom of it."

Henry returns a minute later, followed by several security officers in full uniform. One of them steps over to us and motions for Maisie to stand. "Maisie Gibbons, you are under arrest on suspicion of attempted murder of Her Majesty the Queen."

"What?" she shrieks as they snap a pair of handcuffs onto her wrists. "But I didn't do anything!"

"Henry, what's going on?" I'm on my feet before I've even registered what's happening.

His arms are folded over his chest as he glares at Maisie with unfiltered anger. "She's been poisoning you through your coffee."

"I haven't!" Maisie says, her voice rising in pitch and volume. "I swear to you. I would never do something like that."

"I know her," I say, and place my hand on his arm. It's hot beneath my palm. "She wouldn't do this." Would she?

I study Maisie again, her eyes wide with terror, mascara already running down her face. Her usual polished facade is crumbling. The two officers begin escorting her to the double doors, and she looks at me over her shoulder as they lead her away. "I didn't do it, Celia! You have to believe me. Please tell me you believe me," she yells before the doors close behind them.

I sink back onto the sofa. "There's no way she did it, Henry."

He sits down beside me and takes one of my hands in his. "I don't want to think so either, but we have to make sure."

"She can't even swat a fly. When we worked together at the Historical Society, she bought a live trap on Amazon and made us release them outside. She never knew how many we killed when she wasn't in the room." I'm rambling, but I can't make myself stop. "Once she nearly caused an accident swerving off the road to avoid a woolly worm." I lower my voice until it's just over a whisper. "She wouldn't do this. I have to believe she wouldn't do this."

"I know." His arm slides around my shoulders, and he tugs me against his chest. I feel the pressure of his lips on the top of my head. "It's not like she doesn't have cause, though. Right?" he says quietly.

I jerk my head upright and look at him. "What do you mean, 'cause'?"

Henry sighs. "Just that you two had a falling out, and she was pretty upset that you didn't support her seeing your ex."

My head is spinning. Could that be cause to kill someone? No. It can't be. No matter how mad she was, Maisie would never resort to that. The implication makes my stomach roil.

"If you're wrong about this, she will hate me forever," I say.

"Yeah, but if I'm right, at least you'll be alive."

I'm standing by the window when Henry touches my arm. I turn to find him holding a ceramic mug full of frothy milk.

"Made this one myself," he says. "One hundred percent poison free."

I take it from him, wincing. "Thanks."

He doesn't turn to go, just stands right behind my left shoulder looking out. "I know what you're thinking, but there's no way this is your fault, C."

I blow on the hot coffee. "I should never have responded the way I did. She's had a rough go of it, what with the dating pool these days, and I should have just been happy that she finally found someone good, even if it was Beck."

Henry takes my elbow in his hand, turning me until I meet his gaze. "Don't. No matter how you responded, it doesn't justify murder."

I squeeze my eyes shut, refusing to let my burning tears escape.

"Besides," he says, "your reaction was perfectly reasonable. He shouldn't have made a move on your assistant, for god's sake."

Outside, snow is falling, completely oblivious to the destruction inside. I wonder how many life-altering revelations a person can endure before they just expire from the shock of it all.

"What about the shooting? You can't think Maisie was behind that," I say, taking a sip of my latte.

"At this point, we're ruling nothing out. She could be working with a group of rogue patriots to eliminate you. She would be the perfect inside man."

I frown at my reflection in the glass. That's not something I want to think about. I may never be ready to think about it.

"I do have some good news," Henry says. "The palace renovations are completed in the west wing. You've been cleared to move back in."

My head swivels toward him. "I thought I couldn't move back until the entire palace was secure."

He nods. "Originally, that was what we were thinking. But we expedited a new system that will be completely impenetrable. We'll use it to surround the entire west wing, at least until the rest of the palace is completed. Besides, with Maisie behind bars, I think we can ease up a bit on security. It shouldn't be hard to get her to talk."

My gaze snags on a single snowflake caught on the cold window. Its intricate details are breathtaking, and I wonder at its ability to be so beautiful for such a short period of time. Here one second, gone the next. What would it take to live like that?

"C?" Henry says, touching my arm again. "I thought you'd be happy."

I don't bother trying to look at him. My head feels like it's full of cotton and way too heavy at the same time. I'm happy, aren't I? This particular type of happiness just feels . . . thick.

"I am," I say, and force a smile. *Or at least I will be. Eventually.*

I turn to scan the great room—its stark, modern furniture, cold tile floors, the lack of warmth and life in the whole place. And yet . . . *And yet.*

"I can't wait to go back." This time when I look at Henry, I allow the smile to reach my eyes. "It's time to move on."

Now I just have to convince myself.

28

"Titanium" - David Guetta + Sia

I'M NOT SURE WHAT the acceptable reaction is to finding out your private secretary and friend is not only dating your ex-fiancé, but also trying to poison you, but I'd like to think that mine is normal.

I twist the tap to add more hot water to the tub. I'm on my second glass of wine, and it really does taste better when you're submerged in a bubble bath. Normally I'd be meeting Maisie at this time of the morning, so yes, I'm day drinking. Fortunately, I'm also alone, so no one needs to know.

My phone rings from across the room, but I ignore it. Rosalind has already called me three times this morning, and I've declined every time. I don't have the mental bandwidth to discuss what happens next. All I want right now is to enjoy this gigantic tub before I lose my chance.

I'm moving back. The thought should fill me with joy, but instead all I can think about is how lonely the palace will feel. Bea is going back to Cambridge, Maisie will be behind bars, and Henry—

It doesn't matter where Henry will be, or what he'll be doing. We never had a real possibility of a future anyway, no matter what either of us thought at any point in the past. Timing is clearly not our strong suit, but maybe that's just the universe's way of showing us that it was never meant to be.

At least we won't be parting as bitter enemies. There's a piece of my heart that will always belong to him, no matter how angry he makes me. And I'd like to think a piece of him is mine, too.

I should start packing my things. I could even be gone by this afternoon. But for some reason, the thought has me wanting to sink to the bottom of the tub.

I don't want to leave. I can admit it. *Why* I don't want to is a different beast altogether.

My phone trills again as I'm drying off, and I roll my eyes when Rosalind's name lights up the screen. Once it goes to voicemail, I see that the previous call was not from her but from William. I have no idea what that monster wants with me, but I'm stupid enough to find out.

"Your Majesty," he says.

"I'm returning your call." I squeeze the water from my hair with a towel and try not to clench my jaw.

"I need your help with something," he says.

"What makes you think I'd ever help you?"

The line is quiet for a full thirty seconds. I'm starting to think he's hung up when he finally speaks. "I've been thinking about what you said. About forgiveness and all that."

I toss the towel into the laundry hamper. "I spoke too soon. You don't deserve forgiveness."

"I don't know what you've heard, but I can assure you—"

"I heard that you tried to have me killed."

Anything he might have been about to say evaporates. I can hear his breathing through the phone. It sends chills up my spine.

"Is that what he told you?" he says.

"He said you had me thrown from that horse."

An abrupt laugh cracks through the tension. "Let me guess—Henry fed you a story about how I was behind everything. You should know that he isn't always the most reliable narrator. I assume you've discovered that for yourself by now."

My heart kicks up a notch. What is he saying? That Henry can't be trusted? That the story was all a fabrication?

"He was so upset by the accident, he convinced himself it was my fault, that I was out to keep the two of you apart. I'll be the first to admit that I wasn't a good father, but I would never try to hurt you, Celia. You have to believe me."

I want to retort that I don't have to do anything, but something holds me back. In all the years I've known William, I've never known him to be violent, and I've certainly never heard him threaten to kill someone.

"You were right, about needing to make amends." He pauses a few more beats. "I'm ready to apologize to my son."

Later that same day, the nausea I'm experiencing has more to do with the butterflies in my stomach than the poison slowly ebbing from my body. My phone call with William is certainly to blame for most of it.

He said it was all a big misunderstanding, that because of the things he did to Henry when he was little, Henry decided he was a monster who destroys everything. It makes sense, I guess. I'm just tired of having to determine whether someone is telling the truth or not. When did honesty become so worthless?

The lift doors open, and William steps into the penthouse. He bows stiffly when he sees me, and I marvel again at the absurdity of our situation. Six months ago, I would have been bowing to him.

He glances around the foyer, but it's impossible to read his expression. Given the animosity between them, I can't imagine he's ever been inside Henry's home before, but stranger things have happened.

The security officer I asked Roberts to station inside the doors meets my eyes. I nod to let him know I'm good.

"Come in," I say, hoping Henry doesn't throw me out on my ass for playing hostess again. More than likely it would be on account of this particular guest, which is why we need a solid plan for approaching him with all of this.

"Is he here?" William asks as we make our way into the flat.

"He left," I say, "and I don't know how soon he'll be back. I thought we could meet in the library, just in case." Henry will need time to come around to the idea of talking to his father. Having him walk in on us in the great room would probably not be the best way to introduce it.

Tundra bounds around the corner at the sound of voices. He offers the duke a panting smile and a paw. William smiles and shakes it. "How you doing, big boy? You remember me?"

Tundra wags his tail and strokes William's leg, begging for more. William straightens, pulls a foil-wrapped box from under his arm, and thrusts it at me. "Here. As a thank you for helping me."

I take it from him. This is the second time he's given me a gift as a token of appreciation. The man at least knows how to say thank you, even if he has trouble with "I'm sorry."

"They're truffles," he says.

"Thank you." I place them on the kitchen counter. "That was thoughtful of you."

We enter the library, Tundra pushing his way into the room first. I hope Henry will forgive us for ganging up on him like this. William waits for me to sit before taking the seat across from me on the sofa.

Neither of us says anything for a bit. He rubs his hands together and lets them hang between his knees. "Do you think he'll do it?" he says finally. "Hear me out?"

I study him for a moment. His face is lined, and I wonder if that's the result of the job, if my own skin will be as wrinkled and leathery as his is thirty years from now.

"I really don't know."

He nods as if that's understandable.

"He told me, you know. About when he was young," I say.

William's head snaps up. He watches me like a wild animal stalking its prey, deciding on the best way to attack. Then his expression clears, and he says, "I assumed as much."

"I'm not going to pretend to have sympathy for your situation," I say.

He rubs his hand over his closely cropped hair, so short he's almost bald. "Didn't expect you to."

"I don't understand how a person can do that to a child—any child, but especially their own. I appreciate your kindness in giving me Tundra"—the dog's head lifts from my lap as he looks up at me expectantly—"but I want to be clear that I'm doing this because I care about Henry, not because I want to help you."

William nods again, his gaze locked on the carpet. "Understood."

"Great," I say, smoothing my dress over my legs. "Now let's talk about the best way to approach this."

William and I have discussed a few ideas but have yet to land on one that I think his son will be receptive to when I hear Henry calling my name. Bloody hell. It's too soon.

Tundra hears him too and bolts toward the door, knocking a tall vase from the coffee table in his haste. It shatters on the floor.

"Tundra!" I say, more exasperated at myself for getting myself into this situation than at my dog. William helps me pick up the biggest shards.

Tundra barks at the door as if commanding it to open. Several seconds later, it does, revealing Henry in the doorway. Tundra jumps up on him, and Henry doesn't push him down, just places his hand on the dog's head as he takes in the sight of William and me on the floor picking up ceramic pieces.

"What. The. Fuck. Is going on here?" he says, poison lacing his words.

"Tundra knocked over a vase," I say. "Don't worry. I'll replace it."

Henry walks over and takes my arm, hauling me to my feet. From the other side of the coffee table, William rises as well. The two men eye each other, one with venom, the other with despair.

"Henry," I say. "Please hear him out."

He tears his gaze from his father to look down at me. "What is he doing here?"

This wasn't how I planned for us to do this. I was going to ask Musa to prepare a nice dinner, or we could have hired a mediator. Anything but this.

"He wants to apologize," I say. There's no use in pretending otherwise.

"Get out," Henry hisses at his father. "Now."

William holds his hands up, palms out. "She's right. I have some things to say."

Henry's jaw flexes, and I squirm under his tight grip. He releases my arm. "There is nothing you could say that I want to hear."

If William is surprised by the hatred in his son's voice and body language, he doesn't show it. Instead, he just looks like a sad father who has missed his only chance to make up the past to his child.

"Can't you just listen to him?" I say.

Henry keeps his eyes locked on William but shakes his head. "The man uses words as weapons to further his own agenda. Anything he told you was a lie."

The duke looks at me, resignation pulling his eyes down at the corners. He shrugs, and I know he's giving up, but I'm not.

"He's sorry for what he did," I try again. "If you would just listen to him—"

"Out. Now." Henry points to the door, his eyes narrowed and dangerous as they stay fixed on his father. "Or I will have you thrown from the terrace." His tone is dead serious.

I can't stifle the small gasp that flies out of my mouth.

William looks at each of us in turn, then nods and slowly walks to the door, disappointment tugging at his shoulders. He may be accepting this, but I will do what I can to heal this rift between them.

Henry marches out after him, probably to make sure he actually leaves. Tundra has disappeared, evidently not interested in listening to the humans argue.

I wave a hand in front of my face to fan it, my blood pumping hot and strong. How could he not even give William a chance? That man is his flesh and blood. He deserves five minutes at the very least. I stalk out of the library, intent on giving Henry my own few cents.

We collide in the foyer. "Omph," I say, clutching my aching nose, which has just met the brick wall of Henry's chest.

"Shit, I'm sorry." He grabs my shoulders and holds me away from himself. "Are you okay?"

I nod, still holding my nose. "I will be." I blink away the tears that formed upon impact and drop my hand. "I can't believe you threw him out like that."

"You have got to be kidding me. I told you I don't want him anywhere near you."

"He only wanted to apologize." My voice is raised, and I know the officer near the door can hear us, but I don't care. I've had enough of Henry's two-faced duplicity. "What will it take for you to forgive him?"

Anger simmers beneath the surface of his skin, a lightning bolt ready to strike. "That depends. What will it take for you to forgive me?"

I flinch and take a small step backward. "That's not fair. Nor relevant."

"You're right. Because my father is a lying, manipulating mastermind, whereas everything I told you was the truth."

"Has it ever occurred to you that maybe he's changed?"

Henry throws back his head and laughs, but it's devoid of humor. "My father is as likely to change as Tundra is to turn into a cat."

"You won't even give him a chance." I don't know why I'm defending William so strongly, except I can't help but feel like Henry's anger toward him is unreasonable, even considering what he did.

"You don't know him like I do." He leans down, and I can see the gold flecks in his eyes. "Whatever persona he showed you—contrite, apologetic old man or whatever—was just a ruse. He's playing you, Celia. That's what he does."

"And what if you're wrong?"

Henry scoffs, his eyebrows flicking upward. "I'm not."

"I know he did awful things—"

"You don't know the half of it."

I throw up my hands. "Then tell me."

"I can't." He shakes his head. "If you would just trust me, we wouldn't even be having this conversation."

"How do you expect me to trust you when you won't even tell me the truth? If you'd told me why I can't trust him earlier, I probably wouldn't have let him in."

"If I had told you, you'd likely be dead already."

I cross my arms over my chest, his words chilling me more than I'd like to admit. "If he's trying to kill me too, why didn't he come in with an assault rifle, or at least a coil of rope?"

Henry shuts his eyes as if he's trying to block out my words. "He's dangerous, C. That's all I'm going to say."

"I'm not listening to this anymore. Come on, Tundra. Let's go to bed." I march toward my bedroom but don't hear that unmistakable click of claws on tile. "Tundra! Come, boy."

He doesn't come. I go into the kitchen just as Henry enters from the other side. Tundra is lying on the floor—apparently he's decided the tile in here is as good a place as any for a nap. I kneel down and shake him gently. "Come on, boy. Wake up."

He doesn't stir.

"Tundra," I say, panic lacing my words. "Wake up, boy."

Henry kneels on the other side and lifts his head. "Hey, buddy. What's going on?"

Tundra remains motionless.

"Oh my god, Henry. Is he dead?" The last word comes out on a sob.

He puts his face near Tundra's. "He's still breathing, but something's wrong. We need to take him in." He pulls his phone out and calls Roberts.

A few minutes later, Tundra is being lifted by several PPOs and carried from the kitchen. "Let's go," Henry says, wrapping his arm around my shoulders. "You can sit with him in the car."

I glance down at the spot where Tundra was just lying. Crumpled beneath him is the truffle box. There are only a few pieces left.

A shaky wail tears out of me. "He was eating chocolate." I thrust the box at Henry.

"They'll be able to help him—don't worry." He tucks the box under his arm and leads me to the door.

The ride to the animal hospital is quiet, Tundra in the back seat between Henry and me, his head on my lap. I stroke the soft fur between his eyes and assure him that he's going to be okay, even though all I can hear is William's voice telling me chocolate is poisonous to dogs.

Once we reach the clinic, I try to explain to the assistant about the chocolate, but my words get lost in my sobs. Henry keeps one arm wrapped around me while he explains what happened. He hands over the nearly empty box of truffles.

"This is what he got into?" the assistant asks.

Henry nods and leads me to the private waiting room we're directed to.

Once the door is shut, I whirl on him. "This is all your fault! If you hadn't insisted on arguing about your father, Tundra would have been in my room and never have gotten into those truffles."

"You think I haven't been thinking the same thing?" Henry sighs and sinks into one of the vinyl-clad chairs. "I'm so sorry, C."

I cover my face with my hands, but it doesn't stop the tears from falling. "He's all I have. I can't lose him."

"You're not going to lose him, baby."

"How do you know?"

"I don't think he had a lethal dose of chocolate."

"How much is lethal? I thought they couldn't have any."

"They can get sick, but a dog Tundra's size would need to eat a lot of it for it to be fatal," he says.

The thought eases the anguish in my heart a little. "So you think he'll make it?"

"Yeah, I'm pretty sure. Come sit." Henry pulls me toward the chair beside him. I sink into it and don't even resist when he pulls my head onto his shoulder.

I wake when the veterinarian walks into the room. He's an older man, graying hair at his temples, tired eyes, but a kind smile.

"Good evening, Your Majesty. I'm Dr. Ron."

I shake the hand he extends. "How is he?" I say. "How's Tundra?"

"I'm afraid he's not good." The doctor's eyes flit to Henry, and I sense them having a private conversation that I don't understand.

"But he's going to be okay, isn't he?"

"We're administering a few different medications. All we can do is continue monitoring him to see how he responds to them. Can you tell me exactly how much chocolate he ingested?"

"The box was full. Maybe around a dozen truffles?"

Dr. Ron's bushy brows draw together, and he looks back at Henry. They share a weird moment of telepathy again.

"I'll be right back," Henry says into my ear. "Stay here."

I don't even have the mental strength to argue that I should be in on any conversation that involves my dog. When they're gone, I start to pace the room. It's small, and it only takes me three lengths to reach the other side.

My arms have become insanely itchy. I scratch them through my sweater. I'm also cold, but I have no desire to put my coat back on. Doing so feels disloyal to Tundra, like I'm going to leave without him or something.

After several minutes, the door opens. I turn midpace, expecting Henry, but it's two PPOs. Seeing them is not much comfort, and I don't greet either of them. I don't have the energy to decide what is proper.

It takes Henry another fifteen minutes to return, and by this point, I have started biting my nails, a nonhabit Rosalind stopped in its tracks when I was six with this awful bite-aversion nail polish. I can feel tiny balls forming on the sleeves of my sweater from my incessant rubbing.

Henry quietly says something to the PPOs, then crosses the room to me. I all but collapse into his arms.

"Where is he? Can I see him?" A series of tiny tremors join forces to shake my entire body.

"Yes, but they want to keep him overnight for monitoring."

Relief surges through my body. That means there's a chance he'll be okay. "That's fine. I don't mind staying."

"You're not staying here, C."

"He's my dog, Henry. I'm not leaving without him."

"And as head of your security, I say it's not safe for you to stay here."

I glare at him through my tears, but I already know it's useless to argue. "I want to see him."

Henry leads me to the examining room, which is occupied by several people in blue scrubs. Tundra is lying on the table, a tube snaking away from his body from a wrapped section of his leg. His breathing is shallow, and I have to put my face right up to his to feel it.

"Is he in pain?" I rasp.

"We're keeping him sedated for now so he can rest," Dr. Ron tells me. "We'll know more in the morning."

"Surely you've treated dogs who've eaten chocolate before," I say, fresh tears squeezing from my eyes every time I blink.

The doctor looks at Henry again, but Henry's stationed himself directly behind me, and I can't see his face. He leans forward and says quietly, "We'll talk about that later. Right now, you need to say goodbye so we can head back home."

I bury my face in Tundra's fur, not even caring who sees me cry. This dog has my heart and is everything good in the world. What's the point in getting up in the morning if he's not there to greet me?

"Don't leave me, boy," I whisper. "You're too special. I love you, and I need you to get better." My fingers stay buried in the black ruff at Tundra's neck, my vision growing blurry from my tears. I think about all of the memories we haven't even had the chance to make yet—hiking trails in the national forests, riding through the streets of the city on King Frederick's Day in an open carriage, movie nights curled up on the sofa sans Henry and Beatrice and anyone else who might try to steal him from me.

He's my dog, and while he may have shown partiality to others at times, I know that deep down he knows he belongs to me. He trusts me to make the best decision for him. But why should he? Despite what I said to Henry earlier, it's my fault he's here.

"I never should have left those truffles out where he could grab them."

"You can't beat yourself up over that," Henry says, his warm hands stroking my back.

"But I should have been watching him," I say. "While he lay suffering on the floor, I was arguing with you over stupid things. He lay there, wondering why I wasn't coming, why I wasn't helping him. I let him down." My voice chokes on a sob.

Henry's strong arms wrap around me from behind, holding me tightly against his chest while I cry. Somehow he manages to turn me around to face him without letting go, and I bury my face into his shirt, which smells so good.

"If I had returned to the palace today like I should've, this wouldn't have happened," I say.

"Shhh," he murmurs into my hair. "You can't blame yourself. You couldn't have known. Besides, he's going to be okay. We just have to trust his doctors."

Our ride back to the penthouse is silent save for the sound the wheels make on the slick road. Sometime during the night it started raining, and if the temperatures were any lower, we'd be traveling on a sheet of ice right now.

I watch the droplets on the window race against one another. Henry is sitting beside me, maybe holding his own race on the other window.

We left Tundra at the vet after they assured me multiple times they'll keep me updated regularly, and if anything changes, they'll call right away. There's nothing else I can do.

"There's something I need to tell you." Henry's voice matches the low rumble of the car engine.

I turn toward him but don't say anything.

"The vet said Tundra didn't consume enough chocolate for it to be fatal. Toxic, yes, but their medications should have helped if that's all it was."

I take a minute to let this sink in. "So it wasn't the truffles after all?"

"That's what we're going to find out."

29

"River" - Joni Mitchell

I**T'S BEEN A DAY** and a half since we took Tundra in, and I just got off the phone with the vet. They said he's fighting like a champ, and as soon as they can figure out what's wrong, they can get him the right medication. Until then, they're doing everything they can.

I've never felt so frustrated before. My hands are tied—there's literally nothing I can do, and it's killing me.

Henry finds me on the terrace, facing the city. "What are you doing out here? It's freezing."

I shrug. I didn't even notice.

"God, Celia. You're going to end up killing yourself before anyone else can." He slips through the sliding doors again and comes back a few minutes later with an armload of blankets and a mug of tea. He hands me the cup, then wraps the blankets around me, tucking the ends under my legs.

"Thanks," I murmur, taking a sip of the hot liquid.

He continues moving around the terrace. After a few minutes, I realize he's starting a fire in the portable fire pit. He scoots it closer to the sofa I'm sitting on. The blaze is warm, and the heat seeps into my bones.

The terrace is huge and stretches the whole length of the penthouse, wrapping around the side of the master bedroom as well. The farthest end has a pool and hot tub, but it's been too cold during my stay to use either. There are cozy groupings of outdoor furniture scattered across the rest of the space.

It's the one spot in the entire flat where memories of Tundra can't haunt me.

Henry sits down next to me on the white sofa. "We need to talk about what happened."

"I'm not ready."

"It's important."

"I said I don't want to." I pull my legs under me a little tighter.

"I got the lab results back on the chocolate."

I swing my gaze to Henry for the first time. "What did they find?"

"As we suspected, he didn't ingest enough chocolate to have that kind of effect on a dog Tundra's size. Something was added to the truffles."

"You think your father tried to poison me?"

Henry doesn't say anything, just stares at the smooth cement floor, his arms resting on his knees. He hands me a sheaf of stapled papers, and my vision blurs as I stare at the words. I hand it back. "I don't know what any of this means."

"There were high amounts of thallium in those truffles."

"Thallium," I repeat.

"It's a tasteless chemical that—"

"I know what it is." I watch a pair of birds swoop across the bright sky like a set of dancers at the ballet. "And you think William was trying to kill me with truffles." It sounds like the plot of one of those cozy mysteries Henry's mum likes to read.

There's a lengthy pause, long enough to answer my question. "There is no way that much thallium could have gotten in there accidentally," Henry says.

"Why would William want me dead? He's the one who *gave* Tundra to me." Just saying his name out loud causes moisture to leak from the corners of my eyes. I miss him more than I thought possible.

"Trust me, it'll be a reason only he understands. The man's a psychopath."

"So this means Maisie is innocent, right?" My voice is the size of a mouse.

"She's already been released."

I shake my head, and hair falls into my face. I don't bother pushing it back. "So then why was I sick?"

"We're still working on getting to the bottom of that. It would be good if we could run a blood panel. I know you were nauseous, but did you have any other symptoms that might have been from the thallium?"

I lean forward and rest my face in my palms while Henry strokes my back through my blanket cocoon. My eyelids are gummy and swollen. I used to pride myself on being a good judge of character, but my track record of late has been anything but stellar.

"Insomnia," I say, trying to remember the past few weeks, but all I can see is Tundra lying on that table. "I remember my feet hurting some."

William tried to kill me. He almost killed Tundra. I try to let that sink in, but it just sits on the surface of my skin like oil. He pretended to want my help reconciling with Henry, gave me a bloody dog, even talked his way into my safe house. Henry was right all along—I shouldn't have trusted him.

I trusted the wrong guy, and my dog nearly died because of it.

"We need to leave." Henry's voice is soft, as though he's afraid of breaking my fragile shell.

"And go where?"

"Somewhere he can't find you."

I wipe my nose with the sleeve of my sweater. "I'm not going back to that cabin."

He shakes his head. "I meant out of the country."

"I'm not leaving Tundra." Henry's a fool if he thinks I'll consider that for a single second.

"There's nothing you can do for him here," he says, his eyes on me. "The vet has the lab results, and now that they know it's thallium in his system, they can administer the proper medications. He's going to recover, C."

I pick at the threads of the blanket in my lap. "I can't leave him."

Henry sighs. "If you don't, you might not be alive to greet him when he gets out of the hospital."

"You actually want me to leave the country? For how long?" My voice is following my panic higher and higher.

"Just until we can catch him."

"How long will that take?"

He sighs and runs his fingers through his hair. "I don't know, C. Hopefully not long."

I watch the city below us through a haze of tears. I can't see them, but I can imagine everyone bustling in and out of the shops, buying last minute Christmas gifts and bottles of wine for their holiday parties. I can almost hear the music jingling from the speakers and smell the gingerbread wafting from the bakeries. There's probably a Santa Claus on every street corner wishing everyone a happy holiday.

"I can't leave," I say. "Not now."

"C, he knows where you are. He's already breached the security once."

Henry doesn't mention that I also let him inside.

"My image is in shambles, Henry. If I leave Wesbourne now, I will lose all credibility as queen."

He pulls my hand between both his own, allowing his warmth to slowly leak into it. "I know. But at least you wouldn't be losing your life."

I feel the magnetic pull of his gaze. "And you can promise that?"

His fingers tighten around mine, and he's silent for a minute. Finally, he says, "I promise that I will do everything in my power to keep you safe."

My heart lurches at the look in his eyes. "I'll think about it," I say quietly.

I expect him to tell me I don't have a choice, that my security is in his hands, not my own, but he doesn't. He simply stands, gives me a sad smile, and says, "Don't stay out long. You'll get too cold." He goes back into the penthouse, closing the glass doors behind him.

I don't know if I'll ever be warm again.

Bea joins me an hour later, wearing a long down-filled coat and a pom-pom beanie. She nestles in beside me on the sofa, stealing some of my blankets to cover her legs.

"Did Henry send you?" I say.

"Why would you think that?"

"Because you're outside, and it's not bathing suit weather."

She came to the penthouse after hearing about Tundra, although I've done my best to avoid her, and everyone else, since.

Sniffing, she takes a drink from the cup in her hands. My own tea is long gone. "Fine. He may have mentioned that you were still out here and that he was concerned."

"Figures."

"He's trying to protect you, you know."

Behind her, the Christmas tree is lit up in the window, the sky already darkening around us. I imagine throwing it over the edge of the terrace railing. I study Bea for a few seconds before returning my gaze to the fire.

"I heard him playing the piano last night at 2 a.m.," she says.

"What's your point, Bea?"

"Just that you might find comfort in finally trusting someone else."

A dangerous fantasy to allow myself. "I'm fine."

"Your lips are blue."

"I deserve to suffer, and to do it alone."

She rests a mitten-clad hand on my leg. "You can't blame yourself for what happened."

"Why not?" I say. "It's my fault."

"Of course it's not. You couldn't have known the duke would do something like that."

I hold my feet up to catch more heat from the blaze. "Except that Henry warned me to stay far away from his father, and instead of listening to him, *I let the man inside*." If Tundra doesn't make it, I'll never forgive myself.

Bea sighs and holds her hands out over the flames. "And you're planning to punish yourself by staying where he can get to you."

I open my mouth to speak but close it again. I twist the blanket through my fingers, knotting and bunching it up.

"You'd seriously do that to us?" she says.

I look at her. Her mouth is set in a firm line.

"I know you don't want to believe this right now," she continues, "but there are a lot of people who care about you. This country needs you. The people miss you, but they also want you to be safe." She brushes a few loose curls out of her face. "Besides, if you die, I'd become queen—and trust me, that's a disaster no one is prepared for."

I finally find my voice again, even though it's hardly more than a whisper. "Tundra nearly died because I didn't want to risk trusting Henry." It's one thing to gamble with my own life. But now I'll always have to live with the reminder that what happened was my fault.

"Better late than never," Bea says.

"I don't deserve to have him watching out for me."

Her laugh tinkles through the air like bells. "I'm not sure if you've noticed, but that hasn't stopped him yet."

"What if he hurts me again?" I study my blanket-covered lap, wishing the answers lay somewhere in the folds.

From the corner of my eye, I see her nod. "He probably will, because that's what people do. But will it hurt any less to push him away?"

I consider her words. If I walk away from Henry now, something tells me it will be for the last time. I'm being handed my third chance, and if I refuse it, it's over for us. "Maybe you're right," I say.

"Don't be ridiculous." Bea smiles. "I'm always right."

Henry is pacing outside the kitchen when Bea and I get inside. The air is so warm I nearly choke on it. He looks up, apprehension evident in every feature.

"Finally," he says as we walk through the great room.

Bea tugs the hat from her head and tosses her blonde curls. "Mission accomplished." She throws him a wink, then heads for her bedroom.

Henry looks at me, his eyes searching my face for answers. "Is she right?"

I dump my load of blankets onto the sofa and step closer to him. My hands are trembling. I don't know if it's from the sudden change in temperature or from the adrenaline pumping through my bloodstream.

Stopping right in front of him, I look up to meet his gaze and place both hands on his chest. His heart is beating as hard as mine is. I lick my lips. "I'm ready."

30

"Earned It" - The Weeknd

PLACING MY FUTURE IN Henry's hands set off a flurry of activity in the penthouse. Daphne was brought to the flat to pack my bags, PPOs bustle around receiving instructions from Henry, and somewhere, a plane is being prepped for us.

In the midst of this carefully orchestrated chaos, Maisie walks in, a look of bewilderment on her face. I'm in the great room, doing my best to stay out of everyone's way, when I spot her. We haven't spoken since Henry had her arrested. I motion her inside while my heart somersaults through my chest. This could very well be the thing that ends our friendship, and if it is, I can't blame her.

"How are you?" I say when she's close enough to hear me over the hubbub.

She nods and throws her arms around my neck. "It was awful. So bloody awful."

"I am so sorry," I say, returning her embrace.

She pulls back and sniffs. "Those cells really need some Lysol. I could still smell the previous occupant, and they told me no one had used it for over two months."

"I hope you know I never—"

She cuts me off with a wave of her hand. "I know. Things have been crazy. No hard feelings." Relief crashes through me. She looks around at the bags being hauled to the door. "Where are we going?"

Henry has allowed me one last visit with Tundra before we leave the country. He's still sedated, but just feeling his heartbeat under all that fur was the reassurance I needed to know that I'm doing the right thing.

Henry and I are flying in a private jet. We haven't been alone since I told him I was ready, and I don't think he picked up on my double meaning. Yes, I'm ready to leave Wesbourne for wherever he wants to take me, but I'm also ready to trust him with my heart.

He was right about William, he was right about the memorial service, and he's put his own life on the line to protect me more than once. If I can't trust him, I can't trust anyone. And in my position, that's not a place I can afford to be.

In spite of everything he's done, I still love him. I will always love him. Unhealthy as it may be, you can't choose who you fall for. And like it or not, my wagon is hitched to that incredibly distracting man now sitting just a few feet away from me.

I watch him from the opposite side of the plane, immersed in papers, sexy nerd glasses on. He's completely oblivious to me. I hope that doesn't mean we've lost our chance forever. For all I know, he's moved on in the time it took for me to get my bearings. But if he really loved me for as long as he said he did, I'm under no illusion that he can turn it off that quickly. I'll simply have to remind him.

Maisie is sitting in the seat across from me, prattling on about her new project: researching laws and regulations concerning Wesbourne's jails and prisons. I tuned her out about five minutes ago, not because it isn't important, but because I have a million other things on my mind, not the least of which is the man across the aisle from us.

I haven't even bothered to ask where we're going. It doesn't really matter. I know that Henry will make sure we arrive safely and that nothing happens to me there. I should've listened to the advice to trust him sooner. It really is quite freeing.

As though he can feel my gaze on him, he flicks his eyes toward me, but when he finds me already looking at him, he relaxes and gives me a secret smile before turning back to the report in his hand. The heat in that look tears through me and sets my heart racing. I feel like I'm back in school and just made eye contact with my crush.

Henry shifts in his seat, then reaches up and loosens his tie. His long, slender fingers unbutton the top button of his shirt, then slip inside the collar to loosen it as well. If not for his slow, controlled movements, I would think nothing of it. But the motions are too deliberate, too calculated, to be anything other than a tease.

If that's the way he wants to play it . . .

I slowly bend over and slip off both my heels, leaving my stockinged feet free to stretch and curl. I keep my eyes on Maisie, who is still going on about prisoners deserving clean cells, but I can feel Henry's dark eyes burning in my direction. I cross one leg over the other, knowing it will encourage my dress to slide up a few more inches. Then I luxuriously stretch my arms overhead and arch my back.

From my peripheral vision, I see him dig his fingers into his hair. I have to bite back a smile. *Two can play this game.* I shrug the cardigan sweater I'm wearing off my shoulders and rub a hand over my bare shoulder. I don't dare look at him, but I imagine sweat breaking out on his skin. Sliding a hand up my neck, I pretend to work out a particularly difficult knot—

"Are you even listening to me?" Maisie's voice jolts me back to reality, reminding me that Henry and I are not alone on this jet.

I quickly drop my hand back to my lap. "Of course," I say. "You want to launch an initiative to clean up the prisons."

She frowns but continues without even catching her breath. I chance a glance at Henry. He has returned to his paperwork, but a devilish grin has taken over his face.

It's still dark when we land, and it takes me several minutes to identify the private flight sector of Heathrow. I shouldn't be too surprised that this is what Henry chose. Outside of Wesbourne, he has the most connections in London.

We disembark, and soon I'm settled into a black town car. After a brief drive, we pull up to a curb, and even in the dark, I recognize the Lanesborough hotel. My heart isn't sure what to do with this information. Some of the best memories of my life happened here, but so did some of the worst.

Henry hasn't told me his plans, and he left in one of the earlier cars, probably to get security set up before I arrive. According to Maisie, some celebrity from the US has booked the royal suite, so at least I won't have to sleep in the same bed where Henry made love to me, then proceeded to break my heart.

The suite I end up in is decorated in soothing blues and greens, with an exquisite Christmas tree in the corner of the living room. I don't realize how tired I am until I catch sight of the massive four-poster bed in the master bedroom.

After unpacking my bags, Maisie and Daphne each retire to their own rooms, and I can finally get ready for sleep. I'm slipping out of my cardigan when a low voice behind me says, "I've been waiting for you to do that since the plane."

A dash of heat climbs my spine, and I turn to see Henry leaning against the door frame, sexy smile in place. The longer he looks at me, the more jellified my muscles become. I want him, more than I've ever wanted anything.

He must read the desire on my face, because he moves into the room, but slowly, like he's testing the risk of me bolting. My heart pounds louder with every step he takes, a bloody snare drum announcing to the entire world what this man does to me.

When he's a few feet away, he stops and pulls his tie from around his neck. "You were a little vixen on the plane." His voice is like sandpaper on my sensitive skin. He tosses the tie onto the floor.

"What does that make you?" I ask. "Magic Mike?"

A grin stretches across his face. He hums in amusement, but it's more of a rumble. "It's been nineteen days since I've given you an orgasm."

I swallow loudly. "You're counting?"

Instead of answering, he closes the distance between us and grabs me. I gasp from the sheer pleasure of having his hands on me again. He leads me backward and pins me against the wall, then kisses me hungrily, like I'm his last meal.

The movement of his tongue isn't slow and romantic, but urgent and desperate. The same overpowering need is consuming us both. He tastes of spearmint and Henry and desire. As he presses against me, I can feel how badly he wants this, how badly he wants me.

He breaks off to kiss his way down my jawline and neck. "You want this, right? It's not just me?"

I suck air into my lungs as he nibbles my ear. "I love you. I've always loved you."

"Except for when you planned to marry fucking Harrison," he mutters.

I roll my eyes, then gasp as he bites my neck. "Don't start."

"And this isn't just a ruse to get information out of me?" He cocks a brow as he looks down at me.

I manage what I hope is a coy look. "Would it work?"

He growls and leans down to my neck again. "Probably."

"I don't need to know anything you don't want to tell me."

It's not until the words are leaving my mouth that I realize just how true they are. I'm content to wait until he's ready to tell me about his father and all of the other things he's keeping from me. It's all for my safety anyway.

I drag him back so that he's looking at me and place a hand over his heart. "I trust you."

His face melts into a welcoming sweetness before he returns his mouth to mine. His groan fills the room, and he presses into me even further. I curl my fingers into his hair, tugging on it and causing him to moan each time.

"Baby, I've been waiting so long," he says into my ear. "I can't wait to see how wet you are for me."

I gasp as a shiver runs down my spine. "Pretty sure my panties were already soaked on the plane."

"Fuck," he moans against my mouth. In a flurry of movement, he pulls up my dress. He stabilizes me with one hand while the other pushes aside the crotch of my damp underwear. "God," he whispers. "You weren't kidding." He slips in two fingers, both satisfying and increasing the ache inside me.

Pressing me against the wall for leverage, he hoists one of my legs up, giving him better access and a deeper angle. I hold back a cry as he strokes my core and uses his thumb to rub circles over my clit. I open my eyes to find his heavy, sensual gaze on me as he watches me come undone by his hands.

"You are so beautiful," he whispers into my hair.

He wraps my leg around his waist and pumps his fingers even harder. My body clenches around them, and the hot ball of need in me expands even further.

"Undo my pants, baby," Henry says.

I comply with shaking hands. I manage to get his trousers and boxers pulled down and his very eager erection freed. I stroke it with both hands, coaxing moans from his lips. "Oh god, keep doing that and this will all be over way too soon."

I smile and rub circles around his tip, and he hisses through his teeth. "Condom."

I reach for the wallet I know he keeps in his back pocket and fish one of the foil packets from it. I'm happy to note they have been in there long enough to have become slightly crinkled, but not so long they've expired. He wasn't lying about me being the last woman he's been with.

His hand is still busy stroking my core, bringing me to the precipice of a bliss so good I'm scared to tumble over it. Working together, we manage to get the condom on. Shield firmly in place, he turns back to me with a dark gaze that swirls my stomach in circles.

"I want to fuck you so badly."

I whimper against his mouth, no longer capable of stringing together sentences.

He slowly slides his fingers out of me, and I whine at the loss of him. But before I can mourn it too long, he drags my underwear down to the floor, then grabs me with both hands and lifts. I wrap my legs around him, and he slowly lowers me onto himself inch by inch.

The feeling is so incredible that I couldn't hold back my cry if I wanted to. Once he's fully planted inside of me, his eyes nearly roll back into his head. I shift against him, trying to find friction, but he holds me in place against him.

"Just give me a second to enjoy this," he says breathlessly.

After what feels like an eternity, he starts walking toward the bed. This creates a whole new world of sensations, and I moan, my head thrown back like I'm starring in a porn movie. He chuckles appreciatively and nibbles his way up my neck.

Once we reach the bed, he gently lowers me onto it without losing an inch of space inside. I am dying for more of him. He scoots me up until I'm resting on the pillows. He pushes himself up on his hands so there's a big gap between our bodies down to the seam of connection.

The angle here is incredible. He pulls back until I'm afraid I'll lose him entirely, but then he plunges home, and this time it's my eyes that roll back in my head. He grins wolfishly and does it again. I want to stroke his chest so badly, but my hands are too busy clutching the sheets.

Henry slams into me again and again, stoking the fire into a raging blaze that will consume us both soon. Supporting himself on one hand, he reaches down with the other to massage my clit. I cry out again, and he continues rubbing circles until I'm a blubbering mess.

Seconds later, a volcano of an orgasm tears through me, causing his to start as well. He falls on top of me, no longer able to hold it back. When it's over, we lie there panting as though we've just run a marathon.

He pushes up onto his arms and looks down at me with a sweet smile. My heart jumps and does a pirouette in the air. This man loves me. I hush the niggling doubt that tries to weasel its way to the surface.

I stroke my fingers lazily up and down his chest. "I missed the feel of your skin," I say.

"Feel me up, baby."

I eagerly devour his bare body with my hands. He swoops them up a few seconds later, pinning my wrists above my head with his own hand while the other gently kneads my breast.

"My turn," he growls.

"That's not fair. You get a longer turn."

"Of course it's fair. I'm in charge."

"Why do you get to be in charge?" I give him a pout.

"Because me in charge turns you on."

I can't argue with that. Allowing him to lead is the biggest aphrodisiac. I squirm beneath him as he licks and sucks on my nipple.

"Hold still," he admonishes, before resuming.

Several orgasms later, we're still lying on the bed, my head on his chest as he gently runs his fingers through my hair. Sunlight streams through the curtains and gives the whole thing a dreamy quality.

I can barely keep my eyes open, but I manage to say, "I wanna get one."

His hands continue stroking my hair. "One what?"

"A tattoo."

His fingers halt where they've become entwined in my strands. "Words I never thought I'd hear from your mouth."

"You have one marking you as mine. I want to be marked as yours."

The breath rushes past his lips. "Fuck, Celia."

"Where should I put it?" I peer up at him and blink slowly, more from exhaustion than an attempt at flirting.

"Where should you— God, baby. I'm not choosing a spot for you to brand yourself."

"Why not? You've branded me with your mouth often enough."

"That was different. Temporary," he growls.

I draw lazy circles on his chest, tracing his tattoos. "Please? Where do you want to be reminded that I belong to you, body and soul?"

He groans and tightens his fingers in my hair. "My first pick is that spot behind your ear." As though I need reminding of its location, he nuzzles it. "But that's too public. You have an appearance to keep up."

"Appearances be damned. I'll get one there if that's what you want."

He shakes his head and slides down next to me. "I have something much more private in mind."

My muscles turn to jelly as he begins exploring my body like it's a treasure map. Finally, his mouth settles on the sensitive spot by my right hip bone. He gives it a gentle bite, and I start to unravel once again.

"Right here," he says, switching to a caress. "This is where you can proclaim yourself mine."

31

"What Else Is There?" - Röyksopp

WE'VE BEEN IN LONDON for just over a day, and I've had more orgasms in the past twenty-four hours than in the entire previous year. Is this what I have to look forward to for the rest of my life? No one should be this lucky.

I smile as I run the washcloth over my body, remembering Henry's hands and mouth doing the same thing. He was gone when I woke up this morning, but he texted to let me know he was just on a run. I check my phone again when I get out to see if he responded to my reply that I'd be in the shower if he wanted to join me.

There are no new notifications, but the lock screen is a picture of Tundra and me, reminding me of how close I came to losing everything. London is a bubble, but it can only protect me from reality for so long.

I'm just hanging up my towel and reaching for my clothes when the bathroom door opens and a deliciously sweaty Henry steps inside. He takes in my naked form and strips off his damp T-shirt in one fluid movement. I'm in his arms before I can blink. He reaches blindly for the shower controls while kissing me fiercely.

"You're making me sweaty," I say around a laugh.

"That's the beauty of a shower," he tells me, capturing my mouth again.

"I just took one."

He chuckles into my ear. "But you didn't take one with me yet."

I take one last bite of my blueberry muffin, then place the rest of it on my plate and brush the crumbs from my fingers.

"You're not going to eat more?" Henry asks.

I shake my head. "Not hungry."

"You barely took three bites."

"I have more important things on my mind," I say, resting my hand on his thigh.

He grins and laces his fingers through mine while polishing off the rest of the muffin. "As much as I love the idea of spending all day in bed with you again, I'm afraid I need to leave today."

My breakfast sinks like a rock in my stomach. "You're leaving me?"

He must catch the unease in my voice, because he grabs both my hands. "It won't be for long. And I'll be back, I promise."

I swallow the words that are begging to come out: *How am I supposed to believe you?* Things are different between us now. He was only trying to protect me before. And now that his father is a wanted man, it's only a matter of time before he's behind bars for attempting to kill me. Any leverage he once held over Henry is gone.

I nod, hoping he can't see the way my eyes have watered. "How long will you be gone?"

"Not long. I should be back in time for dinner tonight. We can't go out, but I'll have the chef prepare something special, okay?"

I smile at his words, I smile when he kisses the top of my head, I smile at his retreating back as he walks out of the penthouse. It isn't until I face myself in the mirror that my smile crumbles, leaving nothing but bitterness and shame in its wake.

What kind of fool am I?

Once again, Henry only lasted thirty-six hours before taking off. We have no hope of building a future together if he's going to leave me every few days. And how long am I supposed to tolerate being kept in the dark? Relationships are meant to go both ways, and if he's not going to tell me what's going on at some point, he can forget about getting anything from me, let alone my heart.

I hold the blinds open and stare down at the London street below. Wellington Arch sits grandly in the park across from the hotel.

I'm being ridiculous. Henry is a savvy businessman. He can't walk away from his duties for long without facing serious repercussions. Expecting him to hole up in this suite just because I have to isn't fair.

The best thing to do is get my mind off him and what may or may not be the start of an actual relationship. I briefly contemplate sneaking out and exploring the city on my own, but along with trusting Henry comes trusting him with my security. Whatever I decide to do will need to be done within the safety of the Lanesborough.

I still have an entire box of financial documents to sort through before we can start implementing Henry's plans for the Royal Estate. That kind of boring tedium will be just the thing to get my mind off the current drama in my life.

I text Maisie, who had the foresight to bring the green box with her, and she enters my suite a few minutes later with it.

"Geez Louise!" She dumps it unceremoniously onto the table in the dining room. "Do you have any idea how heavy that thing is?" She perches her hands on her hips.

I cock a brow at her theatrics and remove the lid. "Might as well get started."

We each begin sorting through a stack, setting aside anything that pertains to the income and expenses of the royal household. When the whole system went digital several years ago, someone apparently decided all physical papers could simply be dumped in a bin with no rhyme or reason to their organization. I mentally stick pins in said person with every page I pull out.

We're only thirty minutes in when I get a crick in my neck that threatens to put me out of commission.

"It's a sign," Maisie says without looking up.

"Of what?"

"You're meant to be lying on a bed like a pampered princess, not sorting through years' worth of financial statements. Why are we doing this anyway?"

I massage the tight tendons in my neck. "Because I need to know exactly how much income the royal household has coming in from its various streams."

"And you didn't think that was something the Privy Purse could handle?"

"Considering the fact that the palace staff is currently being paid from my own trust fund because of their fumbling the budget, no I didn't."

She lets out a faint snort. "Fair point. What's this company—WJCS Enterprise? I keep seeing it pop up everywhere."

I take the page from her hand. On this statement alone are listed five sizable deposits they made into the royal household account. "That must be the private Sutherland income," I say.

Before I can hand it back to her, her eyes go wide as she scans another document. "Holy smokes. That must be some income. Look at this." She gives me the second page without taking the first back. She doesn't even look at me. She's already engrossed in the next one.

The statement she's just handed me lists several more deposits from WJCS Enterprise, but these are much larger—likely the reason for her shock. They're more than double the other amounts, which weren't small to begin with.

"What does he *do*?" we both wonder aloud.

I glance up at Maisie. She lowers the paper in her hand to meet my eyes. "This is weird, right?" she says. "No one makes that much money without something shady going on."

I hedge a laugh. "Not necessarily true, but it's also not likely the duke had time to be running billion-dollar companies while also ruling a country."

She nods. "That is a *lot* of zeroes."

"Do you think any of that belongs to the royal family?" I say. If it does, that would solve most of my problems.

"I'm not sure." Her voice drifts off as she looks over yet another page, and she shakes her head. "These deposits are insanely large, and there are multiples every month. No wonder the Privy Purse was content to sit around on their asses all day. There was no need to do anything." She hands me the statement without looking to see if I'm planning to take it.

I scan through it, and I must agree. These amounts are much larger than what one could reasonably expect from a Wesbournian estate these days. With the cost of property taxes, modernization, and the amount of repairs old manor homes take, there's often little to no income left at the end of the month. Or, as was the case with Maison de Lierre, it costs to run it.

I set the pages down and look at Maisie, waiting until she glances up. "What are the odds you could use your witchery to figure out exactly where all of this money was coming from?"

A slow grin spreads across her face. "And here I've just been waiting for you to ask." She holds up a finger and wags it. "But it will cost you."

I shoot her a droll look. "What do you want now?"

"A steady stream of coffee." She's already frowning at the next page in her hand. "And a raise if I'm right about this money coming in illegally."

Now it's my turn to snort. "You're lucky you get paid these days. I wouldn't push it."

Maisie leaves and returns to the suite with her laptop a few minutes later. I'm still trying to work out the kink in my neck. I haven't heard from Henry yet, but he's only been gone for two hours. Is it too clingy to send him a text saying I miss him? Probably. But damn it, I do miss him. There's no reason I can't tell him that. Besides, it might make him hurry back a little faster.

I'm typing out a message when another idea strikes me. "I'll be right back," I tell Maisie, before slipping into the bathroom. I peel my dress off and stand in front of the mirror in nothing but my bra and thong. Holding my phone out, I snap a photo. When I look at it on my screen, I feel seven shades of stupid.

My thumb hovers over the delete button, but I remind myself that Henry and I are in a relationship, and even if we're not committed yet, it's completely fine to send him almost-nude photos of myself. I attach it to the text and hit send.

When I get out, Maisie is typing away faster than I've ever seen her. I'm a little surprised to see that there's no smoke rising from her fingers.

"I'd ask how it's going, but I'm a little scared to stop you," I say.

She grimaces but doesn't slow down. "Not well. You wouldn't believe the number of decoys this guy has in place."

I bark out a laugh as I sit down. "Like father, like son, remember?"

She shakes her head. "Henry's was nothing compared to this."

"Care to explain?" I ask.

"For starters, Henry just hid his companies within shells. This one uses shells too, but everything's encrypted."

"Meaning you can't get into it?"

"Meaning I'm not *supposed* to be able to get into it," she corrects.

"Oh, god." I rest my forehead on my crossed arms. "You're doing illegal things again, aren't you?"

"It's not illegal until I gain access to their servers."

I squeeze the bridge of my nose. "I'm going to go out on a limb here and say that you fully anticipate doing that at some point."

A malicious grin creeps over Maisie's face, the screen casting it in a blueish glow. "That would be correct."

"Lord save us all. If this hits the press—"

"Don't worry," she says. Her fingers haven't missed a beat yet. "I know how to cover my tracks."

"It's the fact that you're leaving tracks that worries me." I unlock my phone, but there is no text from Henry yet.

"Hey," she says, "you want to know, don't you?"

"Yes, I definitely do." And I might know of a better way to get that information too, one that doesn't require illegal means. I pull up Henry's contact listing on my phone and press the call button.

"What are you doing?" Maisie's fingers halt on the keyboard. There's panic lacing her voice.

"Relax," I say. "I'm just going to ask Henry where the money comes from. That way, I'll save your keyboard from burning up and you from going to jail again."

"Oh my god, please don't let me go back there." She clasps her hands in front of her. "It was so dirty and smelly. No amount of antiseptic could have made it tolerable."

"You're not going to jail, Maisie." I point to my phone, which is still ringing. "Hello, whole point?"

She sighs dramatically and leans back in her chair. "I don't think I could survive another prison stint. The first one almost did me in."

I'm about to fire back another retort, but Henry's voicemail kicks in. "Hey, it's Henry. I'm probably too busy having fun to answer, but drop your info, and I'll get back to you. Maybe." I can practically hear him winking through the line. He better not be out having fun, or we will be having words when I finally get ahold of him.

"Hey, it's me," I say when the beep indicates the start of the recording. "Maisie and I are going through those financial papers, and I have some questions about WJCS Enterprise. I thought it might be faster to just ask you. It's not a big deal"—Maisie's horrified look says otherwise—"so just get back to me when you can. Talk soon. Bye." I end the call, already regretting my decision to not say "I love you."

"So I should keep working?" she asks.

"Yeah, at least until he calls me back."

Which shouldn't take long. He didn't say he wouldn't be reachable. He would have told me if he'd be in meetings all day and unable to talk.

Images of him in the back of an ambulance flash through my mind. *God, please let him be all right.* He has to be okay. He probably just walked away from his phone for a bit and missed my call and text message.

It's nothing to worry about.

Seven hours later, "not worried" isn't how I would describe myself. I pace the living room and check my phone for what must be the thousandth time this hour. I've called Henry repeatedly since that first call and sent him a handful of messages, and all of them have gone unacknowledged.

Maisie left the suite hours ago. She still hadn't managed to track down the source of WJCS Enterprise's profits but decided that her own suite would be more conducive to her search than being around my apparent "lack of common sense and ability to sit still."

There's a brisk knock on the door, and my heart jumps into my throat. But when it opens, it's only a smiling woman in a server's uniform. "I've got your dinner ready. Would you like for me to set it up over there?" She gestures to the dining table.

My heart takes a high dive back down to my toes. Henry's not here, but hey, at least the dinner he ordered is. I smile at her and nod. "That would be wonderful. Thank you."

She sets up an exquisite meal, complete with a bottle of DRC La Tâche Grand Cru and a cream puff tower drizzled in chocolate sauce. "There you are," she says, wiping her hands on her apron.

After I thank her, she leaves me with my dinner for two. The only thing missing is my companion. I snap a picture of the spread and send it to Henry.

> **Me:** Good thing I'm hungry.

It's nothing but a bald-faced lie. I couldn't eat if you bribed me with cookie-dough-stuffed cookies. This entire meal is going to go to waste, unless by some miracle Henry walks through those doors in the next few minutes with a ravenous appetite.

No longer to my surprise, he doesn't. Not that hour, the next, or the next. I've fallen asleep on the sofa when the buzzing of my phone wakes me up. It's been attached to my side all day long, something that hasn't ever happened before.

I unlock the screen, then flinch when the light hits my eyes.

> **Henry:** I'm so sorry, babe. I've been swamped all day. I love you, and I'll see you tomorrow. xx

That's it. No explanation, aside from a vague "swamped." No mention of my nearly nude selfie. I check the time. It's just after midnight. He waited fifteen hours to reply to my first message.

I fall asleep wondering if I'm the biggest idiot in the world.

32

"So Long, London" - Taylor Swift

I NOTICE TWO THINGS when I wake up. First, the bed beside me is still glaringly empty. I'm pretty sure I would have woken up had Henry come in during the night, but the fact that he's still gone makes me irrationally irritated. The second thing is that my phone is ringing relentlessly beside me on the nightstand.

Assuming it's Henry, calling to tell me he's on his way, I answer it without checking the screen. Instead of Henry's voice, I hear Maisie let out a garbled screech on the other end.

"Good morning to you, too," I say groggily, sitting up. "You're going to have to repeat that."

"I found something!" she says again.

"God, Maisie. What time is it?" I attempt to rub the sleep from my eyes.

"Who cares? I found something huge. You are going to want to see this right away. I stayed up until early this morning, and—"

"Seriously? I'm not sure it was that important."

"Oh, it was. Trust me. This is way bigger than we initially thought."

I'll admit she has my curiosity piqued, but I'm not ready to face whatever intel she has gained without some caffeine first. "Give me about twenty minutes to get up, then I want to hear all about it." I swing my legs to the floor and stand up, stretching the kinks from my back.

"I'll be at your door in exactly twenty, so you'd better be ready," she says before ringing off.

I roll my eyes and toss my phone onto the bed. She probably discovered that William has a sheep farm and keeps them on property that belongs to the Royal Estate. I stumble to the en suite kitchen, hoping our private butler has already brewed a pot of coffee.

He has, bless the man, and after grabbing a cup, I return to the main living room. In the center of the coffee table, there's a giant bouquet of white hydrangeas. I slip the card out and flip it over to read the message.

I'm so sorry, babe. I'll be back soon. xx H

I stifle a groan. He's already regurgitating phrases, and we're not even to the possibly-having-an-affair stage of the relationship.

I'm still annoyed, but the flowers are a nice touch. At least he didn't forget about me in the midst of his important business dealings. I take a quick shower and do the best I can with my hair. I'll have Daphne arrange it later, after I relieve Maisie's blood pressure.

I'm honestly surprised she isn't already banging down the door. I glance at the time on my phone. Our call ended twenty-two minutes ago, but she must have underestimated the amount of time it takes to get from her suite to mine.

While I'm waiting for her, I order eggs Benedict and fruit for breakfast. I'm starving after skipping dinner last night. Fifteen minutes later, the knock on the door isn't Maisie; it's my food.

It's not like her to be late. I press the button to call her while spearing a strawberry with my fork. It rings half a dozen times before her voicemail message kicks in. Maybe she left her phone in her room. But why isn't she here yet?

I'll give her a bit more time. She may have gotten caught up on her way up here. Or fallen asleep in the elevator due to her late night. I can have Roberts send someone on his team to check on her if she's not here soon.

Twenty minutes later, I've finished my breakfast, and Maisie still hasn't shown. Now I'm getting worried. I've called her twice more, but she's still not picking up. Henry also hasn't shown his face or called, but that's starting to feel like old news.

I open the door into the foyer, which immediately grabs the attention of the handful of PPOs standing out there. They all bow when they spot me. I smile and nod. "Good morning," I say, turning to Roberts. "I'm a bit worried about my assistant. She said she would be here nearly an hour ago, but I can't get ahold of her."

He gives me a stiff nod. "We'll check it out. What room is she in?"

I tell him Maisie's room number, and several PPOs head for the elevator. A tingle of apprehension shoots through my veins. Roberts must sense my distress, because he places a hand on my elbow. "Can I get you anything, Your Majesty? A cup of tea maybe? Or help you to the sofa?"

I shake my head, then change my mind. "Actually, that sounds great," I say, allowing him to lead me back to the living room. "You haven't heard from Henry, have you?"

His face remains emotionless as he says, "Not since he left England, no."

I twist sideways so quickly my elbow falls from his hand. "He left England?"

Small furrows form on his brow. "I assumed he told you."

"I had no idea," I say through my teeth.

"He had some business back in Wesbourne, he said. He left yesterday morning."

"Yesterday *morning*?" It's taking all of my self-control to keep from shrieking. "Did he say when he'd be back?"

"Not to me, ma'am, but I was under the impression he didn't plan to be gone long."

Roberts ushers me to the sofa, and I sit, but my mind is whirling. If Henry left England yesterday morning, he had to have known he'd never make it back in time for dinner. A flight home would take no less than six hours. There's no way he could have done back-to-back flights in the same day and still made it in time.

This whole thing feels eerily familiar. I'm starting to wonder if he was planning to leave me here the whole time. *Get Celia to London, where we can barricade her inside a hotel so she stays out of the way.* How could I have been such a fool?

But until I hear the words from Henry, I have to assume the best: That he never intended to be gone so long. That he does love me.

Roberts comes back a few minutes later to say that they weren't able to locate Maisie and to ask if I want him to contact the local authorities. I tell him to wait while I call her one last time. She doesn't pick up, but a few seconds after I disconnect the call, my phone pings with a text message.

> **Maisie**: Eloping with Beck. Sorry for not telling you sooner. xx

Only one thing comes to mind as I read her words: *What the actual fuck?*

She and Beck are *eloping*? It sounds like the most un-Beck-like thing to do ever. It takes the man ten minutes just to choose a pair of socks to wear. Eloping would be comparable to bypass surgery for him. And what about Maisie? She isn't the girliest girl in the world, but she definitely wants a big poofy dress and cake.

Maybe I don't know people as well as I thought I did.

"Ma'am?"

I startle and see that Roberts is still waiting for my answer. "Sorry," I say, running my fingers across my forehead. "Maisie just texted me. She's fine. She left and forgot to tell me, I guess."

Roberts gives me a quick bow and heads back to the foyer.

I slump into the sofa cushions. She could have at least told me what she discovered before jettisoning off to get married, for crying out loud. She could have at least invited me to said wedding, but we both know watching Beck stand up and vow to love another woman for the rest of his life isn't exactly how I'd prefer to spend my day.

To fill my time while I wait for Henry to return and tell me what the heck is going on, I turn on the news. It seems the only thing newsworthy to have happened in Wesbourne in the past two days is her queen fleeing the country. Even the real news outlets are showing screenshots from the gossip sites and forums, mostly of people speculating that it's either a big conspiracy of some sort, or that I'm the world's biggest coward and left because I know something they don't.

Is this really what they think of me? That I would desert them if the worst came? I gave up everything to become their queen, to save our country from destroying itself. Do they think that was easy, or that I want to live a life in the spotlight, where everyone criticizes every single thing I do—including how often I wear the same pair of shoes?

They can hate me all they want, but I can't let them believe I would leave them to fend for themselves. I took an oath to serve my country to the best of my ability, and that includes boosting public morale. If I need to put myself in danger to show them I am on their side, that's what I'm going to do.

I step back into the foyer. If Roberts is surprised to see me again, he doesn't show it. He has been trained in military-grade emotional repression, a course I wouldn't mind taking myself.

"Can I speak to you?" I ask.

He nods and follows me into the living room, shutting the door behind him.

"I need to get back to Wesbourne," I say. "It's important." He opens his mouth, probably to parrot back some robotic response about the danger of leaving, but I stop him. "As queen, it is my job to be there for my people. I can't hide out in a hotel in London like funds in a foreign bank account."

His voice comes out gruff. "I'm afraid my orders are to keep you here under any circumstance."

I'd like to kill Henry's orders. "I understand, but as your queen I'm asking you to go against those orders and take me home. My people need me."

He frowns, and I can see the dilemma in his eyes. I wonder if he's thinking about the way Davies lost his job for breaking orders to help me. I can't assure him it won't happen to him as well, but Henry will have a whole lot more to deal with from me if he tries.

"I would like to clear it with Lord Henry first, if it's all the same to you, ma'am."

I nod. "Be my guest." *And good luck getting ahold of him.*

Roberts holds the phone to his ear for a minute, then lowers it without speaking. "He's not answering."

"He's too busy to worry about this right now," I say. "I'm fully confident you can get me back to Wesbourne safely. Henry is too, or he wouldn't have left you in charge."

He grunts softly in response. "I don't know, ma'am."

"I will handle Henry, if that's what you're worried about. The palace is finally secured anyway. You can take me there, and it will be safer than the Lanesborough."

Roberts focuses on a spot on the wall, still frowning. "I don't like it, but I don't think I can say no to my queen."

Relief courses through me. "A very insightful thought," I say, allowing just a trickle of humor into my voice.

He looks down at me, not finding this funny at all. "We'll have to charter another plane."

33

"Clarity" - Zedd + Foxes

ROBERTS HAS ARRANGED FOR a car to be at the airport, waiting to pick me up. It isn't until I'm sitting in the back of the SUV that the implication of what I'm about to do hits me.

I haven't been back to the palace since I was nearly shot and killed there. When I close my eyes, I can still hear the screams and smell the fear in the air. They've been improving security since then, but what if it's not enough?

My fears are ridiculous. It's only a matter of time until William is behind bars, and there will be more than enough PPOs around to protect me should anything happen. I take a deep breath and smooth my skirt.

Everything is going to be fine.

I don't know what I expected being back in the palace would feel like, but it wasn't this. Everything is as normal as life in a palace can be. It's like no one got the memo that the monarch survived multiple attempts on her life and is no longer staying under this roof.

Staff members bustle through the halls like their job is on the line if they don't move in a fast trot. The cluster of black suits surrounding me draws more attention than I do, and when someone recognizes whom they are protecting, they immediately stop what they're doing and bow their heads.

I've asked to be escorted to my suite. From there, I will figure out how to let the people know that I'm back and that nothing is going to keep me from serving them. The residential wing is still under major construction, although Roberts assures me all the security measures are already in place. The rest is simply cosmetic repairs.

The number of staff members in the halls declines as we enter the corridor leading to my private living quarters. I step inside, and even though it's been nearly a month since I've been here, it's as if nothing has changed. Fresh flowers dot every surface like always. Either someone has been replacing them throughout my absence or Roberts sent word that we were on our way.

Rather than the musty, stale smell you expect when a place has been closed up for a while, the air in here is clean, fresh, and heavy with florals. I walk into the bedroom, expecting to feel joy upon seeing my own bed again, but a wave of melancholy washes over me instead.

Moving back in here means moving out of Henry's flat. No more sleeping on his sheets or running into him in the kitchen as we're both getting our coffee. No more game nights or movies in the home theater. It's time to get back to my normal life.

A housemaid walks out of the bathroom and startles when she sees me. "I'm so sorry, Your Majesty." She bobs into a curtsy. "I didn't realize you'd arrived."

I smile and set my handbag on the bed. "The suite looks lovely. Thank you."

Her face brightens. "Would you like for me to let Lord Henry know you're here?"

My smile melts away. "Henry? He's at the palace?"

"He's been here for a few days, popping in and out."

I'm sure the confusion must be evident in my expression, so I do my best to pull my features back to neutral. "I think it might be better if I surprise him, don't you?"

"Of course, ma'am," she says. "Would you like for me to locate him?"

"That would be great."

She gives another curtsy and leaves the room.

What in the bloody hell is Henry doing at the palace? I was under the impression he had business in Wesbourne. Lord knows he has enough companies headquartered at the Atlantis. So what could he possibly have to do here?

A prickle of unease shimmies down my spine. Things aren't adding up.

Maybe he's simply overseeing the renovations at the palace, preparing to implement our new plans for the Royal Estate. Relief nearly cripples me as the idea takes hold. I was on the verge of spinning a new narrative, one that didn't paint Henry in a flattering light. Trusting him is proving harder than I anticipated.

I take a quick shower. When I step out of the bathroom, the same housemaid is waiting for me in the sitting room. Her name tag reads *Julia*.

"I've located his lordship, ma'am. I can take you to him if you're ready."

I'm ready, all right. Ready to rip that smug head from Henry's shoulders for leaving me in London without a single word about what he's up to. I've had time since I learned he was here to realize that, despite how relieved I feel, I'm also upset by the way he treated me. Again.

We walk down several more corridors in the residential wing, proving my theory about him overseeing the renovations. The maid stops and motions to a door in a hallway I'm unfamiliar with. "I believe he's in there, ma'am."

I thank her and step through the door into a large room hung with paint cloths. You'd think after having lived in the palace for over six months and having spent a good portion of my childhood here, I'd be more familiar with the place, but there are still plenty of rooms I've never seen, this being one of them.

It's dark in here, the only light coming from the three arched floor-to-ceiling windows. They must be at least fifteen feet tall. The furniture has been covered and moved to the center of the room, away from the exterior walls. It appears to be a large hall or ballroom, but evidently one that isn't used much, given my unfamiliarity with it. It must be where the construction teams are focusing their current efforts.

I move farther into the room, wondering if maybe the maid got it wrong. I don't see Henry anywhere, although the space appears to branch out in both directions in a T shape. The air smells sharply metallic, but I don't hear the sound of tools or people talking. Is everyone on a break right now?

"Henry?" I call out. The corner of a framed painting catches my eye. It's propped against a nearby table, both covered by drop cloths. I lift the cloth, and the former Queen Helena stares back at me. As I drop it back into place, it releases a cloud of dust into the air.

Coughing, I wave it away from my face. "Henry?" I try again. I'm about to turn back to the door when he appears from one of the side wings.

"Celia? What the hell are you doing here?" He stops once he sees me, his form silhouetted by the windows behind him. He glances down the other wing of the room before returning his gaze to me.

It hasn't even been that long since we last saw each other, but god am I thirsty for a drink of him. He's as gorgeous as ever in a blue suit, his shirt unbuttoned at the collar. The sun cuts a sharp shadow across that jawline I once despised for its effect on me.

"I could ask you the same thing," I say, walking toward him.

Something I can't identify crosses his face. He reaches for my hands and tugs me against him. His breath is warm on my neck where he nuzzles it, his faint stubble causing goosebumps to form down my back. "What are you doing here?" he asks again, quieter this time. "You're supposed to be in London."

"Wesbourne needs me. I can't stay locked up forever." My anger is already seeping away. "Why didn't you tell me you were at the palace?"

"I haven't just been here," he says. "I planned to be back in London the same day, but things kept cropping up."

I rise up on tiptoes to press my lips against his. "I missed you."

He smiles and returns my chaste kiss, but I can't help but feel like I've walked in on something.

"I missed you, too," he says into my hair before pulling back to look at my face. "But it's dangerous for you to be here."

"Let's not have that fight again. Please?" I lock my fingers together behind his neck. "Roberts does an amazing job, and I did everything he said." *With the exception of staying in London.*

Henry takes a deep breath and glances behind me again. When he looks back at me, a smile is folded into the creases around his eyes. "So a leopard can change its spots?"

I smack his arm. "I can follow directions. As long as they don't interfere with my own plans."

One side of his mouth jerks upward as if pulled by a marionette string. "That sounds more like it." He leans down to rub the side of his stubbly jaw against my neck.

I squirm to get away. "I should have trusted you a long time ago. If I had, Tundra might not have gotten sick." I plan to head to the vet's as soon as I'm done here.

Henry gathers me close, stroking my back in warm, even movements. "You can't know how things might have turned out. William would probably have found another way to get to you."

He releases my waist, but only to slide both hands around my jaw, cupping it and pulling me closer to him. His mouth is warm and tastes like spearmint, and I'm immediately on a bullet train to a raging libido. He brushes his tongue against mine. I groan, and he moves one hand to my hip to keep me from sinking to the floor.

Why did I wait so long to do this? We wasted so much time. Now, when I'm about to move out of his penthouse, I finally come to my senses. What a waste of a perfectly good shower.

"Take me to bed and do dirty things to me," I say.

He chuckles into my ear. "Yes, ma'am."

I gasp when he nips my earlobe. "Promise you're not going to run away again?"

"Promise," he whispers. "I never wanted to run, you know."

"Could've fooled me."

He pulls back so I can see the furrows in his brow. "I've been yours since the day we met."

I offer him a knowing smirk. "We met when we were babies."

"You were a baby. I was a strapping two-year-old."

My laugh trips out as a snort. "*Strapping*? What are you, eighty years old?"

He pinches my waist, which makes me bend in half to avoid his tickling fingers. "Plenty of people say 'strapping.'"

"Not those born in this century. Besides, you don't remember meeting me for the first time."

"Sure I do. You were wearing a poofy lace dress. I thought you looked like a cake."

I gape at him and jab my fingers into his armpits. He grins and grabs my wrists.

"The first time I saw you, I thought you belonged to me," he says. "When I turned five, my mum told me the truth."

I smile and run my thumbs over those cheekbones that have turned me into a puddle more than once. "Don't be stupid. Of course I belonged to you."

Henry leans down to capture my mouth once more. Is this what normal people get to experience all the time? I'm not just floating on clouds—I am soaring.

A sound like clapping chops through the fluffy whiteness of my happiness. I block it out to get more of Henry, but he must think it's worthy of attention, because he breaks off the kiss. I feel him stiffen, so I turn around to see what he's looking at.

The Duke of Sutherland is walking toward us, clapping his hands and wearing a smile that could shrivel the bravest of hearts. "Congratulations. It's about time, isn't it?" he says.

A chill permeates my skin and doesn't stop until it reaches my bones.

34

"Haunted" - Taylor Swift

HENRY MOVES QUICKLY, PULLING me behind him and shielding me with his body. I want to pummel William with my fists, but Henry keeps both hands on my waist, probably to prevent me from doing something just like that.

I want to ask a million things—starting with "what kind of monster hurts a dog?" and ending with "why do you want me dead so badly?"—but my mouth has completely dried up. I couldn't get a word out even if he were holding a gun to my head.

Henry does not seem to be struggling with the same affliction, although he doesn't say any of the things I'm dying to ask. Instead, he says, "Father, give us a moment? Celia was just leaving."

I was?

Henry appears calm and collected, but when I slide my hand up his back, his muscles feel rigid.

"Nonsense," William says. "It's time to celebrate. I only wish I'd known you two were back together. I would've brought champagne."

As far as I can see, William isn't carrying a gun. He's standing in the most nonthreatening way, hands at his sides as if he's simply popping in for a family gathering. But if the atmosphere in here is any indication, this is no ordinary reunion. Air shouldn't crackle if you so much as flinch.

Henry keeps his hands on my hips while facing his father. "It would be best if you left now," he whispers to me.

I'm about to object when I remember my decision to trust him. "Okay." I reach up to plant a kiss on his cheek. "Come find me when you're done here."

I move toward the door, but William takes a few steps closer. "Not so fast, Your Majesty." He says the words like they taste bad. "I think it would be best if you stayed."

"Leave her out of this." Henry's voice is cold steel. "Celia, go."

I stay frozen in place, wanting to obey Henry but not trusting the look in his father's eyes. William makes the decision for all of us. He pulls a pistol from his waistband and waves it toward me. "You're not going anywhere."

Bloody fucking hell. My heart leaps from my rib cage and is doing its best to break free of my chest. I've never stared down the barrel of a gun before, and I now understand the deer-in-the-headlights thing. I couldn't move even if I thought it was a good idea.

"What are you doing?" Henry spits out. He looks mad enough to tear the head off anything in his path.

The duke waves the gun, motioning me toward Henry. "Stand a little closer, sweetheart. That way I can cover you both."

I do as he directs. Henry grabs my arm and tugs me against his side.

"Now," William continues, as if we're having a casual conversation over tea, "I couldn't help but overhear that you two have finally reconciled your differences."

"That's none of your business," Henry hisses through his teeth.

"On the contrary, you know I just want what's best for you."

"Save your breath. No one here believes that bullshit."

William ignores him and goes on. "And I, of course, am looking out for Her Majesty's best interests, too." He paces a few steps to the left, then turns and walks to the right, keeping his gun pointed at us the whole time. "I can't help but wonder how she would feel if she knew everything."

A sickening sludge is oozing from my stomach through my limbs. *No. Please don't let this be real.*

"I will do whatever you want. Just let Celia go," Henry says. He is clasping my arm hard enough that it will probably leave a bruise.

"She can leave soon enough. But first, I think you owe it to her to tell her the truth." William turns his cold green eyes on me. "Don't you?"

I don't dare look away from the gun, but I say quietly, so only Henry can hear me, "What is he talking about?"

"I don't know. He's a lunatic," he says under his breath.

"Her Majesty has yet to learn what it means to mind your own business," William says. His voice has turned malicious, and all I can think about is how often he's hidden his true feelings from me.

"I don't know what you're talking about," I say.

"I think you do." The duke takes a step closer. "Earlier this year, you started a petition to increase port security. That ridiculous notion wasn't going anywhere until you also stole my throne. And then you had to poke a dozen holes in the financial records."

Dread coils in the pit of my stomach like a cobra. I desperately hope I'll be able to find a bin to be sick into if it comes to that.

"You now know firsthand the impossibility of running the palace and all its staff on that meager thing they call a Civil List. Try raising a family on that." His lips curl in disdain. "But the entire country would have had my head if I had laid people off or asked for taxes to be raised." His chuckle sounds like ice rattling in a bucket. "You found that one out for yourself."

Neither Henry nor I dare interrupt his diatribe, but I can feel Henry's muscles roiling with restraint.

"So, as you were about to find out before I kidnapped your lovely little assistant"—William barks something over his shoulder, and two large men step out of the shadows, clutching a figure between them—"I did what I had to do."

"Maisie!" I shriek. I try to fling myself at her, but Henry's hand clamped tightly around my arm prevents me from going anywhere.

"Stay here," he says. For the first time, I recognize fear in his voice, not just anger.

I curl back against his side, wishing I'd never left London. I make eye contact with Maisie across the room. A piece of silver duct tape is stretched over her mouth. She looks more irritated than scared. I guess she's not eloping with Beck after all.

"As I was saying," William continues, "one does what one must when people are depending on you. Again, you yourself have discovered this. It's unfair to judge the means when you don't understand the motive. For instance, Jean Valjean stealing a loaf of bread to feed his sister's starving children—should he have been thrown in prison for trying to save lives?"

Henry can no longer hold his tongue. "Father, she doesn't want to discuss *Les Mis*. None of us do."

William cackles. "Then I guess it's a good thing I'm the one holding the gun, isn't it?"

I can only stare at the duke in astonishment. How is this the same man who sat beside me and said how badly he wished he could earn his son's forgiveness? The same man who gave me a dog just to thank me for sitting with him through the hardest time of his life?

William starts his pacing again. "As you were about to find out after this little wench accessed our private servers"—he pinches Maisie's cheek, and she jerks away from him—"I have a lucrative side business." He turns back and glares at me. "Very lucrative. Until you stuck your nose in where it didn't belong."

My heart and stomach have taken up a new address down in my feet. I swallow against the cotton in my mouth, but it doesn't do any good.

I can already sense where he's going with this, even if I can't predict the exact words coming out of his mouth.

"Our incompetent government tried to score favors by pushing your stupid motion through, meaning drugs could no longer be imported into Wesbourne. You thought you'd won." A gleam comes into his eyes. "But the war is far from over."

Henry has stiffened into a marble statue beside me. "That's enough. Let her go."

I put my hand on his arm. "Actually, I think I want to hear this." The pieces are already falling into place in my mind. I'd rather wait and see the whole picture, even if the image makes me vomit.

"You should have known we'd find another way," William says. "Insidion is simply too profitable to take off the table. It took us some time, but we eventually learned how to manufacture it ourselves."

I scrunch my eyes shut, trying to block out the horror I'm feeling, but it's crawling all over me, black as night. William has been the one importing insidion all along. How many other people leading this country—people I thought I could trust—are in on it?

I turn to Henry, who is still frozen by my side. "Did you know about this?" *Please say no, please say no.*

William's cackle echoes through the room. "Know about it?" He throws his head back as he laughs, sending a chill up my spine.

I consider the distance to the door. Will I have time to make it through before he shoots?

His next words evaporate any thoughts of escape. "Sweetheart, he's been chief of operations for the past six years."

"Lux Aeterna" - Clint Mansell

I'VE HEARD PEOPLE DESCRIBE the feeling of time stopping, but I've never actually experienced the world halting on its axis like this before. Dust motes sluggishly float through the air. Sound has evaporated from the room. The silence is so thick it starts to ring in my ears. Or maybe that's the alarm bells in my head, telling me that I'm in more danger than I've ever been in before, and the only way to survive is to get out of here.

But my feet are glued to the floor, like I'm standing ankle-deep in fridge-cold peanut butter. I open my mouth to speak, to call for help, to sob hysterically, but my voice box has malfunctioned. Nothing comes out.

From my position as an ice sculpture waiting for sunshine, I see movement behind William. At first I think they're here to kill me, because why not? I've evaded death so often, staying alive has grown uncomfortable.

But as my eyes bring the figures into focus, I see that they're wearing uniforms. Dark green uniforms. Bulky vests over their chests. Belts loaded with weapons. Guns aimed at us.

They creep into the room, and someone yells something, but my ears seem to be full of sealing wax. I can't hear anything but muffled shouting. My fingers are still clutching Henry's arm, and when I notice, I try to make them release their grip, but it's like they've been welded on and we're now one, his arm and me.

I watch the uniforms approach the way you witness things in a dream—from a distance, remote and disconnected. Two of the officers train their weapons on William and hold their aim until he finally lowers the gun. They wrench his arms behind his back and snap metal cuffs on his wrists.

This is finally over. They're arresting the duke, who is behind the insidion production and distribution *and* the attempts on my life. His face is pulled into an ugly scowl, which he first directs at me, then his son.

Henry still has a hand on my arm, holding me tightly to his side, but his attention is on the uniforms headed toward us.

They stop beside us, and Henry releases me. As my hand drops away, I look down to find several finger-shaped bruises on my upper arm. I slowly raise my head, which seems to be full of marbles at this point, in time to watch Henry put both hands in the air while they pat him down.

His jacket sleeves slide down as he endures the humiliation of having his entire body searched. A flash of color catches my eye, and I recognize the friendship bracelet I gave him on his left wrist.

This realization drags my eyes to his face. I haven't looked at him since William's words drove straight into the castle that was my heart, sending it crashing to the ground in a haze of smoke and ash. I haven't dared look, because I'm terrified of what I'll find there. My heart might be ground zero right now, but I'm afraid Henry's carrying a nuclear bomb to obliterate even the rubble.

When I meet his gaze, his eyes beg me—plead with me—for something. His mouth moves, but I can't hear a word he's saying. I watch as they twist his arms behind his back, just like his father's, and put him in handcuffs. His eyes haven't left my face, but I don't understand what I see in them.

Henry and William are led out of the room, Henry's eyes staying fixed on me for as long as possible. I just don't understand what he wants me to know.

It isn't until they're gone and the remaining officers ask if I'm okay, if I have any injuries, if I need to sit down, that I realize I can hear again. I shake my head and request to be escorted back to my suite. Right now, it's the only place where I'll have a chance of making sense of what just happened.

Before we can leave, Maisie launches herself into my arms. I'd completely forgotten she was in the room. The duct tape has been ripped from her mouth, leaving it red and swollen. "Oh my god," she wails. "I thought I'd never see you again."

I force my arms to wrap around her, but they respond with the stiffness of a robot's. *Up, over, pat, pat, pat.*

Strong hands grip me from behind, and I jump, half expecting to find that William has somehow escaped and come back for me. It's only Roberts. He manages to detangle Maisie from me and pass her off to another PPO standing nearby. Turning back to me, he says, "Are you okay, ma'am?"

I nod and shiver. Goosebumps cover my entire body. I'm not sure I've ever been this cold before. "I will be," I manage to say.

"Let's get you out of here." He takes my elbow. After we've left the chaos of the officers gathered outside, he says quietly, "Just so you know, we had surveillance in the room the entire time. You weren't in any danger."

That must be meant to comfort me. So then why does it feel like my soul has been ripped from my body?

"Thank you," I mumble when we reach the door to my suite.

Roberts nods and gives a small bow. "Just remember," he says, "not everything is as it seems." With that, he turns and walks back down the corridor, his steps muted by the heavy pile of the carpet.

There are so many ways to interpret what he's just said, but I do not have the mental bandwidth to think about it at the moment. In fact, I can barely get inside my suite. When I do manage to open the door, it takes the last of my energy to drag myself to the bed and crawl in.

If anyone needs me, this is where they'll find me for the next indefinite amount of time. It's the only place I can handle being alive.

The only place I can process the fact that I've just been betrayed. Again.

36

"Need You Now" - Lady A

I WAKE TO THE sound of thumping in the sitting room of my suite. Stumbling out of bed, I look for something to use as a weapon, since it appears I've been abandoned by my security team.

When I step out, instead of an intruder, I find my luggage stacked around the space. Daphne pokes her head up from behind a large suitcase she's wrestling into submission. "I'm so sorry, ma'am. Did I wake you?"

I shake my head, even though she did, and wrap my arms around my waist. The events from earlier are slowly trickling back into my conscious.

"They brought your things back from the Atlantis. I would have put them away, but I didn't want to disturb you."

"That's fine. Thank you, Daphne," I say, rubbing my arms.

She drops the bags in her hands. "Are you cold? I can fetch some tea for you."

"That would be great, actually." I sink into the sofa as she leaves and scan the room. Daphne will have my things all put away properly in less than an hour. I wish I could do the same with my life.

There's still a faint ringing in my ears, and it's like my entire body has received a major dose of lidocaine. I can't feel anything. The nausea still hasn't completely disappeared. I'm sure finding out that the man I love is behind thousands of deaths didn't help, either.

I once heard that the better you think you know someone, the easier it is for them to fool you. I guess I'm living proof of that.

Had you asked me eleven years ago what could make me stop seeing Henry the way I did, I would have said nothing. I loved him so fully at that point and wouldn't have believed there was anything that could possibly change the way I felt about him.

But there's always something—for everyone.

People deny it, because they want to believe they are good enough to love unconditionally. And while plenty of couples are able to work through issues like infidelity or the loss of a child, plenty more can't. And for those who do, there will still always be something—something they haven't even considered—that could do it for them. Something that would break them.

This is my thing.

Fifteen-year-old Celia would have refuted it, because she wouldn't have believed Henry capable of it. But twenty-six-year-old Celia has seen sides to him she never imagined existed. This is simply another cog in the wheel that makes up the man I thought I knew.

Chief of operations. God.

I reach for the throw blanket folded over the back of the sofa, and as I do, I see a box tucked in with the luggage. I immediately recognize it as the one that lived under Henry's bed, full of childhood mementos. Someone must have thought it was mine and grabbed it.

I kick it, and it scoots across the rug. Stupid box. Stupid boy.

Stupid girl for thinking that who a person is at seventeen is any indication of who they'll be as an adult.

The door opens, and Daphne returns with my tea. "Here you go, ma'am." She hands it to me, her eyebrows pinched in concern. I wonder what stories are circulating among the staff.

"Would you like for me to finish unpacking your things?" she asks.

"I would actually like to be alone just now."

"Of course, ma'am." She bobs into a small curtsy and heads for the door. "I'll get this cleared away while you're at dinner."

I can't tell her I won't be at dinner. I don't know how I'm going to handle showing my face anywhere for the foreseeable future. I feel like a grieving widow, but I don't even have a body to mourn, just a tainted memory.

So much for showing my people that I'm fine. First I have to *be* fine.

I unzip the nearest suitcase and lift the clothes out. Daphne would probably prefer to do it herself, but my hands desperately need something to do, or they will reach over and grab that box and tear apart every photograph inside.

As the stack of clothing on the coffee table grows, so does my resentment toward Henry. Now that the numbness is wearing off, I'm left with a blinding anger. Isn't it enough that I lost him twice? Did he have to completely annihilate what was left of my heart in the process? How long had he been planning this particular attack?

The image of his face as he was being arrested flashes through my mind. That wasn't his plan at all. He wanted me out of there before William could confess anything. Maybe he was hoping to keep running his father's empire for years while keeping me in the dark. Maybe was planning to wait for the perfect moment to tilt my world off its axis.

But the more I think about it, the more the niggling feeling I have increases. I'm missing something. There was something in Henry's eyes, a fear I've never seen before. Fear of what? Being arrested? Life in prison?

The questions are relentless and show no mercy. Somehow, I should have known. I should have seen the signs. Was there an indication of who he would become when we were kids? A clue I should have recognized?

There must have been signs. No one, especially a teenager, is able to hide everything that well. I toss the sweater I'm holding onto a pile and reach for the keepsake box. The answers must be inside.

I fill my lungs with air before removing the lid, as though that can somehow protect me from its contents. I've gone through them before, but so much has changed since my first perusal.

I start with the pictures. They seem like they'd be the most likely indicators something was going on with Henry that I missed. But I don't know what I'm looking for. A parcel of drugs in the background?

I scrutinize every photo, analyzing Henry's smile in each one, looking for slight variances, anything that would indicate what he was doing when we weren't together. I find nothing—not a single clue as to why he did what he did. The only thing the pictures do is remind me of the happiest years of my life.

I still remember what was happening when each picture was snapped. The time his mum told us we had to make cookies because we'd emptied the cookie jar too quickly. Neither of us had a clue how to bake anything, so we mostly watched the palace chef and snuck globs of dough when she wasn't looking. Olivia stood in the kitchen doorway, camera in hand, grin on her face, as we swiped each other's faces with flour.

The time we were meant to be conjugating French verbs but were taking turns doing our best Barney Stinson impressions instead. The time Henry wanted to experiment with his new Bunsen burner and ended up nearly setting the library on fire.

Every single memory makes me smile despite my best attempts not to. We had the best times together, and nothing that has happened since can dampen that. Henry might have turned out to be a liar and a drug dealer, but he was the best friend I could have hoped for back then.

Not every story has a happy ending.

There's a photo he took of me making his friendship bracelet. I'm sticking out my tongue as I braid the strands, so mature for an eleven-year-old. I picture it on his wrist earlier. Surprisingly, the colors haven't faded much over time, still the same vibrant blue, green, and orange from the photo.

I wonder why he had it on today. It was childish when I gave it to him, but he wore it to make me happy. Maybe he wanted the reminder that he used to be a good person.

His face as they cuffed him still haunts me. Desperation clouded his features. I wish I could figure out what he was trying to tell me. He kept saying the same thing over and over, like he knew I couldn't hear him. Maybe he wanted me to call a lawyer for him? Get rid of proof tying him to his crimes?

I replay the scene in my mind, closing my eyes so I can get the details right. I picture the look in his eyes, the movement of his mouth, doing my best to lip-read his words. His look was so focused, so intent, like he was willing me to read his thoughts.

All of a sudden, everything clicks together at the same time.

The look on his face.

The bracelet.

The person I thought he was.

The phrase he kept repeating.

He wasn't saying anything out loud. He was mouthing words he didn't want anyone else to hear.

Trust me.

37

"Go Solo" - Tom Rosenthal

TRUST HIM.

How the bloody hell does Henry expect me to do that after everything he's put me through? Sure, he had explanations for those things, but what if they were nothing but lies?

And we both know they're more than likely lies.

I push the box aside and rest my head on my knees. I'm circling back to the same mindset I had just a few days ago. I made the decision to trust Henry no matter what, and at the first sign of trouble, I've already abandoned him and reverted to accusing him of everything I absolved him of.

But dealing insidion? Being part of the force I've actively been working against? No one could expect me to trust him in spite of that. No one except Henry himself.

A picture peeks out from the stack in the box, a shot of him I took with his camera. He's probably sixteen in it, smiling shyly at me. His hair was more tousled and boyish then, and it fell over his forehead, just brushing his brows. He was always pushing it out of his face. There's a softness in his eyes in the photo, and I wonder if he already knew he was in love with me when it was taken. No one else has ever looked at me quite that way.

There's a tight knot in my chest, and if I press on it, tears will flow. So far, I've managed to keep them at bay. But looking at the love shining in Henry's eyes is taking a sledgehammer to that knot. I stick the picture back in the box and put the lid back on.

No matter what he's done, I will always love the boy he was, and I know that boy still lives inside him. So for the sake of that boy, I'm going to trust him. I'm going to trust that there's an explanation for what happened. Maybe it was another one of William's mind games or a stupid plot meant to undermine me. Whatever the story is, I am choosing to believe that Henry will come home and explain everything.

I just have to wait for him.

It takes three days. Three endless days of questioning everything, of calling myself a fool, of almost packing my bags and getting the hell out of Henry's flat. Because yes, I decided the best place to wait for him was at his penthouse. Of course, when I made that decision, I assumed it would take a few hours for him to get back with a simple explanation on his tongue.

But as the time ticks by, my doubts grow, and I wonder if maybe William was telling the truth after all. Maybe Henry is currently awaiting trial.

I could find out from any one of the PPOs in the foyer, or from Maisie, but for some reason, that feels like disbelief. And if I'm going to put myself through the agony of waiting and believing, I'm going to do it right.

Tundra is recovering well, and I've been visiting him at least once a day. He's still at the vet clinic, but he's supposed to come home this weekend. If Henry still isn't back by then, I'll have to return to the palace.

I'm in the great room of the penthouse, signing some documents Maisie dropped off this morning, when the door opens. I assume it's Roberts with a security update, so I continue scrawling my signature.

When I finally look up, my hand flies up to cover my mouth. I've imagined this moment so many times. Never once did I expect it to be like this.

Henry has definitely looked better. His hair isn't styled and is on the verge of falling into his eyes like it did when he was younger. His face hasn't seen a razor in days and is slowly growing a dark beard. There are lines around his eyes that weren't there before. His shoulders slump with a new heaviness.

I lose my grip on the files in my lap. Several of them slide off my lap and clatter onto the floor. Henry looks up, his eyes growing larger. Apparently, no one warned him that I was here.

He stops at the edge of the rug in the great room. "What are you doing here?" His voice sounds weighed down, like Atlas with the entire world on his back.

There are a million things I could say right now, a million words that could fill this space between us. I choose one. "Waiting."

Several beats pass. "For what?"

"You."

Pain crosses his face, and he brushes it away with his hand. "C—"

"And an explanation."

There's a sizzle of something in the air, the way you can smell rain while the sun is still shining. He takes one more step, crossing the boundary between hall and great room.

We are now in the same room. After three days of endless torture, it feels too good to be true.

"What makes you think there is one?" he asks.

Not taking my eyes from his, I push the papers on my lap aside. They fall to the floor with the others, but I don't care. I stand up and take a single step in his direction. "Because I know you."

The ache he must be feeling rises up and pours from his eyes. He pinches the bridge of his nose. "Or maybe you just thought you did."

His words echo my own thoughts from earlier so closely that I have to fight the urge to cry out. He can't mean that. "You owe me the truth," I say.

Sighing, he drops his hand. "I owe you a whole lot more than that." He turns and walks to the kitchen, then returns a minute later holding a glass of amber liquid.

"I'm willing to settle," I say.

He tosses the alcohol back in one swig. "What if it's not what you want to hear?"

Tears press against my throat, but I swallow, hoping they'll disappear. "You asked me to trust you."

"You heard what my father said. It was the truth."

Henry's words cut deep, past sinew and muscle, straight to the bone. I didn't realize how much I was banking on it all being fabrication. I swallow again and take another step.

When I decided to trust him, this was not the scenario I imagined. Not even close. What happened to the easy explanations and commiserating together over his asshole of a father?

"No." It comes out firmer than I expected, as though there's an invisible band of steel strengthening my spine.

A joy-drained laugh slips past Henry's lips. "What do you want me to say, C? Nothing he said was a lie. I'm part of my dad's drug empire. A big part. And I have been for a long time."

"You're lying."

He shakes his head and returns to the kitchen, this time bringing back the entire bottle of whiskey. "You want the truth? Here it is." He pours another glass and drains it. "My father threatened to hurt you if I didn't do what he wanted. There. That's the story."

"I don't believe you." It's my turn to shake my head. I can feel permanent lines etching their way into my forehead like steel on stone.

"Doesn't make it any less true."

"You wouldn't do something like that."

"Something like what?" There's a flash of fire in his eyes. "Dirty business to keep the girl I love alive? Fuck yes, I would."

"Children *died*, Henry!" My throat burns hot, but I will not let the tears fall.

He sets the bottle on the table without taking his eyes from mine. "He would have killed you."

"My life is not more valuable than theirs." I fight the sobs clawing their way up my throat. How could he?

He clears the distance between us in the time it takes me to blink, his minty breath suddenly close enough to brush across my face. "To me it is. I know that doesn't make me a hero, but I never wanted to be one." His eyes are liquid onyx. "I only ever wanted you."

He plunges his hands into my hair, making me gasp, and yanks me against him. His lips meet mine, and I whimper at the contact. Devouring me, he pulls me closer with every flick of his tongue.

He walks me backward across the room, his mouth never leaving mine, and I don't know where we're going until I feel the cool press of the piano against my back. He drops my mouth, but only so he can suck on my earlobe, my neck, my jaw. His hands are everywhere now that he has me trapped.

I push at his jacket, and he releases me long enough to toss it to the floor. Then those large, warm hands are back, moving across my body like he's a painter and I'm his canvas. I gasp when he lifts me high enough to set me on the piano. He pushes between my legs, spreading them apart, and I cannot get enough of him.

I arch into him as he uses his warm mouth to explore. Fire courses through my veins, spreading like a disease into every last inch of me. Under my palms, his shoulders ripple. I dig my nails in as he bites my nipple through my dress.

Sliding his hand up my dress, he pulls my stockings off. He greedily reaches for my panties, not even bothering to remove them before sliding his fingers inside. "Damn it, Celia," he groans. "You are going to be the death of me."

I angle my hips to give him better access, which he takes without hesitation.

"I hope you're ready to be fucked hard," he says before increasing the speed of his fingers.

I clench around his hand, aching for him with a hunger so I can't imagine it ever being satiated. He uses his thumb to rub circles over my clit, drawing me to the edge so fast.

I ride his hand shamelessly, not even bothering to muffle the sounds rising from my throat. He murmurs encouragingly in my ear while driving deeper and deeper into me. He curls his fingers like he's unlocking something, and just like that, he unlocks me.

I scream as the orgasm rips through me. He chuckles into my hair and continues stroking me until I come back down.

When I finish, he presses a kiss to my hair. The scent of him and the hot fire still coursing through my blood already make me crave him again. He slides his wet fingers out and grabs my panties, dragging them down my legs. When they're off, he gently spreads my legs farther apart. "Lean back on your hands," he says, his voice rough as sandpaper.

I do as he says, positioning myself on top of the closed piano lid. He pushes my dress up to my waist and grins wickedly at the sight of me. "Fuck yes," he says, and licks his lips. He pushes my thighs out even farther. I'm so grateful for yoga at this moment.

He leans forward and buries his face between my legs, kissing his way up my thighs and tracing my bikini line with his nose. I gasp at the first flick of his warm tongue. I can't help crying out when he slides it along my opening, slowly at first, then increasing in intensity and speed.

The sensation is so intense I beg him to stop. He ignores me and continues torturing me with his tongue. It's both not enough and too much. I can't drag his head closer because I'm holding myself up with my hands.

Finally, he thrusts his tongue inside, and I buck against him. He holds me in place with his hands on the crease of my thighs and licks and sucks and kisses me into oblivion.

I use the piano as leverage to push against his mouth, needing him closer and deeper. He complies by using his tongue to tease me and his fingers to knead me deeply. He pulls back briefly to say, "I want to feel you climax around my tongue, baby," then plunges it back inside me.

Within seconds, I'm teetering on the edge again. Then I crash over, this orgasm even stronger than the last. I push against him, taking everything he will give me.

When it's over, he lifts his drenched face and grins. "You're incredible."

He fishes his wallet out of his pocket and pulls out a condom. Quickly unbuckling his belt, he pushes his pants down, giving me a great view of his very eager cock.

After rolling on the condom, he says, "You'll have to come down for this one." He helps me off the piano. "But I have another idea." Leading me over to the dining table, he pulls out one of the chairs.

He sits down, then pulls me onto his lap, facing him. "Comfortable?" When I nod, he says, "Good. Now ride me, baby."

I stand and position myself over him, then slowly sit back down, taking him inside me as I do so. It takes a couple of tries to get him as deep as he can go, but when he's there, bloody hell, it feels good.

I'm already sore, but it's way too delicious to stop now. Using his shoulders for leverage, I push myself back up, and he groans. "Fuck, baby."

He means it as an expletive, but I take it as a directive and begin moving faster and faster. He matches my thrusts with his own. I throw my head back as the pleasure builds. He slides the side of my bodice down far enough to release one of my breasts, taking it into his mouth with long pulls.

I can feel myself tightening around him, winding tighter and tighter as he rams his cock into me. I scream his name as my third climax hits, and he releases my nipple as his own follows right behind. We cling to each other until it's over, and by then I'm too exhausted to move from his lap.

He laughs softly as he runs lazy fingers up and down my back. "That was quite the welcome home." He nuzzles the spot behind my ear, the one he knows makes me swoon every time. "What other dirty things did you have in mind?"

38

"All of Me" - John Legend

T HE SUNSHINE HAS LIED again. From inside the music room, it looks like a balmy day, full of sun and crisp air, with not a single snowflake on the ground. In reality, it's cold enough to turn my veins into icicles.

The sound of laughter behind me teases at my attention, and I turn from the bow window, my fingers tangled in Tundra's fur. My mother and Olivia are sitting at the table behind me, deep in conversation. With everything that's happened this year, I'm glad they have each other.

The Duke of Sutherland is awaiting trial without bail. Henry thinks he will be sentenced to no less than twenty years for his crimes. Henry himself got off with fifty hours of community service, a price he's more than happy to pay for his participation.

He's been working with the authorities for the past three years, trying to gather enough evidence to put William behind bars. His father is a genius and not to be underestimated. He had the entire operation designed so that all leads pointed back to Henry himself.

It took most of Henry's time and energy to finally be able to bring the entire empire down. The base of their operations was at the palace the whole time, right under my nose, and I never suspected a thing. In exchange for his cooperation and the risks he took to do it, the judge granted him leniency and a quick trial.

The press have their hands full covering the nest of maggots Henry's revelations uncovered. They're currently too busy to worry about my love life, something I'm all too grateful for.

My eyes find Henry on the other side of the room, talking to Beatrice. The two of them have their backs turned to me and their heads bent over something. Bea's tinkling laugh fills the air again, and I smile. It's good to see them as friends instead of worrying that there might be more going on between them.

Henry's plans in the new year include selling the majority of his businesses to fund the necessary steps we need to take to set up the income streams for the Royal Estate. When I balked at this, he said it was the least he could do, considering the investments he made were with money from his father's insidion ring. He is also having a memorial erected in honor of all of the children who overdosed on the lethal drug.

I walk back to the table in the middle of the room, the remnants of Christmas dinner still strewn over its surface. Tundra trots along beside me, fully back to his goofy self. We kept the staff bare bones today so that as many of them as possible could celebrate with their families. We've been fending for ourselves, and it shows. Cleaning this mess up is going to be a chore.

I sit in the chair next to my mother and set my glass of port onto the table. She turns to me and smiles, clasping my shoulder in her warm, firm grip. I place a small peck on her cheek. The air between us has thawed since her big revelation, even if we still have a long way to go. We'll get there.

Thanks to her, we have big plans to redeem my image with my people. I also have an interview scheduled next week with the most promising candidate for press secretary to come across my desk yet.

Bea twirls her way back to the table as well, resting her arms on the back of an empty chair. "Should we take this party to comfier seats?" she asks.

Henry approaches me from behind and bends to plant a kiss behind my earlobe. His hands find their way to my shoulders as his lips stray farther down. I do my best to stifle the moan that awakens in my throat. "Let's ditch the lot of them," he whispers.

I grin as heat climbs my neck. I slide my hand up to his, twining our fingers together. "Soon," I say, turning to meet his kiss. We keep it chaste—our mothers are in the room, after all—then follow Bea to the sofa and chairs clustered around the fireplace. Tundra settles his head on my lap. He's never more than a few feet away from me at all times.

Henry stokes the fire with a poker, and the blaze roars with newfound oxygen. There's a quick knock on the door. It opens to reveal Davies in his classic black suit. I bolt to my feet, and Tundra gives a surprised whine.

Henry stands, a giant grin on his face. "Looks like one of your Christmas presents has arrived," he says to me.

I look back at Davies in confusion. "I don't understand." Then I spot the familiar earpiece in his ear. "You rehired him?"

Davies offers his own smile in return, a bigger one than I've ever seen on him before. "It's an honor to be back in your service, Your Majesty. I just wanted to say happy Christmas."

I want to hug him but know that would be uncomfortable for both of us. I settle for shaking his hand. "Thank you so much for everything you've done for me."

He nods. "It's been my pleasure, ma'am." The twinkle in his eye tells me he really means this.

"You should be celebrating with your family, not stuck here," I say.

"Tyson is with his mum and her relatives. I'll see him later this evening. There's nowhere I'd rather be than here, ensuring your safety."

"Hopefully the days of high vigilance are over." I chance a quick glance over my shoulder at Henry, but he's deep in conversation with Rosalind. Worry lines pucker his brow. "But your loyalty will never be forgotten."

A red flush tints Davies's cheeks through his bristly stubble. "There isn't anything I wouldn't do for my queen or country."

"I know." It's taken me a while, but I'm finally recognizing that there are those whose commitment to Wesbourne rivals my own—men and women who lay their life on the line to protect not only her citizens, but also her monarch. I will never view my security team as a burden again, not when they are jeopardizing so much for me. "Happy Christmas, Davies."

He bows once and leaves as quietly as he came.

I move back to the sofa, taking a seat next to Olivia this time. Bea and Rosalind are still speaking in hushed tones with Henry. Olivia smiles at me, but sadness lurks in her eyes. She just found out her husband was the mastermind behind a large drug operation, responsible for thousands of overdose deaths and the ripping apart of far too many families.

"How are you doing?" I ask, stroking Tundra's head.

"Better today." She gestures around the room. "This is helping get my mind off things."

"I'm glad." I reach for her hand. It's cool to the touch. "You're welcome here anytime."

Henry and I haven't talked about the future yet. There hasn't been time, between his hearing and preparing for the holidays this past week. But regardless of where we stand, Olivia will always be like a second mother to me. Besides, the palace was her home for most of her life. She belongs within its walls.

"Thank you," she says. She reaches for the bracelet on my wrist. "This looks familiar."

I twist it so she can see it better. "Henry and I made them for each other one summer."

"Ah, that's why. I've seen him wearing his recently."

A firework of bliss explodes in my heart. I don't think he's taken that friendship bracelet off since the day I found it in his box of things. I don't know what it symbolizes for him, but for me it's a sign that my gut was right. He has always been all of the things I thought he was. The boy I adored and the man I love are one and the same, no matter what has happened these past ten years.

I found my own bracelet a few days ago and eagerly slipped it on. Until I get a tattoo, it's the only way I can think of to symbolize that I'm his, completely and irrevocably.

"I'm so glad he has you," Olivia says.

I realize that my eyes have wandered to Henry of their own accord. I pull them back to her, blushing. "I'm the lucky one."

She fumbles with the wedding ring she still wears. "I also want to apologize for my husband's actions."

"You have nothing to apologize for. You're not responsible for what he did."

She looks at me with watery eyes. "I feel like I should have known somehow."

I understand that feeling, despite it being illogical. "He was brilliant at covering his tracks."

"He was." She sniffs and dabs at her nose with a tissue. "I still don't understand how he was poisoning your coffee. Henry tried to explain it to me, but my brain hasn't been functioning the same recently."

Memories of the thallium poisoning threaten to make my dinner rise in my throat. I shove them away. "He had thallium added to the vanilla syrup in the coffee shop." Which means I am far from the only one who has been suffering the adverse effects of his far-reaching power.

Olivia clucks beside me in sympathy. She bears no blame in any of this, but it can't be an easy truth to live with.

My phone buzzes on the table in front of us.

Maisie: Happy Christmas!!!!!!!!

Attached is a picture of her and Beck in the most atrocious sweaters I've ever seen. I snicker and show the photo to Olivia.

"Oh my," she says, covering her smile. "Those are . . . unique."

I slide the phone back onto the table as Bea claps her hands. "Who's ready for presents?" she squeals.

Henry sits beside me and puts his arm around my shoulder as we exchange gifts with the people we love. Being with him, actually *with* him, in public is still such a new sensation that I feel a bit like a preteen with her first boyfriend. Heat grows in the space where our thighs are pressed together, and the way his fingers trace imaginary lines over my shoulder is extremely distracting.

"Leave her alone, Henry," Bea says, watching me unwrap the gift she's given me. "She'll never get it open at this rate."

Our gift exchange continues until the pile under the tree is gone. "This is one of the best Christmases ever," I say, sliding my hand up and down Henry's thigh, relishing the way he jerks when I get too close to his groin. The port has loosened my reserve, and I snuggle into him, no longer caring who sees us displaying affection. Let the world know I love this man. I'd shout it from the pinnacle of the palace if I could.

"It's not quite over," Henry says. His voice rumbles under my ear from where I'm cozily leaning against his chest. "I still have one more gift." He shifts me off and stands.

I glance over at the tree, but the floor beneath it is empty.

Instead of walking away to retrieve anything, he kneels in front of me and takes my hands in his.

Oh my god. It's the only thing I can think, because I know what happens next in this story.

"Celia, you are the most incredible woman I know. You are so brave and dedicated and passionate. You would do anything for those you love.

Watching you on fire should be considered one of the wonders of the world.”

Tears well up in my eyes, and there's no way to stop them from spilling over.

“I know we haven't talked about what the future holds for us,” Henry continues. “I know our relationship has been unconventional in every single way. But I've spent most of my life in love with you, and I don't want to go another day without waking up next to that beautiful smile.”

He slides his hand into his pants pocket and pulls out a small velvet box. “We've done this once before. That time, the only answer I got was a nod. I'm hoping you'll be a little more enthusiastic this time.”

Laughter rings throughout the room and reminds me that we are not alone. The giant, insurmountable lump in my throat has also joined us.

“Celia Eleanor, queen of my heart and my country,” he says, then pauses. He's fighting tears of his own, but there's a smile at the corners of his mouth. “Will you marry me?”

He pops open the box, displaying an exquisite ring. It's not the diamond-and-emerald one he used to propose when we did it for king and country, but it's stunning all the same. I cover my mouth to keep my sob from becoming audible.

“Say yes already!” Bea says.

I hiccup-laugh and meet Henry's gaze. “What a ridiculous question. Of course I'll marry you.”

He seals his mouth to mine before I even have time to process what's happening. I barely register the pop of the lid shutting on the box before his hands are threading through my hair, holding me in place as he gives me a taste of what's to come when we're alone.

“Get a room,” Bea groans.

“Beatrice,” Mum scolds, but there's a smile in her voice.

Henry and I pull apart, grinning like idiots at each other. God, we must be repulsive, but I don't care. He slips the ring from the box and holds it out. “You sure about this?”

"Don't give her a chance to back out, dude," Bea says.

"I've never been more sure of anything," I say.

Henry slides the gold band onto my finger and kisses my hand just like he did the last time. The action might be the same, but my heart couldn't feel any more different.

"To the start of forever," he says.

Need more Henry & Celia? Download a spicy bonus chapter that follows their second wedding at https://jessicajude.com/castles-we-sto rm-bonus

What's next? Read the conclusion of Henry & Celia's story in Crowns We Save!

Thank you for reading *Castles We Storm*! If you enjoyed this book, it would mean the world to me if you left a review, even if it's short. Reviews are like tips for authors, and every one helps!

xoxo Jess

P.S. Want to discuss my books, dissect Easter eggs, and spiral with other like-minded readers? Join my exclusive reader groups on Facebook and Discord. We'd love to see you there! You can also join my email list at jessicajude.com/newsletter to receive updates and exclusive bonus content!

Also by Jessica Jude

Thrones We Steal Trilogy
Thrones We Steal
Castles We Storm
Crowns We Save

Hand of Revenge Series
Ace of Betrayal
Queen of Vengeance
King of Obsession
Joker's Endgame

A group of wealthy friends plays poker to determine the victims of their weekly revenge plots. What they don't bargain on? Falling in love with the people who could destroy them.

Embers of Us Series

Flare (coming 9.15.26 – pre-order now!)

About the Author

J ESSICA JUDE LOVES NOTHING better than sending her characters on an emotional roller coaster of love, angst, and drama, but in reality her life is very ordinary, drama-free, and probably boring to anyone watching. (Which would be weird. And creepy.)

She married her high school sweetheart at nineteen. Being an author is a dream she's had since she was six years old and wrote her first book, which was ten pages long, about a girl named Mary getting lost in the woods. (It was never published, but good news: Mary was eventually rescued.)

When she's not writing, Jess is reading, reading about writing, or eating ice cream. In another life, she would live in England in a sprawling manor house with hidden passages and secret stairways, but for now, she's content with her old brick farmhouse in the Midwestern United States.

Still a fan? Here are some ways you can ~~stalk~~ stay connected!
https://jessicajude.com/newsletter
Instagram @JessicaJudeBooks
Threads @JessicaJudeBooks
TikTok @JessicaJudeBooks